FOUR HISTORICAL NOVELLAS

Cowboy Christmas Homecoming

Mary Connealy
Ruth Logan Herne
Julie Lessman
Anna Schmidt

GILEAD
PUBLISHING
Wheaton, IL

Cowboy Christmas Homecoming
Published by Gilead Publishing, Wheaton, IL 60187
www.gileadpublishing.com

ISBN: 978-1-68370-012-8 (paper)
ISBN: 978-1-68370-013-5 (eBook)

Longhorn Christmas © 2016 by Mary Connealy
A Cowboy for Christmas © 2016 by Ruth Logan Herne
Last Chance Christmas © 2016 by Julie Lessman
Connie's Christmas Prayer © 2016 by Anna Schmidt

Scripture quotations are from the King James Version.

Editor: Barbara Scott
Cover and Interior Designer: Larry Taylor

Printed in the United States of America

Contents

Last Chance Christmas

Julie Lessman

For by grace are ye saved through faith;
and that not of yourselves: it is the gift of God.
—*Ephesians 2:8*

CHAPTER ONE

Last Chance, California
Fall 1885

*S*helter, *food, and babies, Lord, that's all I ask.*

Grace O'Malley peered out the window as the railcar groaned to a stop in front of a tiny train station, her stomach rumbling louder than the iron wheels on the tracks. Hand to her queasy middle, she peeked up at an azure sky tufted with cotton and expelled a guilty sigh, almost forgetting her most important prayer.

And a decent job?

"Last Chance, California!" the conductor bellowed, and the railcar erupted in a flurry of activity. Grace's abdomen responded with a loud growl, turning the heads of several people despite all the commotion.

"Hungry?" an elderly woman asked with a sympathetic smile, relieving Grace's embarrassment over the mortifying trait that plagued her since she'd been a child—a growling stomach whenever she was nervous.

"Not really," Grace said, her smile wobbly at best. Oh, how she wished she could say yes! But her days of untruths were behind her. She drew in an unsteady breath. *Just like my days in a saloon.*

The woman patted Grace's hand, her rheumy blue eyes soft with understanding. "A new babe for you and your husband then?" she whispered. "Causing a wee bit of morning sickness?"

Grace blinked, her cheeks suddenly toasty. *Goodness, if only!* But the only "morning sickness" Grace had ever known was from stale cigar smoke and late hours at The Red Dog Saloon in Virginia City.

"Second call for Last Chance!"

Relief flooded her as she welcomed the interruption, saving her a response as she collected her valise. Offering a final smile, she inched past the woman toward the exit when the cry of an infant snagged her attention. Arms flailing, the child squalled in its mother's arms while the poor woman herded two toddlers to the door. Compassion propelled Grace forward to assist.

"Landon, no!" the mother shrieked when one toddler escaped, plowing straight into Grace's skirt.

Delighted, Grace dropped her bag and swooped up the runaway, her giggles merging with his as she snuggle-kissed his neck. "I think I may just gobble you up, little man," she said with a squeeze, "but first we need to follow your mama off the train."

"I am so sorry!" Cheeks blooming bright red, the young mother reached to take her son.

"Don't be," Grace said with a smile, cuddling the imp. "I love children, so I'm happy to help."

The pinch between the woman's brows eased, and with a tired nod of thanks, she turned to usher her family from the train.

Clutching the squirm-worm to her side, Grace retrieved her bag before hurrying after the boy's mother, pretending for one blissful moment the little dickens belonged to her.

But that was never to be.

"It's called amenorrhea," the doctor explained when pregnancy eluded her after eloping with Gabe at fifteen. She'd always known her "womanly time" was different, twice-yearly instead of monthly, but she'd always believed she'd have children despite the doctor's awful prognosis. *Barren.* Nonetheless, three years of marriage had produced little but heartbreak, and when Gabe died in a mining accident, she was left with nothing.

No husband, no income, *no babies.*

A delicious giggle feathered her cheek, and her gloom instantly vanished. Alighting onto the platform, she couldn't resist a playful whirl or two, Landon's giggles taking flight along with her blue calico skirt, which billowed in the dusty air. Flush with laughter, she delivered

Landon to his mother, who'd already handed the baby to a silver-haired woman of striking resemblance.

"I can't thank you enough for your help," the young mother said, the gratitude in her eyes edged with fatigue as she took the toddler from Grace. "Can my parents and I offer you a lift?"

"I'm not sure," Grace said, scanning with a hand to her eyes, stomach cramping at the possibility that Eileen might not even live here anymore. Her last letter was over a year and half ago when the young mother was expecting her fourth child and begged her to come. But the prospect of a saloon girl paying a visit to a pastor's wife had been too painful to consider, especially since she'd lied to her childhood friend, claiming to be a "teacher."

Only not in any school.

Gripping her valise, she squared her shoulders. *But . . .* she was a new creature in Christ according to Maggie Mullaney, a young nurse who tended her wounds after a barroom brawl. Sweet Maggie's ministrations had not only helped heal Grace's body, but also her soul, instilling a hope for a new beginning. One last chance to make things right.

In Last Chance, California.

Her lips tipped up at the corners of her mouth, the irony of the town's name not lost on her. It had, in fact, been a motivating factor in even considering a visit to a friend she hadn't seen in years.

Prophetic, she hoped. And God's will, she prayed.

"I'm looking for the parsonage," Grace said with a crimp in her brow when she saw no sign of a steeple on the dusty main street lined with a hodge-podge of buildings and pines. "I was hoping it would be in walking distance, but I don't see anything that even remotely resembles a church."

"That's because the Last Chance Chapel is on the west hill, tucked away in the trees," the silver-haired woman explained, joining her daughter as she jiggled the baby. "You must be here to see the McCabes. Are you a relative?"

The McCabes. A silent sigh seeped out. Eileen was still here!

"No," she said too quickly, loud enough to mask another noisy churn of her stomach. "Just a friend of the family hoping to help out." Anxious to avoid further probing, Grace started for the west edge of town, lifting a hand in farewell. "Thank you for pointing me in the right direction."

"If you're here to help, they'll be mighty glad to see you," the woman called as Grace picked up her pace. Offering a wave, Grace rounded a building that appeared to be a saloon, given the familiar tinkling of a piano and several bleary-eyed cowboys who stumbled out.

"Hey, pretty lady, where you off to in such a hurry?" one of the men slurred, and Grace bolted down the wooden sidewalk without a glance back, hand plastered to her straw bonnet to keep it from blowing off. Ducking around the mercantile, she backed up to the side wall, hand to her heaving chest.

A wagon rumbled by, and she jerked from the building, spotting a steeple through the trees in the distance. Praying Eileen would welcome her despite the lack of notice, Grace finally arrived at a white clapboard church tucked among a scarlet copse of red maples. The sight literally stilled her soul. A shaft of sunlight illuminated the wood-shingled roof like the finger of God leading her home. Behind it at the top of a hill, a log cabin peeked through the pines, a lazy curl of wood smoke rising from the chimney to fill the air with its welcome scent.

Gaze flicking back to the church, she decided a chat with the Almighty might be wise. "To hedge my bets," she said, then ruefully glanced up. "Forgive me, Lord—gamblers and saloons are part of my past, not my future, so please don't let Eileen turn me away."

Grace gingerly approached the cherry-red door as if she were trespassing, the whiff of wood shavings tickling her nose. Sidetracked by the wonderful smell that reminded her of her grandfather, she tiptoed around the corner to see a makeshift workbench beside a stack of lumber. Memories of Grandfather's carpentry shop tugged, and breathing in the heady scent of cedar and lacquer, she knew this was a sign from God.

She was finally home!

Grateful she was alone, she slipped into the dim church, blinking to adjust from blinding sunlight to stained-glass shadows. One of the shadows moved, and she froze, then gasped when she realized the moving silhouette was on a ladder in the far corner. True to form, her stomach joined in with a truly ferocious growl, and the poor man jerked so fast, his ladder teetered for several horrifying seconds before his can of stain shimmied off, crashing to the floor.

Right along with her hopes.

Eyes round with surprise gave way to a tic in a hard-sculpted cheek as he slowly descended, the clamp of a steely jaw not a good sign.

Grace gulped. *Finally home?* Gnawing the edge of her lip, she groaned—along with her stomach.

Maybe not . . .

CHAPTER TWO

Colton McCabe gingerly stepped into a sea of mahogany stain, thankful he'd taken the time to put a tarpaulin down. His mouth sagged. This'd teach him to get testy with the Almighty in his own house. He'd been so lost in his mental "negotiations" with the "Boss," he hadn't heard the door open, too busy badgering God for divine assistance in caring for four small children and a woman with a broken leg.

He squinted at a small figure who appeared as stiff as a pew and bit back a smile, wondering how such a tiny body could make so much noise without saying a word. "Can I help you?" he asked, unwilling to take a step closer lest he track stain across the floor.

"I am *so* sorry," a guilty voice whispered, its owner emerging into the light like a doe from the shadows. "I thought I was alone."

"My fault, not yours," he said, swabbing the soles of his boots with an old rag. He tossed it over a rung and approached a young woman who looked ready to bolt. Eyes wide, she took a step back, hand splayed to the bodice of her faded calico dress as if he were Beelzebub himself. Swiping his palms on his work pants, he offered a warm smile. "I would have greeted you if I'd heard the door, but I tend to get lost in my work." He extended a hand, his smile inching into a grin. "Name's Cole McCabe, and I'm the pastor here at Last Chance Chapel."

She shook it so quickly, it was barely a touch, the blush in her cheeks a nice complement to golden hair the color of winter wheat. "I'm Grace O'Malley, Pastor McCabe. From Virginia City?" She paused as if expecting recognition before more pink dusted her cheeks, setting her face aglow like an angel. "It's a true pleasure to meet you," she said softly, her pale blue eyes the exact shade of her bonnet. "Especially after all the good things I've heard."

His laughter—all too rare of late—boomed through the church. "You've obviously been chatting with the Irish contingent in our fine community, Miss O'Malley, known for more than a bit of the blarney, but I'm glad to welcome you to our fair town. How may I help you today?"

Her smile faltered as she peeked up beneath a fringe of honeyed lashes. "Actually, Pastor McCabe, I was hoping I could help you."

His brows lifted in surprise. Help *him?* His smile twitched, thinking this was one speedy answer to prayer.

"You see," she continued, those blue eyes searching his, "I'm a childhood friend of your wife's, so when Eileen sent a letter last year asking for help after the baby was born, I wasn't able to come until now."

He blinked, all air whooshing from his lungs.

"I know this is a surprise since I didn't notify her I was coming . . ."

A surprise? The horrendous ache he'd tried so hard to dispel seared through his chest with a vengeance. *No, this is a blow to the head with a two-by-four, Miss O'Malley.*

"But my departure from Virginia City was rather sudden, you see . . ."

Cole's eyelids closed. Yes, he knew all about "sudden."

"So I hoped—well, prayed, really—that Eileen could still use my help."

Eileen. The woman he'd been privileged to marry. A woman of God with a heart so pure, she'd been a beacon of light that helped chase away the darkness in his own sorry soul. God knows he hadn't deserved her, and yet she'd married him anyway, giving him nine wonderful years, four beautiful children, and in the end—her very life.

Gut twisting, he reopened his eyes, loathe to tell Miss O'Malley that her friend now resided on the other side of eternity, as if saying the words would revive his grief all over again. The very grief he'd worked so hard to hide for the sake of his family and congregation for well over a year. But tell her he would, even offering lodging for the night if need be.

"I won't stay long," she said in a rush, as if sensing his hesitation. "You see, I was a teacher in Virginia City, and Eileen wrote such wonderful things about your t-town, I decided to resettle here. So I h-hoped to accept her kind invitation till I could find a home of my own. And, of course, I promised to help in any way I could."

Promised. His eyelids weighted closed again. Yes, he'd promised Eileen something, too. Something his aunt's broken leg had made nearly impossible since caring for her and his children took so much of his time. Precious time he'd once devoted to making furniture to earn the price of the promise he'd made to his wife.

"I want a piano for Christmas, Cole," she'd whispered on that fateful day he'd lost her, her voice so frail, he'd barely been able to hear. "For our girls to play . . . like I did when I was small." She'd clutched his hand then, as if expending all her energy in a plea he could never deny. "Promise me, Cole, please. Give them music for Christmas . . . just in case."

Just in case.

"If you need to discuss this with Eileen, I totally understand . . ."

As if the mention of her name had conjured up her, Eileen's sweet face appeared in his brain like a vision, smiling that serene smile that always assured him God was at work and all would be well. In his mind's eye, he saw her touch her fingers to her lips and blow him a kiss like always whenever he left to work in his shop. And in one violent thud of his heart, he knew. Knew deep down, as if Eileen herself had whispered into his very soul.

Grace O'Malley was not just an answer to his prayer.

She was an answer to Eileen's, too.

He drew in a breath redolent with wood stain and the lemon oil he used on the pews and carefully expelled it again, his lips curving in the barest of smiles tinged with melancholy and awe. He vaguely remembered Eileen mentioning a long-lost friend, but he'd soon forgotten since his wife never brought it up again.

Until now.

He reached to tug Miss O'Malley's valise from her grip, the stillness of the sanctuary underscoring the peace that slowly seeped into his soul. He ushered her out of the church into the blazing sunlight, grateful for God's hand in his life.

"I assure you, Miss O'Malley, your help is not only desperately needed, but deeply appreciated as well. Maybe not by my sweet Eileen," he said softly, his tone hushed like the moment as he quietly closed the door, "but by the family she left behind."

Chapter Three

S *weet mother of pearl, now I've done it!* Shutting the bedroom door, Grace sagged against it for what seemed like an eternity, palms fused to the wood as if she were sweating glue. When she finally stumbled to sit on the bed, she was still in shock. Not only over the pain of Eileen's passing, but that Pastor McCabe had asked her to stay. No more than six weeks, he'd said, until his aunt could care for his daughters again.

Sweet mercy, one of which is a baby!

At his request, glimmers of joy had penetrated her grief over Eileen, *along* with prickles of guilt. *Especially* when he'd asked her if she could cook on their way up to his log house at the top of the hill.

"Oh, absolutely!" she'd fibbed, desperate to convince him she could be a big help.

"Good to hear," he'd said with an easy smile far too handsome for a minister. "I put a stew on for dinner, but Aunt Millie is the real cook who keeps us all fed, so she'll appreciate someone who knows her way around a stove."

Grace almost choked as he explained the family's routine from sunup to sundown.

Sunup?

Stove?

Gulp. The only time she'd seen a sunup in the last ten years was when a fight broke out at The Red Dog, and the girls were up till dawn, putting everything to rights. As far as a stove, Harvey never allowed "his girls" in the kitchen since their services were needed in the bar from noon until the wee hours of the night when he closed down.

Oh, she was "excellent" at pap she supposed, the watery gruel she made for little Molly, the baby her coworker Andrea had given birth to in the room they'd shared upstairs. A baby herself at fourteen, Andrea went to work for Harvey after her parents died of cholera, a situation that grieved Grace to no end. Harvey was one of the few saloon owners with a heart, requiring no more from his girls than entertaining downstairs and dancing with patrons. Even so, Grace hated to see Andie trapped in the same hopeless life that Grace herself was forced into when Gabe died. Andie was the little sister Grace never had. So when a no-count cowboy left her with child, Grace borrowed money from Harvey to send mama and baby back East to live with Andie's aunt. She released a wispy sigh. And no matter the cost, the loans for Andie and others like her had been well worth it.

Until Harvey passed away, leaving The Red Dog to his greedy brother.

"Uh, Pastor McCabe?" She'd mustered her courage at his front porch, no longer willing to lie. "Before you take me in, there is something I think you should know."

He'd stopped at the base of the steps to give her his full attention, the kindness in his face making it easier to do what God had called her to do.

"I . . . told Eileen I was a teacher in Virginia City . . . b-but that's not exactly true."

He blinked, shifting her heavy bag from one hand to the other. "You didn't teach school?" he asked, confusion ridging his brow.

"Uh, not exactly . . ." Her belly rumbled loudly, underscoring a truth that wouldn't be easy to hear—*or* say. "I mean, I *did* teach," she said quickly, cheeks burning as much as the half-truth she'd written to Eileen, "but not in a school. I taught music to women I worked with . . ." The lace of her collar bobbed as she swallowed her shame, her words trailing to a whisper. "In a saloon . . ."

The man had just stared, no noticeable change in his features whatsoever except the rapid loss of blood in his cheeks. Petrified he'd turn her away, she had babbled on about how a woman named Maggie led her back to God, assuring him she no longer worked in a saloon.

"I see," he'd said with a patient nod so befitting a pastor. A barely perceptible smile had lifted the edge of his mouth. "Then we'll just keep that between us for now."

For now.

Drawing in a deep breath thick with the aroma of coffee and stew, she surveyed the bedroom Pastor McCabe had assigned to her for her stay. From the brass double bed to the blue-and-white chintz curtains, she was painfully aware this had been his and Eileen's bedroom. Cheeks hot, she averted her eyes from the blue patchwork quilt to an exquisite mahogany bureau with matching mirror. As if in a trance, she moved closer, heart drumming as she surveyed a picture of Eileen and Pastor McCabe on their wedding day, their faces filled with joy. Eileen was arrayed in a snow-white gown as pure as the woman who wore it.

Unlike you, a thought taunted, and tears threatened as she replaced the photo.

Tap. Tap. Tap.

Grace whirled around at the sound of a knock on the door. "Dinner in five minutes," Pastor McCabe called. "There's fresh water in the pitcher on the bureau to wash up."

Her stomach churned right on time. *This is it, then.* The moment of reckoning when she needed to win the approval of Eileen's family. Aunt Millie was napping with the little ones when they'd arrived, and the other girls were at school, expected home soon. So he'd shown her around the small farm with pride, pointing out the milk cow along with a fair number of chickens and pigs. She'd grinned outright when he'd introduced her to Sassafras, "as bullheaded a mule as God ever created."

"Just as soon buck ya as look at ya." His wink had surprised her. "Good thing I'm more bullheaded than he is."

Smiling at the memory, she assessed herself in the mirror, pinching her cheeks before unpinning her hat. "Oh, drat," she whispered, flaxen curls springing wild from a bun once neatly pinned, now as disheveled as she.

"Land's sake, Sadie Grace," she muttered in a tone reminiscent of Mama, "you're here to tend to a family, not dazzle cowboys at The Red Dog." Melancholy crept in at the thought of her mother, whose death had altered Grace's life at the age of ten, resulting in her running off with Gabe to escape a drunken father.

"I know, Mama," she whispered, the thought of her mother's no-nonsense practicality helping to unravel some of the knots in her stomach.

Swiping her eyes, she corralled stray curls with extra pins, then tilted her head right and left, satisfied she appeared like a proper lady. "Okay, Lord, wish me luck!" she prayed with a nervous smile, face flaming over a petition more suitable to poker than prayer. "I m-mean . . . bless me, Lord," she quickly amended, hoping her former habits and speech wouldn't be apparent. With a firm tug of her bodice, she straightened her dress and smoothed out her skirts, determined to meet the family with a fresh "burst" of confidence.

Which is exactly what her hope did when she opened the door.

"It's about time!" A young girl of eight or so heaved a noisy sigh as she flicked a butterscotch braid over her shoulder. "Afore we have to reheat the stew."

"Sarah Margaret," her father said firmly, "Miss O'Malley is our guest, young lady, so I suggest you apologize."

Grace worried the edge of her lip, slowly sinking into her chair.

"*Now,*" her father ordered when his daughter didn't comply.

"Sorry," she muttered, "but I wish Mama was here instead."

Her father fixed her with a sober stare as he dished out stew. "I know you miss your mama, sweetheart, but that's no cause to be rude. Next time you'll go to your room—"

"No!" Grace interrupted, spasms in her heart along with her stomach. "I mean, this is Sarah's home, Pastor McCabe, and I understand how she feels." Her gaze flicked to Sarah's cold one, and it was all Grace could do to hold back her tears. "I wish your mama was here, too, sweetheart, because I know how it feels to have someone you love stolen away. My mama died when I was about your age, and it leaves an awful big hole in a person's heart."

A sudden sheen softened Sarah's gaze, flooding Grace with such compassion, she reached to squeeze the child's hand. "I know it hurts, darling, but I promise the hurt gets easier to bear with time. But you know what? Your mama's love never changes, 'cause it's still powerfully strong up in heaven, where she's praying and watching over you right now."

Sarah's lower lip quivered, and when Grace felt a tiny squeeze back, love bloomed inside like a garden of hope.

"Is she watching me, too, Miss O'Malley?" the young girl next to Grace asked, blue eyes brimming with a childlike joy that coaxed a chuckle from Grace's lips.

"Yes, you, too, sweetheart, and please—call me Grace." She gave her a quick hug. Her gaze lighted on a solemn little tot no more than three, then on an older woman who shoveled stew into the mouth of a precious baby. "Just think! All of you have your own personal angel watching over you just like my mama watches over me." She picked up her spoon and flashed a brilliant smile. "So if we don't want any thunder in heaven," she said with a wink, "we best eat our stew." Grace tucked into the steaming bowl with gusto, stifling a delicious moan over the first real meal she'd had in days.

"*Ahem.*" A smile squirmed on Pastor McCabe's lips. "I suspect we'd hear a wee bit more grumbling over no grace at meals, Miss O'Malley, given this is a pastor's house."

Grace blinked while the stew turned to sludge in her mouth. She swallowed with an awkward duck of her throat, the noisy gulp merging nicely with the growl of her tummy.

"Uh-oh, I think it's already started," Sarah said with a giggle, her pixie grin unleashing more chuckles all around. "Was that your stomach?"

Grace's smile was sheepish at best, cheeks steaming more than the stew. "Uh, yes, unfortunately, so please forgive me. I guess I'm so hungry, I forgot about grace."

"Indeed," the pastor said with a definite twinkle before he bowed his head to offer thanks. At his amen, spoons clinked around the table, allowing Grace to dive back in.

"Aunt Millie—meet Miss Grace O'Malley, a friend of Eileen's who's here to help till you're back on your feet."

"Don't need no help," the woman said with a grunt, her curt words rife with warning.

"We both know that's not true," he said gently, patiently buttering a golden-brown biscuit. "Doc Morrow wants absolute rest for that leg if it's going to mend properly, especially after your fall last week, attempting to get out of bed on your own." The concern in his voice veered into a jest. "Doc said you're lucky you didn't damage it further, but I told him your bones are as hard as your head."

More giggles circled the table as the woman's lips gummed into a thin line.

The pastor tendered an apology with a trace of a smile. "This is my aunt, Miss Mildred Crabtree, but we call her Aunt Millie, and I promise she's not always this *crabby*."

The woman issued another grunt. "Don't need no help," she muttered again, this time singeing him with a decidedly "crabby" look before stabbing a piece of meat in her stew.

"Glad to meet you, Miss Crabtree," Grace said loudly to deflect the noisy nerves in her middle, "and I'll need help as well since this is your house, so we're in the same boat."

"Humph, a sinkin' one far as I can tell, and my leg's broke, missy, not my hearin'."

Grace quickly turned to the baby. "And who's this?" She tickled the child's chin, tension dissipating as always in the presence of an infant.

"That's Abby, and I'm Becca," the little girl next to her said through a mouthful of stew.

"Why, thank you, Becca." Grinning when Abby tugged Grace's finger into her mouth, Grace peered around Becca to the toddler. "And who are you, sweetheart?"

"That's Ruthy. She's three, but she don't talk no more." Becca shoveled in more stew, her declaration freezing the smile on Grace's face.

With dark curls the exact shade of her father's, the tiny girl stared at her bowl as if lost in its depths, emanating such a deep sadness, Grace felt a cramp in her chest.

"Ruthy seems to have taken it the hardest." Pastor McCabe spoke quietly. His telling gaze met Grace's with a sobriety that ached to her very soul, whooshing her back to the year of her mother's death when she herself had been no more than an empty shell.

Ker-splat!

All heads whipped toward Abby, who'd managed to slam Grace's dinner on the floor in a gooey mess. Grace launched to her feet in a panic, toppling her chair with a loud crash. The noise apparently frightened Abby because the poor thing cut loose with an ear-splitting wail, arms thrashing so hard her baby bottle took flight, shattering on the floor to join Grace's dinner.

"Blue blistering blazes!" Grace shouted without thinking, her appetite suddenly as depleted as the empty bowl at her feet. Little-girl gasps broke into a fit of giggles as she snatched the baby up, soothing her with rapid-fire pats on her bottom while she crooned in her ear. "That's okay, sweet pea, it was my fault, not yours."

Pastor McCabe righted the chair. "No, problem, Miss O'Malley. If you'll just attend to the baby, I'll take care of this." He steered them into Grace's bedroom. "There are fresh towels in the bottom bureau drawer to clean up Abby, along with clean diapers."

"I am *so* sorry!" Her eyes begged forgiveness as she cuddled the baby. "It seems I always cause you a mess." Her belly rumbled an apology of its own.

The seeds of a smile twitched on a generous mouth obviously proficient at disarming situations with humor and ease. "Things do tend to spill when you're around, Miss O'Malley, I'll give you that." He picked a pea from his daughter's hair before his gaze met hers with a kindness she'd seldom known. "But if that spilling involves laughter in a house that's had all too little of late, then that's a beautiful mess in my opinion, so spill away."

"Thank you," she whispered, not used to gentleness from a man.

He turned to go, then stopped to nod at her dress, drawing her eyes to splatters of stew all over her bodice. "Oh, and when you clean Abby up, there's a bit on you as well."

Heat toasted her cheeks as he closed the door, leaving her to survey herself in the mirror. She bit her lip, not sure who wore more gravy, the baby or her.

"Mess, indeed." She nuzzled Abby's cheek, enjoying a bit of heaven despite the cold sticky feel. "But nothing we can't handle, right, buttercup?" Breathing in the sweet scent of talcum powder and stew, she closed her eyes to treasure the moment, her sigh of contentment happily merging with Abby's goos. "At least not while I have a baby in my arms."

CHAPTER FOUR

I understand the good Lord done answered your prayer, Cole, and sent you some help." Tilting back his chair in Cole's office at the back of church, his best friend Tom O'Shaughnessy sported a crooked grin above a clean-shaven jaw. He hiked a boot up on the rung of Percy Smith's chair, the gleam in his eyes a sure sign he had tomfoolery on his mind.

Literally.

"Hear tell she's a wonder in the kitchen, too," Harve Fernell piped up, the jest in his tone hard to miss now that the board meeting was over.

A wonder? Cole ignored them both, making a great show of recording the final minutes. *Not exactly the word I'd use.*

"Oh, she's a 'wonder,' all right." Percy lounged back in his chair, revealing a paunch Cole suspected came from too many beers at the Diamondback Saloon. He propped his boots on Cole's desk. "According to Millie, it's a holy wonder she hasn't burned down the house yet."

Cole sent his friends a half-lidded warning he was pretty sure they'd ignore while he shuffled his notes into a neat pile. "Pardon me, gentlemen, but this meeting is adjourned, and I might remind you Miss O'Malley was not on the docket. So you can all rest on the subject because the lady is just fine, thank you."

"*Whoooeeee,* that goes without saying," Percy said with a wink, apparently not in any hurry to get home to his wife. "Fine, indeedy. Why, I believe the good Lord may have sent you an angel straight from heaven."

Harve elbowed Tom with a grin. "'Cause ol' St. Pete probably kicked her out afore she could start up a fire."

His friends chuckled and Cole finally joined in, shaking his head. "Miss O'Malley is a friend of our family who hasn't had a lot of call to learn domestic chores, but she's learning."

I hope.

Cole filed away his notes, anxious to go home. His mouth crooked. *If I still have one.*

"Either way," he said, "the lady has been a blessing to my aunt and children."

"And you?" Tom eyed him with a razor-thin edge of something in his tone. *Jealousy?* Most likely. Cole suspected he was smitten after only one conversation with Grace last week.

Cole stared him down, determined his best friend—and everyone else—knew he had no romantic interest in Miss O'Malley. Period. She was Eileen's friend and nothing more. "Of course she's a blessing to me," he said, tone too sharp, "because now I actually *have* the time to provide for my family and congregation."

Kneading the bridge of his nose, he expelled a weary breath. "Look, Tom, Grace—" Heat scorched the back of his neck. "Miss O'Malley," he corrected, "is merely a guest in my home kind enough to care for Millie and the girls, so if you have an interest, I suggest you pursue the lady on your own and not draw me into the mix, all right?"

The strain in Tom's face eased into a smile. "Good to know. She's a special lady."

"Yes, she *is*," Cole emphasized, fighting the itch of a smile while he reached for his hat. *If cooking, cleaning, and safety aren't part of the measure.* "So if you gentlemen don't mind, I think I'll call it a day."

Harvey ambled over to the window to squint up at the log cabin. "Well, it's still standing, and I don't see no smoke, so maybe supper's the only thing that'll get scorched tonight."

Laughter followed as Cole tugged the brim of his hat low lest they see the concern that shadowed his smile. "Good night, boys. See you on Sunday."

"If not before," Tom said as he and the others filed out, his meaning clear when he sent Cole a wink.

Waving them off, Cole locked the door and started up the hill, enjoying the balmy evening. He glanced up at the log cabin Miss O'Malley had almost burned down on her second day, and a shiver licked up his spine. Just like a grease fire had licked the kitchen curtains last week, threatening everything in its path. His family. His home. The brainless woman who'd told him she could cook. The *same* woman who'd single-handedly set his aunt's recovery back weeks, according to Doc, when Millie reinjured her leg trying to put out the fire.

He exhaled a slow and arduous breath, grateful he'd been chopping wood when it happened rather than down at the church or in town. The cabin was his pride and joy as a carpenter, as pretty as a picture with window boxes and shutters, roomy and comfortable and a far cry from the clapboard shanty assigned to the prior preacher. Determined to provide the best for his bride, Cole was a craftsman who'd designed and built it himself with help from Eileen's brothers, sons of a banker in Tulsa who wanted to make sure his daughter lived well. This suited Cole just fine because he sure didn't want to take one dime from the town for what some might see as an extravagance for a preacher. Nor did he want to be beholden to a town that had viewed him with suspicion when he and Eileen first arrived.

But his carpentry skills—if not his preaching—soon won them over when he turned the old church building into the finest church in the county, devoting countless hours over the years to make it everything a house of God should be.

Strong, beautiful, holy, and pure.

Just like his Eileen.

Laughter drifted from the windows as he approached home, the absence of smoke billowing out along with it a very good sign. He sniffed the air for the smell of anything burnt, but only inhaled the sweet aroma of apple pie that caused his stomach to rumble. He offered a silent prayer of thanks that Millie now supervised whenever Miss O'Malley stepped foot in the kitchen. Who knew? She might even learn to cook yet. His mouth quirked. As long as she stayed away from meat loaf baked into a lump of charcoal or oatmeal he could use as chinking.

No doubt the woman's so-called skills in the kitchen were slim to nil, but somehow she'd managed to bring a little sunshine into his children's lives if not decent food and clean clothes. Nonsensical games and an endless repertoire of stories had harvested more smiles out of Sarah and Becca in two short weeks than he'd seen in the last year. She'd even managed to coax a laugh or two out of his crotchety aunt, whose recovery mode up till now had been akin to a wounded grizzly's.

And although his precious Ruthy still never uttered a word, Cole could see that Miss O'Malley had managed to light a tiny spark in his daughter's usually vacant eyes, no matter how faint or infrequent her smiles. He shook his head. A hazard in house and hearth, maybe, but the woman was truly a touch of God's grace at a time when his family sorely needed it. A smile curved his lips.

Amazing Grace, indeed!

Washing up at the pump, he noted the fresh crop of weeds invading Eileen's garden, reminding him how meticulous she'd been at tending both her vegetable patch and her home. Melancholy swooped in like a turkey vulture, picking at any semblance of happiness he managed to attain. He bent to take a long cool drink from the water bucket, able to slake his thirst, but not the parched feeling in his chest that he'd never find another wife or mother as perfect and pure as Eileen.

More giggles took flight from his chintz-curtained windows, and his thoughts returned to Grace, whose love of babies and devotion to children definitely went above and beyond. "A special lady," Tom had called her, and Cole supposed she was. Certainly a pleasure to look at and a joy to be around, she was perfect for Tom, a bachelor for whom briquette meat loaf might be a treat. But a pastor needed more from a wife than a pretty face. He needed a woman with a pure heart and staunch character who could nurture and care for his children with the same excellence as their mother. He swiped a sleeve across his mouth to sop up the water, wiping his melancholy away along with it.

No, Grace O'Malley was definitely no Eileen, but at the moment, she was exactly the breath of fresh air his family needed. Even *if* it took the place of a clean house and fresh laundry, so he supposed he couldn't complain. Gaze snagging on long johns flapping in the breeze, as pink as the red dress fluttering beside, he shook his head as a baby's squeal pealed in the air.

Or maybe he could.

Chapter Five

"Beans again?" Sarah flung her head back, brows pinched in agony. "For crying out loud in a bucket, don't you know how to make anything else?"

Potholders in hand, Grace paused, her cheeks hotter than the casserole she'd just set on the table, the only dish she'd mastered in a near month of meals.

"Sarah Margaret McCabe—apologize this instant, or you'll go to bed *without* beans." Pastor Cole—or just plain "Cole" as he'd asked her to call him—rose up like a thunderstorm, as if stormy gray eyes and a jaw of steel wasn't enough to intimidate an eight-year-old with a sudden aversion to beans.

"Sorry," Sarah mumbled, mouth flat as she picked up a fork to impale her dinner.

Nibbling her lower lip, Grace silently spooned a pile of beans in front of Abby, unable to resist a kiss to the child's cheek. As always, the scent of talcum powder calmed her as she reached for a biscuit, attempting to discreetly remove the burnt bottom. No matter how hard she tried, she couldn't seem to master the cookstove.

Bowing his head to give thanks, Cole gave Grace just enough time to rip another burnt bottom off a biscuit for the baby. When he said "amen," she'd composed herself enough to send a gentle smile Sarah's way. "I'm sorry, Sarah, but I thought you liked my beans, especially since it's one of the few things I don't burn."

"The only thing," Sarah grumbled, jabbing at the beans on her plate.

"At least they're not black," Becca offered in a matter-of-fact tone, spinning the charcoal biscuit bottom she'd cut off like a top.

"Well, I love beans." Cole sent Sarah a pointed look.

"I used to." Millie grunted.

"And the biscuit ain't so awful bad." Becca decapitated another burnt one. "Once you get past all the black stuff." She paused, looking up with a squint, not a bit of malice in her sweet freckled face. "Is there anything you *can* do real good? You know, that you don't fry to a crisp?"

Cole started to hack, and Millie scowled as he lunged for his water. "Sure hope you didn't swallow one of those charcoal wafers—that awful taste will haunt forever."

Grace ignored Millie's comment with a secret smile. "Well, as a matter of fact, Becca, there are a few things I can do, and I promise, there's no burning involved."

"Really? What?" Cole blinked, completely unaware he'd just insulted her.

"Well . . ." Grace caught her bottom lip against her teeth. "I may not be all that good in the kitchen, but . . ." She peeked around the table, their wide-eyed anticipation almost making her giggle. "I'm told I can sing and dance, and I do play several instruments."

Silence reigned as mouths dropped open around the table.

"Perhaps we'll have music after dinner," she said in a breezy manner, gaze homing in on Sarah with a flutter of lashes. "That is . . . if *everyone* eats *all* their beans."

Never had food disappeared so quickly. The girls flew through their chores in no time, shimmying into their spots around Grace's chair in their nightgowns, all ready for bed when the party was over. Grace smiled. They were as fidgety as the crowds at The Red Dog on Saturday nights, when she and the girls entertained on the piano and fiddle. Even Millie's dour attitude seemed improved as she rocked in her chair, excitement in eyes usually narrowed in disapproval.

"How are you gonna make music if you don't have an instrument?" Sarah asked, the suspicious squint of her eyes reminding Grace a lot of her Aunt "Crab."

"You'll see," Grace said with a smug look, slipping her hand into the pocket of her calico dress to draw out the battered harmonica Grandpa carried during the Civil War. Fingering it with care, she closed her eyes and began to play, the poignant and haunting sound of "When Johnny Comes Marching Home" filling the cozy room with a sweet hush. Lowering the harmonica, she began to sing and as always, her voice caressed the lyrics with a reverence she reserved for Grandpa, the only man who'd never disappointed her with his love. The last note of the song lingered in the air like the smell of wood smoke, evoking a strange silence she seldom heard at The Red Dog.

"Where on earth did you learn to play like that?" Cole whispered when she opened her eyes, the deep respect in his tone warming her more than the fire.

She gave a tiny shrug. "My grandpa taught me everything I know. He always said music was like the finger of God, touching our souls."

She blinked to deflect sudden moisture, her smile full of the sweetness his memory always called to her mind. Swiping at an errant tear, she shook off her melancholy with a sassy wink. "But how 'bout we liven things up?" Their cheers launched her into a lively rendition of … "Old Susanna" that had everyone singing along, except for baby Abby, who dozed on her daddy's lap.

"Daddy, dance with me!" Sarah shouted, tugging on his arm.

Lumbering to his feet, he put a finger to his lips and carried the baby to bed, quietly closing the door behind. He returned to spin Sarah around and around, unleashing a cascade of giggles as Grace finished the song.

"My turn, my turn!" Becca shouted, jumping up and down like Grace had fed her Mexican jumping beans for dinner. Cole whirled her to another tune, his laughter rich and low as it rumbled through the parlor, causing an odd flutter in Grace's stomach. When he put her back down, Becca staggered to and fro, dizzy and whooping like a drunken cowboy.

But when Ruthy scampered off Millie's lap and held hands up to her daddy, Grace's heart turned over. A slow, easy grin slid across his handsome face, and the strait-laced preacher gave way to a man wild and free. Dark curls askew and a shadow of beard that lent a rakish air, he scooped Ruthy up with a snuggle growl to her neck, eliciting a rare squeal of delight from the little girl who seldom smiled.

"Daddy, can you dance with us like we're ladies?" Sarah asked when he and Ruthy sat back down. "You know, like they do at the town social?"

"Uh . . ." He cuffed the back of his neck. "I . . . don't really know how to dance like that."

Grace glanced up, jaw dangling. "What? Didn't you dance at your own wedding?"

"Humph. Not well," Millie volunteered, smile flat as her knitting needles clicked away. "Poor Eileen limped for a week."

A ruddy blush validated his aunt's jibe. "I'm afraid she's right, so perhaps it's best to limit my dancing to just spinning you girls around."

"Horsefeathers!" Grace laid the harmonica aside and extended her hand, ignoring the stunned look on his face.

"W-What are you d-doing?" he stammered.

"Teaching you and your daughters to dance, Pastor McCabe," she said with an impish smile, too caught up in the tease to consider the close proximity they'd share.

He was shaking his head before she finished her sentence. "Oh, no, I'm afraid some things are better left undone."

"Daddy, *please*?" The older girls begged in unison while Sarah heaved Ruthy off his lap.

Grace bit back a grin when Becca yanked on his hand without mercy, tugging him up to do her bidding like he was Sassafras at the end of a rope.

"Ten minutes," he threatened, jaw clamped despite a tight smile. "And then it's time for bed, understood?"

Their squeals rose to the rafters as Grace stood in front of Cole, hesitating with a sprint of her pulse she hadn't expected. Swallowing hard, she peered up beneath half-lidded lashes, suddenly overwhelmed by his height. Barely coming to his shoulders, she gave him a shaky smile, certain she'd get a crick in her neck.

"All right, girls," she said, voice annoyingly breathless as she took Cole's hands in hers, "the boy positions one hand on the girl's shoulder blade like this, then holds her other at eye level like this." She forced a bright smile, the touch of Cole's work-roughened hands causing her stomach to churn. Heart thumping, she guided him through each step, her gaze fused to his feet to avoid the intensity of those piercing gray eyes. "It's basically a box pattern to a count of three," she explained, counting loudly to drown out the ruckus in her tummy. "One-two-three, one-two-three . . ." She peeked up with a shy smile. "See? Not too hard, right?"

"Till I step on your toes," he said with a shuttered gaze, his husky tease almost buckling her knees.

"Which," she said, jerking away with a flash of heat, "is why you will now practice with the girls while I provide the music."

"Coward," he said softly, as if for her ears alone, the glint in his eyes almost roguish as he swept Sarah into his arms, leaving Grace trembling as she began to play.

"All right, girls," he said when he'd danced with them all, "it's time for bed."

"But I'm too excited to sleep!" Sarah said with a pout.

"Just one more song, please?" Becca's face puckered in a plea.

Grace met Cole's gaze. "A lullaby might help them sleep," she suggested meekly.

He pinned her with a probing stare that tumbled her stomach, his sobriety barely tempered by a shadow of a smile. "One. Last. Song." He emphasized each word before reclaiming his rocker.

Closing her eyes, Grace began to play "Amazing Grace," grateful for the one hymn that never failed to soothe her spirit. And she needed soothing right now—*desperately*. Like the girls, she was too keyed up to sleep, but for entirely different reasons. What in heaven's name had she been thinking, attempting to teach Cole to dance? One touch of his hand, one look into his eyes, had stirred such turmoil within that she feared their comfortable friendship would never be the same. Even now her heart drummed out a traitorous beat despite the sweet and soulful sound of her favorite hymn, painfully aware he was watching, mere feet away.

When her hands began to quiver, she lowered the harmonica to sing, only to stutter on the lyrics. She felt her face flame, and unbidden, her lashes lifted, her gaze colliding with his. The connection lingered with such intensity, the very air seemed to crackle and hum. Cheeks ablaze, she swiftly looked away, terrified he'd sense the unsettled feelings that had taken her by surprise. Dangerous, impossible feelings, unwanted, and most certainly uninvited. Feelings that at that exact moment made her want to flee both this house and the unexpected attraction that now burned in her soul.

The plan had been for her to stay past Thanksgiving, only two weeks away, when Millie could take over again. But because of her own ineptitude with the fire, Millie's recovery was now slated for mid-December, and Grace only hoped she could bear it till then. Another month of his easy smiles, his teasing laughter, and his tenderness toward a family who adored him and deserved so much more than she could ever give. And something she could never have. She gripped the harmonica in her lap.

Lord, help me! What am I going to do?

And then the answer came so softly, simple and pure in the lyrics she sang, imparting a tender peace to her soul.

"The Lord has promised good to me, His Word my hope secures; He will my Shield and Portion be, as long as life endures."

Tears stung as hope sprang anew. Because of *his* amazing Grace.

And, oh . . . how sweet the sound!

CHAPTER SIX

"Blast!" A rare swear word reverberated through Cole's shop at the back of the church, where blood pooled from a jagged splinter impaling his palm. A noisy sigh of regret blustered out. "Sorry, Lord," he muttered, wiping the blood off with a clean cloth before removing the splinter; he was in far too dangerous a frame of mind to work on Mrs. Merriweather's furniture.

But he had no choice. Christmas Eve—the delivery date he'd promised in exchange for her piano—was only six weeks away. He repositioned the plane, mouth in a tight line. And if it took working every single night until late, he swore Millie and his girls *would* find a piano in the sanctuary on Christmas Day, just like he promised Eileen.

Eileen. His mind wandered to the woman who'd possessed his thoughts day and night for over a year, and he missed her all over again. Her pure heart, her devotion to God and family, her keen mind that knew Scriptures better than he did. And the excellence she put into everything—cooking, cleaning, sewing, providing a safe environment for her family.

Unlike someone I know.

He expelled another heavy sigh, scattering sawdust into the air as he sagged over his worktable, head bowed, and arms corded from bearing his weight. No, that wasn't fair. Grace O'Malley wasn't like Eileen, true, but she had talents all her own. She could sing; she could play music.

Eileen sang.

Eileen played music.

"No!" He slammed a palm to the table, not really sure if he was talking to God or to himself. All he knew was this morning he woke with a weight on his shoulders, and nothing had been right ever since. Not his thoughts, not his work, not his mood.

Not his feelings.

Yesterday every thought had been consumed with keeping promises—to Eileen, to God and his congregation, and to his family. To be the man, pastor, friend, father, and nephew God wanted him to be.

But today? His shoulders sagged all the more. He couldn't stop thinking about Grace. Of the way she'd felt in his arms last night, the sparkle in her eyes when she'd teased his children, coaxing them into eating beans and getting ready for bed without complaint. The way even Millie—or Mildred as she'd instructed Grace to address her since "she wasn't family"—was softening up, despite the fact Grace was nothing short of a catastrophe as a homemaker. His lids dragged closed as if they were lead.

The near fire that almost destroyed his home.

The damage to Millie's leg from trying to put out that very fire.

The food poisoning from making a salad with the poultry knife.

The scorched trousers from an iron she went off and forgot.

The crystal bowl she shattered with boiling water.

The pink long johns.

Not to mention indigestion from countless recipes botched and burned.

Before he could stop it, his lips curved in a faint smile while he expelled a tenuous breath. If ever there were an accident waiting to happen, Grace O'Malley was it. His smile dissolved. But now the accident had happened to him. He pinched the bridge of his nose and stifled a groan.

He was attracted to her. And the guilt was eating him raw.

Guilt over feelings for another woman.

Guilt over feelings for a woman his best friend planned to court.

And guilt over feelings for a woman who was the worst possible candidate for a wife and mother. For pity's sake, she could barely cook, barely knew Scripture, and had repeatedly put his children and home in danger.

Not to mention my heart.

Frustration spilled out of him as he thumped a fist on the table. "Lord, how the devil did this happen?"

"That's what I'd like to know."

Cole spun around so fast, he knocked the plane off the table; it landed on his foot and a streak of pain contorted his face. "For crying out loud, Tom, don't you ever knock?"

Tom strolled in, hands in his pockets as he shot Cole an annoying grin. "Did, old buddy, but as usual, you were too deep in thought to notice." He sat and crossed his boots on the worktable with a clunk. "Why were you so deep in thought anyway—a message from God?"

Heat singed Cole's collar, and he swiftly stooped to pick up his wood plane, hoping Tom wouldn't see the flush that burned his cheeks. He stalled to give his face time to cool off by placing the plane back on the shelf just so, perfectly spaced between his other tools in a shop kept far more meticulous than his house.

"Something like that." He turned back to sweep sawdust off the table.

Yeah, like, "Open your eyes, Pastor, and flee the temptation."

The thing is, he'd never seen Grace as temptation before. Till now, she'd just been one of the girls, as giggly and wiggly as Sarah and Becca whenever they horsed around.

"But that can't be Christian, stabbing a worm through the eye!" she'd shrieked one morning when he'd taken them fishing, gawking like an exorcism was in order.

"I promise you, they don't feel a thing," he assured her, shaking his head when she imitated worm screams that ended up in a giggle fest with his girls. He dangled the hooked worm over her head, and she squealed louder than Abby, blue eyes snapping with tease as she threatened him with a fishing rod.

"Touch me with that slimy thing, Mr. Preacher, and I'll burn your dinner on purpose tonight."

His laughter had echoed through the valley with his daughters' as he cast his line into the deep. "I'll have you know this 'slimy thing' will provide our dinner tonight, young lady," he'd said with a mock scowl that slid into a wink. "And burnt on purpose or not, it all seems to come out the same, Miss O'Malley—charred to a beautiful crisp."

His stomach had hurt from laughing that day, something that happened a lot when Grace was around. Be it a baking lesson with Millie where Grace sported more flour on her face than the girls, or a game made up by Grace called wobbly boots where he swung the girls around and around to see who wobbled the most. Rain or shine, the woman had a bag of tricks and fun that never failed to make him smile.

Even when she'd taught his girls to play poker with dried beans.

"Grace taught you what?" he'd shouted one day after the girls had been trapped inside during a week of rain.

"Jackpots," Becca said in total innocence as she proudly displayed the handful of beans she'd won. "And Grace says I'm a natural."

"Did she now?" He'd homed on in Grace with a glare intended to singe her cheeks, but she'd only blinked as if she couldn't understand the flaw in teaching a pastor's children to gamble.

"You're teaching them *poker*?" he'd hissed in her ear when he'd pulled her aside, wondering if the woman truly had cotton in her head like Millie always said.

"No, of course not." She'd given him a look more cherubic than Abby's. "Gambling is with money, Cole, and this is only beans." He'd near bit his tongue to battle a smile when she'd declared with a wiggle of brows that at least these beans couldn't be scorched.

Shaking off the memory, Cole wiped his hands with the rag, grateful to focus his full attention on Tom. "So, what brings you here today, my friend?"

It was Tom's turn to flush as he batted an ear, tone too intense for a friend who usually took things in stride. "I need advice about a woman," he said with a crease in his brow, his serious manner almost laughable if Cole didn't suspect the woman was Grace.

Battling a prickle of jealousy, Cole perched on the corner of his table, arms in a tight fold. "Grace?"

Tom blasted out a noisy sigh. "Who else?" he said with a crack of a smile. "You and I both know I've never had trouble with women before, but blue thunder, Grace has me all tied up in knots, you know?"

Yes, he knew. Unfortunately.

Rubbing the grain of wood on his chair, Tom peered up. "You know how long I've been wanting to call on her, Cole, but hang it all, seems like whenever I broach the subject after church, she bolts up that confounded hill faster than a coon up a tree stalked by a dozen dogs."

Cole cemented his lips to ward off a smile.

"And when I finally cornered her last week to invite her to the Thanksgiving social this Sunday? She acted like I'd asked her to a blasted saloon, cheeks as scarlet as that pretty red dress she wore last week. You know . . . the one with the lace collar?"

Cole shifted uncomfortably. Yes, he knew.

"Well, it took some mighty fast talking, but I finally got her to say yes."

Cole's heart stopped. *She said yes?*

"So what I want to know is," Tom said with a squint, "is she that shy around you?"

Grace's image from last night suddenly alighted on his mind, firelight flickering over her beautiful features. Any other time he could've answered Tom's question in the negative, because once past the awkwardness of their first meeting, Grace blossomed in the midst of his family, no matter their resistance. Her gentle grit and boundless fun had banished all shyness, her ability to laugh at herself disarming his entire family. So yesterday he could have honestly responded that no, she wasn't shy around him.

Until last night.

From the first tremble of her hand during their dance, to the moment she'd stumbled in her song and lifted her gaze to his, a spark had sizzled between them that changed everything in one ragged catch of his breath. The deep stain of pink in her cheeks, the shy, skittish look of a doe in danger, the eyelids sheathing closed as if she feared he'd notice the tension that now hung thick in the air. Mid-inhale, oxygen had swirled in his lungs at the notion she might be attracted to him. And then whooshed right back out when he recognized the same feelings in himself.

Nerves twitching, he snatched his canteen off the shelf and took a deep swig before handing it off to Tom, striving for a composure he didn't feel. "Sure, at first, just like with you, but now she's like one of the family, sometimes louder and rowdier than my own girls."

"No kidding?" Tom took a drink and handed it back, a lovesick smile marking him as a goner.

Just like me if I don't cut these feelings off at the pass.

"Yeah. So give it some time and patience—she'll come around."

"I sure hope so." Tom released a quiet sigh, smile lingering. "I'll tell you what, my friend, I'm not sure how you keep from falling for a woman like that when she's right under your nose, but I thank God because I sure aim to make her my own."

"Good," Cole said, mood suddenly as flat as his smile. "Because Doc says he'll cut off Millie's cast mid-December, and I'm not too sure how long my house'll be standing with Calamity Jane under its roof."

Rising, Tom chuckled and shook Cole's hand. "Appears we both have a vested interest in this suit, Pastor, so I trust I can count on your prayers?"

"Oh, you bet, old buddy." *Nonstop.*

"Good." Tom clapped Cole on the back and headed out, tossing a grin over his shoulder. "Because between your prayers and my charm, I'm hoping the lady can't resist." He gave a quick salute before closing the door.

"Yeah . . ." Cole lapsed into a vacant stare, expelling a noisy sigh. "Me, too."

CHAPTER SEVEN

*P*lease, Lord—*let dinner be perfect!* Prayer pinged around Grace's mind like corn kernels in the wire popper. Her worry was making her as nauseous as the burnt smell from the popcorn she'd incinerated this afternoon, filling the cabin with the awful stench of failure.

Her hands shook as she took the cherry pie out of the oven— Cole's favorite, according to Mildred—bubbling through a lattice crust that was golden brown. She'd followed Mildred's recipe to the letter, even checking the oven every two minutes for nearly an hour to make sure it didn't burn. Sweat beaded her brow as she carefully laid her masterpiece on the windowsill to cool, hoping it would dispel the gloom that shrouded her day.

"It still itches," Becca whined, scratching at the baking soda paste Mildred had instructed Grace to put on Becca's poison ivy. The poison ivy she'd contracted in a game of follow the leader after Grace rolled down a hill, squealing 'round and 'round to the bottom. The *same* bottom where Sarah barreled over a stinging nettle plant, prickling her hands.

Grace's repentant gaze flicked to Ruthy huddled in Mildred's lap, her unblinking stare focused on her sisters as they itched and moaned. Thank God the silent little girl had just watched as usual rather than joining in on Grace's inane antics or she'd be itching, too.

"When will the burning go away?" Sarah wanted to know, not a bit happy to have baking soda paste caked on her hands like her sister.

"Soon," Mildred soothed, her razor-thin glance underscoring her opinion that Grace was more of a child than the girls she cared for.

The door swung open, admitting a cold blast of air along with the man who'd stolen Grace's sleep, causing a shiver to pebble her skin that had little to do with the weather. Cole bolted the door again, then tossed both hat and coat on the rack, cheeks ruddy from the bitter wind.

"How's my family?" His eyes quickly scanned the room as he made a beeline for the blazing hearth where the fire crackled and spit.

"Awful," the girls said in unison, their woebegone looks a perfect match for Mildred's "Grace-be-gone" scowl.

"I have poison ivy," Becca said, "and Sarah has stinging nettle."

Cole blinked, palms midair as he warmed them by the fire. "How in tarnation did that happen in November?"

"How do you think?" Mildred punctuated her accusing tone with a curt nod at Grace.

The roaring fire had nothing on Grace's cheeks when Cole's gaze flitted her way. "Grace? What on earth happened?"

"We had a picnic," Becca explained. "We raced rolling down a hill, and Grace won."

Sure I did. A lump the size of the dumplings she'd made for dinner bobbed in Grace's throat as she avoided Cole's stare. *The prize for idiocy!*

"A picnic?" Cole's sharp tone sent Grace scurrying to rouse Abby for supper. "In the dead of November?"

"We were bored," Sarah said while Grace bundled a sleepy Abby in her arms, the scent of a sweet baby soothing some of her guilt. "And Grace said she could fix that."

"She fixed it all right." Mildred's rocker picked up speed. "But good. Imagine a grown woman teaching 'em to roll down a weedy hill like boulders, and just as dumb." She grunted. "It'll take forever to pick burrs and sticks off their coats alone, much less heal 'em up." Her gripe lowered to a growl that rivaled Grace's stomach. "Doesn't have the sense God gave a goat."

"What on earth were you thinking, Grace?" Cole first squatted to assess Becca's rash, then Sarah's before he rose to prick her with a piercing stare.

"Humph. Not much." Mildred pressed a kiss to Ruthy's unscathed cheek as if grateful she escaped the peril of Grace's bumbling care.

Avoiding Cole's eyes, Grace slipped Abby into her high-chair, nudging a cooled plate of chopped chicken and dumplings toward her before meeting his gaze. "I'm sorry, Cole," she whispered, stomach plummeting at the disappointment she saw. "It's been so dreary and the girls have been inside so much, I just thought a winter picnic might be fun."

"Fun." Mildred scowled. "Could do with less of that and a little more care."

"Millie!" Cole's stern tone surprised even Grace. He washed up before lifting Ruthy from Mildred's lap. "If it's all the same to you, I'd like to enjoy a peaceful dinner with my family." He seated Ruthy with a tired kiss, then sniffed the air, no doubt smelling the tinge of burnt popcorn along with cherry pie. "Hmm, something smells awfully good." He helped Mildred hobble to the table, her crutch clunking on a floor now littered with twigs, burs, and baking soda paste.

"Mildred gave me her recipe for cherry pie." Grace's voice was tentative as she brought dinner to the table, praying the pie would redeem her somewhat. "And there were plenty of canned cherries in the cellar, so I thought I'd give it a try."

"Well, that's certainly my favorite." Polite approval laced his tone as he poured milk into everyone's glasses per his routine. "So other than cockleburs, poison ivy, and stinging nettle," he said with a hint of jest, "how was the picnic?"

"Good!" Becca reached for a biscuit, automatically sawing the burnt part off. "We ate cornbread and raisins on the bluff over the river." She shuddered. "But it *shorrrrre* was cold."

"But no ants, right?" Cole gave her a wink and took his chair, bowing his head for grace. "Lord, we give thanks for this meal, for our family, and for Grace, without whom I wouldn't have time to be in my shop to put food on the table. Amen."

His aunt poked at a dumpling before taking a nibble. "Doc came by today and said he might take the cast off sooner, maybe first week of December." She plopped the entire dumpling in her mouth with an air of pride, as if "Aunt Crab" was the one who propped pillows, kept the cast dry during daily sponge baths, or relieved the itch with a bellows. Grace bit back a smile.

"That's great news, Millie," Cole said. "Soon we'll be back to normal."

Normal.

Grace jumped up to retrieve the pie, the ache in her chest reminding her that no matter the laughter and love all around her, she wasn't family and would soon be gone. But between Flossie's offer of a job waiting tables at Last Chance Café and an attic room at Mrs. Monroe's boardinghouse in exchange for Grace's help, at least she was on the threshold of a new life. Not the one she'd always imagined, maybe, but certainly better than before.

But . . . till then, she was determined to win this family's favor. Setting the pie on the table, she feigned nonchalance when everyone ooohed and ahhhed, her manner deliberately casual as she handed out dessert. But the moment Cole complimented her, she lost the fight, the approval in his eyes warming both her heart and her cheeks.

When everyone had been served and coffee poured, Grace spooned pie into Abby's mouth, delighted when the little girl lunged for more. Chuckling, Grace dumped a small piece in front of her while Cole moaned with every bite, the sound actually fluttering her stomach.

"Frog freckles," Becca said with a thorough lick of her spoon, "this has to be the bestest pie ever, don't you think so, Aunt Millie?"

All eyes converged on Mildred, and for several thundering heartbeats, the room was silent. And then, the tight purse of the woman's lips slowly curved in a smile as thin as the air in Grace's lungs. "I'd say it's a downright miracle given the hands that baked it."

Grace couldn't help it—she grinned, the backhanded compliment the most praise she'd ever received from the woman with the scowl.

"Better than angel food baked in heaven, for dead sure." Sarah swept her tongue over her plate in wide sweeps, eyes closed in a show of ecstasy. Once she'd licked it clean, she laughed at Abby, who wore cherry juice head-to-toe, complete with cherry pulp caked on her lashes.

"Well, Grace, I'd say your dessert was a real succe—" Cole started to raise his coffee in a toast when Sarah screamed. Her fork dropped as she reached for Abby, who jerked back in her chair with a wheeze, face deathly pale.

Cole shot up so abruptly his chair crashed to the floor. In a blur, he swooped Abby up and gave several sharp blows to her back with the heel of his hand, the fierce calm of his manner belying the leach of blood from his face.

As if in a trance, everyone stared in horror while Cole continued to pound, Abby's tiny body limp like Ruthy's rag doll over his arm. Ruthy started to cry, and the sound was eerily foreign for a child who never spoke. Heart hammering, Grace snatched her up, silently rocking her while prayers pummeled her mind. *Please, God, don't let Abby die . . .*

With a final thud of Cole's hand, something pinged off the floorboards, and with a gasp, Abby's face went from near blue to mottled red as she flailed and bawled at the top of her lungs.

The most glorious sound Grace ever heard!

It was then Grace noticed the tremble of Cole's hands as he clutched his daughter, thanking God over and over while he buried his face in her neck. Sarah and Becca rushed his legs in a whimpering hug that brought him to his knees, water welling in his eyes as he embraced them all. Thrashing wildly, Ruthy scrambled from Grace's arms to join her sisters.

"What happened, Daddy?" Becca said, voice quivering as much as Grace's body.

He pressed a kiss to each of their heads before he rose. "A cherry pit, most likely." He scanned the floor until he found it. "Thank you, Lord, for saving our sweet girl's life." He held up the pit, gaze awash in a sheen of gratitude. "This, my precious daughters, is the grace of God against the hand of evil, so never forget the boundless mercy of our Father above."

"Bring my girl to me," Mildred said, arms outstretched and tears streaking her face. The family gathered around while Grace stood inert, her body lifeless and her mind vacant. She ached to hold Abby, to breathe in her scent and whisper love, but that was a privilege lost. "Double-check for pits," Mildred had warned, but Grace forgot, too excited to win this family's trust.

Only she'd lost it instead.

Again.

"I'm so sorry," she whispered, but no one seemed to hear, their laughter, love, and relief surrounding them. Something she wasn't part of. Nor ever would be. Because as Cole had so painfully put it, this had been "the grace of God against the hand of evil."

Sleet slithered through her veins. *The hand of evil.* She opened the door and silently slipped out.

Hers.

CHAPTER EIGHT

"Come on, little angel," Cole whispered to Abby, tugging her from Millie while Sarah and Becca cooed and tickled her feet. "Daddy'll put you to bed." He pressed a kiss to her soft curls before noticing the table littered with dirty dishes. "Girls, let's get things cleaned up, and I'll read you a book, all right?"

He was met with shouts of glee that reminded him just how little time he'd spent with his girls of late, devoting most evenings to working in his shop. Taking advantage of Grace's presence to keep his promise to Eileen.

Grace.

He glanced at the kitchen, but she wasn't there, her absence as noticeable as the churn of his stomach over the disaster she'd almost caused. She was probably hiding away in her room, he suspected, and his jaw automatically compressed. *As well she should.* The moment that cherry pit shot from Abby's mouth, his concerns about her ability to care for his children were confirmed. Why hadn't she taken greater care with that pie or mashed Abby's piece as usual? *Because she's not responsible enough, that's why.* Snatching Abby's bottle on the way to her room, he silently berated himself for leaving his family in the hands of a woman who was a menace.

And a blessing? He paused while unpinning his daughter's wet diaper, the thought so out of the blue he knew it wasn't his own. Abby gurgled, reminding him of the peals of delight that always rang out whenever Grace changed her, the bond between them as thick as the triple flannel pieces Grace insisted on using. Even if it meant more washing for her.

46

"I want Abby to feel warm and snug," she claimed, twirling his daughter around and around in a giggle dance that soon had the older girls begging for one, too.

Sometimes the woman seemed little more than a child herself, a playful scamp so full of mischief and challenge Cole felt compelled to constantly cover her and his family with prayer.

Grace is an answer to prayer.

For a second time, Cole found himself hesitating before tossing Abby's dirty diaper and clothes in the laundry pail, the voice in his head diffusing his anger. Okay, yes, there was no question Grace had fulfilled a need in his family. He tugged a fresh nightgown over Abby's head before settling into one of the several rockers he'd built. But sometimes he wondered if all the calamity was worth it. Laughter drifted in from the parlor as Abby closed her eyes to drink from her bottle, and in two creaks of the chair, he had his answer.

Yes.

Grace's stay had been worth it if one counted giggles and smiles where few had been found before. And love. Lots and lots of love that helped fill the gaps left by both their mother and father, a man who was gone more than he was home.

The moment Abby stopped suckling, Cole carefully laid her in her crib with a soft kiss, suddenly anxious to alleviate Grace of the guilt he knew she must be feeling. Silently closing the door, his gaze skimmed parlor and kitchen before peeking in her empty bedroom.

"Where's Grace?" he asked Mildred, but she only shrugged, knitting needles flying while Ruthy snuggled at her side.

"Haven't seen her since Abby choked," Becca said, drying a dish as Sarah washed, both girls peering over their shoulders. "But her coat's gone, Daddy, so maybe she took a walk."

"Maybe she did," he muttered, grabbing his jacket. "Girls, I need to find her, but I shouldn't be long." Buttoning his coat, he turned up his collar and opened the door.

Closing it again, he searched the porch and yard, but the only shadows he saw were moonlit trees swaying in the chilly breeze. He squinted down the hill at the darkened church and instantly knew that's where she'd be. She knew where he kept a key. What he hadn't anticipated, however, was the anguished sound of her weeping when he opened the sanctuary door.

"Grace?" His voice was no more than a whisper, but she obviously hadn't heard given the sobs that wracked her body with a violence that tore at his soul.

"Grace," he whispered again, sliding into the pew, her agony quickly becoming his own. She jolted with a gasp that trembled into a sob, and with a wrench in his gut, he tugged her to his chest, stroking wild curls as impulsive and uninhibited as the woman herself. He whispered into her hair, the scent of lavender luring his eyes closed. "It wasn't your fault."

"I-It w-was," she stuttered, jerking back as if to convince him, her wild-eyed stare fracturing his heart. "I almost killed your daughter, Cole, and I'd rather die than ever hurt Abby or any of your children."

"I know." He stroked the line of her jaw like she was one of his daughters. Only she wasn't. She was a woman who'd managed to stir his emotions without his being aware. "It was an accident," he said quietly, "and I don't blame you at all."

At least, not anymore. The thought took him by surprise, halting his hand against her skin. His breath snagged as he stared, his prior anger and irritation suddenly nowhere to be found, replaced instead by a deep-seated gratitude for the woman in his arms. "Grace." He lifted her quivering chin with a gentle finger, coaxing her gaze up so she could see the affection in his. "You are appropriately named, Grace O'Malley, for you have been a touch of God's grace in our lives when we needed it most." His mouth curved in a tender smile. "A challenge at times, yes, but I assure you, the good far outweighs the . . ." His lips twitched. "Challenge."

She swiped at her eyes, looking so much like a little girl, he wanted to hug her all over again. "Do you . . . do you really m-mean that?" she whispered, her frail question muffled by a noisy groan of her stomach.

His grin came as naturally as breathing. "Yes, I really mean that."

He fished his handkerchief from his pocket and dabbed at her cheeks, finally offering it to her. She blew her nose so loudly, he grinned again, suddenly struck by a sense of childlike innocence he seldom encountered in a woman. An innocence that suddenly stuttered his pulse, drawing his gaze to full lips now kissed by her own tears. Jarred by the jolt of attraction he felt, he scooted back.

"I promised the girls a story before bed, but I wanted to make sure you were all right." He nudged her chin up again, giving her his best parental smile. "You are, aren't you?"

She nodded with another sniff while those unruly curls bobbed in assent, and without thinking, he deposited a kiss to her forehead, totally unprepared for the sudden sprint of his pulse. Against his will, his eyes closed, lips lingering far longer than they should. But when his mouth skimmed to her temple, he could do nothing but drink in the silky touch of her skin, the intoxicating scent of her hair. A sense of panic seized him when he realized his shallow breathing was in tandem with hers, and shooting to his feet, he stumbled back.

"I need to go, but stay as long as you want." He swallowed hard, guilt and shame pummeling his brain.

"Not sure how you keep from falling for a woman like that when she's right under your nose, but I thank God because I sure aim to make her my own."

Tom's words stopped his blood cold, cooling the heat of desire that coursed through his veins. Heaven help him, he didn't know either, but by the grace of God, he would stop these feelings, one way or the other. Stepping out of the pew, he turned, steeling his will for what he needed to do

"Grace, I have a favor to ask," he said, sidestepping any mention of the damage he'd almost done.

She sprang to her feet, the earnestness of her manner all but breaking his heart. "Anything, Cole," she whispered, eyes shining with a caring that constricted his ribs.

He looked away. "I . . . I made a promise to Eileen before she . . ." He swallowed hard, unwilling to utter the words that had altered his life forever. "To give my daughters and Millie a piano for Christmas, which is why I've been working so hard. You see, Mrs. Merriweather is selling me her Steinway for a fair price, in conjunction, of course, with furniture commissioned. Unfortunately, I'm behind on the final piece, so I'll need every spare moment to finish . . ." His throat convulsed several times before he met her hopeful gaze with a stoic one of his own. " . . . before you leave." The words hung thick in the sanctuary, not unlike the attraction that stifled his air, and he saw the light die in her eyes as she gave him a dull nod.

He forged on. "Which means, I need to take advantage by working late and through dinner every night till you leave, so if you can save me a plate, I'd be much obliged."

She nodded again, the motion almost listless for a woman who usually lit up a room.

Jaw compressed, he gave a firm tug of his hat. "You've been a godsend to my family, Grace," he said quietly, chest cramping when he realized this was the last time he'd ever see her alone. "And I can't thank you enough for all you have done."

Those perfect lips curved in a sad smile while she hugged her arms to her waist, as if barricading herself against that same awful ache that throbbed in his own chest. She made a valiant attempt at a jest with the faint glimmer of tease. "*All* I have done, Pastor McCabe? Including the daily threats to your family and home?"

He scratched the back of his neck with a sheepish grin. "Well, not all, maybe, but most. You have my word."

Her lips blossomed into the sweetest of smiles he'd grown to cherish and love. "Well, it's only two more weeks, I suppose," she said softly, tucking his handkerchief in the pocket of her coat as she reclaimed her seat in the pew. "And then your house will be safe forever."

"Indeed." Smile stiff, he bid her good night and headed home, an unexpected emptiness seeping into his soul as he quietly closed the door. *Safe forever.* Yes, his house, certainly. He hunched further into his coat as he made his way up the hill.

And, God willing, his heart, too.

CHAPTER NINE

"Miss O'Malley?"

Grace started, the sight of Tom O'Shaughnessy towering over her with a cup of punch in his hands jarring her from her reverie. A blessing, for sure, since the reverie had been focused on Cole across the sanctuary as he chatted with Pastor Daniel McCoy and his wife, Libby, close friends from the next town. Since Last Chance Chapel was a good-sized building with movable pews now lined against the walls, it was the perfect place for a Thanksgiving service and social for both congregations. So when Tom offered to fetch her some punch, Grace had taken full advantage of the crowd to watch the man she'd barely seen all week.

The same one who'd turned her world completely upside down.

She could hear his rich laughter over the shrieks of children who darted in and out of the sea of adults, the sight of Abby dozing over his shoulder melting Grace's heart. He was such a good man, so full of fire for family and faith, his sermons always stirring her with their passion and depth.

Just like the touch of his lips had stirred her soul not one week ago.

At the memory, a gloom stole the joy of the day, reminding her that despite the care and desire she'd seen in his eyes in this very sanctuary, there was no place for her in his family or in his life. He'd made that abundantly clear, distancing himself from her presence as thoroughly as he'd distanced his heart.

"There's always a crowd at these events, so it's hard to hear over the chatter and noise." Tom handed her the punch, his volume high, no doubt, to make up for her lack of attention. "If you like, we can talk someplace quieter, like Flossie's for a cup of coffee since the social's almost over. Then maybe dinner after?"

Grace paused, unable to douse the look of hope in his eyes. She glanced to where Cole was laughing with Pastor McCoy while Becca and the Turner boy darted around his legs in an apparent game of tag.

"I already checked with Cole," he said quickly, as if worried her hesitation meant she might say no. "So you have a free night if you want. He said he was overdue for dinner with his family anyway."

With Mildred at home with Ruthy, Abby asleep over Cole's shoulder, and the older girls enjoying games, there was no reason for Grace to stay. Releasing a frail sigh, she looked up at the man who wanted her company, even if his best friend did not.

"I'd like that." She gave him a polite smile, convincing herself it wasn't a lie. After all, she needed to distance her heart from Cole, too, and at the moment, Tom seemed like the best way to do that.

"That's great!" He grinned ear to ear, and Grace couldn't deny he was a handsome man who'd certainly gone out of his way to gain her attention. Offering his arm, he ushered her to the front door, fielding comments and slaps on the back on their way through the crowd. Retrieving their coats, he helped her on with her wrap before donning his own, then opened the door. He grinned and gave a salute to someone across the room, and Grace couldn't resist a peek over her shoulder.

Her gaze collided with Cole's, and her heart stuttered, the look on his face appearing as stiff as her own. With a nod of acknowledgment, she turned and followed Tom outside, the cool air a welcome relief to the heat she felt in her cheeks.

"I'll bet it's nice to get out of the house for a change, isn't it?" An eager smile lit his face as he carefully led her toward town, the warmth of his hand helping to ease the chill in her heart.

"Yes, it is," she said with a gentle smile, more grateful for Tom O'Shaughnessy than she ever believed she would be.

More than you'll ever know.

Cole's smile faded the moment Tom and Grace headed for the door, his good mood suddenly disappearing.

"Everything okay?"

He glanced down at Daniel's wife, Libby, a sprite of a woman who never missed a thing. The moment he'd introduced her to Grace, the two had chatted like old friends, just like Libby and Eileen used to do, making Cole homesick for the camaraderie the couples once shared. They'd been closer than siblings, and he missed that more than he realized. He forced a smile. "Sure, why wouldn't it be?"

Libby peered up with a squint that told Cole she didn't intend to let it go. "I'm not sure, but you haven't seemed yourself all day, and I couldn't help but notice you scowled when Tom and Grace left.

He blinked, suddenly annoyed she had read him so well. Shifting Abby on his shoulder, he welcomed the baby's warmth as she curled against him. "I'm just tired, Libs, that's all. Up till midnight every night trying to finish Mrs. Merriweather's furniture before Christmas."

"You need help?" Daniel asked.

"No, I'm on schedule, Dan, but thanks. Just trying to get as much done as I can before Grace leaves, so I can help Millie more when she gets back on her feet."

"I like Grace," Libby said, studying him with a boldness that only close friendship afforded. "She's a sweet girl, and by the frown on your face when she took off with Tom, I'd say you like her, too."

Cole bristled, suddenly anxious to round up the girls and head up the hill. "Of course I like her, Libby, she's been great with the kids." His mouth quirked into a smile to deflect the raw nerve that she struck. "It's the house, the food, and the children's health that haven't fared quite so well, but even so, she's a good woman."

Before Libby could ask more questions, he called to Sarah and Becca, telling them it was time to go. He faced Libby and Daniel, tone apologetic. "Sorry to hurry off, but Millie and Ruthy are alone, and Abby needs to nap in her bed."

Libby touched his arm and spoke in a gentle tone. "Not only is she a good woman, Cole, but it's pretty obvious she's in love with you, too."

"Daddy, I don't want to go," Sarah whined, and never had Cole been more grateful for a child's interruption.

"Aunt Millie and Ruthy have been alone all day, and we need to take them some cookies and put Abby down. So please get your sister because we're leaving."

Groaning, she trudged away to fetch Becca, giving Cole the perfect opportunity to leave. He extended his hand to Dan, ignoring the pursed look on Libby's face. "Dan, it's been great to see you again, and I look forward to our joint Christmas service," he said with a firm shake. He gave Libby a side hug, feeling guilty for ignoring her comment. "Libs, I like Grace; I do," he whispered for her ears alone, "but not only is she not the type of mother I want for my children, but my best friend wants to court her, so I don't have a choice."

Libby fixed him with a probing stare, the clamp of her jaw a sure sign she didn't agree. "Eileen was the best mother I ever knew, Cole, but sometimes God has something different in mind, so I sure hope you don't miss it."

"Daddy, we're ready." Sarah and Becca saved his clipped response, but not the heat that crawled up the back of his neck. Nodding to both Libby and Dan, he ushered his girls toward the vestibule to put on their coats and bundle Abby in a blanket. He offered a handshake to Harve and Percy, thanking them for volunteering to lock up after things were cleaned.

Plodding up the hill, the girls jabbered nonstop, chattering about all the fun they'd had.

"Is Mr. O'Shaughnessy bringing Grace home?" Sarah suddenly asked, reminding Cole how shocked the girls had been when Grace left with Tom.

"Yes." He picked up the pace, brightening his tone. "He plans to court her."

Becca skidded to a stop. "But Grace is ours, Daddy! Why aren't you courting her?"

The question of the day, apparently.

Cole huffed out a weary sigh while he herded the girls into the house, systematically hanging up their coats. "Grace is just with us for a season, Bec, and when Aunt Millie gets her cast off next week, Grace will have to leave."

"But, why?" Sarah wanted to know, the mournful slant of her brows a clear indicator she didn't agree. "Grace is part of our family, Daddy."

"No, she's *not*." His curt tone drew everyone's gaze. Closing his eyes, he massaged his temple, ashamed for snapping at his family. He expelled a heavy sigh and gave them a feeble smile. "I'm sorry, girls, but let me put your sister down, and I'll explain." Laying Abby into her crib, Cole quietly closed the door, then squatted to draw them close. "I'm going to miss Grace as much as you, but Aunt Millie will be back on her feet soon, so it's time for Grace to begin her own life. And," he emphasized before Becca could object, "Tom is hoping it will be with him, so we need to let her go and not mention it again, understood?"

With sad-eyed nods, both girls turned and trudged to their room.

"How does chili sound for supper?" he called, hoping to entice them with a favorite meal.

"I don't care," Sarah said, flopping onto her bed.

"Me either." Becca moped, shutting him out with a click of the door.

"Don't expect sympathy from me, because I think you're being a dolt."

Cole spun around to stare at Millie, his jaw agape. "What are you talking about? You can't even stand the woman."

Millie scooted Ruthy off her lap, planting a noisy kiss on top of her head. "Go see your sisters, darlin', so I can have a word with your mule-headed father."

Searing Millie with a look, Cole stooped to give Ruthy a squeeze. "I love you, sugar-pea," he whispered, heart aching when she slipped out of his arms without even a hint of a smile.

He blasted out his frustration. "Now how in tarnation did I become the bad guy here?" He dropped into his rocker and put his head in his hands.

Millie's voice had its usual edge. "You know, Cole, I couldn't abide that girl when you brought her home. Thought for sure God had slapped the Four Horsemen of the Apocalypse into one little filly, never knowing what disaster she was going to inflict next." The loud squeak of her rocker meant she was picking up speed. "But I was dead wrong."

His head shot up, jaw unhinging for the second time in as many minutes. "What?"

Her lips compressed into a thin line. "Truth is, I'm a stubborn old goat who didn't want anybody taking my place with my babies, especially not some pretty little thing with more cotton in her head than brains." Her lips began to gum like always when she was about to swallow some pride. "But after sweet Abby choked on that pit and Grace came home without an iota of that infernal joy she's always a bubblin' around, well, the Lord and me had a talk. And I don't mind sayin' he brought me up short. Told me in no uncertain terms that this cotton-head girl was a gift to this family, and if I didn't start treatin' her right, I was cuttin' off my nose to spite my own face."

Cole could only stare, mouth hanging open like that dolt she'd accused him of being.

The scowl on Millie's face suddenly softened, and Cole swore he saw a glint of tears. "I didn't want to give her a chance because she was here with my babies instead of Eileen, but it don't take a blessed genius to see that woman was plumb good for us all." She sniffed, then thrust her chin up as if to ward off more tears, her crotchety manner back in place. "So if you let her waltz out that door and take up with Tom, then you're a bigger dolt than I thought."

Cole groaned and rubbed his face with his hands. "She's an accident in the making, Millie, and nothing like the mother I want for my kids." He hung his head, closing his eyes as his voice faded with futility. "And nothing like Eileen."

"No . . . no, she's not," Millie said quietly, the squeaking commencing once again, "but Eileen's gone, son, and I believe God sent this woman to take her place or he wouldn't have had the two of you fall so all-fire in love."

"I *don't* love her," he hissed, the very notion scaring him silly. But the moment the words left his mouth, he knew they were a lie. His shoulders slumped as he put a hand to his eyes. "For the love of God, how did this happen?"

Mille emitted a raspy chuckle. "By just that, Cole—the love of God. A gracious God who binds two people together in devotion to him. Just like he did for me and my Sam and then for you and Eileen. And looks to this old woman he's afixin' to do it again."

Cole ran shaky fingers through his hair, his breathing as jerky as his pulse. He raised his head, panic contorting his face. "But what if she doesn't love me? What if she wants Tom?"

"She don't," Millie said with a certainty that stilled his soul. "You may be one fine preacher, Pastor McCabe, but I'd say you're plumb witless if you don't see the longing in that cotton-girl's eyes." She shuffled in the rocker and pounded her crutch on the floor. "Now git me to my room so I can rest these old bones. You and the Lord done worn me plumb out."

A slow grin spanned the whole of his face at the thought of Grace in his life—and his heart—forever. "Have I told you lately, Millie, just how much I love you?"

"Yeah, yeah, yeah." She shot him a sour look, but he didn't miss the rise of color pinking her cheeks. "Don't tell it to me, preacher boy, tell it to the girl with cotton in her head.

CHAPTER TEN

"Oh my goodness!" Grace caught her breath outside the café, her gasp rising in a puff of warm air as white as the flakes drifting from the sky. "It's snowing!"

Her words billowed into the crisp, cold air like the wood smoke from the chimney pipes along Main Street. Without a second thought, she darted into the snow-covered street to twirl around with outstretched arms and palms up as if she could capture every heavenly crystal.

"I just adore snow," she breathed, her words tinged with the same awe she'd known when Maggie had convinced her she was no longer that saloon girl laden with sin but a new creature in Christ.

Though your sins be as scarlet, they shall be as white as snow.

"You look like an angel," Tom said softly, standing so close that Grace's breath snagged in her throat. He gently brushed snowflakes from her cheeks, the tenderness in his eyes chilling her more than the ice doilies melting on her skin.

"I s-should really g-get h-home," she said with a falter in her voice, heat flooding her cheeks at the mistaken notion that Cole's home belonged to her.

"Absolutely." Tom offered his arm with a patient smile, and she took it, relieved when he launched into entertaining stories of growing up in Montana where blizzards were the norm. She chuckled at the appropriate places, of course, but her eyes always strayed to the top of the hill, where lamplight glowed in windows as if calling her home.

If only.

"Grace, I had a wonderful time," Tom said when they stood on Cole's porch.

She glanced up, unwilling to qualify anything as "wonderful" that didn't include Cole. "It *was* a nice evening," she said softly. "Thank you for the lovely dinner."

He moved in close. "Only the first of many, I hope," he whispered, his look of affection stealing her air. "Because the truth is, I'd like to court you, Grace, so may I?"

"Uh . . . well, uh . . ."

Grace jumped, hand to her chest, when the door whooshed open.

"Oh, you're back—good." Cole latched a hand on her arm and tugged her in. "The girls refused to go to bed till you got home, so thanks, Tom, for taking good care of her."

"Sure, no problem," Tom said with a definite strain in his voice, the tight bunch of his jaw a sure sign there was, indeed, a "problem." His gaze flitted to Grace, softening the frown on his face. "So, as to my question, Grace—may I?"

Her stomach gurgled loudly, and she swallowed hard, keenly aware of Cole's hand on her arm. "I . . . I . . ."

"Grace!" Becca darted from the bedroom with Sarah on her heels, nightgown flying as she toppled Grace out of Cole's hold.

In mirror-like motion, both men grabbed to steady Grace with equal force. "I *have* her," Cole emphasized in a steely tone that loosened Tom's grip. "You'll have to talk tomorrow, Tom, 'cause we really need to get these kids to bed."

"Sure," Tom said with a pinch of lips. He tipped his hat to Grace, unseating a dance of snow from the brim. "Thanks again, Grace. Talk to you tomorrow."

She barely had time for a nod before Cole heaved the door shut, whirling a flurry of flakes into the parlor.

"Sweet Sunday sassafras, it's snowing!" Becca raced Sarah to the window.

"Isn't it wonderful?" Grace hurried to join them, grateful for the reprieve from the tension at the door. She felt a tug and glanced down to see Ruthy rubbing sleepy eyes while dangling a tattered ragdoll. Lifting her up, Grace propped her on her hip and pointed out the window. "Look, Ruthy—the first snow of the season!"

The little girl's body went rigid, and Grace's heart constricted at the harsh catch of Ruthy's breath.

"Mama!" Ruthy whispered, voice hoarse as she thrashed to skitter down Grace's coat. Bare feet slapping, she sprinted to the front door, pounding her tiny fist in a panic. "Mama, Mama!"

With a hitch of her pulse, Grace met Cole's confused look with one of her own, rushing to Ruthy's side. Cole swept her up while Grace attempted to soothe her. "Ruthy, what's wrong?"

But the little mite only bucked and lunged for the door, almost leaping out of Cole's arms. "Mama, Mama . . ."

"It must be the snow," Grace said, opening the door wide to show Ruthy everything was all right. "See, sweetheart? It's just snow—like God is sifting sugar to bake you a cake." She scooped up a handful, tasting it before offering some to Ruthy. "Mmm . . . try it!"

Ruthy stilled for a taste, then started wiggling again, stubby arms straining toward the snowy steps. "Mama, Mama . . ."

"Ruthy darlin'," Cole pleaded, "please tell Daddy what's wrong."

Frantic to help, Grace snatched the girl's coat off the rack and slipped it on her tiny body. "Cole, bring her out on the porch for a moment, will you?" She flew down the steps to the yard, whirling around with arms stretched high to catch snowflakes with her tongue. Becca and Sarah giggled when she wobbled to a stop. "See, Ruthy? Snow is fun, and tomorrow we'll build a snowman and fort to show you how much. But first . . ." She waggled her brows. "How 'bout a snow angel to guard our house?" Not waiting for an answer, Grace plopped into a snowdrift with a squeal, flapping arms and legs in wide arcs.

"Mama!" Ruthy almost vaulted to Grace.

Grinning, Grace hopped up and dusted off her coat, totally unprepared for the onslaught of emotions when Ruthy leapt into her arms with a sob.

"Mama used to make snow angels with us," Sarah said from the door, her tremulous tone nearly breaking Grace's heart.

"I love you, Ruthy," Grace whispered, "and everything will be all right, sweetheart, you'll see." Lashes lifting, Grace's gaze collided with

Cole's, and goose bumps pebbled her skin at the glow of love in his eyes. And for one erratic skip of her pulse, she pretended that look was meant for her as well as his daughter.

"Okay, monkeys, time for bed." Cole stamped his feet at the door before latching a hand to Sarah's and Becca's necks, their giggles leading him to their room.

Grace followed with Ruthy, the little girl's hold so tight, Grace could do nothing but settle into the chair and rock her to sleep while Cole prayed with her sisters.

"Will you sing 'Amay'?" Becca's sweet voice drifted across the room after Cole deposited kisses and tucked them both in.

"Of course, sweetheart," she said quietly, the faint squeak of the rocker in perfect harmony with the haunting sound of Amazing Grace. Cole's silhouette watched from the doorway, and Grace closed her eyes, desperate to focus on her favorite hymn rather than on him.

Long after Ruthy fell asleep, Grace stayed, removing the little girl's coat before she finally tucked her in. She deposited a tender kiss to each of their heads. "Good night, my sweet angels," she whispered with a sting of tears. *How I will miss our precious moments together!*

Quietly closing the door, Grace was grateful all lamps had been doused, indicating Cole had also turned in. Unbuttoning her coat, she glanced at the hearth where he always slept in his clothes on a cot, firelight flickering over his lean body as she tiptoed to hang up her wrap.

"Don't. Please."

She spun around, heart ramming her ribcage as his shadow rose. Her voice came out as a croak. "What?"

"Don't take your coat off," he whispered, his unhurried approach turning her mouth to dust, too dry to utter consent. "I'd like to sit a spell outside and talk if it's all right."

Without another word, he carefully rebuttoned her coat while her body went stock-still, the action robbing her of air till she thought she couldn't breathe. His gaze burned into hers as he reached for his jacket and slid it on, snatching a blanket before opening the door. He nodded for her to go out, then followed behind, tugging his gloves on to sweep snow off the swing.

Blood pounded in her ears as she sat, and her chest constricted over what he was about to say. *Oh, Lord, he's going to ask me to leave early, I know it, and that's going to break my heart!*

Body trembling, she hugged her arms to her waist and scooted to the edge, almost jumping out of her skin when he sat right beside her. She could feel the heat of his body, warming her more than the blanket he carefully tucked around them both.

"Grace," he said softly, the whisper of her name languishing like a ghost in the winter sky. "This is awkward, I know, but . . ."

Her chin began to quiver as she squeezed her eyes shut, moisture pricking in them over the words she expected to hear. *I want you to go.*

"I don't want you to go . . ."

With everything in her, she fought a rising sob to no avail. It pushed past her lips in a shudder that shook her body to the core, causing Cole to bundle her close. He tugged her tighter with every heave, but it only made her weep harder, the agony of leaving this family she loved—this man she loved—too painful to bear. She'd known this day would come, but she'd hoped somehow, someway, God would see her through.

I will never leave thee, nor forsake thee.

Cole nudged his handkerchief into her hand, and she gave a shaky nod, allowing God's Word to calm her as she patted her eyes. "I understand," she whispered. "Mrs. Monroe said I'm welcome to move in anytime, so I'll pack my bags tomorrow."

She froze when he cupped her face in his hands, the intensity in his eyes fusing her to the spot. "No, Grace," he said with a tender smile, "I didn't say I want you to *leave*—I said I want you to *stay*."

She blinked, mind as foggy as the clouds of breath swirling into the sky from her gaping mouth. "S-Stay?"

His low chuckle tingled her skin as he traced her jaw with the pad of his thumb. "Yes, I want you to stay."

Her heartbeat skyrocketed. "To t-take c-care of the children? B-but . . . b-but your aunt is almost well—"

"No . . ." Her heart stopped when he moved in close while he feathered the side of her face with the tips of his fingers. "To take care of me," he whispered. "I love you, Grace, and I want to marry you." He kissed her cheek with such tenderness, her eyes fluttered closed.

"Marry me on Christmas," he whispered, "and help me give my family the best gift of all."

Her lashes lifted as her lips quivered into a wobbly smile. "Oh, Cole . . . are you sure? Because heaven knows I'm not a good cook."

His chuckle caressed the side of her face with a warmth that spread all the way to the tips of her fingers and toes. "Completely," he said, teasing her with a playful kiss to the tip of her nose, "as long as Millie keeps you out of the kitchen."

CHAPTER ELEVEN

Have to admit—wasn't sure you'd show." Squatting in front of Mrs. Merriweather's new hutch, Cole looked up, polish rag limp in his hand.

Tom ambled in with a grunt, flinging his coat on the rack. "Me either," he said with a one-sided smile, dropping into a chair to hike boots on the table. "Finally figured Grace's heart wasn't mine to lose, so that kind of steals the thunder out of making my best friend pay."

Cole winced as he swiped his brow with the back of his hand. "Yeah, well, I guarantee I've paid plenty these last few weeks, old buddy, achin' clean through when one of the people I respect most turns his back on me." He paused, eyes in a squint as he studied the man who'd long ago offered his friendship no matter the cost. "Thanks, Tom."

Huffing out a sigh, Tom scratched the back of his head. "Yeah, well, it's bad enough to lose the prettiest gal in Last Chance to the likes of you, preacher boy. Figured it was plumb stupid to lose my best friend, too."

Grinning, Cole continued to buff out the hutch. "Well, look at it this way—at least the good Lord spared you from charred food."

An easy grin wended its way across Tom's lips. "I must admit, there is that one small consolation. I'll be eatin' better than you." He propped hands to the back of his neck. "So, tonight we deliver the hutch, eh? And a week early, too. There's gonna be some mighty happy folks come Christmas morning, in your family *and* in this church."

Cole polished the wood till it gleamed like a mirror, reflecting the contented smile of a man whose future gleamed just as bright. "No doubt about that," he said softly, throat clogging with emotion at how much God had blessed him with a woman who was nothing like he'd wanted, but everything he'd ever need. His smile tipped.

Including a piano teacher.

"She may wreak havoc in the kitchen, but Millie says when it comes to music, she's a mighty talented woman, your Grace," Tom said with a hint of longing.

My Grace. Cole's chest rose and fell in gratitude. *And all because of God's grace.*

"She ever tell you where she learned how to play and sing like that?"

Cole pretended not to hear, focusing hard on one of the drawers. *Yeah, The Red Dog Saloon.* His mouth thinned. The only dull spot in a future that was shiny and new. But like Cole had told Grace the day she arrived, they would just keep that between them for now.

"Pastor McCabe?"

Cole spun around, caught off guard by a swarthy-looking stranger at the door in a satin vest and expensive black duster sprinkled with snow.

"I'm Colton McCabe. What can I do for you, Mr. . . .?"

The man strolled in, and the smell of tobacco and beeswax followed him, his waxed moustache too wide over a smile Cole didn't trust. "Crocker—Doyle Crocker, and it's not what you can do for me, Pastor McCabe," he said, pushing his duster back to rest a hand on the hilt of his gun, "it's what I can do for you."

"And what's that, Mr. Crocker?" Cole tossed the polish rag into a bucket before he eased into the chair behind his desk, facing the man with a calm fold of his arms.

"Help clean up your congregation. You see, I'm here to collect something that's mine—a pretty little saloon girl who ran off owing me a fair amount of money."

The biscuits Cole had for dinner roiled in his stomach, and for once it wasn't because they were burnt. He studied the dandy before him with a cool smile. "The only saloon girls here, mister, are down at the Diamondback Saloon."

"Not this one," the man said, reaching inside his coat to produce an envelope he flipped onto the desk. Cole's expression never wavered as he recognized Grace's free and fluid handwriting, but his stomach more than made up for it when a smirk slid across the stranger's face. "Found this letter buried in one of my girl's room, and it would appear

Songbird Sadie has been playing house with you, Pastor."

Cole shot up like popcorn kernels in a scorched pot. "Get out—now! I don't know any Songbird Sadie, and I don't like your tone."

"Pretty harsh words for a pastor, but can't say I blame you." His black eyes glittered with greed. "I was mad as a peeled rattler, too, when Sadie Grace O'Malley ran out on me, stealing that pretty voice and face of hers from my customers, especially with a sky-high debt she'd promised to work off."

Tom bounded to his feet, fists clenched at his sides. "You're flat-out lying! Grace O'Malley is no more a saloon girl than I am."

"No?" The lowlife produced a folded piece of paper from inside his coat and leisurely opened it, chucking it on the desk. "Then s'pose you explain why her signature is on this IOU to my brother, promising to pay off her debt with her wages from The Red Dog Saloon."

Ignoring the shock on Tom's face, Cole snatched the paper, stomach plunging when he saw the amount. He threw it down and fished a key out of his pocket to unlock the desk drawer he'd built as a steel-lined safe for the church's funds. Bypassing the church lockbox, he snatched up a burlap bag and hurled it on the desk, eyes harder than the silver coins inside—a year's worth of scrimping to keep a promise to his wife. "That's three fourths of what she owes, so take it and get out of here. I'll send the rest when I have it."

Laughter boomed through the tiny workshop, as sinister as the grin on the man's face. He nabbed the sack, chuckling as he counted it out. "Sorry, Rev," he said, tucking it and the IOU inside his coat, "but Sadie's the top hurdy-gurdy girl in Virginia City, worth twice as much as all the others, so I aim to take that pretty songbird with me till she's paid off the rest."

A tic pulsed in Cole's temple as he stood, voice as steely as his stare. "Get this and get it good, mister—you're not taking Grace O'Malley anywhere. I already know about her past and it's behind her now, so I will see to her debt in a timely fashion once I make her my wife."

Surprise widened the man's eyes before he flashed a full set of yellow teeth. "Is that right? Well now, you're obviously a pastor who holds to forgiveness, McCabe, seeing you're willing to bed a soiled dove."

Cole's body turned to stone, the man's words like a fist to his gut.

Crocker's brows rose, his vile laughter defiling the awful silence his declaration had wrought. "Now, don't tell me you didn't know, Pastor? Why, I'd think after samplin' her wares, you'd know you got yourself a well-trained pigeon."

Fury exploded inside of Cole like a match to a keg of powder, blinding him to the fact he'd just vaulted the desk and slammed a fist to the man's jaw. The burn of knuckles to bone jolted him from his rage, and with a harsh gasp of air, he realized Tom was holding him back.

"He's not worth it." Tom's urgent tone brought Cole back to himself. "One look at the scum will tell you he's lying."

"Am I?" The lowlife staggered to his feet, hate glinting in his eyes as he wiped blood from his lip. "Why don't you ask her then? Since she was so all-fire honest about working at The Red Dog, ask her how she paid off some of her debt?"

Cole's eyes shuddered closed, the weight of Grace being impure almost more than he could bear. A saloon girl was bad enough—dancing and entertaining men to entice them to drink—but a soiled dove for a pastor's wife? A woman who'd sold her body to men?

"Talk to her," Tom said quietly, handing Cole his coat. "I've got some money put away, so I'll run and fetch it for Grace, then I'll be right here if you need me."

Cole nodded and handed Tom the key to his safe. "Lock up before you go, if you will," he said, ignoring Crocker as he donned his coat on his way to the door. He was totally silent as the lowlife followed him up the hill while needles of sleet pelted Cole's face without mercy. Like the needles of pain piercing his soul, where there was no mercy to be had. *Why, God?* He slogged through the snow like an old man in a blizzard, thick white drifts dragging him down as much as his traitorous thoughts.

Soiled dove.

Scarlet woman.

Lady of the night.

A silent groan stuck in his throat as they approached the house, the lively sound of a harmonica in direct contrast to his mood. "Grace?" He stuck his head in the door, and for once the smell of burnt biscuits failed to produce a smile. His ribcage constricted as he looked at Grace giving Sarah harmonica lessons while the other girls huddled around, and his heart swelled with love for the woman he'd hoped would be their mother. "Can I have a word with you, please?"

"Daddy, you're home!" Becca jumped up to dart for the door.

"Not yet, darlin'." He stooped to hug her, Grace's welcoming smile wrenching his gut. "I still have work to do, but first I need to talk to Grace."

Eyes suddenly somber, Grace handed the harmonica to Sarah. "Just practice like I showed you, sweetheart," she said, slipping on her coat. She blew them a kiss before closing the door. "Cole, what's wrong?" she asked, her smile vanishing."

Cole suppressed a shudder as Doyle slithered out from the shadows. "Why, hello, Sadie, good to see you again."

Grace's body went cold, heart seizing when Crocker appeared, the evil in his laugh chilling her blood. He mounted the steps slowly, yellow teeth bared in a grin like a wolf on the kill. His eyes raked her head-to-toe with a lecherous look that made her skin crawl, and when he reached the top step, she stumbled back, the door as hard and cold as Doyle's gaze.

"Respectability agrees with you, Sadie—you almost look like a real lady."

A scream rent the night, and she realized it was hers when Cole slammed Doyle against the post, knotted fists buried in Doyle's duster like meat hooks. His deadly tone was one she'd never heard before, shocking her almost as much as Doyle's presence. "You talk to her like that again, and you'll be limping back to Virginia City with broken bones." He shoved him back, clunking Doyle's head hard against the post just as the door flew open.

"Daddy, is everything all right?" Sarah stood barefoot, face pinched in worry. "We heard Grace scream."

"Everything's fine, darlin', just go inside." Cole tugged on one of her braids before carefully closing the door. He turned to Grace with a guarded look, chest rising as he drew in a deep breath. "Grace, I know you were a saloon girl because you already told me, and now I know you owe this scum a heap of money, which I'm more than willing to pay. But he said something else, so I need to ask you . . ." He shoved his hands in his pockets, head bowed enough to shadow his eyes. "Are you a . . ." His Adam's apple ducked as his voice lowered to a whisper. "Soiled dove?"

The very words jerked a gasp from her throat, making her feel as dirty and vile as Doyle. Water immediately welled in her eyes as she clutched arms to her waist, the violent shake of her head sending rivers of tears cascading her cheeks.

"No!" she whispered, the sound boiling into the frigid air like a hiss. "Harvey never required that of his girls, Cole, I promise."

"But then ol' Harvey died," Doyle said with a snicker, "and the new owner did, Songbird, now ain't that right?"

The look of suspicion in Cole's eyes sliced right through her, shuddering her body and shivering her words. "Y-Yes, Cole, but I refused, I swear!"

Doyle cackled. "And you believe her? A woman who danced, drank, and satisfied men for money?" He sneered. "I should know—she sure satisfied me."

"That's a lie!" she screamed, desperate to vanquish the doubt and shock she saw in Cole's face, his stone-like stance painful proof he wasn't so quick to battle for her honor. "He forced his way into my room, Cole, intending to rape me, but I ran away."

"Yes, yes, that's right," Doyle said with a chuckle, his sarcasm as thick as the snow on the ground. "This little mite of a woman was able to fight me off, Pastor, so if you believe that, then you sure in the devil deserve a soiled dove for a wife."

Grace's heart lurched when Cole turned away with a hand to his eyes, his shoulders sagging as much as her hope. "Cole, I swear—he's making it up!"

"Now that's as big a tale as her saying she weren't a soiled dove, Rev, so she's hardly fit to be a pastor's wife. *Especially* when I spread word the angel you intend to marry is a fallen one who's had, you might say, a fall from *grace*." Doyle turned back to Grace, the stench of moustache wax making her sick. "You ran out on a debt, Sadie girl. Sure hate to have the sheriff lock you up till you make good. Your fine pastor here paid most of it, but there's still some to go, so I'm takin' you back. Get your things—*now*."

"She's not going anywhere," Cole said, his voice dangerously low. "Grace—go inside and tend to the children while I get this lowlife the rest of his money." He waited, head to the side as if to make sure she opened the door. "*Now*," he said sharply, "and lock the door."

She scrambled inside and secured the latch before hurrying to the window, hugging the girls to her skirt as Cole disappeared down the hill. Whipping the curtains closed, she buffed Sarah's arms with a strained smile, thankful Millie had gone to bed early. "Sarah, sweetheart, would you mind getting the girls ready for bed? And close the door so we don't wake Aunt Millie, all right? I'll be in shortly to say prayers."

"Sure, Grace." The girls tore off for their bedroom in a rush, stopping at the door to blow her a kiss. Moisture burned her eyes as she blew one back.

Love beareth all things, believeth all things, endureth all things . . .

Quietly lifting the latch, Grace stepped outside to confront her past, stomach turning at the smell of smoke. A cigarette glowed red in the dark as she silently shut the door, back pressed to the wood. "I'll pay you the money, Doyle, I promise."

He rose from the swing, low laughter snaking around her like the reptile he was. Strolling forward, he tossed the cigarette into the snow. "Well, well, Sadie Grace, I have to say your siren song sure cast a spell. Ain't never seen a pastor bewitched by a daughter of sin before."

Grace clutched the knob, ready to dart inside if he got too close. "I have a job at the café lined up, so I can make payments until the debt is paid. And I'll even pay more, I promise." She hated the panic that wavered her words. "So please—can't you just leave us alone?"

She gasped when he lunged, gripping her hand on the knob with a pressure that made her wince. "Now you listen here, Songbird, if you don't leave with me tonight, I'll not only ruin you in this prim and proper town of yours, but the pastor and his family as well, so if you feel anything for this man, you best heed my words."

Grace turned away from the foul odor of his breath, limbs buckling along with her heart. Her eyelids closed at the truth of Doyle's words. She'd seen the doubt in Cole's eyes, a doubt she'd see forever if she decided to stay. But the worst was that Cole would be ruined, along with his family, and although he was willing to pay off her debt, the price was too high.

For the man she loved.

And the family she adored.

"I need time to pack and say good-bye," she whispered, body numb from the only decision she could make.

"I'll give you twenty minutes while I have me a drink at the saloon and then I'll be back, Sadie girl, so you best be ready, ya hear?"

Heart comatose, she opened the door to the only real home she'd known in a long, long time, full of laughter and love. And in that exact moment, she knew it needed to remain that way. And it wouldn't if she stayed.

Greater love hath no man than this, that a man lay down his life for his friends.

"I'll be ready," she whispered, heart breaking when the girls' laughter floated in from the other room.

To love as never before.

CHAPTER TWELVE

Tom crashed through the door of the workshop, and Cole shot up from his chair. "Is it true?" Tom whispered, the angst in his tone matching Cole's own.

"I don't know." Cole sank into his chair and put his head in his hands, unable to think clearly for the fog of pain clouding his mind.

"Well, you're not gonna believe some no-good polecat over Grace, are you?"

The disbelief in Tom's tone both riled and shamed him, tripping his temper. "It doesn't matter if I believe her or not, Tom. I'm a *man of the cloth*," he hissed. "How can I make Grace the mother of my children when some lowlife is threatening to drag her name through the mud and my girls along with her, rumor or no?" He stood and shoved the chair out of the way, slashing his fingers through his hair as he paced back and forth.

"So . . . what are you going to do?"

The question stopped him cold. He hung his head, then bashed a fist to the wall. "I don't know, but one thing I *do* know—I'm giving that scum his money and send him packing. Wit*hout* Grace." He glanced up. "Did you bring it?"

Tom nodded and fished a packet of bills from his coat, tossing them on the table. "Take what you need."

"Thanks, Tom, I'll pay back every dime, I promise." Cole counted out the remainder of Grace's debt, then handed the rest back. "Because I may not be able to marry the woman, but I sure as the devil can redeem her debt."

"You mean like God did for you?" Tom said in a measured tone.

Cole froze. His friend's statement pierced him straight through, sapping his strength. Body shaking, he dropped into his chair before his legs gave out. "Yes," he whispered, gaze trailing into a lost stare, "just like he did for me."

Tom paused. "Only his redemption came with both forgiveness *and* a new life, Cole, something you don't seem inclined to give Grace."

That got his attention. Cole bludgeoned his desk. "It's different with Grace!" he shouted. "I was a new man when Eileen and I came to Last Chance, so my past had no power to hurt. But Grace's past is too fresh, too questionable, too able to damage my family." Frustration swarmed the back of his neck as he stared, frantic to convince himself as well as his best friend. "Tell me, Tom, how can I do that to Eileen, the mother of my children—the godliest woman I've ever known? How can I bring a woman of questionable character and past into my family, into my bed, when Eileen came to me so unblemished and pure?"

Tom studied him, the utter calm of his manner in stark contrast to the frenzy of doubt whirling in Cole's brain. When he finally spoke, the compassion in his words lanced Cole's heart, unraveling all the fear and angst in his chest. "Eileen did," he said quietly.

Cole's eyelids shuddered closed, as heavy as the lead in his gut. That's right, she had. She'd married him, believed in him when he was no more than a gunslinger and gambler whom God salvaged from a heap of garbage, as many notches on his belt as sins in his heart. She'd married him and brought him into her family, into her bed, helping him to be the man God called him to be. A pastor with a painful past—who could teach others about a God who offered a joyful future. A God who could transform a gunslinger into a new creature, where old things are passed away.

Behold I make all things new.

Even a saloon girl, soiled dove or no.

Pinching the bridge of his nose, Cole shook his head, a faint laugh rasping from his lips. "I think between the two of us, the wrong one has been preaching from the pulpit."

Tom's chuckle eased the tension in Cole's shoulders. "Naw, where do you think I learned it?" He paused, the humor fading from his eyes.

"So, I'll ask you again, Pastor McCabe—what are you going to do?"

For the first time since Crocker darkened his door, Cole actually smiled, feeling a surge of strength he knew wasn't his own. "Like I said, I'm gonna find that scum, give him his money, then send him packing." Wrapping a string around the bills, he slipped them inside his coat before opening the door, shooting a grim smile over his shoulder. "Right before I make that woman my wife."

"Kinda hard to do with her in Virginia City, Pastor." Doyle strolled into Cole's office with a low chuckle, the smell of alcohol in his wake.

Cole slammed the door hard, his good mood suddenly as foul as the lowlife before him. "I already told you, Crocker, she's not going with you." He hurled the money from his coat pocket onto the desk before taking his chair.

"Sure she is, Pastor. She's up there a packin' right now. Then Songbird and me will be on our way."

Fury carefully contained, Cole propped his feet on his desk with a cold smile. "That's where you're wrong, Crocker, so take the money and run before I change my mind. Or else."

Crocker's laughter rang out, teeth glinting as bright as the Colt 45 on his hip. "Or else what? Some namby-pamby preacher boy is gonna make me?"

Cole's body calcified as he rose, arms hovering at his sides in a habit formed years ago. "I'm going to say this one more time, Crocker. You're going to take your money, sign the IOU over to me, then get on your horse and leave—*without* Grace. *Now.*"

"Am I?" The man grinned and picked up the stack of bills, flipping through them before slipping the stack into his vest. "Suppose I tell you what *you're* going to do, preacher boy?" he said with a casual draw of his gun, motioning toward the drawer safe. "Open it real slow. *Now.*"

Venom pulsed through Cole's bloodstream, but he tempered it while he met Tom's unblinking gaze. With a slow nod, Tom tossed him the keys, and Cole snatched them midair, fingers twitching like the tic in his jaw. He unlocked the drawer and pulled it open, revealing the church's lockbox.

Which completely hid the holster and gun behind it.

Crocker smiled at the sight of the box. "Well, well, what do we have here?" His smile hardened. "Open it."

Unlocking the box, Cole shoved it across the desk, his poker face masking the rage simmering inside.

"Well, looky here—looks like I struck me some gold." Chuckling, Doyle rifled through with the barrel of his gun.

Click.

"Lead, too," Cole whispered, tone as deadly as the cock of his gun.

Crocker grinned and cocked his own weapon, black eyes glittering with pleasure. "Now, now, Pastor, is that any way for a man of God to act?" He distanced himself slowly, gun trained on Cole. "But then again, who's better prepared to meet his Maker?"

"Put the gun down, Crocker, and I won't hurt you."

Crocker's laughter bounced off the office walls. "No doubt about that. Never met a preacher who could shoot to save his soul."

"Yeah? Well this one can, right, Cole?" Tom's voice held a hint of humor despite the tension in the air. "Or maybe I should say 'Rattler?'"

Crocker snickered. "As in Rattler *McCade?*" His teeth flashed yellow. "If you're gonna steal a gunslinger's name, McCabe, at least get it right."

"Couldn't," Tom said, placing hands to the back of his neck. "Had it legally changed from McCade to McCabe, ain't that right, Cole? Too many trigger-happy upstarts just itching to make a name."

Crocker's eyes narrowed to slits. "You're lying."

"Nope. Preachers can't lie," Tom said. "Pert near as bad as gamblin' or shootin'."

"Shut up!" Crocker hissed. His eyes flicked from Cole's face to his gun, his fear as potent as the smell of smoke and sweat he'd ushered in.

Cole never moved a muscle, finger on the hammer of his Colt with the same deadly precision that had taken many a man down, earning him a name he'd worked so hard to forget. *Don't do it, Crocker,* he silently begged, but instinct told him Crocker was as foolish as he was corrupt.

The barest twitch of Crocker's eye confirmed it, and stifling a rare curse, Cole squeezed the trigger.

Kaboom! Crocker howled when his gun hurtled across the room, gouging the wall before it clattered to the floor in a wild spin. He stared in horror at his bloody knuckles that Cole had only nicked on purpose.

Aim steady, Cole hurled his handkerchief at the man. "The next one won't be quite so friendly. Now wipe up your mess before it gets all over my floor." Cole tossed his pen on the desk along with the ink from his drawer, then nodded to Crocker's vest. "Put the IOU down real slow-like and sign it 'paid in full' along with your name, real pretty. Then you're going to take your money and your stench and never come back, you got that?" Cole eased onto the edge of his desk, shocked at how natural the gun felt in his hands when pointed at a man rather than a makeshift target in the woods.

Crocker's hand shook while he did as Cole instructed.

"And one more thing." Cole wandered over to retrieve Crocker's gun. "You'll get this back when Finn McShane sends word you're back in Virginia City, staying out of trouble." Crocker's eyes narrowed over mention of the man who'd saved Cole's soul through a poker game. Finn was one of the most respected men in Virginia City and a formidable foe if you were on the wrong side of the law like Crocker.

Locking the cashbox and Crocker's gun in the safe, Cole singed the lowlife with a half-lidded glare. "Because if you ever threaten Grace or her reputation again or anybody comes looking for C.R. McCade in Last Chance, I'll know who's to blame, and it will be *your* last chance to be a whole man, if you get my drift. Understood?"

Crocker nodded and backed toward the door.

"Good. Now get out of here and don't come back."

Crocker fumbled with the knob, hurling the door open against the wall with a crack.

"Bad manners on top of being a fool," Tom said as he shut it again. "Rattler sure suits you, though, Cole. Just like a diamondback, you never lose your speed."

"Can't," Cole said, strapping on the holster and gun he seldom wore anymore, "McCade had too many enemies."

Tom cocked his head. "Think he'll cause any trouble?"

"Naw." Cole moseyed over to the window, peering outside where

Crocker's horse had been tethered. "Cowards like Crocker only pick on the weak and defenseless." His gaze flitted up to his cabin where Grace was waiting. "And that's not Grace anymore." He reached for his hat. "Mind locking up, Tom? Let's deliver the hutch tomorrow 'cause I gotta help a woman unpack."

Tom chuckled. "Sure thing, and give her my love, will you?"

Cole tipped the brim of his hat with a wide grin, hand on the knob as he opened the door. "Not a chance, old buddy."

Chapter Thirteen

Cole sprinted up the porch, heart pumping so fast, he was out of breath. But not from exhaustion—from sheer gratitude to a God who'd blessed him beyond measure. First by saving his sorry soul, then with a gift like Eileen and their children. And now all over again with the greatest Christmas present of all.

The gift of Grace.

Stamping the snow off his feet, he banged on the door while absently jiggling the knob, surprised to find it open after he'd instructed Grace to lock it. "Grace?" He scanned the cabin while he hung up his coat.

"She's gone," Millie said from her bedroom door, grief in her eyes while weeping filtered out from the girls' room.

"What do you mean she's gone?" he shouted.

She stared, eyes rimmed raw, as if she'd been crying, too. "I mean her things are gone, Cole, and she left a note telling us good-bye."

His heart plunged.

"Daddy, Grace is gone!" Becca sobbed, all three girls darting into the room to clutch at his legs.

"Where's the note?" he rasped, voice breaking.

Millie nodded at the table. "Borrowed Sassafras. Said she'd leave 'em with Libby and Daniel."

He moved forward in a daze, her letter trembling in his fingers as he read it.

Dear Cole, Millie, and Precious Ones,

I don't want to leave, but I love you too much to stay. Please forgive me. I'll leave Sassafras with the McCoys. Thank you for the best months of my life.

All my love forever.

Grace.

"Why d-did she g-go, Daddy?" Sarah said, face slick with tears. "I thought she loved us."

"She does love us, sweetheart," he whispered, grazing the parchment with his fingers before carefully tucking it in his pocket. "More than you possibly know."

"Can you bring her back?" Sarah asked, the hope in her eyes stirring his own.

"Yes, darling, through the grace of God, I can." He squatted to hug them. "Go back to bed, and I'll be back as soon as I can." He rose to usher Millie to her room. "And, Millie, I need you *off* your feet and *on* your spiritual knees, praying we get her back."

"We'll pray, too, Daddy." Sarah reached for Ruthy's and Becca's hands.

"Good girls—counting on it." He blew them a kiss and opened the door, jerking it closed when he spotted Sassafras at the steps, stamping, snorting, and saddle askew.

And eerily empty.

Chest constricting, he descended the steps to calm both the disgruntled beast and his own frenzied thoughts, slowly mounting the mule to coax him back the way he had come.

Please, Lord, keep her safe.

Following the tracks behind the house, Sassafras plodded on, his sporadic brays the only sound in a wonderland of white, where everything was pure, perfect, and new.

Just like Grace. The thought whispered into his mind as gently as the snowflakes floating from the sky, and Cole pressed on, desperate to find her before the snow covered her tracks.

"Grace!" he shouted, the blanket of white muffling the urgency of his tone. Squinting hard, he called again and again, every second an eon as he peered into the blustery night.

Until the tracks suddenly ended.

Right before a gully.

"Grace!" Heart thundering, he vaulted as if Sass had bucked him off, too, and peering into the ditch, he saw her, body splayed like Ruthy's rag doll, silent and still.

"Grace!" He scrambled down in a stumble slide and pressed two fingers to her neck, his own pulse leaping for joy when he felt a steady beat. "Thank you, God!" He ripped a glove off and stroked her cold face. "Grace," he whispered, "please wake up." Assessing her limbs and back, he removed his other glove to warm her face with his palms. "Grace, can you hear me?"

Her soft moan may as well have been a choir of angels—so great was his joy—and when her lashes fluttered open, he felt like singing along, too. "C-Cole?"

"Yes, darlin', I'm here." He brushed his lips to her cheek, cool as porcelain as he breathed his warmth against her skin. "Grace, I don't think anything's broken, but how do you feel?"

Her eyelids drifted closed for several seconds before she opened them again, her shallow breaths rising into the sky like his hope. "My l-left leg hurts, so it might be sprained."

"Well, Sass and I'll get you home, but first . . ." He cradled her face, a rush of love swelling his ribcage as moisture stung in his eyes. "I love you, Sadie Grace O'Malley, and I want you as my wife and mother of my children."

A groan parted from her lips as she shook her head, the motion making her wince. "No, Cole, you and the girls deserve better—"

"I know," he whispered, "and God's given it to us, sweetheart—in you."

Water pooled in her eyes. "But Doyle—"

"Is *gone*," he stressed with a firm look, potent with the intense need to protect and provide. "Back to Virginia City to never bother us again."

A tear dribbled down her cheek and into her hair. "B-But the d-debt—"

"Is paid in full, my love." He caressed her jaw with the pad of his thumb. "Just like God did for us, Grace, both you *and me*. 'For ye are bought with a price,'" he quoted softly.

A sheen of wonder shone in her eyes. "'Then old things are passed away and become new,' just like Maggie said."

He grinned. "Yes, ma'am, and God bless Maggie wherever she is."

Grace reached to touch his face, fingers soft against the bristle of his jaw. "I can hardly believe you still want to marry me," she whispered, lips wobbling into the sweetest of smiles. "Especially since I can't cook to save my soul."

"Yes, ma'am," he said, his breath warm against her skin as he brushed a tender kiss to her cheek, "so it's a good thing God did it for you."

CHAPTER FOURTEEN

O ne toe on that floor, Missy, and I'll feed you nothing but beans."
Grace froze, foot dangling off the bed, itching for the feel of wood.
The odds of which were as likely as a smile from Millie, who glowered
at the door with Grace's coat in hand.

Normally, Grace would secret a smile at Millie's crusty tone, no
longer intimidated by the crotchety woman she'd come to love. But not
today. Not after being forced to stay off her feet for a solid week of quiet
and rest. Nope, she was more than a little testy herself at being banned
from most activity, whether playing in the snow with the girls or dancing
in the parlor with Abby. For mercy's sake, today was Christmas and her
wedding to boot, so why in the name of St. Nick couldn't she at least
hobble down the aisle?

"Millie, please," she pleaded, hoping the jut of her lower lip might
wheedle mercy out of a former foe who now allowed Grace to use her
family name. "It's my wedding day, and my leg feels fine, I promise, so
a wee bit of walking is not going to hurt."

"No, but this hairpin will," Millie huffed, barreling into the room
so fast Grace hurdled back on the bed in the white silk dress Millie had
made. Tossing the coat on the bed, Millie plucked a flower wreath from
the nightstand and secured it on Grace's head with a hairpin, making
Grace wince. "I've got my work cut out for me as is, young lady, teaching
the likes of you how to cook. Don't need to lose another week 'cause
you're too stubborn to stay abed."

Grace couldn't help it—she grinned. "Stubborn? That's a little like
my cornbread calling the kettle black, isn't it, Millie?"

Millie's eyes narrowed, no doubt to deflect the twitch of her smile.

"There's only room for one stubborn woman in this house, Missy, and I was here first."

"She giving you trouble again, Millie?" Handsome in his best suit and coat, Cole strolled in with Abby swaddled in a blanket for the trek to church, his slow smile tumbling Grace's stomach. Giving Grace a wink, he handed Millie the baby. "Because I'll be happy to handle it."

"It's time, it's time!" Sarah said with a squeal, flying into the room with Becca and Ruthy like a prairie twister of giggles, love in motion as they bounced onto Grace's bed in their coats. "Time to become our mama!"

Mama. At the sound, tears welled in Grace's eyes, her watery gaze connecting with Cole's as she hugged the girls close. "I love you," he mouthed, and she could do nothing but weep. *Oh, Lord, why have You blessed me with so much love?*

Because I have called thee by thy name, and thou art mine.

A sob broke from her throat, and Cole quickly tugged Ruthy from her arms, shooing all the children to the door. "Plenty of time for hugs and kisses later, girls, so wait in the wagon with Aunt Millie please, and we'll be right out.

Giggles and shrieks echoed through the house as they raced out, followed by Millie who stopped at the door to shoot a rare smile over her shoulder. "Best enjoy these last few days of rest, cotton girl," she said with a smirk, "'cause you got a busy life ahead."

When the front door closed with a click, Cole grinned. "Ah . . . the blissful sound of silence," he said with a low chuckle, helping her on with her coat. "Millie's right, you know. You best enjoy the quiet while you can, Miss O'Malley, because it's something a mother almost never hears."

"Silence is overrated," she said with a soggy smile. "I prefer the blissful sounds of being a mother if it's all the same to you, Pastor McCabe."

"Maybe," he said, buttoning the coat up to her chin. "But the sounds of being a wife?" He swept her up in his arms and nuzzled his nose into the crook of her neck, coaxing a heady giggle from her lips. "Those are a few of the sounds I'm looking forward to." With a teasing smile, he carried her to the wagon and tucked her in beside the girls in the back, all of them snug in a blanket while they sang Christmas carols on their way down the hill.

"It's about time," Tom said when they arrived at the church, smile broad as he helped Millie and Abby down from the wagon. "The natives are restless, anxious to get their pastor hitched."

"Not as anxious as their pastor," Cole said with a chuckle, lifting his girls down as he gave Grace a wink. "Everybody inside except the bride." He swept Grace up last with a quick kiss to her nose.

"A girl should be able to walk down the aisle at her own wedding, you know," she said when they were alone, attempting a pout.

His husky chuckle did funny things to her tummy. "Nope, Doc says no weight on that ankle for another few days, Miss O'Malley, so you'll just have to settle for my arms." With a whisper of a kiss to her cheek, he carried her into the closed-door vestibule and helped tug off her coat. "Besides, how many girls get carried down the aisle in the arms of the man who adores them?" He hung up her wrap and handed her a dried flower bouquet Millie had placed on the hat shelf, then shifted her in his arms. "I love you, Sadie Grace O'Malley," he whispered in her ear, his words warm and so very full of hope. "And you are the best gift to my family, this Christmas and forever."

Her eyelids jerked open when she remembered the gift of a piano that would now have to wait. "Oh Cole, can you ever forgive me for ruining your promise to Eileen?"

Gaze tender, he caressed her face with a smile. "No forgiveness necessary, darlin', because our God has already covered it all.

"Joy to the world, the Lord is come . . ."

Grace went completely stiff in Cole's arms, heart seizing in her chest. Not from the sound of the congregation singing a Christmas carol, but from the rich tingle of notes that rippled and flowed along with the voices. Eyes wide, she dug her fingers into his arm. "Is that—"

"A piano, yes, my love," he whispered.

"But how?" she rasped, moisture blurring her eyes.

Cole's smile was achingly tender. "The second best Christmas gift this year, darlin', sent by Eileen from above." He gently skimmed her face with his fingers, the sheen in his eyes evidence of the blessing of God in their lives. "Mrs. Merriweather donated the piano to the church for now, Grace, till I can pay off what I owe as soon as I can."

She gasped, fingers trembling to her mouth. "Oh, Cole . . . truly?"

The doors whooshed open with the scent of Christmas pine, and the congregation swelled to their feet in song and deafening applause, causing Grace to sob uncontrollably in Cole's arms.

"And wonders of his love, and wonders of his love, and wonders, wonders of his love."

"Merry Christmas, Grace," he whispered, "because the greatest gift is you."

"Oh, no," she said with a quiver, tears brimming over with the love of a Savior who had never let her go. "It's the gift of grace to all whom God loves!"

"Amen to that," he said with a grin, giving her a wink as he carried her down an aisle strewn with pine boughs and holly. "The gift of 'Grace,' indeed."

A Cowboy for

Christmas

RUTH LOGAN HERNE

And now abideth faith, hope, charity, these three;
but the greatest of these is charity.
   —1 Corinthians 13:13

CHAPTER ONE

Ellensburgh, Washington
November 1889

"Will we have food, Mama?" The hope in Beth's voice did more than stir June Harper's resolve as she and two friends hurried west on the Seattle road. It pushed her to make a decision she'd been putting off for weeks.

Either she would get the job to gather potatoes at Hugh Stackman's sprawling Central Washington ranch, or she'd accept one of several unacceptable proposals she'd received in the last two months. One way or another, she was determined that her children would have a warm fire and food on the table before months of cold settled in. Her friends Anna and Caroline had come to a similar crossroads as winter loomed.

"And bread and jam for Christmas?" wondered Amanda. She was smaller and had a hitch in one leg, making her slower than her older sister, so June carried her along the worn, wide path. Amanda clutched a collection of rags against her chest. June had tied them together and pretended the clutch of tattered cloth was a doll. With no needle and not even a length of thread, she didn't have the means to fashion even a faceless toy for her beautiful girls, but the good Lord had gifted them with ripe imaginations and quick wits.

Wits went dull on empty stomachs, though, and the Harpers hadn't been offered food or shelter in two days. The tent city that lay in what used to be a house-filled neighborhood in Ellensburgh, Washington, was growing colder and damper, leftovers of the July 4, 1889 fire that destroyed a huge part of the city.

"The harvest is truly great, but the laborers few: pray ye therefore the Lord of the harvest, that he would send forth laborers into his harvest." The poignant passage became more meaningful as they trudged west on the well-traveled road.

June's friend Anna walked beside her. Anna had one child, Samuel, age five. His pale cheeks and hollow expression were regularly seen among the hundreds of families displaced by the fire. Many families had given up and left, wandering east or heading west, desperate to begin again.

These three women had no money to go anywhere, but they had one another, and the support of a friend was sorely needed in troubled times.

The well-established ranch owner had posted a need for labor. Like Ruth of Bible times, June, Anna, and Caroline intended that at least two of them would get hired. The third would mind their five children, and if Hugh Stackman was a kind man, perhaps he'd allow them to glean in his fields once the best tubers had been harvested.

A flat-bed wagon was pulled up to the road running parallel to the new railroad tracks linking Ellensburgh to the Puget Sound. The river ran the same way, three modes of transportation marking changing times.

A brawny man stood on the wagon bed, handing out burlap sacks to some, dismissing others. June studied him, trying to discern his choices. He picked men and some women, so it wasn't a choice based on gender alone. The oddity of that struck her, but as she watched from down the line, she noticed that the few chosen women were comely . . . or would be if they had time to bathe and primp in proper fashion.

These women didn't have that luxury, but there was a certain sameness about them. Not too big, not too small, and all attractive.

June's mood soured because even without benefit of a mirror for long days and weeks, she knew the woman begging for work now bore little resemblance to the seamstress who used to sit at a machine at Hansen Needleworks.

As they edged closer to the decision maker on the wagon, she considered her marriage proposals one by one.

Could she make that choice? Marry someone who was after one thing, and one thing only, and live her life as a lie?

"Is there any roll left, Mama? Just a scrap will do." Beth's voice, so soft. Not begging, because she was a kindly child and never whined. The wistful tone said she was simply hungering.

Defeat weighed on June. She drew back her shoulders and tried to stand tall and look strong as the man's gaze raked all three of them. How had it come to this, that the lives of her children, and her own, might depend on the opportunity to pull potatoes from rich loam?

And yet, it had.

The farm overseer scanned the three women head to toe, and when his gaze lingered longer on June than was proper, she told herself he was probably hesitating for a good reason. And then he pointed. "You."

He motioned June to the front and handed her a sack.

"And you." He bypassed Caroline and motioned to Anna. He handed her a sack, too, and as Anna moved toward June, June watched the man's eyes roam Anna's shapeless dress.

Her heart ticked harsher in her chest because she'd seen that gaze aimed at her before by unseemly men.

"Seven more! I'll take seven more, and then the rest of you need to be on your way. No lingering here!"

He chose the final seven quickly.

June didn't dare turn to read the disappointment on the varied faces behind her. If she'd tarried two minutes longer, she'd have no work. Who would have ever thought two minutes to be of such import?

And yet they were, today. And perhaps tomorrow, too, depending on the workload. She kissed the girls a quick good-bye. Anna did the same as Caroline gathered the children for the long walk back to town.

"Ten cents a sack—no underweights. The scale is in the field. You're responsible for getting your sack to the scale. It will *not* be coming to you. If you need help, that will cost you." He aimed his gaze at several women, including June and Anna.

Anna didn't shrink against June, although June was pretty sure she wanted to. Anna was a scrapper, despite her diminutive size, and she drew herself up, ignored his look, and leaned closer to June. "I have my knife with me. Do you have yours?"

Oh, it was a sorry day when misfortune meant homeless mothers needed to carry self-protection, but the three women had made a pact within forty-eight hours of the fire. They would share time, resources, and wisdom, and one of those first bits of sage advice was to carry protection. And so they did.

"I do. My intent is to avoid a need to use it."

"As is mine," Anna replied in a soft, low tone. "But intentions are not always of choice, and I've made sure it's readily available this day."

They boarded the wagon that would take them out to the field, and if it wasn't for the discomfort with the overseer, it would be a perfect day. A chance to work, earn a day's wage, and put money by.

June Harper was now a harvester.

She had taken great pride in her schoolwork as a child, in her sewing as a young mother, and now she determined to do her best as a gleaner. She would give it her best because the more she did and the faster she gathered, the quicker all their children would eat.

As the wagon pulled away, Caroline turned the children around, herding them back toward town. Perhaps along the walk they would find fresh greens to munch, but the chill, wet autumn had muddied the road. Still, it was a hope because it would be long hours before June and Anna returned with dimes in their pockets.

Across the broad valley, a laborer directed a thick-bodied horse along the rows. The horse pulled a golden yellow machine, a ray of sun in a field of wan plants and late-season weeds. The horse and man moved in perfect rhythm, not too fast, nor too slow, as if in tandem with the day and the machine.

A potato digger.

Never had June heard of such a thing, but the evidence lay at her feet along the row. Piles of freshly dug potatoes now lay ready for removal, with weeds and plant parts marking the opposite side of the row. As a woman who loved the clever operations of a treadle sewing machine, June understood the marvel of the mechanism that had laid neat rows before her. Each person was given a row, and when the sack seemed to weigh fifty pounds, the harvester delivered it to scale, then carried it to the wagon by the road.

Anna was quick and busy, but fifty pounds was a heavy load for someone her size. But for June, after carrying Amanda so often, the sack was bulky but didn't seem as heavy as it looked. "I'll carry while you gather; we'll team."

"That's not fair to you," Anna protested.

June leaned down and smiled as she twined her first sack closed. "But it's quicker, and if we combine our efforts, we'll make more money."

"Then I am properly hushed and busily filling sacks," Anna agreed.

Sack by sack June hurried up the rows to weigh them, as fast as some men and faster than others. Back and forth she rushed, and when the first wagon was as full as the horses could carry, another wagon was drawn up to the front. Two men unhitched the team, rehitched them to the loaded wagon, and drew it forward.

The overseer pointed to two men and June. "You, you, and you. Climb aboard for help unloading."

"Me?" June stared up at him.

"I called you, didn't I? You hauled faster than most of the pants-wearers I hired on, so yes. You. There's a six-bit bonus for the unloaders."

Seventy-five cents. With Anna still loading bags in quick fashion, that seventy-five cents would come in handy. She climbed onto the wagon seat.

The two men hopped onto the load behind her. One shared a hunk of dried meat with the other. She could hear them chewing and talking softly.

They offered her nothing.

Maybe that was just as well. Getting too friendly with some strange man could be misunderstood, and a woman alone couldn't afford to be misunderstood. The wagon pulled up to a much larger wagon meant for road travel.

The overseer set the brake, climbed down, and gave the horses a small offering of grain to crunch on while June and the two men unloaded the potatoes. Then the overseer pointed around back of a large building. "The necessary is around that corner, if needed. You two are going to toss the bags from one wagon to another and lay them crosswise to steady the load. You." He pointed to June. "Your job is in the first barn."

The barn?

Unease prickled June's spine. "I thought I was unloading. With them."

"You might be able to tote a quick bag, but tossing them is men's work. I'm going to show you how to sort the second kind into sizes, and when this first field is done, the rest of the women will join you. Women are better sorters. Quicker with their hands. But I need a team leader to make it run smooth, and you seem like a take-charge person."

She was.

She followed him into the barn. Doors were open on all four sides, allowing light. Tables were set up on an angle in the middle, with small chutes fashioned along the outer edge. At the end of each chute was a stand for a burlap sack. The man showed her the sorting method. After watching him demonstrate, it all began to make sense.

Perhaps the burly overseer hadn't picked the women for their looks. There was a plan to the action, a plan she hadn't seen. She breathed easier, knowing that. She'd grown suspicious since the fire. Life had changed in a matter of hours, and survival brought out the worst in some and the good in others.

By the time the next wagon pulled up, she'd become efficient at sorting and was able to school the first group of women. By midday they were harvesting the fancier potatoes, and a group of sixteen women worked together to quickly sort, chute, and bag the golden tubers in easier-to-handle, twenty-five pound bags. As they worked, June saw another image.

An image of people, working like the gears of a machine, like that bright-toned potato digger in the field, each part doing their job to make the task quicker and easier. They were pieces of a puzzle, and coming together, they made a complete picture with a common goal of efficient production.

She broke away midafternoon to use the necessary, her mind full of the wonder of cooperative labor, humble potatoes, and fancy-painted machines as she crossed the weedy expanse of yard.

A hand grabbed her arm from behind and held tight.

A second hand clapped over her mouth. "Don't scream."

Oh, she'd scream, all right, if she could. But she couldn't and her mind quickly went to her choices. June and her friends weren't stupid. They'd practiced this scenario since becoming homeless because there was an unfortunate segment of society that equated desperate with promiscuous. Once her initial fear ran its course, practiced reason came to the rescue.

"You wanna make more money for them kids, pretty lady?" The overseer's stench and breath turned her stomach, but his words said he wasn't necessarily planning to force her, but more likely looking for a paid service. "I've got an extra six bits with your name on it, Junie. Six bits buys a lot of bread for gimpy kids."

Gimpy kid?

Anger didn't just bite her.

It roared to life within her.

He wanted a harlot. He wanted to pay for favors, and he'd called her precious, beautiful, God-given child a wretched name.

Gritting her teeth, June stomped down hard on his foot with her heel, and even with his boot on, he howled in pain.

He let go of her in a quick hurry, but June didn't run.

Oh, no. June Mary Harper wasn't a runner. She snatched that tiny knife from its pouch along the seam of her dress and whirled on quick feet.

And then she stalked him, backing him up as she strode forward, her sharp knife gleaming in her right hand. "You filthy pig." She raised her hand higher, and the overseer actually tried to run backward. He tripped over an upraised root from a nearby tree and fell to the ground like an overstuffed sack of his own potatoes. "Does your boss know of your lecherous ways? Does he know you skulk about, grabbing defenseless women when they're away from a crowd? Does he know you're willing to pay for the very blessed union of two people in sanctified marriage?"

"He does now."

June turned.

A not-too-tall but thoroughly imposing man strode out of the barn. He carried a small whip in one hand, and the anger on his face indicated he wasn't afraid to use it.

The man on the ground scrambled up. He faced the approaching man.

There was nothing strong about the overseer now. He trembled like a young pup, newly chilled. "She misunderstood, boss. You know these women; they're desperate, and they throw themselves at you because their brats are starving. They'll do and say anything to make money, mark my word."

The man . . . *the boss, he'd said* . . . drew near. He snapped that whip so close to the overseer's leg that the heavy man jumped, and so did June. "You've got ten minutes to pack up your things and get out, and don't bring your ugly face and uglier ways back to the Stackman Ranch again. You hear me?"

"For her?" The overseer sent June a disgusted look. "You'd throw away a man who's been in your employ for seven years for the likes of her?"

The whip snapped again, and this time it caught enough of the overseer's leg to slice a clean rip in his baggy pants. "For her or any other woman disgraced by a lowlife like you. Any woman on Stackman land is under my protection. Now go."

Shock deepened the lines of the overseer's face. He gulped, stared at June, and then at his former boss in disbelief before he started moving. And then he left, feet dragging and head down.

June's heart had gone into overdrive when the cur laid hands on her. The sudden respite brought realization to mind.

Close. So close . . .

She bent over, suddenly faint. And through the quick rush of blood to her brain, a strong but kind voice penetrated, wondering if she was all right.

She wasn't. She hadn't been for a long time. But right now, in this moment, the forces that had been winding like a precision timepiece for months, came together and ground to a halt.

June cried.

Hugh Stackman could handle a lot of things, and he liked to prove that on a daily basis. He and his brother had defied the odds and driven twenty-eight head of cattle into the valley a dozen years before, a pair of teenagers bent on making a fortune in the mines but finding their fortunes in land and beef instead.

The long-time bachelor had no idea what to do with the crying woman in front of him. And what if others spotted them? What would they think? Did he care what they thought?

Oddly, yes, this time he did.

He grabbed her hand and led her toward the house.

She dug in her heels instantly and struggled.

He turned, wondering what to say. What to do. Was he about to make a bad situation worse?

Blue eyes, damp with tears. A tanned face, unusual in a woman, but circumstances had left so many homeless this past summer. Tanned skin had become its own mark. Dirt streaked her cheeks because working potatoes was a dirt-crusted task, yet that same dirt helped protect the potatoes in storage. "I've got tea in the house, and he tore your dress. I thought to fix it before you go back."

She followed his gaze, saw the rent, and if he'd expected more tears, she surprised him. "I have but two dresses. This one I was wearing during the fire, and one other, given by the kindness of a stranger to clothe the naked, and now your impudent farm manager has torn one of them? Give me that whip and I'll let him know what I think of that."

Hugh didn't give her the whip because he was pretty sure she meant every single word. "But he didn't hurt you? I mean—" He stumbled over the question, searching for appropriate words.

"Other than degrading me, offering me pay for my marital services, and ruining my dress? Oh, no." She impaled him with a sharp look. "I'm just fine, as you can see."

She wasn't fine, and unless he missed his guess, she was tempted to cry again, but that might be because she was spittin' mad.

Well, that made two of them because he'd just fired one of his more experienced workers at harvesttime when he needed all the help he could get. That was a problem for later. Right now he wanted to calm this woman down. While doing so, he'd make sure the whip was up, out of reach, because he'd seen her with that knife.

Impressive.

"Come inside with me. My sister can help mend your gown."

"Your sister lives here?" Suspicion deepened the question and for good reason because Lily Stackman had stayed close to home since coming north and few knew of her existence.

"She does. Listen." Hugh yanked off his hat and scrubbed a hand through his hair. "Stuff like this doesn't go on here, and I sure don't want word to get out that it does, Mrs. —?"

"Harper."

"Unless you want me to bring the law down on Hinckley. I can do that."

She stared at him, as if weighing her choices, then sighed, and when she did, he figured it was about the saddest sigh he'd ever heard. She squared her shoulders, hiked her skirt above the weeds, and quick-stepped toward the house. "And then it becomes his word against mine and less time to work and make money for two hungry little girls. There's faint promise in starvation while standing on principle."

Starving children?

He caught her arm as they neared the steps, but when she turned to smack him, her eyes met his.

She paused as their gazes locked.

He read pain and sorrow and guts and grim determination in her steady look. But what he didn't see, and what he had a sudden, inexplicable urge to change, was the lack of joy in any part of her expression. "Your children go hungry?"

"Mine and many others," she told him quietly. She stared at him. "How can you not know the reality that exists so close?"

He frowned and scrubbed his chin. "We helped right after the fire, and then it was nothing but work for the next several months as it always is for a farmer or a rancher. And I'm both." He stared beyond her, before he drew his gaze back. "I knew there were people seeking work, Mrs. Harper, which is why I posted the flyers. I knew nothing of starving children."

"Hugh?" Lily called his name softly from a nearby window. "Is something wrong?"

"Lily, this is Mrs. Harper, and she's had a scare."

"A scare?" Lily knew far too much about scares and the reality of foolish people, but she'd lived a hermit's life for long years and the timidity of that showed in her voice.

"A scare?" Mrs. Harper glared at him, and Hugh was pretty sure the heat in that expression might be singeing his socks right about now. "I believe what I had was an attack, sir."

"A frightening attack." He said the words low, not wanting to upset this woman any more than she'd already endured.

He longed to soothe her.

Why?

He had no idea, but the negative emotions in her eyes seemed wrong.

She should be smiling.

She should be making biscuits and honey for her children. For all the children.

The thought of starving children clamped his gut.

Hugh Stackman and his brother knew hunger as children. Their self-absorbed father had spent copious amounts of money on women and spirits and left his wife and five hungry children to beg scraps. Of the five, there were three left. Hugh, Jacob, and Lily. The thought of children going hungry nearby, while his fields lay rich with harvest, shamed him. But first things first. "Lily, can you fetch a needle and some thread?"

He stepped ahead of Mrs. Harper and opened the door. She glanced around, her eyes reflecting a mixture of worries and nerve, but when she lifted her eyes to his once more, he sensed the barest hint of trust.

She walked through the open door.

Chapter Two

Two things surprised June instantly.

The modestly outfitted, large log cabin was neat and clean.

Lily Stackman had an ugly scar covering the lower side of her left cheek.

June glimpsed it briefly before the other woman, just about her age, she surmised, disappeared into another room.

The aroma of cooking food filled the air, and June's stomach gurgled like a freight train firing up.

A pot of soup simmered on the broad cookstove, a treasure not often seen outside of a restaurant kitchen. A pot of beans sat cooling nearby, and the scent of warm honey marked a hank of ham roasting in its juices.

Above all that, the salty, pungent scent of biscuit dough wrapped itself like a blanket around the other food smells.

A part of June wanted to grab everything in sight and dash off with it to feed the remaining displaced people back in Ellensburgh.

Another portion of her thought to be sick because the onslaught of smells took her long-empty belly by surprise. That part won, unfortunately.

She stared around, gut-clenched, unsure what to do.

"You're sick."

Lily wrapped an arm around June and hurried her outside. Long minutes later, she settled June into a rocker on the porch, brought her some tea, and took the thread in hand to mend the shoulder of June's dress.

"You're too ill to work," Hugh declared, now that she was settled on the porch and not caught in unseemly circumstances around back.

"I'm not one bit ill," June shot back.

"Evidence to the contrary says otherwise." He pointedly looked toward the rear of the house.

She took another sip of the bracing tea and faced him. "Lack of food and a sudden combination of smells brought on a temporary upset stomach. My system is no longer accustomed to rich odors and scents, and your kitchen is ripe with some of the nicest ones I've smelled in a long time. But my stomach is more delicate now, and that's probably true of most of us."

"There are many who hunger?" Lily seemed to have forgotten her marred face now that she'd busied herself helping June. "The fire was months ago. I would have thought all was settled, and I'm sorry to be mistaken."

"There are dozens of us, many with no families except for their own hungry children. Like mine."

"You have no husband?" Lily asked softly. She bobbed the small needle back and forth along June's shoulder in a quick, not-too-tight overstitch.

If by husband, Lily meant a man who'd vowed to stand by his wife through thick and thin and work to provide for his family as the good Lord advised, then no, but she'd lost that part of her marriage long before illness claimed the man himself.

"Influenza took him nearly eighteen months back. I am a seamstress by trade, although my current clothing barks opposition to that claim, no doubt. But I'm accomplished; but when the needleworks burned and they chose not to reopen, my job was gone. My home was gone, too. My two girls and I escaped with the clothing we were wearing and a few dollars that didn't stretch very far. And now, harvest." She raised her gaze to Hugh Stackman's. "Your offer meant a great deal to my friends and me and many others."

"You don't think it beneath you to harvest after a profession of note?" Hugh asked.

Rather than answer his question directly, June quoted a Scripture. "So she gleaned in the field until even, and beat out that she had gleaned."

"From the book of Ruth," Lily noted. She smiled, and when she did, a good part of the ugly scar disappeared in the joyful crease. "There is much comfort to be taken in wise words, regardless of age."

"Comfort for some. Not all." Hugh Stackman stood. He paced the porch twice, then came to a stop before her. "We want to help. Lily, my brother, and me. How best can we accomplish this?"

"Food, shelter, and work," answered June. "The chance to make money is a marvelous thing, but with winter approaching, our tents won't offer enough warmth, and the city has so much of its own repair to do, those left on the fringes are in a difficult position."

"Hugh."

A hollow note tightened Lily's tone, and June recognized fear in her voice.

"You can help from here, of course."

Compassion. Tenderness. Kindness. Those three qualities weighted his words as he addressed his sister.

It had been a long time since anyone had treated June with that kind of gentleness. Her husband had initially, but years of hard labor had taken their toll on him. He'd died an unhappy man, feeling sorry for himself, almost welcoming death, a fact she would never share with her beloved daughters. In the end, she had to remain strong enough for all of them.

Until the fire.

"Is it possible to enlist aid from others?" June wondered as Lily tied off the final stitch. "I didn't mean for this to all fall on your shoulders."

"Perhaps God did." Lily spoke softly again, but with a new firmness.

"Simple coincidence and timing, sister." The rancher's note of dismissal shrugged off Lily's words. "But knowing this, we can't turn our backs."

June stood, a tiny flicker of hope renewing her strength.

Hugh leapt off the rail to steady her, but she didn't need steadying any longer.

Then she looked up into prairie-brown eyes—gold, tan, and gray, all mixed together—and June realized she might need steadying after all.

Her heart sped up. Her breath caught. Her hands felt warm, then hot, then cool and damp, an adolescent reaction to a man's kindness, and a rich man besides. A woman who stoops to dig potatoes has no business getting heart sensations by the gaze of the handsome landowner.

Lily's words flooded back: the sweet story of Ruth and Boaz, and Ruth's care for Naomi in her time of need.

But this wasn't ancient times. This was modern-day Washington with all the busyness and work involved in settling new lands, and June Harper had no intention of tucking herself anywhere near Hugh Stackman's bed to catch him in a marriage. Yes, he was treating her with unexpected kindness and seemed sincere in his desire to help, but a man who hid his scarred sister from society and shrugged off God was best avoided.

Infirmities were part of life. They weren't punishments meted out by a wrathful God, and she'd treated little Amanda no differently than she treated Beth, despite her bad leg. Yes, Amanda had to work harder to do things, but in the end, that would strengthen her daughter. Or so she hoped.

"I must get back to work. I'm making no money for my family by being so graciously tended. Mr. Stackman, Miss Stackman, I thank you for your kindnesses to me."

"Are you able to work?" He thrust his cowboy hat back onto his head, and June had to wrangle her heart into serious submission when he did.

"When one has no choice, one is always able to work," she told him. She hurried down the steps, across the weed-riddled field, and back to the barn.

Anna caught sight of her when she entered, and she read the concern in her friend's eyes, but this wasn't time to speak of what had transpired. There would be time enough for that on the long walk home. Right now, there were potatoes to sort, and June took her place back on the line, sorting as quickly as her hands and hollow belly would allow.

When the light grew dim, Hugh Stackman and two other men appeared to hand out the day's wages. A different ranch hand had taken over the ledger abandoned by the fired overseer. He had a solid look about him; the other man looked much like Hugh. As June and Anna moved closer to the front of the line, Hugh Stackman approached them, and June's pulse began to race again.

Stop it, heart!

June's heart ignored her command, fickle organ that it was, and as the ranch owner drew closer, he tipped his hat down to shade his gaze from the east-facing sun. "The rest of the day has gone all right?"

"It has."

"Good." He shifted his gaze to Anna, clearly awaiting an introduction, and who wouldn't? Anna was beautiful, petite, lively, and engaging, even under dire circumstances. "My friend and coworker, Anna Menendez."

He reached out his hand. "Thank you for coming to work today, Mrs. Menendez. We're grateful for the help. And can you both be here tomorrow?"

"Gladly." June answered for both of them because Anna seemed unusually tongue-tied.

"I'd like to meet with both of you and a few others to come up with a plan for the displaced."

"Meet with us?" Anna frowned in confusion. "But we mean to work, of course."

"You will have work, although not perhaps the same work as today. My brother and I," he motioned to the second man, a little taller and broader in stature than Hugh. "Have things to discuss tonight, and with your help in the morning, perhaps we can put a plan into action, Mrs. Harper. Per your suggestion."

Anna stared at her, as if wondering what she'd done, which, of course, was nothing except fight off an attacker and possibly accuse the wealthy landowner of disassociation with the very people buying his goods.

Other than that she'd done nothing. Nothing at all.

She extended her hand as she would in other circumstances. Yes, it was dirty, but it was dirty from honest work—farm-dirt—and if a man of the land stood in fear of his own soil, that revealed a great deal.

He took the offered handshake and did not let go. Her heart tripped faster.

A beautiful connection.

The strong grip of his hand over hers, the warmth of understanding in his gaze . . . ridiculous reactions to a momentary surge, but the sheer pleasantness of his attention brought heat to her cheeks.

"My brother, Jacob." He nodded to the man at his left, and although he seemed reluctant to leave go of her hand, he did it. "Mrs. Harper and Mrs. Menendez."

The younger Stackman took her hand, also, but when he shook Anna's hand, his gaze brightened. "I'll look forward to speaking with you both in the morning." He turned slightly toward his brother. "I've checked with four others and sent a rider to two more. We should have a room full of people first thing."

"Good." Hugh turned back toward them. "Until morning, ladies." He strode off, mounted his horse, and moved upland.

Anna pretended to swoon while curious glances came their way from those in front of them and many behind. "I cannot wait to hear the story of how you single-handedly managed to win a rich man's heart in the space of minutes. A noble feat."

"There is no need for such a story." June kept her voice low and hid her emotion intentionally. "It is simply a tale of identified need and a call to action."

"Oh, there is need all right," Anna said happily. "He is in the need for love, sure as I'm standing here. He might want to help for other reasons, but loaves of bread for the hungry don't put that light in a man's eye. Credit me with brains enough to know that."

Anna couldn't be right.

Could she?

And yet, didn't June feel exactly the same when she looked up at Hugh? She shook her head. It was simply a preposterous feeling brought on by being neglected too long and driving the reins of life independently. And Anna didn't know the whole story. When she heard of the way he tucked his sister away, with few knowing of her existence, she'd see things differently.

The new overseer counted coins into June's hand, and when she received as much as Anna, she shook her head. "I was indisposed for a short while, so my pay should be less."

The man showed her the paper ledger. "The boss has initialed this right here, ma'am. What the boss says, I do."

And there is was, alongside her name, a firm H.S. declaring her wages.

A benevolent heart at war with itself.

She recognized that in him because she struggled in much the same way. But when she tucked the coins into her tiny change pouch and secured it to the inside pocket of her dress, its weight smacked of success.

At that moment she didn't care how far she'd fallen in society's stature, because stature put no food in her children's mouths or money in her pockets. Work accomplished that, and today, she and Anna had pocketed several dollars in pay. There would be bread for dinner, if there was any left to be found at this late hour, but if not, there would be a grand breakfast.

She remembered the rich smells of the Stackman house, overwhelming her weakened system. If she rose from these impoverished times . . . *when* she rose from these times, she quickly corrected herself . . . she would never take the thought of "daily bread" for granted again. She and her children would thank God mightily for what they might have expected as their due in the past.

Desperate measures had taught her a great deal, but the jingle of coins in her pocket bought temporary respite. Having work for at least two days meant she wouldn't have to accept anyone's offer of marriage for the moment, and that in itself was a huge relief.

———

"Being mad at yourself won't get things done quicker and makes you fairly unpleasant," Jacob noted when the Stackman siblings finally sat down to supper that night. "We can make plans in the morning and put them in motion."

Jacob meant well. And he made sense. But he'd been young when their family's fate took a sudden downward turn, and he'd been given a more easygoing nature besides.

Hugh hadn't been easygoing in two decades, and the thought of children suffering with empty stomachs while his fields had lain rich with second-harvest potatoes, cabbage, and fruit struck him hard.

"Go easy on him, Jacob." Lily passed bread to her brothers. "He takes too much on his shoulders, but if you'd seen Mrs. Harper's countenance today, how green she turned just smelling good food, you'd feel much the same."

"I'd like to give Hinckley a piece of my mind and a good thrashing," Jacob answered. "Now it makes me wonder if there have been other instances. Perhaps this was the only woman who had the courage to call him out."

"I can't deny wondering the same." Hugh directed his attention toward his dinner plate, but June Harper's face came back to mind. The anger and hunger mingled beneath an intelligent reserve. He read strength in her expression and heard resolution in her voice, but it was her eyes that captivated him. Bright blue softened with pale gold and ivory flecks, not enough to hint green, but enough to flash and sizzle. "We'll talk with all the hands tomorrow and revisit standards of behavior. There is no room for depravity here. But first we'll meet with the neighbors and the ladies."

"Aren't you hungry, Hugh?" Lily laid a hand on his arm, a hand just as tanned and hardworking as his. "Or have thoughts of others stolen your appetite?"

It had, but to ignore Lily's work would hurt her feelings. He ate some ham, but his mind couldn't dismiss the image of hungry faces. Gaunt cheeks. Lackluster hair.

He left the table soon after and took a lantern to the porch that overlooked the wide valley. They'd driven a cattle stake north as teens, looking for their good fortune in the mines of the Cascades, but they'd found land first. Broad land, lush enough, but not too wet, a land meant for cultivation.

They hadn't needed to go further west to the mines after all. They'd set up shop in the valley, expanding yearly, and as their herd and expertise grew, so did their fortune. Over the last fifteen years, they'd bought out several neighbors and had created a good trade with the Yakama Nation. Folks thought well of them, and Hugh appreciated that, and the new railroad ties had opened a wealth of expansion in both directions. But while he paid scant attention to empty words offered by foolish preachers, his mother had taught him to do unto others. To give of himself. To share of life's bounty.

He'd obviously failed this past summer, but with winter approaching, he couldn't fail now.

Lily found him on the porch. She pulled her shawl snugly around her shoulders and drew up next to him. "We are blessed."

When he grunted, she elbowed him none too gently. "You're quite stubborn in these matters, but it's true. We are blessed, and it's good to share of those blessings. Food and shelter are easily taken for granted until you know the lack firsthand. Then they are greatly missed. But you can't blame yourself. You didn't know of their plight."

"I should have."

She sighed, her expression reflecting worry for him, but Hugh knew the truth. He'd seen the destruction of fire firsthand as a young teen. He'd watched the wooden buildings flame like oiled torches in the brisk Nevada winds. Wasn't that the very reason he'd ordered bricks for the coming spring, so they could build a brick home less likely to burn?

And then in the daily rush of sowing, harvesting, weeding, and calving, he'd pushed the plight of those who'd suffered the outcome of the great Ellensburgh fire out of mind. His heart grieved, thinking of it.

"We'll help now. We'll help fix this, all of it," Lily whispered. She pressed his arm lightly. "The president has just made us a state of the Union, Hugh. We are part of the new world our mother used to speak of. We'll share Thanksgiving with those in need and celebrate the new fortune of statehood."

"After the potato harvest, of course." Jacob came through the door behind them, and Hugh had to smile.

Leave it to Jacob to stay practical.

The oldest Stackman turned and nodded. "We're on borrowed time, I know that. The easy fall gave us time for these late spuds to mature, and a bumper crop it is. But instead of having these ladies work the fields or the barn, I think we can pay them to organize what's needed first and most. They're directly involved. They'll know what to do. And then we provide them the means to do it with the help of our neighbors and businesses." He turned back to Lily. "I didn't mean to thrust you into the middle of this. If you prefer to stay out of it, I'll understand." The decision to stay tucked away had been hers. The decision to change that status must be hers as well.

She stared beyond him, the ugly scar marring the lower left side of her beautiful face directly in his line of vision.

He'd stopped seeing it long ago, but Lily never had. She'd shied away from so much of life after the fire, and they hadn't pressed her. She'd been young when they came here. So young.

She drew a breath and linked an arm through his. "I am done hiding."

Jacob looked at Hugh, and Hugh looked right back.

"Half the town doesn't know I exist, and most of the workers pretend I don't, but in the way of people, I'm sure there's talk. I'm not a child anymore."

"No, but you're still under our protection," Jacob reminded her.

"Which I cherish, but no longer need," Lily told him softly. "It's time for me to shrug off what's happened before and embrace our future. And if that means enduring a few odd looks, then it's time I did just that. Beginning with the meeting tomorrow."

Hugh wanted to argue out of habit, but he couldn't.

Lily was right. No longer a child, it was time to seize the opportunities that came her way. They'd sheltered her for a long time. Letting go wouldn't be easy. He picked up the lantern he'd brought out to the porch. "I'm going to take a look around back, then turn in."

"I'll walk with you." Jacob shoved his hands into his pockets and strode alongside. Sometimes he'd whistle as they walked.

Not tonight. Tonight they circled the paddock and the two sprawling barns in silence. He expected his brother was thinking about the scheduled meeting. He knew he was. As he tried to wrangle his thoughts to planning, the image of June Harper, facing him with smudged dirt on her cheeks and hands, kept invading.

She'd quoted Scripture to him, the book his mother had loved, the story of Ruth, a widow.

He knew the story well, told to him as a boy at his mother's knee. He could recite much of it from his early days.

But it had meant nothing until today when Scripture came to life in a woman of courage.

In normal times he'd go back to the house and hunker at the table, two lanterns chasing shadows, pouring over books and ledgers and plans, but tonight none of that won his attention because June Harper had grabbed hold of his mind hours before and hadn't let go.

Stake Carmody came around one side of the far barn while they approached from the other. Stake had signed on early with the brothers, and he'd been on the payroll from the moment there was one. He moved forward quickly and faced the Stackmans. "That business today. With that woman."

"Mrs. Harper."

"If that's her, then yes. I don't think she's the only one, and if you want me to hand in my notice for not realizing what a low-down, no-good skunk of a man Hinckley was, I'll do it."

"Plenty of blame for us to share, Stake." Calm by nature, Jacob leaned against the fence.

"I was in charge of the work crews. I shoulda had better control all around."

"We're wiser now, and we'll keep better check on things," Hugh told him. "And we're going to talk with all the men tomorrow—make ourselves clear. This wasn't on you, Stake; it's on all of us. The ladies will be back tomorrow. We're going to find housing for those going without."

"Housing?"

"For the winter. Yes."

Stake frowned. "They said they're out on the streets?"

"From the fire, yes."

"And you're sure they're being up front with you?"

Hugh had no reason to think otherwise. "Why wouldn't they be?"

"No big reason. I just heard tell of a couple of women who got themselves hitched up with well-off men after that fire, like they were gold diggers, looking for a way up the ladder. And they found it. I'm just wondering if these women are like those. Not that I know a whole lot about women."

"No one does, Stake, but I'll keep my eye on them."

"It pays to, Hugh. Least that's what I've heard."

"Gold diggers?" Jacob made a face once they'd continued on. "Potato diggers, yes. I'm pretty sure the women worked just as hard and maybe harder than the men today. And they surely worked as fast."

"I get his point." Hugh surveyed the last fenced area. All was calm. "Folks with a plan often have ulterior motives, and it's best to be on guard."

"The only ulterior motive those women have is food on the table and a roof over their heads. You're being ridiculous. And so is Stake. I'll see you in the morning." Jacob trudged inside while Hugh let the silence of the night enrobe him.

The hills and valley filled with sweet noise on spring nights, but the chill of fall quieted the plateau.

He could hear his own breath in the chilled, still air.

Was June a gold digger?

He didn't think so, but he carried the responsibility of not just himself and this ranch on his shoulders. Jacob and Lily's futures and happiness were tied up here, too. Stake was cautious by nature, he knew that. Still, maybe quiet caution was called for, although when June's face flitted through his brain, the way she stood up to a weak, spineless man, he didn't feel the least bit cautious or quiet.

CHAPTER THREE

"Are you ready, Anna?" The wind had picked up slightly. The day hinted of cooling temperatures, but the fall had lasted long and been surprisingly warm to this point. June moved around a circle of remaining tents tucked in the curve of a woodlot.

"Yes." Anna leaned down and kissed her son good-bye. "You be good for Caroline, all right?"

He nodded, clinging tightly to the hank of bread in his hands. "I will, Mama."

She hurried to June's side. They walked west, side by side. "It's nice that we don't have to drag the children up the road today." Anna tugged her wrap closer against the lingering chill. "It's good to know there's work for us and that the little ones can stay behind with Caroline."

"And that she is good with them and has money for provisions, which makes everything easier," June agreed.

"I—" Anna paused and moved to the right as a buggy approached from the west. And when the buggy came to a stop, so did the women.

Hugh Stackman jumped off the front seat lightly. "No need to walk all that way, ladies. I should have said we'd come by for you."

"Come by for us?" June darted a look from Anna to him. "Why would you have said that or we think it, Mr. Stackman?"

"Because it's the right thing to do," he told her. He met her gaze and extended a hand to help her up into the seat.

That look. Warm and serious and helpful and kind. She took his hand and stepped up between the wheels. The horses stayed calm, and when he helped Anna up as well, he waited until they were tucked into the seat, then asked, "All in?"

"We are, yes."

"Yes, thank you."

He smiled at her. Right at her. His gaze went past Anna and caught hers, and she had to tamp down her pulse all over again, which wasn't easy with Anna giving her an "I told you so" nudge in the side.

He climbed back up, directed the horses forward, and when he got to a widened stretch of road, he turned them in an easy half circle and headed back toward the ranch.

Anna leaned close to June's side. "Like a pair of grand ladies, aren't we?" she noted softly.

June couldn't stretch her imagination quite that far. "With tattered clothing and unwashed stockings."

Anna rolled her eyes, but they both knew there'd been little ability to wash up this past week. "I prefer my whimsy to your more prosaic variety."

"I do, too," June whispered, then laughed softly. "My own thoughts are far too full of reality these days."

She gazed out beyond Hugh's broad shoulders. The dullness of November had taken over the countryside, but the fertile valley still teemed with life. Stackman cattle roamed several areas. A hog farm had been set up south of the railroad line, and half a dozen pens filled with porkers lined a long dirt drive.

A parade of wagons, stacked high with hay bales, trundled east toward the depot. Stackman hay, she supposed, being sold for the growing horse and cattle population along the coast.

Wagon after wagon moved by them, and each driver tipped his cap toward Hugh Stackman.

Silent, he drove the team north along their farm lane. June spotted the cabin in the distance, and the cozy image of the timber-framed house, tucked against a thick forest of upland trees, seemed like home. It wasn't any such thing, of course, but June almost thought the solid dwelling called to her.

Two small wagons and one buggy stood east of the porch. Beyond that a small corral held a couple of horses she hadn't seen there yesterday.

Jacob met them at the base of the stairs. He helped the ladies down and directed them inside while Hugh took care of the horses.

Gentler smells filled the air today, and June shot Lily a look of gratitude.

Several people were seated in the front room. They all looked up when June and Anna walked in, as if eyeing displays at a museum. Anna generally didn't mind being the center of attention, but today, when both women knew they'd had little chance to clean up properly, even Anna shrank within herself.

"Ladies, please have a seat." Jacob motioned them to a pillow-topped wooden bench. "Lily's bringing tea."

The room had gone silent when they walked in, and it stayed that way for long ticks of the clock. The gathered men and one woman stared at June and Anna, who kept their eyes downcast as they accepted tea from Hugh's sister. And then, when the silence seemed ready to burst, Hugh strode in, tossed a pair of leather gloves onto a shelf, and grabbed a chair. He plunked it right next to June's end of the bench and offered quick introductions.

"Mrs. Harper and Mrs. Menendez, these are my neighbors and friends, Chad and Martha Doherty, Blake Morgan, and Irwin Kettleberger. And over here we have Kip Barton and his father Jack. They were gracious enough to drive over here today to meet you. We've given them a rough explanation of the circumstances, and our goal is to help those left homeless by the fire. We'd like the two of you to direct things if you're so inclined."

"Direct things?" That brought June's gaze up pretty quick. Anna's, too. "What do you mean? What are we directing?"

"We've got two bunkhouses between us with no one wintering over," said Mr. Kettleberger. He waved toward a younger man across the room. "We share bunk space with the Doherty place. It's good-sized, okay to sleep ten, but more comfortable for eight, I'd say. And Blake Morgan's father just built an extra house and passed away before he had a chance to spend more than a month in it, and Blake figures a family or two can put up there for the winter. And then we've got a full pantry larder that's been put by after a good year, and pork and beef between us, but we're all busy working our places."

"If you two ladies can coordinate who can stay where and who needs what, we figure if we can get folks through the winter, there should be enough businesses recovered and rebuilt in town by April or May to offer jobs again."

"And them that gets jobs can be on their own again," added the older Barton.

"You're offering food and lodging? But there are nearly thirty people, including the eight of us. Three widows and five children." June faced them frankly. "That's a lot of food and a lot of space."

"Well, it's none too fancy," said Chad Doherty. "While our bunkhouse ain't nothin' special, it's got a sound roof and walls and a stove to keep things from freezing over the winter."

"Ours is about the same," added the younger Barton, "and holds eight. When the workers come back in the spring, we'll need to put them up, but that's a ways away."

A lot could happen in four or five months; June knew the truth in that. "And in the house, Mr. Morgan?"

"No mister, ma'am, just Blake is fine, and I'd say four to six could put up there easy. My wife and me have two scrappin' boys and my dad loved them, but he liked to walk away from their crazy now and again. And then he passed almost as soon as the house was done, and while that's been a source of sadness, it seems providential that someone could use a warm, dry place to overwinter."

"And that leaves eight to put up," June mused.

"We've got a double bunkhouse here as well." Hugh had put his chair right beside hers, and she'd been talking back and forth, pretending that meant nothing, and all the while wondering if he'd sat by her on purpose. He turned her way. "I figured if you and your friends stayed here with the kids, we'd be able to offer the protection of the Stackman Ranch. It's not easy being a widow with children, and Jacob and I would be honored to step into that void."

Living here.

With Hugh Stackman right at hand, and a band of cowboys bunking nearby.

Yesterday's ugly scene flashed in her mind—Hinckley's ugly sneer and uglier proposal.

Her palms grew damp, and her breath hitched. She had to work to detach herself from the nasty image, and when Hugh Stackman laid a big, strong hand over hers . . . in front of everyone . . . she found herself able to breathe again. "Safety of women and children will be of utmost concern, of course." His words gave her unexpected assurance.

She understood his unspoken message. He was promising that nothing like yesterday's altercation would occur again.

Could she believe him? But if not, couldn't the very same thing happen in the tents lined up in the lee of the woods, and there would be no big, strong cowboy protection at hand? Sure it could and had already if rumors were to be believed.

Lily seated herself at Hugh's other side. "For I was a stranger, and you took me in." She murmured the sweet words from the gospel of Matthew. "For my part, I will love having women and children around. It would be a great joy to me, Mrs. Harper, Mrs. Menendez."

"June." June reached beyond Hugh and tried not to notice that he smelled of wool, horse, and hay mixed with pure Washington fresh air. "Please call me June."

"And I'm Anna." Anna stood, shook Lily's hand, then sat back down. "I think this is an excellent idea, and if you're quite serious about June and I coordinating the efforts of so much kindliness, I for one would be happy to do it? June?"

Anna was always ready to jump in, feet first, and June tended to think too much, so what choice did she have? "I agree, and I thank you all. I can't deny we've been wondering how we'd survive the coming winter, putting our faith in God to see us through. And he has surely done so this day."

"Hugh, I've got an extra buggy if the ladies need it for transport to get things accomplished." Irwin Kettleberger made the offer from his seat.

Hugh looked at her. "Can you drive a buggy?"

"Yes," said June.

Anna shook her head no. "But I'm a quick study, and you can't learn any younger."

"I know your wagons are full up of hay hittin' the rails to ship west to Seattle, and I've got an extra buckboard," noted the older man. "That would come in handy for movin' folks into a place quick like because this nice spell is bound to break soon. When it does, there ain't no tellin' what Mother Nature's got in store for us, but if it's winter, it's likely to be cold, wet, and messy, and that's the truth of it."

"I'd appreciate it, Irwin."

Lily rose and retrieved a tray of biscuits and jam. She circled the room with it.

A few folks winced when they noticed her scar. A couple of them seemed to deliberately *not* look at it. And two others seemed to not notice at all. As Lily circled the room in her simple, cotton gown, June read the sheer courage behind the young woman's look of practiced confidence.

The room cleared quickly, most taking their biscuits with them.

Hugh disappeared, then returned with paper and pencils. "If you can make a list of folks who would fit well together, that would be a help. And then a list of supplies. The bunkhouses have straw ticks on each cot in need of refilling. I can make sure there's fresh straw at each site, then if folks pile up the old straw, we can cart it to the near side of the barn out of the wind. We've dropped many a calf in the lee of that barn."

"Hugh, I've got an idea, if Jacob can spare you for the day," Lily said.

"Spare me?"

She nodded and put a hand along June's arm. "Mrs. Harper—"

"June, please."

Lily smiled. "June doesn't know which farm is which, and it makes more sense if you take her around rather than have her get lost. Then if Anna doesn't mind staying here, she and I can get our bunkhouse ready. And then the two ladies can approach the others knowing exactly what's offered with little waste of time."

"I've got Marty handling the potato harvest with Ben, and the last potato field is fully turned," Jacob added. "As soon as the hay wagons return, we'll reload them for the next train to Seattle. It's a sound idea, Hugh."

Nervous anticipation fluttered along June's spine, and when Hugh saw the sense of the offer, her stomach got nervous again, but for very different reasons. He turned her way. "Shall we head out? It will take a little time between farms."

"Of course." She felt Anna's smile behind her back and didn't dare turn, because the idea that Hugh Stackman might be interested in a penniless widow stretched conjecture to the extreme. But when he held her hand a moment too long after helping her up into the buggy, a part of her wanted him to keep on holding her hand, like say . . . forever?

He released her hand and climbed into the buggy, offering just enough time for her to gather errant thoughts and stuff them away.

She wasn't born yesterday. A married woman with children understood much of the ways of the world, and engaging in a flirtation with a man in close surroundings was a dangerous precedent. She wasn't a young girl who believed in the sweet lies and empty promises that fell from some lips. She'd lived that choice once. She would never live it again. Better to be alone, raising her girls on her own, than be caught in a loveless arrangement with a man who cared more for himself than anyone else.

She trained her gaze on the road ahead, but studied the surrounding land as they progressed. "This is all Stackman land?" she asked when they came to a newly fenced border. Just outside the fencing sat a small, white house in need of significant repair.

"It is now." He directed the horses along at an easy pace, not pushing. "Harrv Bedloe had this place but then got old and sick and couldn't keep things up."

"So you bought it for a bargain."

He rubbed his chin, looking skeptical. "When there's a sight of work to be done, I can't say the word bargain entered into the arrangement, but it worked out the way I hoped."

She bet it did. From all she'd heard, things had a way of working out Hugh Stackman's way, and June was pretty sure that didn't happen by accident. He turned the buggy into a farm lane stretching north, and when he pulled up at the bunkhouse, she hopped down before he had time to fully set the brake. He came around the back of the wagon and seized her hand. "That was dangerous. If those horses spooked, you could have been caught between the wheels and dragged. Are we in that big a hurry?" He stared at her in confusion, then dropped her hand and stepped back. "I am not the enemy here. Am I?"

She dropped her gaze, embarrassed. At that moment, she'd thought of him just that way.

"Mrs. Harper, I don't know what you've heard."

She winced, because she'd heard plenty over the last several years, that's for sure.

"And I promise, you don't even have to make yourself like me."

Like him? She hadn't been able to get the strong, handsome rancher out of her mind since meeting him yesterday.

"But most of what's said is untrue or grossly exaggerated, so if you would kindly give me a chance, I'd be grateful."

Was she foolish to believe him? Or foolish to believe what came from envious lips around Ellensburgh? "I am unaccustomed to being around people of substance, it seems." She raised her chin and met his gaze. "For reasons of my own, I tend toward skepticism."

He didn't seem insulted by her words. "I entertain my share of that as well. But for the moment, can we lay that aside and work together to get folks settled?"

"Why are you doing this?" There. She'd said it. She'd asked the question right out. "You profess no faith in God, and you have nothing to gain. I must ask," she went on more gently, "for to bring people into a situation that may or may not be wholesome is a heavy responsibility upon me and Anna. When I take this offer back to a crowd of displaced people, they will be quick to seek shelter, and need can then become a downfall. So I need to know, Mr. Stackman. Why are you reaching out to the fallen now? At this late date?"

Nothing was ever easy. Hugh had discovered that at an early age—that things and people were not often what they seemed.

This woman appeared genuine. She was smart, intuitive, and focused on caring for her family and others at her own expense. Her appearance attested to that.

He released her hand and moved toward the bunkhouse, silent.

He didn't owe her answers. He owed no one anything. He'd come to this land with nothing but a stake in cattle and two younger siblings. He'd built his home, his ranch, and his life with their help, and if he wanted to share a little here and there, it was no one's business why.

"When something needs to be done, I do it," he told her. He kept his tone short and tight. "You brought a need to my attention yesterday, one I hadn't realized. We have means to help, and so we do. That's the end of it."

It should have been, but this woman didn't brush off easily, and he wasn't too sure if that was good or bad.

"And I have your word that there is no ulterior motive?" June pressed.

"Will you take my word?" He faced her frankly. "Or will you continue to let seeds of doubt poison your thoughts?"

To his surprise, she didn't argue. "I do exactly that," she murmured, then moved beyond him into the long, narrow bunkhouse. "It is an unseemly habit of doubt that I must learn to conquer because this mistrust isn't of God, is it?" She peered at him, but didn't seem to need an answer, which was just as well because the whole God nonsense wasn't anything he cared to debate. People came, they existed, they died, and if they were lucky, they left a positive mark on the land. End of story.

"I do apologize, Mr. Stackman."

"Hugh. Please. Just Hugh." He felt tired saying it, as if asking her to treat him normally expended too much effort, or maybe it was because she made him think of things he'd cast aside long ago.

She worried her lower lip with her top teeth, just a little, just enough to make him wonder what it would be like to worry that pretty mouth on his own time, and wasn't that an interesting turn of events? Here she was, concerned about people's safety and ulterior motives, and he was contemplating a delightful ulterior motive all the while she convinced herself there was none.

"Hugh."

She said it softly, and he melted inside.

He'd never sought love these past ten years. He'd kept himself too busy building this, acquiring that, and taking responsibility for Jacob and Lily, but now, gazing into sapphire-blue eyes and hearing his name from the prettiest lips he ever did see, a longing swept over him.

He smiled. Just that. He smiled at her, and let his gaze linger for long, slow beats. "So, June."

"Yes?" She held his gaze, too, a two-sided affair if ever there was one.

"I think this will do to keep folks sheltered and warm for a few months. Don't you?" Did he lean closer?

Or did she?

He wasn't sure, but the urge to put his lips on hers swept over him as strong as anything he'd ever desired in over thirty years of living.

"Hugh, is that you?" Chad Doherty's voice splintered the moment. A few seconds later Chad strode into the bunkhouse, happy to see them. "I was hoping you'd show the ladies the way, because as easy as it seems to tell one place from another if you're familiar with the area, it becomes another situation when you're not." He crossed to the standard-model Franklin stove across the room. "Now my missus knows this old stove ain't a bit good to bake with, but it's all right to cook on, so she said she'd do an extra measure of bread daily to help out. Eight folks, give or take. That's a lot of bread to produce on a stove meant for heating and not much else."

"That's a generous offer." June stepped forward and took Chad's hands a lot easier than she'd taken Hugh's. Hugh was almost insulted when a thought struck. Taking Chad's hands meant little, which meant holding his meant more, and that thought put him right back in mind of the kiss he'd just missed.

But that was most likely a good thing, he realized, as Chad shut the bunkhouse door and they moved back to the wagon. They couldn't afford to complicate things.

Too late.

His conscience offered a common sense nudge.

This is already complicated, and now you need to simplify things.

Simplify? He helped June up into the buggy, hauled himself up into the seat beside her, and realized that there was precious little chance of simplifying any of this.

CHAPTER FOUR

S he'd almost kissed Hugh Stackman.

Right after she lectured him about motive, she'd been ready to lean that little bit closer and see what kissing Hugh Stackman would be like, which was exactly the reason she should take up quarters somewhere other than the Stackman ranch. Someplace with a geographical distance from this man, and she was determined to do just that. But at the end of the day, when they drove up the lane to the Stackman cabin, Caroline, Anna, and the kids were all there.

"Mama, we've got a house to live in!" Beth raced her way and grabbed her around the legs in a big hug. Amanda followed more slowly, but with equal excitement.

"It's nice and snug, Mama." She peeked up at June with all the innocence of time gone by. "It's so very special to me." Round-eyed, she gazed at her mother with an intensity and gratitude far beyond her few years.

June's resolve melted away. She swallowed angst and a large bite of pride as she nodded because these girls had already dealt with so much. "The Stackmans are very generous people."

Hugh moved up behind her. She didn't have to turn to know it. She'd know it without the blended scents of leather, hay, and a light tobacco scent that hinted a fondness for a pipe. She'd know it because when he drew near, dulled senses flew to high alert like a bird seeking flight.

"Your children, June?"

That voice, deep and still, a reflecting pool, holding much unseen beneath the surface. She nodded. "Yes, Hugh."

Did he smile when she used his name? Did it please him? She didn't turn to find out. "This is Beth, and this is Amanda."

"Ladies." She felt the motion of his raised arm as he tipped his hat behind her, and the way the girls smiled meant he'd smiled first. Still, she kept her gaze on her beautiful daughters. It was safer that way.

"And my friend Caroline Harders and her children, Beau and Mary. And this is Anna's son, Samuel."

Caroline moved forward and extended her hand. "Thank you, Mr. Stackman. The kindness extended by you and your neighbors will not go unblessed."

She felt him stiffen behind her.

Hugh didn't like talk of blessings or faith or Scripture.

A man of no faith?

June moved forward with the girls, breaking the connection for the moment, knowing it would come again, but she couldn't relocate the girls now that they were here. Hopes and dreams had been nonexistent in their lives for a long time. She had no right to dash the new gleam in their eyes because of her lack of self-control. And that meant she needed to shelve the attraction.

"Anna, did you tell the folks at the encampment what's happened?"

Anna shook her head. "Some were working, but Jacob and I went to get Caroline and the children so they can get settled. And with them here, you and I can go back to the woods with the buckboard and talk with everyone."

"With dark coming?" Hugh shook his head. "I can't have you two out on a dark road. What if bad weather came up? Or you had trouble with the horses? But I do see what you mean. If folks are working, this could be difficult." He drew his brow tight. "We'll ride at first light before people have left for work. And even if they have, we can make the offer and let them decide. Are there many with jobs?"

"Less than a handful," June told him. "Still, any employment is a blessing unwisely sloughed off."

"Work's mighty important when you've got a family." He turned toward Anna. "I'll drive you ladies over first thing, and we'll get this part squared away. Then for those who'd like to take shelter, we can use the buckboard to bring them up the road."

Such an old-time saying for a modern man. "Up the road" as if the multi-mile span was around the corner, but in big country, that's how it was.

June clasped her hands at her waist. "I can drive the buckboard. I am fully capable, and I'm sure you have important things that draw your attention."

He shifted his gaze to her, and there it was again. Her heart hummed as if singing a tune. Her fingertips buzzed in time. Her muscles went lax. And then he nodded. "You're right. I'll have Jacob escort you into Ellensburgh, and he can help with the move." He turned back to the others and touched the brim of his broad, black cowboy hat. "Welcome to the Stackman Ranch, folks."

And then he left.

She should be relieved that Jacob would be with them. Wasn't that exactly what she wanted, to maintain distance from the oldest Stackman?

Not wanted, she decided, as she helped the children get their bedrolls organized. *Needed.* And she shouldn't have worried because for the next two weeks she didn't catch sight of Hugh Stackman at all. Not in the morning. Nor in the afternoon. And not even in the night, although her eyes strained for a glimpse.

Nothing. It was as if Hugh Stackman had disappeared, never to be seen again, and by the weekend before Thanksgiving, she was near bursting with questions she didn't dare raise.

She spent her time helping Lily in the kitchen and hand stitching blanket tops by lantern light. The bunkhouse had few windows. Light was scarce. But the box heater warmed the large room, and there was no scarcity of firewood, unlike the plains where she'd been raised. Who'd have thought a simple stack of firewood would be such a treat? On broad open plains where nothing but scarce cottonwood and buffalo chips heated the long winters, the lack of cozy shelter had been the norm.

Lily approached the women on Saturday. "Is it your custom to go to services on Sunday?"

"It is, but we realize we are here by your grace," June told her. "Caroline, Anna, and I have talked, and we don't want to put you or your family out any more than we've already done. We can pray here together."

A mix of relief and disappointment shadowed Lily's face, but then she nodded. "May I join you?"

"Yes," said Caroline.

"Of course." Anna bobbed her head in quick assent.

"Absolutely." June answered in time with the others, making them all smile.

"I haven't been in a long time," Lily told them. She pulled a shawl closer around her shoulders as if cold, but the bunkhouse was quite warm. "To a church service that is. Not since . . ." Her voice wandered. She shrugged one slim shoulder as if expecting them to understand, and anyone looking at her face would understand. "And then we moved here and life was quite busy, and I was happy being back here, off the road, out of the hustle and bustle."

"But now you're thinking of stepping out." June met her gaze. "It's like that once you get a taste of community again."

"I want courage again." Lily faced them, hands out. "I lost it a long time ago, and Hugh and Jacob took such good care of me, but when you've lost a precious part of your being, it becomes vitally important to find it again. When Old Feather comes down the mountain in the fall, we talk."

"He is Yakama?" June asked. The Yakama tribe had gathered for a fall celebration in this broad valley for generations, long before new settlers flocked in.

"Yes. We do business with them as they remember their past and we crowd in with our future. This year he told me that to find what is lost means we must look hard, and not just away, but within. And then you came to work here, and I think God is showing me that there is a way back to that old courage, that young Lily. But not without some effort on my part. So I will pray with you now at your services if I may, but at some point, I want to walk into a church like I did as a child. My head held high, my eyes cast forward. Because when God looks at me, it is with no pity." She squinted slightly. "He sees beyond the scars to the sweet soul. And if I can find the courage to go out on a regular basis, I think others will start to see me as God does. Beyond the scars."

Her words humbled June.

To go through life with a raggedly scarred face was a trial. June had been fretting about temporary circumstances that had changed her life. Hearing Lily, she realized her shallowness. Lily's circumstance was never-ending. "Your goals show a great amount of courage, and we'd be happy to walk into church with you, anytime."

"Soon, then. But tomorrow, I'll come over here and we can pray together. With the children."

"Who may be noisy," Caroline warned. "Even when shushed."

Lily laughed, and June realized it was the first time she'd done that in her presence. "I'll be glad of the noise, honestly. We're three adults, living and working in too much grown-up quiet. Their presence gladdens us." She started to go, then turned back. "Hugh has been gathering cattle in the high country and bringing them down a level with some of the men. They'll be back for Thanksgiving on Thursday. Can we all celebrate together? I know we won't all fit into the house, but I thought if the day was mellow, we could cook ahead and gather in the barn around the sorting tables? Unless the men have plans to eat elsewhere, and then we could just use the house, but I think most will stay."

"That would be lovely." Anna picked up Samuel and kissed his little cheek. "Lily, we have so much to be grateful for, and it would give us a chance to thank you and your brothers."

Lily shook her head instantly. "No, please. You have no idea how wonderful it is to have you here, so I'm thanking you. Let's save Thursday for thanking God. I need no thanks, and it would just embarrass Hugh, and then he'll go all quiet. After nearly two weeks of being in the hills and sleeping in cold conditions, I expect they'll be ready for a great meal or two and a warm place to lay their heads."

Rounding up cattle.

June hadn't thought of how the cattle up top must be gathered and brought down to winter over closer to home. It made sense, but beyond that, her mind flew to Thanksgiving, and it had little to do with a fine feast.

Hugh would be back.

Yes, she was foolish to think about him this way. It was adolescent and sophomoric and boasted folly for multiple reasons, but her heart seemed to care nothing for the sensible. It beat faster and stronger each time she pondered the coming holiday, and as the week bore on, she cooked, baked, and cleaned the barn with Lily, pretty much thinking of nothing else.

He'd thought of June every minute.

Hugh directed the nearest herd dog to come by once he opened the last gate. He remounted his palomino gelding and moved ahead, leading the way with two cowhands bringing up the rear.

A flood of gently plodding cattle pushed through the opening, not in any sort of hurry. He liked cattle. He liked their mostly easygoing nature, although he had two bulls that made him look sharp whenever he was in their presence. But the cows were primarily passive creatures, rarely aggressive, unless their babies were endangered. Then even the most amiable cow could turn into a fighting machine.

They'd found the remains of one cow and two calves up top. Cougar kills from the looks of the tracks embedded in the soft ground of late autumn. The cougars rarely came this low looking for food and never this time of year. In March and April, after a bad winter, yes. But not now, and the reason he thought of that was the laughing voices of children, playing on a huge mound of straw in the closest barn. He moved the horse closer, guided him through the near gate, and when Alfred motioned that he'd close the gate, Hugh steered the horse nearer.

And there was the woman who'd occupied his thoughts for thirteen days, watching the children, laughing right along with them.

His heart clenched. So did his hands on the reins, and Buttergold shied back in question.

She turned.

He paused the horse.

Her eyes sought his, and he knew it was no use. He'd gone on the roundup, needing to set her aside, needing to come back stronger and more able to keep his distance. He wasn't what a woman of faith needed, and what if Carmody was right? What if she was a gold digger, playing a part to win a wealthy man's heart to ensure her children's future?

He swung down out of the saddle and walked forward.

Would she meet him halfway? Or make him come the distance? And which would be better?

He didn't know.

And then she smiled.

When she did, none of it mattered. Not Carmody's warning, not her diffidence, nor her bravado. He strode forward, warmed by that smile, and grasped her shoulders, knowing he shouldn't and just as sure he couldn't resist. "June."

"You've come home."

Those words. That face, that smile, the children laughing and sliding down the straw pile behind her. When he was young, he'd never had the chance to do things like that once the fire had stolen the laughter out from under him. He'd taken on a man's responsibilities as a lad and never shirked them once, but hearing the children and seeing the light in June's eyes pushed him to think ahead rather than back, and he couldn't remember that last time he'd done that. Not about people that really mattered.

She reached up and covered his hands with hers.

His heart leapt again. "I have come home, and it was a long, cold, and wet roundup."

"You need food and rest." She held his gaze and looked worried, as if anxious for him, and that made his heart beat sharper yet. "Perhaps we should make tomorrow's celebration smaller, so you and the men can rest."

"Tomorrow's celebration?"

"Of Thanksgiving," she reminded him, and if she hadn't, he probably wouldn't have given the day an extra thought. "That's why you came back today, of course. To celebrate our gratitude tomorrow?"

He hadn't thought of a calendar or the day or thanking a nonexistent being for anything, and the look of disappointment in her face indicated she'd read his expression.

"Well." She stepped back, still smiling, but not the same. Nothing close to the same. "Lily is quite excited about it, and we wouldn't want to disappoint her."

She cared for his sister's feelings, but rebuked his, and what could he say to that? A man didn't pretend belief he didn't have, did he?

Could you pretend for such a prize as her?

He watched June back up another step and wished he could, but falsehood didn't become him. He'd been raised to be an honest man in the face of his father's dishonesty, and to offer pretense now was impossible. But as June took another step back, he desperately searched for a different answer and found none.

"Mama, I can slide so far!" The littler girl had scrambled up the straw pile as quickly as any of the other children. He watched her, curious. She couldn't walk as quickly, nor run as fast, but climbing offered no problem. He watched her sail down the straw, arms up in complete abandon, then he studied her gait once she rose. Hobbled, back and forth, a slight lurch with each step, but then back up the straw, quick as a mouse scurrying up tree bark.

"Well done, Amanda!" June clapped for her when she slid down again, enjoying the children's fun as if it were her own. And maybe, as a parent, it was.

He walked away, not even saying good-bye. What was the point? He wasn't going anywhere, but the chasm between them was as deep and strong as the attraction, and he had no right to pursue things with such a breach. He knew it and she knew it, and why couldn't their hearts just muster along?

He slept soundly that night but woke early. Jacob and the small crew were seeing to chores for a couple of days to give the roundup crew time to work out the kinks of sleeping on cold, hard ground. The warmth of the cushioned bed wrapped itself around him, but the sound of voices pulled him downstairs.

Fresh-baked breads sat cooling on an extra shelf Jacob must have erected. Pans of this and pots of that stood about, and as he came through the front room, one of the men was carrying a large covered dish down to the cold cellar. The room and the house smelled like a feast should smell, a mix of sugar, spice, and roasted meat.

"Is it that late?" He peered outside deliberately, teasing. "Dinnertime already?"

"It's so good to have you home!" Lily hugged him, then shooed him aside. "Now the coffee is there in your favorite pot and freshly made, but the ladies and I are doing a service this morning for all who wish to attend, so we wanted a head start on some things for a midday dinner and then a time of rest for everyone. Except for essential duties, of course."

His ears heard one thing. "A service?"

"A prayer service, yes."

He stared at her, wondering why she had the right to look so happy. Why didn't she resent God as he did? Or shrug him off as nothing of consequence, an illogical father-figure who offered no comfort or reprieve? Was she too young to hang tight to the anger that grabbed hold of him and refused to let go? Anger at a careless father who abandoned his family for love of mining and money and loose women? And deeper anger at the supposed God who pledged his love for mankind, and left his people to perish in fire?

Or is your cold, hard fury because of the circumstances that had you out of the house when the fire swept in, stealing the precious breath of your mother and baby sisters? A lad yourself, working to put food on the table for others.

"You don't have to come, Hugh. I know how you feel about all this, but for me it is different. It's always been different, and when I see women with June's courage and Anna's humor, I want to charge in and grab hold of what I'm missing. I want to be brave and bold enough to walk down an Ellensburgh street and not worry about the stares. I want to walk into church and have people see me as God sees me, but the only way to do that is to get them accustomed to seeing me. And I think doing church services with the ladies has been helping."

"You've done this already?"

She released his arms and moved to the stove with swift, sure movements. "We have, and the children are mostly good and so sweet.

But it's not mandatory, of course, and if you'd like time to just rest and relax here after being on the trail for so long, that's understandable."

His sister never pestered him about faith. She read her good words quietly and sometimes made notes, but she never foisted her innocent beliefs on him or Jacob.

Shame knifed him, because while she'd quietly embraced her faith, he'd let it be known that he found belief in God to be a waste of time and intelligence. She never challenged him or called him out. She took the high road, exactly as she was doing today, and the shame spread wider when he realized it.

Hugh poured his coffee and stepped onto the broad side porch. Jacob or someone had mowed the weeded field separating the house from the sorting barn, and despite the coolness of the day, he saw people moving about in the large building. And then someone closed the west-facing door.

What were they doing? Or, better yet, what were they hiding?

He slipped from the porch, walked along the north face of the barn, then turned to walk south again. He came to the wide-open east door and looked in.

The potato sorting slabs were scrubbed clean. Pots of late wildflowers and tall grasses decorated the two long tables. An odd assortment of plates was set out, with an odder selection of silverware. A tub stood nearby, with a small stand set up inside the wide bucket mouth. Beyond that a makeshift table had been erected on wooden sawhorses. Five smaller plates were set on this table. A children's table, he realized, and as he had that thought, June's youngest limped into the barn carrying a stack of cotton squares for napkins.

"Hullo." She peeked up at him, unafraid, but none too sure, either. "I brought these for Mama."

"Perfect." He set his coffee down, took the squares from her, and set them on the long tables. "You're Amanda, right?"

"Yes, sir." She bobbed a tiny curtsy, and her rosy cheeks dimpled. When they did, it was June's face smiling up at him. She held up four little fingers. "I'm this many, and Beth is five, almost six. I like your house. A l-l-lot. It's big and pwetty and Miss Lily is so nice to everybody!"

She sighed as if happiness totally overcame her. "It is so very beautiful here."

It was.

The verdant hills, the mountain backdrop, the broad, rich valley, ideal for production . . . the sum of the parts was an amazing gift they'd stumbled upon, thinking they'd use their cattle for start-up costs of a mining operation.

He knew he was home the moment they began their initial descent, and he'd been happy here ever since. "Thank you. I'm glad you like it, Amanda. May I see your left boot, please? Just for a moment?"

She frowned and sighed. "They're a bother, Mr. Hugh."

"I'll help."

"Fank you!" She sat right down on a straw bale, kicked her foot out, and let him unfasten the boot. "It's really, really tight right now, and Ma says I'm between Beth's old ones and some new ones, but new ones will be a pretty penny."

When times were tough and money tight, shoes could be a prohibitive expense. He remembered that from childhood. Seeing Amanda's troubled look reminded him of how far he'd come. If he needed boots or shoes, he rode into town and bought them. Or he ordered from the catalogues Lily loved to get, and the boots would be delivered right to the post office, made in his size. It was an amazing world when you had cash in hand to pay your way.

He glanced around the barn. He wanted to experiment with her shoe, but nothing he saw was just right, so he cut two hands full of straw and stuffed them in her boot. He measured, then added two more hands full. *Better.*

He put the boot back on her foot, snugged the laces, and had her stand. "Can you walk for me? Please?"

"Walk where?"

He laughed because it was a very good question. "Just anywhere. I want to see if the boot is easier on your foot when it's stuffed."

"A stuffed boot is a funny thing that feels even funnier," she told him, but when she walked around the barn, her limp was decidedly less noticeable. "Can we unstuff it now? It prickles me. Please?"

"We can." He removed her boot, shook out the stuffing, then dusted off her stocking. He replaced the boot gently, and then he set her down on the floor. "How's that feel now?"

"Better without prickly stuff!" She grinned up at him and took hold of his heart right then and there. "I've gotta go help Mama. It's almost time for prayers." She grabbed his hand. "Come on! You can sit with me, and Mama will read to us!"

How did one tell a small child no? He had no idea, and since words failed him, he followed her out the door and around to the bunkhouse.

Four lanterns hung from the studs. It wasn't light, but it was light enough, he supposed. With few windows, the long room seemed dark and dim.

At the front stood a table with a Bible and another lamp, filled and trimmed with care.

He understood that. He'd been crazy careful of anything that might start a fire once he was given the chance to make choices. The woodstoves and chimneys were located away from wooden walls to keep them from getting too hot. The best lanterns, the best beeswax, the highest quality lamp oil. Nothing with a flame next to anything that could tempt a fire.

His mother had taught him well, but when an entire street goes up in flames with fierce Pacific winds, there was little to quell the awesomeness of its fast-moving power.

June entered the bunkhouse from the other side. If she was surprised to see him in Amanda's grasp, she didn't show it. The other women followed with the children. Half-a-dozen cowboys came in behind them, including Stake Carmody. The men removed their hats as they stepped inside, as if arriving in a real church building. The women took seats quietly to his right, with the men filling in behind.

Some sat on cots and some stood. As June held up the Bible, a hush fell over the group. She read from the Old Testament, then the New, and then asked Carmody to come forward and read the Gospel.

He glanced around, then pointed to himself. "Me, ma'am?"

"If you've a mind." She smiled at him, and Hugh might have felt the tiniest stab of disconcertment when she did.

"I can do that." Carmody walked forward and didn't look the least bit suspicious as he took the Bible, turned, and faced the group. When his eyes lit on Hugh, he winced slightly. He read the passage she'd marked, and when he was done, he handed the book back. "That was a mighty nice passage to pick, ma'am. In light of all that folks have lost this year, seein' the Savior through Simeon's and Anna's old eyes is a treat."

"Amen." She took the Bible back, Caroline rose and offered a prayer of thanksgiving, and then they all stood as if they knew they were supposed to, so Hugh followed along.

Anna began singing. Caroline and June joined in, as well as several of the men. It was a simple song. Pretty chords on Stake's guitar and an easy, thoughtful melody. As Hugh listened, little Amanda leaned against him. As naturally as if he carted youngsters around every day, he picked her up.

She smiled her thanks, laid her head against his chest, and popped a thumb into her mouth.

His heart went tight.

Pearl had done much the same thing before they lost her. She'd tuck her head against her big brother's neck and ease into slumber with her thumb in her mouth.

The others sang soft words, following the music—words that recounted the highs and lows of life and dealing with them.

The verses touched him, but not as much as the child taking rest against his chest. She watched her mother, leading prayers in the front of the room, and seemed completely content to cuddle in the safety of his embrace.

"It is well . . ."

The words again, convincing.

"With my soul . . ."

Did he have a soul? And if so, did that mean there was a celestial governance? A heaven and a hell, much as his mother had believed? And the grace of an almighty father?

Surely not.

And yet . . .

Hearing the words, feeling the music, listening to the heartfelt testimony of two old folks who had been waiting for a Savior, something nudged open inside him as if making room.

"Are you so very hungry, Mr. Hugh?"

Amanda whispered the words against his neck as he carried her outside, and he had to smile. "Famished."

"Mama said we had to wait, but then she said if we're too hungry to wait, we might have a roll. Do you fink Miss Lily would let us have a roll?"

"She's a soft-hearted thing, so yes. Shall we go together?" He peeked down at her and her cheeks dimpled.

"Yes! And maybe we can snuggle by the fire and tell stories? I l-l-love telling stories!"

He toted her inside the house as the women bustled around the log-sided kitchen, making preparations. Cheerful voices and delicious smells set his stomach growling. He nipped three rolls from one of the baskets and took Amanda into the front room. Midday sun shone brightly on the south side of the cabin. He repositioned the broad corner chair to catch the light and sat down.

June's youngest daughter scrambled into his lap, chewing her roll and chatting between bites. As he sat with her, munching soft, yeasty rolls and whispering stories of old like his mother had done decades before, the combination of soft bread, a small child, and old stories stretched open his crotchety heart even more.

CHAPTER FIVE

"Here you are!" June folded her arms across her middle and smiled at them from the doorway a quarter hour later. "I wondered where you'd gotten off to, Miss Amanda. I see you have a fine escort, so I will worry no longer."

"I should have told you she was with me." Hugh frowned. "I didn't mean to cause you concern, June."

"It seems motherhood comes with concern firmly attached, so we've come to expect it," she assured him. "I lost track of her in the busyness and wanted to make sure she was fine. Which she is." She started to step back toward the kitchen, but he called her name. Softly. So softly.

He held out a hand. Just that. Such a simple gesture.

Kitchen noise beckoned her from behind, but here, in the quiet of the front room, a man's hand reached out for her.

She answered the summons, took his hand, and knelt alongside the chair. "Are these good stories we're telling?" She kept her voice soft because it seemed a time for soft-spoken words.

"They are. The stories my mother shared with me and Jacob and my sisters."

She met his gaze then and sighed. He'd had his share of loss too. The shadows in his face said as much, but the words confirmed it because there was only one sister now. "I love old stories and the joy of passing them on, but I like to make up new stories, too."

"Do you make up stories, June? For the children?"

She laughed and gave his hand a light squeeze before letting go and standing. "For them as well as me. I love pretending. I love seeing what could be and reaching for it. Imagining it. And I want the girls to have

137

great imaginations and marvelous thoughts of doing whatever they'd like to do. I see this great West as a place for women to not only find their way, but chart their way. And that's an important consideration when raising daughters in a man's world."

"Now you sound like a suffragist."

"Wonderful!" She smiled when he looked slightly aggrieved, and she leaned forward. "We are in new times at long last. We have doors opening before us, even as men like Hinckley believe they can run the world and our lives through craven deals. You heard the words of Anna in the Gospel message, how she saw that baby Savior and proclaimed his birth far and wide. And later on, at that cross, it was women standing vigil with Christ's mother. All but one disciple ran off, but the women stayed, crying and praying until the end. So yes, I'm a suffragist, and not so much for me but for them." She ruffled Amanda's curls. "I believe the country will go as Wyoming went, and we'll all be voting before long because an imbalance of power is in no woman's best interests. And I've got a lot at stake with two daughters to raise."

"Are you ever unsure of yourself, June?" Hugh asked as Amanda wriggled to get down. He let her go, then stood. "Do you have answers for everything?"

"Far more questions than answers, but I've learned some lessons in my twenty-seven years, and they've been life's best teachers. I don't trust as easy."

He grunted, which might mean he felt the same way, or he was just plain grumbly.

June continued, "I'm not afraid to forge my own path. Make my own choices. And every one of those choices puts Amanda and Beth first. And that's the crux of it, Hugh."

"Mama, can we go help some more?"

June paused Amanda with a quiet hand. "I do believe you need to thank your new friend for spending his morning with you when he surely had many other things to do, sweetheart."

"Fank you so much!" She grabbed him around the legs and hugged him tight, and when he reached down and hugged her back, June's heart twisted open, like a rusted-well faucet. Children benefitted from the love and example of a good man. A man could and should bring a core difference to a family.

Her girls had never known that difference, but Amanda's reaction to Hugh demonstrated what life could be like in ideal circumstances.

But did the perfect conditions even exist?

June was pretty sure they didn't.

Amanda hurried out, not letting her listing gait slow her down.

June followed and paused in the empty kitchen as the other women arranged food in the nearby barn.

This kitchen was such a grand room for food and gathering. To think that Hugh had built this, *all of this*, with Jacob, so the siblings could take care of themselves as they matured.

A man with foresight and honor and no heart for God.

She started forward.

Hugh's hand stopped her from behind.

She turned.

His embrace didn't take her by surprise. It took her by storm, as if all her life she'd been waiting for this man, this moment.

He drew her back into the other room out of sight in case someone dashed into the kitchen for something.

And then he sighed, holding her the way she'd always longed to be held. Not just in the throes of desire, but in the strong, confirming arms of a man who knew himself and his goals, if not his heart.

"I won't apologize for holding you, June. And I won't guarantee it won't happen again." His voice sounded gruff, as if he knew he should be sorry and wasn't.

"I am as guilty and as delighted, it seems, but you are wrong, Hugh." She stood back and gripped his hands. "It cannot happen again, despite our feelings, because I am in a compromising situation here. I am living on your land, by your largesse, and a woman with children can't afford the look of impropriety. You know this as well as I."

"There's little to be considered improper if I make you my wife." He drew her back toward him. "I believe all of this becomes quite proper indeed."

If he made her his wife?

Not if he asked, or desired, or requested.

If he *made* her Mrs. Hugh Stackman.

Oh, she wished for a better choice of words from such a marvelous person, but no one was going to make her anything, ever again.

She stepped back again. And then again.

And then she turned and slipped through the kitchen door, leaving him standing there, the big oaf.

Should she have to explain the insult? Shouldn't he realize that a woman isn't just made a wife, but courted, cherished, and beloved?

She crossed to the big barn and entered through the door on the far side.

The feast was set out. Caroline and Lily were making the huge bowl of eggnog to celebrate the day of thanksgiving, and the children were dashing about the far end of the barn, pretending to be cowboys.

Hugh came in as she crossed the room to help with the serving.

He didn't look her way. She knew because she kept an eye on him with her peripheral vision, pretending, of course, to pay no attention to him at all.

Make her his wife.

In a pig's eye.

And yet, when he came through the line for the delightful array of food, the thought of his embrace and what it meant . . . and being his wife . . . were the *only* things on her mind. Beef and corn pudding and rolls and cake meant nothing at that moment, because when he'd held her, she wanted nothing more than to stay in his arms forever.

But not on those terms.

———

A scorned proposal?

Hugh spent the first week after Thanksgiving stacking wood and rigging fence, refusing to think about June but unable to think about anything else. In the end they had tight fencing and extra wood and he hadn't gotten June . . . *or tucking her in close to his heart* . . . out of his mind.

And then he chopped more wood, even though the last thing they needed was more wood, because he and Jacob and the men had set by six full cords in the midsummer lull.

But he chopped it because he needed to be doing something vitally busy and mindless. Then he spent a few days riding fence, then chopped more wood, because he absolutely, positively wasn't going to spend these early days of winter working right up there at the house where he'd either be seeing June, hearing her voice, or worse, catching a whiff of that soap-and-water clean scent with a dash of fresh vanilla.

She'd hugged him back. Would she have kissed him, too?

He'd kissed a few women back in the day, and while he wouldn't say he had a wealth of experience, he was well-traveled enough to know when a woman anticipated a kiss.

June wanted a kiss as much as he did.

But now what was he to do? She wouldn't have him. She'd made that clear, and the fact that she was less than five hundred feet away all day and all night was driving him mad.

On top of that, she didn't even have the courtesy to avoid him.

No!

She was up at the house this minute, creating fruit cakes with Lily, and studding them with chopped fruit and nuts, an old-fashioned nod to the upcoming holiday.

And they'd planned sugar cakes for the children, trays of cookies, and *lebkuchen*, a spicy bar she'd been taught to make by neighbors on the prairie.

Carmody had dropped all pretense of mistrust and now ran errands for the women like a trusted pup.

The cowhands washed their hands every night, and if Lily set out a tray of baked goods, the house was filled to bursting with the women, kids, and cowboys looking for some home-cooking and feminine attention.

June treated him with respect.

And nothing more.

And it was killing him.

Jacob rode up on the back of Young Susie. He pulled up tight, stopped, and stared at his brother. "We've got enough wood for two years. Stop chopping."

"Idle hands get into trouble."

"There's strapping to be fixed, leather to be oiled, and a pile of other chores waiting at the barn and the house. Unless . . ." He peered closer and sighed. "You don't want to be by the house."

"Busy enough here."

"With wood we don't need." Jacob sighed again, on purpose, Hugh was sure of it, and then he climbed off his horse as if it was the last thing he wanted to do. "You're avoiding June."

"There's no avoiding anyone up at that house. It's been invaded by so many people a man can't sit down long enough to get his boots off or tug them on without someone interrupting his train of thought or climbing on his lap to hear a story."

"You said you liked kids."

"I like them well enough when they're in someone else's house."

"Well, you're the one who invited them here, I believe."

"Here, yes." Hugh pointed in the direction of the bunkhouse area. "Inside? No. That was Lily, one hundred percent Lily. And now there's barely room to breathe."

"For a few months, sure. But then they'll all be gone. That should make you happy."

"Having them gone won't make me a bit happy. What's more I think you know that." He swung the broad ax repeatedly, punctuating his words. *Chop. Chop. Chop.*

"I might have thought you'd be looking at courting Miss June about now, but you didn't so I figured you weren't interested. Because you sure don't act interested."

"I'm full-well interested!" He set the ax down carefully because what he really wanted to do was throw it, full steam. "She's the one who's not interested, and she won't have me."

"You asked her to marry you?"

"Yes."

"And she said no?"

Hugh paused, then glared. "She said nothing."

"She gave you no answer?" Jacob scratched the back of his head, perplexed. "That's not like her."

"It's very much like her, and I'm of a mind to say so."

"When did this happen?"

"Thanksgiving Day."

Jacob's mouth dropped open. It looked like it took a fair bit of work for him to shut it, and then he faced his brother head-on. "You proposed to June on Thanksgiving Day after only knowing her . . . seeing her . . . a handful of times?"

"A body should know when he loves someone, shouldn't he?"

"So you told her you loved her . . ."

Hugh hadn't done any such thing. He shook his head.

"You didn't tell her you loved her?"

"There wasn't time. One minute she was hugging the stuffing out of me, and the next minute she was walking away."

"So." Jacob folded his arms and held Hugh's attention. "What happened between the hug and the walk?"

"She said we couldn't be doing this again, and I said we could if I made her my wife. And then she walked away."

"You said what?"

Jacob's face changed. So did his posture. He rolled his shoulders back, then scrubbed a hand to his face like he did when the cows refused to walk through a gate.

"You heard me."

"That was your proposal?"

Hugh thought hard and shrugged. "Well, we never exactly got to that part full-on. She made up her mind and turned and walked away."

"You didn't think a fine woman like June might like some courting? Some old-fashioned wooing? Because while you might be the older brother, when it comes to women, I think you need more than a few pointers. One thing I know for certain is that women don't likely want to be made to do anything."

"That's not what I said."

Jacob narrowed his eyes at him for good reason because that was exactly what he'd said.

"But that's not what I meant."

"I expect she'd like to know that. Gently and kindly and without grumbling, because I've got to tell you, living with you the past two weeks hasn't been a bit pleasant."

"You think it's pleasant for me?"

"I don't think anyone looking at your face would make that mistake, believe me, but that's your choice." His brother climbed onto Susie's back. "If you're truly interested, you need to show her. Kindness and tenderness go a long way, big brother. And I expect June could use her share of both." He turned the horse around and rode off easy, checking fence.

Was Jacob right?

He lifted the ax, then set it down again.

He hadn't actually asked June, had he? He'd made an announcement, as if she should jump all over it, and that made him a presumptuous jerk. What woman in her right mind wanted to be tied down to a presumptuous man?

June, he hoped.

He put the ax away in the barn, pulled down the piece of wood he'd been quietly shaping since Thanksgiving, and began sanding and buffing it. The small slab needed to be perfectly smooth to avoid chafing, and as his hands worked the wood, he began to plan something that had nothing to do with farms or cattle or increasing annual profit, but everything to do with love.

CHAPTER SIX

L ily patted dough balls into shape before nestling them in a broad, low pan to go into the lower, hotter oven. "You're quiet, June. Even for you. Are you feeling all right? Has something saddened you?"

"I'm fine." June sent her a pert smile, a smile she'd pulled out and dusted off after that Thanksgiving embrace and its disastrous aftermath. "And we're enormously grateful to be cozy and warm and making preparations for Christmas with you and your brothers. Perhaps if I'm quiet, it's because I'm thinking ahead to what spring will bring. I need to find work, and if Hansen Needleworks isn't reopening, I must check for another position. Maybe one that isn't based on sewing, although my skills lie in that direction."

"A lot to think of," Lily agreed, and then she paused. "I envy you."

June made a face and scoffed.

"No, I do. You have such purpose in everything you do, and ever since I was little, since the fire," she waved toward her face and the scars that June rarely noticed anymore. "I've been cared for."

"Being loved is not a bad thing, Lily."

"It's not, but it's easy."

June glanced around the lovely log home. "Keeping a house and a home and cooking for a crowd of men isn't what I'd call easy."

"There's work, yes, and I enjoy it, but that's not what I mean." She pondered a moment, then shrugged. "I mean having the choice to take care of myself."

June rolled her eyes and Lily acknowledged her action as she began reshaping balls of dough. "Okay, I know life isn't easy, and your life has been full of pitfalls, but it has made you a marvelous person, June. And I'd like a bit of that character-building for myself."

A marvelous person?

She didn't feel marvelous. She felt restless and testy and downright grumpy during a time of year when she should be singing God's praise and thanking him for abundant blessings. She was healthy. The children were healthy. The homeless had food and shelter and box heaters. This was so much more than they'd anticipated a month ago.

And still it wasn't enough, and it hadn't been enough since Lily's brother had held her in the shelter of his broad, strong arms on Thanksgiving.

. . . make you my wife . . .

The words had stung then, for good reason, but now she'd had a full fourteen days to get over the sting and miss the man.

Perhaps he didn't mean his words to be as businesslike as they sounded, as if she were nothing more than a good cattle deal come to pass. As if the joy of loving was a simple expectation. It wasn't. Love and marriage were never easy and rarely convenient, and without a shared commitment to God and each other, how could it work? And did he really mock her suffrage leanings?

She bit back a tell-tale sigh and beat a cool, flour-and-water mixture into a pot of chicken drippings to make rich, roasted chicken gravy, perfect for the yeast-dough rolls Lily had fashioned. "Lily Stackman, I think you have enormous character."

Lily's expression disagreed.

"You fought your way through a dreadful trauma as a child, you were brave enough to make the trek north, you helped your brothers establish a holding that rivals no other in the valley, you're nice to Indians and homeless folk, and you have a gentle manner about you that brings children running. A faith that moves mountains and a giving spirit. What more could you want, dear Lily?"

"Experience."

She said the word so softly June almost missed it.

"A chance to get out of the house and live life. To go places, do things, see things."

"And your brother forbids this?"

Lily's chin rose up quickly. "What?"

"Hugh doesn't allow you to go places. Is he worried for you? Or embarrassed?"

First Lily stared, then she laughed, and then she winced. "Oh, I'm so sorry you have that idea of my wonderful brother. Hugh has been after me to get out and see things and do things for years. Not when I was younger and the stares were hurtful, but as I grew older he and Jacob kept nudging. No, it was my choice, my fear holding me back. My fear of rejection and talk and conjecture. And then you came along. Hugh told me how you brandished that little knife against Hinckley, and how he shrank down before you. Hugh said it was like watching Joan of Arc in action, and that he was overwhelmed with pride that a woman would stand up for herself that way. Like our mother did so long ago."

"He said that?"

"That and more, and our Hugh is not one given to talk overmuch, but he did that day. And then you were here, and I started seeing as he did, that it is so much better to grab hold of life and make your way."

"When one has little choice, it's not so much honor as necessity," June said softly.

"But that's just it." Lily slipped the trays of rolls on the warm oven top to rise before baking. "The necessity becomes the honor because there are so many choices along the way. To make the right ones is truly living the Word, don't you think? But if you never step out enough to have choices, one loses that opportunity to not quote faith, but to live it."

"Oh, Lily." June reached over and grasped her floury hands. "I wish I were half as good as you make me out to be. I'm not, but your words hearten my soul. As for you, let's do this thing together. We can drive to town, we can visit stores, we can go to church. If you're of a mind to get out and be seen, then I've a mind to go with you. And how the children would love a trip to Ellensburgh to see the pretty Christmas wreaths on every door. The red bows on every streetlight. Although they'll see goods in store windows we can ill afford, but still, the experience will be wonderful."

"You don't think I'm foolish? Or seeking trouble?"

"Neither," June declared, "and in my years on the earth, trouble finds us whether we seek it or not, and if you've a mind to get out and about, we'd love to join you. I think it's good, dear Lily." She reached out and hugged the other woman. "When shall we go?"

"Monday?"

"We'll have to set aside candle-making until Tuesday," June teased.

"Which is why I need to step out," Lily admitted, "because I have become too steeped in scheduling every detail of my life, and there is much to be found beyond the details."

"Good and bad," June reminded her.

Lily nodded. "I'm ready."

Was she? June wasn't so sure, but she understood Lily's desire to begin a life put on hold years before. Lily had lived cloaked in fear, with her brother steeped in anger. If having three women and a clutch of cute kids had helped Lily gain the courage to try something new, that was good.

Now if it had only worked the same on her angry and stubborn brother.

June walked out to the bunkhouse once the stew was settled for heating. Caroline and Anna had taken over lessons with the older children, and she and Anna had started piecing quilt tops in their quiet moments. She approached the bunkhouse and paused.

A wide wreath decorated their door. Constructed of native evergreen branches, the deep shades of green shown vibrant against the dull brown of old wood and winter grass. A ribbon wound through the wreath, a little faded in spots, but at those spots, pine cones had been fastened to the greens.

It was a thing of beauty, and she picked up her step appreciably as she moved forward. She pushed open the door and walked in. "I love the wreath you've made for the door. It was just enough to make me yearn for Christmas!"

Anna looked at Caroline.

Caroline returned the look and shrugged. "We made no wreath."

She crossed to the door, tugged it open, and whistled softly. "Well, isn't that a thing of beauty. And look." She pointed toward the front door of the Stackman house. "There's one there as well."

"Jacob? Or Hugh? Or one of the stockmen?" Anna wondered.

"You heard nothing when someone was fastening this to the door?"

"We took a nature walk to see the cows and the horses and came in the other door. So maybe they put it up while we were gone."

"They must have. And it's beautiful." June touched the woven ribbon and traced its path around the greens. "It brightens the soul, doesn't it? Long dark nights and short days, but the light of Christ is in our lives."

"And an endless supply of lantern oil." Caroline adjusted the wicks to allow greater light while the children practiced numbers and letters. "That is my dream come true right there—the chance to give light as needed, where it is needed."

"The joy of simple pleasures," Anna agreed.

"But who do we thank?" June asked the other women. "Is it supposed to be a mystery?"

"I love mysteries and surprises," caroled Beth. "They are my favorite, especially at Christmastime!" Her voice rang with anticipation, and since the loss of her father almost two years before, she'd been a quiet, inward child. But today her young voice brightened with excitement.

"We have so little," Caroline whispered to Anna and June. "Will they be disappointed in our celebration?"

"Not if we're not," June answered sensibly. "Our joy will be theirs, and they're content with little things. It is the more mature who trouble themselves over how much of this and how many of that. If a handwoven wreath can bring such joy, we'll be fine. As will they." She nodded toward the children and picked up her work from earlier. "Lily has a desire to go into town on Monday. She wants to step out, to see and be seen. I told her we'd bring the children and go along."

"They'd enjoy that." Caroline minded lessons while Anna and June stitched pieces together. "But is it a good idea, June? Really?"

"Courage begins in unexpected places," she answered softly, because she wasn't one bit sure herself. "Why not the streets of Ellensburgh?"

"Jacob, can you take this kettle of stew to the bunkhouse for me?" Lily indicated a kettle on the stove with her chin. "The men are eating up here, but the women are staying put."

"They're eating over there?" Hugh didn't try to hide the surprise in his voice. "Why?"

"June feels like they're imposing on us, filling the house with so many people each night, and the children, of course, love to glean attention. They felt it was better to keep the commotion down."

"Exactly what Hugh was saying earlier," noted Jacob, and earned a glare from his brother.

"I didn't mean for them not to come. I was simply stating a fact."

"More like a wish that has now been granted," Jacob reminded him as he picked up the hot handle on the cast-aluminum kettle with a thick, folded towel. "That should make you happy."

It should but it didn't because now that he'd decided a course of action, June could at least follow her normal patterns of behavior, but no. Being a woman, she shifted her focus midstream, and he'd have to seek her out.

"Give me the stew." He reached out a hand and took the kettle from his brother. "I have something I need to give June, so I might as well drag supper over while I'm at it."

"Anything you say, big brother."

Jacob smirked.

Hugh ignored it, grabbed hold of the handle, and nearly burned his leg in the handoff.

"Hugh, are you all right?" Lily called from the far side of the kitchen when he bellowed, but he was all right, so he hadn't really needed to bellow at all. He'd just felt like it.

"Fine." He walked through the door. Jacob closed it shut behind him, and he strode across the mowed strip separating the house from the barn, listing to one side with the weight of the pot off one arm.

The wreath left him little room to knock so he set the stew down, rapped on the wood, and lifted the kettle again.

Caroline answered the door. "Hugh, why thank you! Here, let me take this from you. How kind of you to bring that by."

"Glad to do it, ma'am. Is June about?"

If Caroline grinned, he didn't see it because she dipped her chin into the shadows. "She is. Come in."

He stepped inside, removed his hat, and when June walked toward him, it had to be the prettiest sight he'd ever seen, and he wasn't talking about the worn, faded dress or the lack of adornment.

Her face, so sweet. Her eyes, bright and winsome. Her hair tucked up but for a few tendrils that slipped down around her cheeks.

"You needed to see me, Hugh?"

Oh, he did, all right, in the worst way possible, and not just on occasion, but daily. And nightly. By his side, through thick and thin, but Jacob's advice had him biting his tongue and biting it hard. "I wanted to try something, June, on Amanda. Can you have her come here and bring me her boots?"

"Of course." She sounded level, as if she expected him to ask about something mundane, but when her eyes dulled slightly, he knew she was a tad disappointed.

Good. Because he wanted her to long for him the same way he longed for her.

Amanda hurried their way and hugged him tight. "Mr. Hugh, did you come for supper? Because wouldn't that be so nice of us? You let us have supper at your house all the time, so we should give you supper over here, too. I fink it is a very good idea!"

"Me, too!" Samuel chimed in from the front of the bunkhouse.

Caroline's kids agreed, and when Beth said, "I'd love that, Mr. Hugh!" what could he say?

"I'm sure Mr. Hugh has things to do," June chided them as she helped Amanda remove her boots. "We're keeping you youngsters over here to give the poor man a little peace and quiet."

"And what if the poor man has had more than his share of peace and quiet for years?" He accepted the boots from her hand and held her gaze. "What if he's ready for a little bit of noise and confusion in his life, June?"

She stared at him, then swallowed hard. She put a hand to her throat, wondering, he hoped, but he said no more. He sat right down on the nearest cot, withdrew the small slab of wood and slipped it inside Amanda's boot. "Amanda, can you put these back on, please?"

She stared at him, then her mother, and frowned. "I just took them off, Mr. Hugh."

He couldn't fault her logic. He smiled, stooped down, and offered his help. "I know, but I'd like to see if this idea works, okay?"

"Okay." He helped her slip the boots on, then laced them for her. And when she stood, she smiled up at him.

"Can you walk over to Anna and back, please?"

"Yes." She walked to Anna quick as a wink, turned and walked back, then stopped. She stared at the boot, then him, then her mother. "Mama! Watch me!" She turned and walked again, quickstepping across the bunkhouse floor, without the tiniest bit of a limp. "I'm fixed!"

Tears filled June's eyes. She watched her little girl walk back and forth without a trace of limp, and when she brought her hands to her face, he thought she might break down.

But this was June, and instead of breaking down, she turned right around and grabbed hold of his hands. "You've done this, Hugh. It's a miracle to us, and I don't know how you knew what to do, but look at her! I don't know how to thank you."

Blue eyes lifted to his. Damp with tears, but not overflowing, he held her attention for a few seconds, then winked. "I expect I'll find ways for that gratitude, June. At the proper time, of course."

He counted her blush as a victory. "Now be sure she has stockings on and don't let her do too much with the wedge in place until she's accustomed to it, or she's liable to blister. And that's never fun."

"But what made you think of this?" June held tight to his hand as she watched Amanda show off her new, even gait. He had a good mind to drop to one knee, right then and there, but he forced himself to wait. Jacob had offered advice, and since he'd mucked up his proposal so thoroughly the first time, a smart man learned to bide his time.

"Horses," he told her. "An uneven gait means a shoe is misworn or gone bad, so I thought what if the same could happen to folks, only inside? If we're off just a little bit, then the feet don't meet the ground the same way. Now they do."

"We practiced, didn't we? On Thanksgiving?" Amanda crossed the room and gave him a big hug. "You used the straw in my shoe and it prickled a lot, but this doesn't prickle at all."

"Good." He stood.

"Aren't you staying?" Amanda stared up at him, so hopeful, and June looked mighty hopeful, too, but Hugh had found out the hard way that if a man sounded too eager, he was likely to get nowhere fast, so he palmed her head and gave June's hand a light squeeze. "Another time. And remember, don't do too much running and hiking at first, okay?"

"I won't!"

He turned back to the door.

June followed. "You sure you won't stay and eat with us?"

He didn't want to leave, and she didn't want him to go, so, of course, he did just that with an easy smile. "I've got things to tend over at the house." He shifted his smile to the happy little girl at the front of the bunkhouse. "I'm glad it worked out. Don't let her overdo, all right?"

"I won't." she folded her arms and half-smiled, half-sighed. "I am beyond grateful, Hugh."

He settled his cowboy hat back on his head and tipped the brim briefly. "Happy to help where I can. You like the wreath?"

Her mouth dropped open. She looked at the full wreath, then him, and nodded. "I cherish it. We all do."

"Well, good. Surprises are nice now and again. Good night, June."

"Good night, Hugh."

She watched him from the doorway. He knew it because he didn't hear the click of the bar dropping into place. He let himself get almost to the porch before he turned.

And there she was, framed in the doorway, watching him.

He smiled.

He tipped his hat one more time.

And then he walked inside.

Jacob might be younger, but Hugh had to hand it to him. He was smarter about women, and if tonight's reaction was an indication, Hugh might win the kind heart of the fair bride after all.

CHAPTER SEVEN

Hugh Stackman might have been sweeter than sweet the past five days, but looking at what she'd just done to his big buckboard on Monday afternoon, June was pretty sure the big, strong rancher was going to kill her.

She studied the wagon wheels, hopelessly mired in thick, oozing mud. The wagon that had been filled with children and women an hour before was now tipped at a ridiculous angle that even the two sturdy horses couldn't fix.

They'd tried every trick June knew to get the wagon righted and back on the wide drive, but the December rains and chill wind finally bested them. So here they were, stranded on the wagon path, muddied, sullied, and dog-tired, a wretched end to what had been a marvelous day.

"Hugh and Jacob have gotten stuck from time to time," Lily assured June as she wrapped the children's shawls and scarves tighter for the long walk to the house. "Hugh was riding fence with Alfred and Stake in the far acreage today, so we might need to find a few of the hands to get us unstuck if he's still in the hills."

"How did I miss that turn?" June studied the curve from the road and sighed. "I thought I banked it beautifully, and we'd had so much fun, and it was a good outing all around. And then . . ."

"You took the turn at breakneck speed and pitched us all into the pit," Anna filled in for her.

"Not breakneck, surely, Anna," Caroline added, laughing. "But most assuredly faster than was prudent at the moment."

"And for the conditions," agreed Anna, but she giggled when she said it. "The horses are unhurt, and while we're a bit muddy, we've had a day of it, haven't we?"

"Oh, we have," agreed Lily, and June loved hearing that note of strength in Lily's voice. Now if she could only go back in time and redo that turn. And what if she'd broken the axle beneath the wagon?

Fixing heavy-duty underpinnings wasn't a small task, nor an inexpensive one. Well, if she'd broken it, it was up to her to pay for it, and that's all there was to it. "I'll stay here with the horses, and if you'd be so kind as to send back help, I'd be grateful."

"I can stay," Anna told her, but June shook her head.

"I was driving. But I'm glad we had a grand adventure, ladies. That part was marvelous."

"And tea at the Copper Kettle." Beth's smile couldn't possibly get wider, but it did when she hugged Lily Stackman. "I've never in my life had such a treat, Miss Lily. Thank you!"

"You're quite welcome, sweetheart. It was a treat for me, too, but let's get you kids up to the bunkhouse and send the men back out here to help your mother before dark."

Long, thin, December shadows were already stretching from the hills, deepening the gray-brown of the extensive plateau. When her friends and the children left her alone, June huddled on the far side of the wagon, out of the wind, as best she could.

Things had been going so well.

She'd had the best five days of her life—Hugh so kindly attentive and nice; Amanda's fine, even gait in the engineered shoes; and the beautiful wreath smelling of Christmas each time she opened the west-facing door.

And now this.

She'd taken the team and the wagon without Hugh knowing.

She'd taken his sister into town to test the waters in the same fashion.

And then she'd made a serious misjudgment on the turn, and here they were, back to square one, which most likely meant he'd boot them off the property. Well deserved, too.

The wind howled louder and fiercer the longer she waited, hinting rain or snow, depending on the overnight temperatures.

"June!"

One clear bellow and she knew it wasn't mild-mannered Jacob coming to her rescue. She straightened and walked around the far end of the buckboard as a second wagon rolled down the lane.

"June!" Hugh was driving, and there were several ranch hands in the back, but he pulled up, set the brake, and jumped down as soon as he saw her, and why wouldn't he? She'd broken every rule she could think of this day, and he had every right to be—

"You all right?"

"I am, but the wagon, Hugh—" She squared her shoulders and faced him. "I'll pay for it, of course, for any repairs. And—"

"I've fixed my share of wagons in my time, and I've bogged equipment in mud more often than I care to remember, and as long as you're all right—"

She was, but she wasn't, because his gaze took in her face . . . her eyes . . . and then dropped to her mouth and lingered there while the hands scrambled forward to right the mess she'd made of his wagon.

His tender, worried look didn't linger long, because if she'd learned one thing these past weeks, it was that Hugh Stackman was a man of action.

He slipped his arms around her and pulled her into a tight embrace, then sweetened the moment by kissing her cheek, her brow, her ear, his lips lingering there as he whispered her name. He pulled back slightly, scouring her face. "You're okay? You're not hurt? And don't play brave with me, June. If you've got an injury, I need to know right now."

"I'm totally uninjured as you can see, although I fear for the mechanisms beneath your wagon."

Hugh released her and then his two big, broad hands cradled her head. Two strong, blunt thumbs stroked her cheeks. "Wagons can be fixed, darlin'. But in all my years I've only found one woman who makes my heart beat faster than a thoroughbred on a dirt track, and I don't wish to lose her to an accident now. You're sure you're fine? Lily said you'd slipped in the mud while trying to get things untangled. I do believe we have a crew of six winter men plus myself and my brother, so why would you think you needed to get things untangled without our help?"

She sighed softly and put her hands up over his. Foolish pride, plain and simple.

"We had a marvelous day in town, but I didn't tell you I was going and you have every right to be upset with me."

"But . . ." He held her gaze. "You had Lily with you, correct?"

"Yes. She wanted to get out of the house at long last, and I agreed to take her, which was fine until that last fateful turn."

"So why would you need my permission for anything? Lily owns as much of this ranch as we do, and if she says something's fine, it's fine."

"You're not upset that I took her?"

"I'm thrilled that she wanted to go," he admitted. "And she said it went well other than a few odd looks from folks, so I knew it was the right time. She had to be ready to weather that attention, and now she can. And that's thanks to you."

She'd done nothing, less than nothing, and when he looped an arm around her shoulders to walk her back up to the house, she started to object, but then she couldn't because he paused, gazing down at her.

His thumb traced tiny circles along the base of her cheek, her chin, and every tiny hair along the nape of her neck rose up, seeking his attention. He caught her gaze, and if his eyes held a question, hers must have offered the answer because his other hand circled the nape of her neck, while the first hand stroked that delightfully sensitive area just beneath her chin.

And then he pressed his lips softly to her face, kissing her forehead and both cheeks.

When the cold wind kicked up, she barely noticed.

"June." Husky and deep, he said her name, then dropped his forehead to hers. "I know I messed this up the last time, but I'd like to try again. June Harper, I love you." He drew back slightly and kissed her cheeks, her eyes, and her forehead again, then pulled her close. "I love you, and I would be happy if you would do me the honor of becoming my wife, and letting me be a father to Beth and Amanda. I'll make you happy, June. I swear to it."

"Hugh." She whispered his name, delighted with his sweet words, but then she breathed. "I want to marry you, too. I've wanted to marry you from that second day, when you almost kissed me in Doherty's bunkhouse, and I was so tempted to throw myself into your arms."

"Darlin', that would have saved us a whole lot of trouble, wouldn't it? We could have called the preacher and been man and wife all this time."

Leave it to a man to jump that far ahead.

How she wished it were that easy. She sighed and leaned into his arms, cherishing the safety net they provided. "I love you, Hugh, but there's a chasm between us. One you don't see as a big deal, but that's exactly why it is a big deal."

She felt the beat of his heart. And then she felt it drift away from her ear when he pulled back.

He met and held her gaze. "Church."

"I've got a responsibility to myself and those girls to raise them surrounded by my beliefs. And while I respect your right to disbelieve, I can't tether myself to it, as much as I want to."

"You'd refuse me over faith?"

Was that what she was doing? She took in a deep breath. "Yes."

He looked sad. So sad.

What right did she have to make a person that bereft? And yet, she'd been married to a man who thought nothing of God and only of himself and his hardships. If she married again, she and her husband needed to meet on even ground, like Amanda's new shoes.

"You told us how a horse walks off-step when his shoes aren't even. Marriage is the same way. If I marry again, I want my husband to love God like I do. To go to church and help with things as needed, and to walk his daughter down the aisle someday. I want a husband who is no stranger to God because life is no stranger to trial, and my faith has gotten me through those trials."

"I can't be something I'm not, June."

Oh, her heart ached.

It broke inside her chest. Every bit of her fiber was screaming at her to say yes and accept this good man.

And yet, she couldn't. "I know, Hugh. Lily told me your mother was a woman of great conviction."

"And we all know what that got her."

"We do." She clasped his hands one last time. "Eternal life."

He dropped her hands. His face . . .

That strong, sweet, square-jawed face—

Went flat. And then it went sad. And when he raised his eyes back to hers, the sheen of moisture said her words affected him deeply. He splayed his hands and lifted his shoulders in a shrug. "God didn't need her in heaven. Or my little sisters, either. But here on earth?" He stared up into the heavens, dark and cloudy on this wind-filled night. "We needed her every single day. And that's what I can't forgive, June."

"I know." She backed up one step, then another. "And until you can, I have to say no, my love. And Hugh Stackman, saying no to you is the hardest thing I've ever had to do." She turned and walked away, knowing she was doing the right thing, and hating that she had to do it.

Hugh didn't come after her.

Chapter Eight

Hugh faced the next few days in a haze of frustration and disappointment.

June's words circled in his brain, but he wasn't a man of pretense, so no solution presented itself.

She wanted a faith-filled man, but she loved him just as he was.

It made no sense, none at all, and once again he'd been thwarted in his proposal and his assumption.

He chopped more unneeded wood.

He rode fence that didn't need riding.

He stared up at stars that seemed to go on forever and wondered why such a subjective thing as faith should take on so much importance.

Old anger surfaced, but with more question now than punch.

Lily made him a list for the mercantile, then decided to go to town with Anna, saving him a trip. With confusion clouding his brain, he could have used a ride into town, so he took one anyway.

He bought leather oil, ordered new shoes for each of the children as a Christmas gift from the Stackman ranch, and ordered two sacks of sweets for the holiday, then made it three sacks because the ranch hands would appreciate one themselves.

He walked.

It was a cold, damp, late December day, not a time anyone would normally choose for an around-the-town saunter. He stood on Fourth Street, gazing left, then right, remembering what the town had looked like six short months before fire razed a large portion of it.

Brick buildings were taking shape, with some already completed. The city had jumped into the aftermath of the fire with grandiose plans.

Now that things had simmered down, more realistic visions were taking hold.

Church spires poked through bare tree branches.

He surveyed the new construction, a testament to human resolve as the town rose from the ashes of destruction. While he paused, the church bells rang out from the bell tower atop St. Andrew's.

His mother loved church bells. She loved hymns and singing and candlelight services. She had an old-fashioned air that he'd respected from the time he was old enough to see how wonderful she was.

He stared at the town, at the buildings, new and old.

The smoke smell that had lingered for weeks was gone now. The ashes had been carted away. New replaced old.

And time went on.

Folks hurried up the walk to the white clapboard church, calling soft greetings to one another.

He eyed the bell tower as new thoughts pushed old anger aside.

The destructive fire had most likely been started by a stray firework from the Independence Day celebration. One tiny mistake had wreaked huge devastation.

And the fire that claimed his mother and sisters was likely started with a lantern left too close to a newborn foal and her mother.

In each case, one tiny mistake.

Was it of God? Was it God's fault?

Or did people simply make mistakes or poor choices?

He observed the midday stream of people filing into the small church, short months after a disaster had hit their town. They weren't holding back. They weren't stuck in an anger-filled past, but then he'd lost so much back in Nevada. If only he'd been there. Or if his no-good, no-account father had taken the lead with his family.

A chill breeze covered him with mist, and the dark clouds predicted an even heavier downpour, but still he didn't move. Surrounded by the new build of a recent fire, he recognized the old fierce anger still controlling his life.

He'd pretty much loathed his father before fire took three beloved lives. Once it had, hatred had formed a hard knot inside him, because no one who was supposed to care about his mother, Pearl, or Celestia was there to save them. Including himself.

He sat down hard on the bench outside the mercantile.

He thought of June, forging on, but with a cheerful disposition. Anna and Caroline, too. And Lily, despite her grievous daily reminder, seeking warmth and direction from her faith.

Anger.

He saw it plain as day at last and wondered how he'd been so blind and bound to it for so long.

Anger had marked his days. Anger had choked up his heart and maybe his soul.

Standing up, he strode with purpose toward the church. The bells paused. To the left of the church walkway, a wooden stable had been erected. In the cover of the rough-sawn wood were four figures: Mary, Joseph, an angel, and a newborn baby, wrapped in swaddling clothes, lying in a hay-lined feedbox.

The sight humbled him.

He had so much to be grateful for, so much to appreciate, yet how much time had he wasted on anger?

Too much.

Joseph gazed down at the baby, a child not his own, with such a look of loving tenderness that the artist must have loved a child along the way. He thought of Beth and Amanda and how precious they were. Was he strong enough to be their father?

Yes.

Could he be faithful enough to stand like Joseph, doing God's will instead of forcing his own all the time?

He could try. He *would* try. He made his decision and headed back to where he'd left his horse, but he made one more stop in the mercantile before heading back to the ranch. He slipped the wrapped box into his saddlebag, mounted Buttergold, and headed home with a less heavy heart than he'd known in a long time. June might still refuse him, but at least now there was room in his heart for whatever life brought him, and if it was a life with that wonderful woman and those two girls, he'd be the happiest man in Kittitas County.

Chapter Nine

"Have you ever seen a more delightful collection of treats?" Caroline hugged Lily as the two women covered one last tray of spiced cakes with a clean length of muslin to keep them fresh. "It is a feast for sure and a reminder of days gone by."

"A house filled with people, fun, faith, and food," Lily replied in kind while June worked nearby. "Who would have considered such a wondrous Christmas just short months ago?"

"Not I, surely." Caroline took the tray of cakes onto the cooler back porch where Jacob had set a small stand of shelves out of the west wind and away from roof spatter. "To be warm, clean and dry, to have food. I've learned to appreciate the simplest of things, Lily. To see my little Beau and Mary with full cheeks once more, laughing and playing, sliding down straw-stacks. That's gift enough for any mother."

"And I've learned the joy of having friends nearby, the strength of women working together." Lily glanced across the room at the clock. "I'm surprised that Anna hasn't joined us with the children. Beth was yearning to make the sauce for the pudding, and she hasn't come over yet."

"I'll check on them." June stood and set the newly mended table cover aside. "Maybe one of the little ones dozed off and that's what's holding them up."

"Thank you, June."

June lifted her shawl down from the hooks inside the door. She began to open the door, then paused. "It's snowing."

"Is it?" Lily looked up from the warmth of the stove. "Oh, it always seems right to have snow for Christmas, doesn't it?"

"I'm not sure why, but you're right," answered Caroline. "It's as if the whiteness coats the world, sweeping it clean, just in time for our Savior's birth."

"Whereas I'd say it's a welcome respite from rain and mud," June told them, smiling. "Prettier and cleaner, and what mother doesn't grow weary of mud by March?"

"A fact, for sure," Caroline agreed, then she waved toward the fresh falling snow. "There's Anna now."

June stepped back and pulled the door wide. "I was just coming to see what was keeping you. But I do believe you've forgotten something. Two things, actually. My children."

"June, I know." Anna waved a hand of frustration her way. "I was having the worst time with Beth. She was giving me all kinds of argument, so unlike her. Would you run over there and see if you can talk some sense into her? Please?"

Talk sense into sweet, mild-mannered Beth?

June pulled the shawl closer and stepped out. "Of course, I'm glad to. I'm amazed she would give you a hard time, Anna. She'll be apologizing right quick, believe you me."

She strode out the door and took the slick steps with care. Snow slipped beneath her feet, and the handrail was her saving grace from falling on the smooth wood. As she made her way down the now-worn trail to the bunkhouse door, she examined Anna's report in her mind. Children often grew testier with age, but Beth had always been such a tender-hearted child. What could have gotten into her?

She hurried in the door, ready to find out the truth, and paused when two smiling faces looked up at her. She swung the door shut behind her and moved forward. "Why are you still here, and what is there to smile about? Did I hear that you were giving Anna a hard time? On Christmas Eve? Ladies, this is—"

"It's my fault, June, not theirs."

Hugh's voice sounded from just beyond the door.

She turned, surprised.

He was smiling, too. At them, then at her. She moved forward. "I don't understand."

"Mr. Hugh wants to ask you something, Mama!" Beth held her tongue, but Amanda could always be counted on to let secrets fly free. "We wanted you to come back over here so he could talk to us all together."

His gaze met hers, and oh, how she longed to offer him the same kind of joy she saw in his face, his eyes, but she didn't dare, because what was to come of it? And did he think tempting her sweet daughters into the conversation would force her to say yes?

He couldn't possibly be that devious, could he? Was she such a poor judge of character still? She pretended indifference and moved forward. "Except we promised Lily we'd help with preparations, and Beth, you especially wanted to help make sauce for the pudding, remember?"

Suddenly, Beth looked uncertain.

Was it because of the sauce or did she expect something different from her mother? June had no idea, but as she reached for their shawls, Hugh took her arm with the gentle strength of a man in love. "We have time, June. Come here."

She shouldn't.

She knew it and he knew it, too, but as he led her forward, she longed to follow him, heart and soul, all the rest of her days. And therein lay the problem.

He drew her to a wood-slatted chair. "Sit. Please."

She sat and the girls scampered forward, and when he handed her a box, she gazed from one to the other, confused.

"It's a present!" Beth grinned, and Amanda pressed her two little hands to her mouth to hold back excitement.

"Oh, Mama, I'm so 'cited!"

"Me, too." Hugh's voice, warm and kind and good. He tapped the box with one finger. "June, my love, the whole intention of a gift is to be opened."

She wanted to leave their relationship as it was. She wanted to hand the box back to him and tell him she couldn't be bought. But it *was* Christmas Eve, and the smiles on the girls' faces reflected a joy she hadn't seen in so long. It meant too much. "For me, Hugh?"

He sat on the bench opposite and nodded, but then confused the matter by saying, "For you, for me. For all of us."

She lifted the pretty cover and set it aside, then sucked in her breath. From inside the box, bound in layers of pretty paper, she lifted a figure. "Mary."

He nodded and set the figure on the small table drawn up next to her chair.

She withdrew the next figure and unwrapped it with care. "And Joseph."

"Oh, he's so handsome, Mama!" Beth reached out a finger to graze the carefully constructed figure. "Is he breakable?"

"He is, so we must be gentle, all right?" She reached back into the paper and withdrew a small wooden feed box, and in that box laid the wrapped figure of a baby. "The Christ child."

"Yes." Hugh nodded, and he settled one hand on her knee, alongside the box. "There's one more figure in there, June."

There was. She lifted the small figure of a papier-maché angel, painted in muted shades of cream, blue, and white. "Oh, Hugh." She held up the delicate angel, then tucked it behind the little family, gazing down in adoration at the tiny child between them. "Hugh, I don't know what to say, and I surely don't deserve a gift as fine as this. We saw these in town when we went shopping with Lily, and they were quite dear, Hugh. Too dear."

"Not for you, June." He reached up and cupped her cheek with one big, strong hand. "And not for us."

For us?

He motioned the girls forward. "June Harper, I've had a very serious talk with these girls of yours."

Oh, she could be sure he did from the matching grins on two little faces.

"And we're of a mind that we'd like to be a family, June. A family that works together and plays together and prays together. So I thought it would be a good reminder of all that if we had a Holy Family on our mantel, not just for Christmas but for always. To remind me of the kind of father I didn't have, but long to be."

Oh, his words . . . his gaze holding hers . . .

He slipped off the bench and took one knee before her. "June Mary Harper, would you do me the honor of becoming my wife? Walking through life and into church on my arm? Working with me, laughing with me, praying with me?"

"Hugh." She said his name softly as the girls waited nearby, their hands clasped. He'd taken a bold step forward. He'd come to meet her more than halfway, and the thought that a man of pride and prominence would openly take that step . . . "You humble me, Hugh Stackman."

"Well, now, humility wasn't what I was after, June." He stood, reached down and drew her up with him. "I'm in mind of love, sweet June. The kind of love that binds a family together all of our days. And if you say yes, Reverend Bickers has promised to stop by tomorrow and take our vows. If that's all right with you, of course."

All right?

It was more than all right. It was all her hopes and dreams formed into the most delightful Christmas gift of all. "It's not all right, Hugh." When he searched her gaze, she reached out, took his whiskery cheeks into her hands, and kissed him right there, in front of her beloved daughters. "I'd say it's absolutely perfect."

His smile—such a smile! Joy-filled and happy, just for her, and then he made it even better by reaching out an arm to draw the girls into their embrace. "Shall we go up to the house and tell the others?"

Beth wriggled out of the hug instantly. "Yes!" Quiet, calm Beth darted free and raced to the door, ready to share their happy news.

"Me, too!" Amanda did the same, and both girls left in a hurry. They let cold air in and warm air out, but Hugh's strong arms protected June from the draft and promised her so much more.

She peeked around his arms toward the open door and the now-empty room. "Hugh Stackman, I do believe you did that on purpose."

"A chance for a few moments alone with my beloved? My beautiful bride?"

Beautiful.

After long months of struggle and hardship, June hadn't felt attractive. Here, in Hugh's arms, hearing sweet words of courtship in his deep, husky voice, the opposite was true. The strength of the man holding her bolstered more than her heart. It lent strength to her soul.

He kissed her face, her cheek, and her hair, an embrace that left no doubt he was a man in love, then he pulled her shawl up close around her. "Let's go home, darling."

Bliss consumed her.

He'd gone the distance for her. No man, nor any other person, had ever done such a thing in all of her days. It felt—amazing. "I'd love to, Hugh."

She tucked her arm into his, and they walked through the bunkhouse door. They strode up the path together, arm in arm, his broad house standing strong in the northwest wind, the winter snows, and the cold, long days of rain.

Lantern light brightened glass windows against the falling snow, a welcoming sight, and when they walked in the door, shouts of gladness greeted them.

She'd come home. Home to her heart, home to Hugh's love, home to the growing faith of a family, and June Harper would never ask for anything more than what God had given her this night. Faith, hope, and love . . . and the greatest of these was love.

Longhorn
Christmas

MARY CONNEALY

And Joseph also went up from Galilee, out of the
city of Nazareth, into Judaea, unto the city of David,
which is called Bethlehem; (because he was of the
house and lineage of David). . . . And the angel said
unto them, Fear not: for, behold, I bring you good tid-
ings of great joy, which shall be to all people. For unto
you is born this day in the city of David a Saviour,
which is Christ the Lord. . . . The shepherds said one
to another, Let us now go even unto Bethlehem, and
see this thing which is come to pass, which the Lord
hath made known unto us. And they came with haste,
and found Mary, and Joseph, and the babe lying in
a manger. . . . The star, which they saw in the east,
went before them, till it came and stood over where
the young child was.

—Luke 2:4, 2:10–11, 2:15b–16; Matthew 2:9b

CHAPTER ONE

Big Bend Region, Texas
November 1865

The trouble with lassoing a Texas cyclone was—now you had a cyclone on the end of your rope.

Then what was she going to do with it?

She dropped a loop over the monster's head and kicked her pony into action.

Her cow pony dodged around a clump of trees as the red cyclone with an eight-foot spread of horns charged. With whip-fast moves, Netty snugged the lasso around an aspen and kicked her horse to get out of range.

Cyclone, a longhorn mama, with a noose tight around her deadly horns, lunged at poor Blue. Her razor-sharp horns swiped at the horse's rump, but she only snared the blue roan's tail. The horse was scared enough she didn't take any notice, not counting running for her life, of course.

Cyclone charged until she reached the end of the rope and was yanked back so hard she flipped over onto her side. Then, like a striking snake, she turned and charged the trees. The yellow leaves still clinging in the late November breeze quivered and quaked.

The longhorn bounced off the trees, then turned back and locked her furious eyes on Netty. A big old hank of horsehair dangled from one horn.

Trembling, Netty stayed atop her dancing horse for a few seconds, shaking so hard she was afraid if she dismounted she'd just sink down to the ground in a heap. Blue quivered beneath her, both of them quaking as bad as those aspens.

Cyclone bellowed and pawed the dirt, then turned to thrash at the trees that held her tight.

Netty took a deep breath and blew it out. She still had to finish this job.

She swung off Blue, clung to the stirrup until she was sure her knees would hold, ground hitched the horse, and turned to do what she'd come for.

"Are you all right, Mama?"

Netty was scared fit to beat all, but her son didn't need to know that. With no one to watch her six-year-old son since Ma died, there was no choice but to bring him along.

"I'm fine, Jeremiah." She looked about forty feet away to a good-sized red oak tree where she'd perched her boy up high—out of Cyclone's reach. Safe until she could finish this and fetch him.

But first she had to save the calf.

Cyclone had busted out of the canyon gate, and Netty'd been glad to see the back of her. As much as she needed every cow, Cyclone, amid a herd of wild, dangerous animals, was the deadliest.

Then today, Netty'd ridden out to hunt food and found a mess.

A desperate, protective mama standing guard over a baby she couldn't reach.

Netty worked hard to save every baby on the place. She and her son's hold on survival was tenuous, and losing a calf, especially a perfectly healthy calf, was serious business.

But she didn't rope Cyclone for money; there wasn't enough of it in the world.

The truth was she couldn't bear the thought of that baby trapped down in a hole away from its mama, dying a lingering death.

Netty strode to the crevice in the jumble of rocks and looked down. The little red-roan calf looked up and bawled piteously.

Carefully, picking a thin ledge for footing, Netty dropped into the hole. It was about five feet deep, not too deep, just too deep for the baby to escape. When Netty wiggled into the notch in the ground, roughly shaped like an upside-down triangle, she scooped up the poor baby and hoisted it high and set it on the ground.

Then a terrible bawl came from Cyclone—she must've spotted the calf—and a snap loud as a gunshot sounded. The rope broke just as Netty finished crawling up out of the hole. Cyclone charged.

"Look out, Mama!" Jeremiah shouted in terror.

Netty dropped back into that hole and landed face down on the bottom. Looking over her shoulder, she saw one of those long horns slashing at her. She flattened against the ground. The horn snagged the coat she wore but didn't catch it. Netty ripped off the coat just as Cyclone rammed her head into the crevice.

With her heart pounding, she flattened and sucked in her stomach to get as low as possible. The maddened cow missed her again.

Cyclone continued to gouge at her, hook with her horn, then shove her head in the hole. Hot breath blasted the back of Netty's neck.

Cyclone pulled her head back, snorted, and dove once more. Pulled back again. The calf bawled pitifully, and that finally turned Cyclone aside.

Netty lay still, gasping for breath. That's when she heard Jeremiah screaming.

What if he climbed down and tried to drive Cyclone off? The cow would kill him.

He shouted, "Get away! Go!"

"Jeremiah, I'm all right." The energy her panic gave her voice echoed from the hole, and Cyclone whirled and slashed down in the pit again. Netty buried her face in rock to keep her head low and yelled with her mouth against stone. "She can't reach me down here. Stay up where you're safe."

Netty sincerely hoped she was telling the truth. Just because Cyclone hadn't managed to snag her yet, didn't mean she might not find a way. "Sit still until she calms down and wanders off with her calf."

It occurred to Netty that there was a nice patch of grass and a spring mighty close. Cyclone might just settle in and stay here forever.

Looking up very carefully, Netty shouted, "Jeremiah, you watch her. Let me know when she's far enough away from this hole for me to climb out."

"I'm watchin', Mama. But the baby is nursing right now. I think they're gonna stand for a while. I could climb down and throw a rock at her."

"No! I lifted you up into that tree. It's got no low branches. You might be able to get down, but how could you get back up if she charged you?"

"Okay, but I don't like it up here." Jeremiah's voice wavered. Her little boy had been acting tough lately. Trying to be the man of the family. Especially since Netty's mother died.

The three of them together had been getting by since Pa and Netty's husband, Ralph, and Netty's two brothers had gone off to war . . . and been killed.

No one would say they'd thrived out here by themselves, but they got by as the years passed and reports came, one by one, telling them another man in their family had died.

And then they'd lost Ma.

Now, Netty was scared every day. The herd was too small to support them. Netty could no longer ride into the rugged, broken hills near their property and round up wild longhorns to add to their holdings, gentle them enough to herd, then drive them to town for a few dollars to buy the things they couldn't grow or hunt for themselves.

There was no one but her to cook and see to the farm chores—gather eggs, milk the cow, see to the garden. It took everything she had in her, which left her with a tiny herd of about six longhorns and three calves, counting Cyclone. That'd been enough before because she could round up a new one or two to keep them going. But now she needed a sight more because she couldn't hunt cows like this anymore. But they had to have some spending money to pay for supplies and taxes.

Jeremiah rode along when she worked. But she could no longer hunt cows. It was too dangerous with him along, and what's more, it was too dangerous without him, because what if she died? Her son would have no one.

And here she was then, tending the cows she already had, and it appeared even that was too dangerous.

Doing her best to stay completely silent, Netty inched her head up. She saw Cyclone's red back, then her massive side. The nursing baby appeared as Netty continued lifting her head.

A bit higher and she could see Jeremiah in the tree. As if the sight of her eased a terrible burden, his shoulders lifted and his head came up. She waved. Her son waved back.

The mean mama had stepped a few yards away and was calmly grazing while the calf nursed, but Netty needed more than a few yards to make a getaway.

Which reminded her, Blue—her roan horse—was nowhere in sight. Probably headed for the barn when Cyclone charged.

Without her horse, escaping from here was tricky. Jeremiah could probably jump into her arms, and they would have to run. But run to where?

There was no shelter for them if Cyclone took it into her head to give chase.

Netty crawled out of the hole on her knees, and Cyclone's head came up. She woofed at Netty and pawed the earth with her front hooves, all without jarring her hungry calf from where it stood eating.

Netty braced herself to dive back down flat, but Cyclone continued eating, apparently satisfied that she had Netty well and truly cornered.

No more than the absolute truth.

Chapter Two

Roy Hollister spotted the saddled blue roan running away from somethin', its reins flying.

Not good.

He was headed for California and had no schedule, nor a thing to do when he got there. All he knew about California was it wasn't here, and he didn't want to be here.

The longer he wandered, the more afraid he was that he didn't want to land anywhere.

The land was broken here north of a big bend in the Rio Grande River. In the last little western town where he'd stopped, he'd heard this country called The Big Bend region of Texas. All he knew was he'd gone as far south as he could get to avoid the cold. Any farther south, and he'd cross into Mexico. Which he might try if California didn't suit him.

He watched the mare race toward a canyon with a solid gate that stretched across the narrow opening. The roan mustang slowed as she reached the gate, then stood, sides heaving, looking through that gate like the answers to all the world's questions lay on the other side.

Roy figured that *answer* was most likely a barn. That's usually where tame horses headed.

He considered riding after the horse and opening the gate for it, but right now his main concern was for the rider.

He backtracked the mustang, leery of finding some cowpoke on the ground with his neck broke. But maybe the rider was fine, just stranded. Or hurt badly enough he'd die without help.

That was the kind of thing that haunted a man later if he didn't look into it. And Roy didn't need any more ghosts.

Riding along, he found clear tracks the horse had left. The ground was rocky, with enough grass for an animal to eat if it was good and hungry—but mostly wasteland. This part of Texas was studded with clumps of prickly-pear cactus as tall as him on horseback, gnarled mesquite thickets, and aspen trees in tight copses with an occasional oak tree towering over everything. It all added to his belief that this was a harsh, unwelcoming country.

The trail twisted around a clump of aspens, and Roy rode right into a longhorn cow who whirled on him, snorted, lowered her head, and charged.

Well, his zebra-dun stallion was a top cow pony, and good thing he was. His horse jumped sideways, while Roy hung on and let the critter dodge hooves and horns and race away until the cow turned back. From a safe distance, Roy spotted her calf. No wonder.

Then he saw something that struck him as mighty odd.

A little boy clung to the branches of an oak tree as if he'd grown up there like an acorn.

"Hey, Mister, my ma is trapped by Cyclone."

A cyclone? Roy looked up. There wasn't a cloud in the sky. He thought it all through and still hadn't figured out what was going on when another voice drew his attention.

"I'm down here."

He looked past that red monster cow—he couldn't ever remember seeing one bigger—and spotted a woman's head pop up like a gopher. Bright red hair, all in a tangle, and freckles on her nose under eyes green as grazing grass.

A shocking sight just sticking up out of nowhere like that.

Then she waved.

And the cow charged her.

Roy had a feeling this was how a cow named Cyclone introduced herself.

The woman let out a short shriek, and her head vanished as she dropped. The cow took a swipe with one horn, plunging it into the ground as if she was digging a hole with it.

The horn didn't come up with a woman stuck on, so the hole must be deep, at least a few inches deeper than one of that mama's horns.

The red-and-white roan calf bawled, and the mama changed into the gentlest creature on earth.

"I can see the trouble, ma'am," Roy hollered. "Let me think how to get the cow goaded away from you. She's not going to herd easy, but I'll find a way."

The lady's head popped up again. "Take your time."

"Yep," the boy added. "We're not going anywhere."

They both sounded mighty calm. He didn't know much about Texas, but he'd been passing through the land that lay between Arkansas and New Mexico Territory—so that brought him to Texas. He'd noticed folks here took things as they came for the most part. Kickin' hard against what trouble Texas dealt out was just a waste of energy and boot leather . . . and you needed both to survive so why waste it.

He was a while figuring it out, but finally he managed to lure the outlaw cow into charging him. He kept his fleet horse ahead of her, but not so far ahead of her she gave up trying to gore him. Her calf gamboled along behind. Roy rode hard until he found another grassy spot, then spurred his horse to leave the cow behind. She—well named Cyclone—picked a spot and settled in to graze.

Roy gave her a wide berth as he circled around to go back. By the time he was behind her, the cow was moving again. In fact, that old battle-ax looked to be making tracks in the direction of the canyon that horse'd been heading for. Old Cyclone had probably busted through that gate to start this whole mess. Now she acted as if all this nonsense had been an afternoon's lark.

He watched her stroll along, heading for home, her calf frolicking at her heels.

By the time he returned to check on the woman, she'd rolled up out of that hole and was running to the tree. She had the boy on the ground fast, then she turned and smiled at him.

Wearing pants. Jeans if he wasn't mistaken. He thought he saw the rivets. He gave his head a mental shake to lift his eyes off the rivets and back on her face.

"If you want to follow us home, I'd be glad to have you for supper, mister."

Which sounded alarmingly like she meant to serve him as the main course.

"It's Roy, ma'am." He touched the broad brim of his hat. She was just barely a ma'am. The boy had a few years on him though, so she must've had him when she was a youngster herself. "Roy Hollister.

"I'm Netty Lewis, Mr. Hollister, and this is my son Jeremiah."

Jeremiah looked nothing like her with his oak-brown head of hair and eyes to match. The boy's skin was brown as a berry tanned in the relentless Texas sun, while her fair, freckled nose looked burned and peeled.

This being November didn't halt the heat of midday. Leastways not most of the time.

"We thank you kindly for helping us," she said. "I was good and trapped, and that old cow looked content to keep me in that hole and Jeremiah treed till kingdom come. You saved us." Her green eyes were wide and her tone was hushed as if she spoke of an act of great heroism.

Well, it beat how he'd been treated back home after the war, as if it was his fault the Rebs'd run over their land and burned their homes and killed their livestock—not exactly a hero's welcome. Her gratefulness lifted his spirits. He had to stand quiet for a moment and just enjoy it.

Then he smiled. "It's Roy, please, ma'am. Not mister or sir. That's mighty formal for a yondering cowpoke."

"Then call me Netty, not ma'am." She smiled, and her teeth shone white, and those grateful eyes flashed like green lightning. "Are you hunting work, mister . . . uh . . . I mean Roy? Because if you are, I'm hiring."

CHAPTER THREE

Netty was *not* hiring.

At least not in the sense that she'd ask him to do work and give him money for his trouble.

And that pretty much described hiring.

She had no money and no idea what had made that offer roll out of her mouth, except she needed help desperately. That had never been clearer than today. And she was so relieved to see another human being, never mind being saved by him, that she couldn't stand to let him *yonder* on.

No money to pay him, but she did have a place he could sleep. That gave her pause. She didn't ever go into the other house. Shrugging off that discomfort, she knew it would be fine to let him use it.

And she'd be glad to feed him. There was no end to food in the rugged hills around her home. She even had a decent supply of flour and coffee, two of the very few things she needed and couldn't get out of this land. Necessary things that she needed cash money to buy.

Maybe she could pay Roy in longhorns. She'd have some to spare if he did his work right—work catching longhorns. Of course, he could just catch them for himself if he wanted a cow to sell.

She didn't mention any of that. Just waited and rested her eyes on the tall man who'd saved her and her boy. He had dark hair—so black it shined almost blue in the sunlight like a raven's wing.

His eyes were light blue, though she hadn't gotten all that close to him, what with him sitting on top of a pretty zebra dun stallion. And up there he looked taller than even he probably was—his shoulders broader and his expression kinder. Though how a horse could affect that, she didn't know.

Roy seemed as glorious to her as an angel descended from heaven. At that thought, she paused to thank God. Angel or man, his presence was a blessing, and she'd not forget that for one moment.

His clothes were worn and none too clean, which was normal for a range-riding cowpoke. His horse was in good shape, with no brutal scars on his flanks, even though Roy wore spurs. And his guns looked clean. Both the rifle in his saddle scabbard and the six-gun he wore holstered looked well cared for. A man who took care of his horse and guns was a man she could trust . . . until he proved she couldn't.

That might be foolish of her, but trust came easier when you were desperate.

"I'd appreciate a meal, ma'am."

"Netty, please."

"Uh . . . yep, Netty. I'd appreciate a meal very much. Your horse is what warned me of trouble. He was running wild, headed for that canyon with the gate across it. I backtracked him to find you."

A wave of some crazy weakness washed over her, and for a horrifying moment she had to fight not to cry. Crying was just a plain waste of time, not to mention salt and water. She didn't want any truck with such nonsense.

"As for a job, well, I'm headed west but in no hurry. Is your husband to hand or another of your cowpokes?"

"Nope, it's just Jeremiah and me. The war took my father, husband, and two brothers. My ma just died a few months ago. I could use the help. Jeremiah and I get along but it's a . . ." She hesitated as she searched for an adequate word for her daily struggles to earn enough to buy her few groceries and keep her taxes paid and deal with the constant battle to fend off loneliness, grief, and the feeling of being utterly abandoned. Plus, the downright terror that something would happen to her, leaving Jeremiah alone in the middle of nowhere without a soul to take care of him. No right word in the world could describe her worries.

"We've got our hands mighty full, Roy."

The tall cowboy nodded and swung off his horse. "You've had a day of it, Netty. Get up with your boy and ride. I'll walk alongside."

Before she could decide if that was something a strong woman would object to, she found herself plunked on the horse, Jeremiah on back hugging her waist with both hands, and Roy starting off toward the canyon. It made good sense. He must've figured her land was nearby.

"It's a couple of miles," she said. "I could go for my horse and come back so you could ride along, but by the time I ride there, round up Blue, and come back you'd've nearly walked there."

"I didn't see a cabin."

"It's inside that canyon fence. It's a box canyon, so with only one gate I can keep my livestock in. My husband homesteaded outside the entrance to the canyon. My pa homesteaded inside over the only waterhole. We control a couple hundred acres of nice grassland that way."

Netty knew she sounded oh so chipper. That was a lie. She was a desperate woman, and before the day ended, he'd know it, too. She rode astride his muscled dun, while he was afoot, so she decided to shut up about it. She decided instead to find out more about him. Make him do the talking.

"So you're headed west. California?"

The man looked sideways at her and smiled.

Almost as if he knew something, like he realized she wasn't being exactly honest about offering him a job. It wasn't a job if she couldn't pay him.

"Yep, in the end. But I'm not a man to push forward and miss the parts of the trail I could enjoy. I've never been in West Texas before, so I'll be happy to spend some time helping at your place and earn some traveling money while I'm at it."

"You've worked as a cowhand before?"

"I've been traveling since the war. Nothing to go home to. It looks like it cost you plenty, too."

Wasn't that about the least could be said about it? "You had no home? What happened? Your voice sounds like the North, and the war was fought in the South."

"We lived in Virginia, too close to the edge of the Mason-Dixon line, so the war spilled over to our side for a time. My folks died while I was gone, and our land was stolen. The girl I thought was waiting for me saw our farm lost and picked a man who looked to have better prospects. Probably wise of her."

Netty decided the girl was a fool, and Roy was well escaped from her clutches.

"Since then I've turned my hand to whatever job crossed my path. I've driven stage, worked a cattle drive, run a livery, and even cooked in a diner a time or two. I spent time working on leather with a saddle maker in St. Louis, and a cartwright taught me his trade in Omaha. I reckon whatever job you've got in mind, I can wrangle."

Maybe that was why he looked at her funny. He'd heard her suspicion that he wasn't up to the job. Well, it was good if he thought that—better than him knowing the truth.

"It sounds like my lucky day, Roy. I am blessed to have you come by when you did. Blessed by a loving God." It seemed wise to let him know she was a God-fearing woman. If that bothered him, better he should decide to move along now, no matter how badly she needed him.

"I'm honored to be considered a blessing from God, Netty. Thank you for saying that. It puts heart into a man. I hope we will work well together."

The first of what he said sounded wonderful. But the last part made Netty uncomfortable because she didn't really think of it as *working together*. She was the boss. She'd give orders, and Roy would take them.

No "together" about it.

Chapter Four

Roy stepped inside the little cabin—honestly, a pretty decent size. One front room set up with a kitchen in one half and a fireplace with a rocking chair on the other. But what was puzzling was the whole room was coated in dust. And the small table had plates on it. He stepped closer. A plate. A cup. And silverware. If he was seeing right, there was still food on that plate, dried and unrecognizable.

The house looked like someone had stood up from that table, shoved the chair back, and walked out never to return.

Years ago.

Nervous about that weird place setting at the table, he went through the room to another built on the back of the house.

It had the same air of abandonment.

A bed, neatly made, but covered thick with dust. A pair of overalls still hung on a nail. Very little else in the room. This smaller cabin had to belong to Netty, didn't it?

He stepped out of the room and saw another door across the hall. He didn't open it. It almost felt as if he were standing on hallowed ground.

An image swam before his eyes of Netty, sitting at the table eating, a baby in her lap maybe, a letter in her hand. She opened it and read the news of her husband's death in the war.

He could see her stand up, shocked, babe in arms, walking out of the home she and her husband had shared to move to the bigger house and her mother's comfort—and she'd never come back.

The pain of it cut through him like a saber.

Really, he didn't know a thing. He ached with his own pain, so maybe he was just laying hurt on her head.

Should he ask her what to do? Was this something that happened so long ago she'd forgotten how she'd left the house? Or was her hurt so bad she couldn't think of it?

Nope, he wouldn't ask her. He'd just move in and get to work on ranch chores. He'd knock the dust off things and clean off the table later, and if Netty didn't bring this up, he'd never speak one word.

He was a man who respected someone else's pain and asked for the same in return.

With a dull plunk, he dropped his saddlebags and bedroll on the floor and considered himself moved in.

That finished, he headed straight out to the barn. Ranch chores were no mystery. He found a chicken coop and gathered eggs. The coop had been built out of pickets and sticks so Netty could move it easily. She must not feed the chickens cracked corn, but rather let them scratch it up for themselves from the grass and weeds. Any bug that wandered into their pen was fair game.

Seemed smart to him. There were a dozen chickens and six eggs so that showed the hens were healthy to produce that well.

Using the tail of his shirt, he gathered the eggs and then headed for the house. With a rap of his knuckles on the back door, he listened for footsteps. She swung open the door a few minutes after.

"Got eggs for you." She plucked them out of his shirt. "Is the milk cow in the barn?"

"Yes. Thank you." Her eyes lit up like he'd given her a bag of Christmas candy. It was late November so Christmas wasn't far off. He wondered what she did to celebrate. Maybe he'd still be here and find out. "The milk cow is in a stall in the barn. I've got hay cut to feed her and . . ."

"I can find it. Have you got a milk pail?"

She reached inside and handed it over, smiling to beat all. "I really appreciate your help. Jeremiah is a little upset over the cow treeing him and trapping me. I wanted to spend a little time with him before I got back to work."

"You stay put. I'll take care of the chores. I can finish up everything in time for supper."

She smiled wider, and it struck a chord in him that brought to mind a church bell he'd rung back when he was a kid. They'd been able to hear it though they lived aways out of town. On Sundays one of the kids rang that bell at just the right time for his family to head in for services.

A purer sound Roy had never heard. And why her smile made him think of it, he couldn't say. But along with that pure sound was the memory of his happy childhood and that led to pain. The pain of the war. The pain of his parents' death. The pain of his fiancé's betrayal.

Pain had sent him wandering, always searching for a new land and a pretty scene. He wanted to explore the whole world. As soon as he stopped in one place too long, his feet itched to head on down the road. They were itching right now.

He took the bucket, turned, and almost ran away from her and that pure smile.

Netty frowned.

She watched his back and puzzled over his strange ways.

Roy had agreed to work for her, helping to ease her load, and she'd thanked him with all her heart and strength and might. But he'd reacted as if talking to her was the last thing on earth he wanted to do.

As if he wanted to saddle up and ride for the hills.

Then he'd turned and run like a man whose hair was on fire.

Maybe that was just the way of a yondering man. Maybe he always wanted what he didn't have.

A character flaw to her way of thinking.

But at least she was getting her cow milked.

She looked at the eggs he'd brought in and decided the man would have the best meal she could concoct. She was a decent cook if she did say so herself.

She looked at the eggs again and headed for the coop. No time to go hunting. They didn't have chicken as a meal much since she was building her flock. But there was at least one shirker in that batch of hens, and she knew exactly who it was.

Fried chicken was that idler's fate.

CHAPTER FIVE

Netty fried the chicken and cooked a few precious carrots from her garden. There was flour enough for biscuits and to contrive a gravy for the arrowroot they ate nearly every day in place of potatoes. With the honey from her beehive and dried fruit from a prickly-pear cactus, she could make a fine, sweet sauce for dessert. She'd serve it with thick cream poured on top.

There was nothing in this meal that would let him know how close she was to disaster—so close she couldn't pay him.

While she cooked, Jeremiah sat on the kitchen floor and played with a wooden horse Netty had carved for him. None of the men in Netty's life had given much time to carving toys for a little boy.

As she worked, she prayed. Like a wind sweeping over her, she soon realized the sin of employing Roy.

It was such a powerful awareness that her hands trembled as she resisted. She needed help so badly. And if they could just gather a few more cattle she could pay him.

She didn't hear the voice of God, she just felt it. Knew it.

The backdoor swung open, and Roy stepped in with a half bucket of milk.

"That smells fine, Netty. I haven't had fried chicken in some time, and then it was at a diner and not a meal cooked by the hand of a pretty woman. I thank you kindly."

Smiling, she fought down her guilt and took the milk from him.

"Wash up over there." She nodded toward a basin. Whatever had sent him running before seemed to be under control now, because he washed up fast and looked expectant for a home-cooked meal.

"Can I help?"

"It's all ready to go on the table. Sit down, Roy. I am more grateful to you than you are to me."

He pulled out a worn, wooden chair and sat down, an eager smile on his face.

She was pretty sure she'd thanked him about ten times already. Although she was as sincerely thankful as a woman could be, she hoped he'd remember her thanks and gratitude when it came payday.

Stuffing down her guilt, she set the golden platter of chicken on the table with an overly sharp crack.

He'd been staring at the food with big eyes, but at the harsh sound, his chin came up and his brow furrowed. "Is something wrong?"

Netty ignored his question and made short work of dishing up the carrots and gravy. The biscuits and honey were already on the neatly set table.

"Jeremiah, wash up so we can eat." Her boy splashed a little water on his hands and dried the dirt on the towel before he raced to sit down.

Netty sat at the foot of her table, which was pushed up against the wall. No use for a lot of seating.

Roy sat at the other end of the table, with Jeremiah between them on Netty's right.

"Can we say grace before the meal?" She needed all the grace she could get right now.

"I'd be glad to say it." Roy paused to let her decide.

"Thank you."

They bowed their heads, and he said a good-hearted prayer that gave Netty hope he was a Christian man with a spirit of forgiveness.

She plopped a chicken leg on Jeremiah's plate, then passed the platter down to Roy.

"I have a confession, Roy." Netty cleared her throat.

"What is it?" He sounded nervous, and why not? She had meant to warn him.

She cleared her throat again. "I gave you a job but . . . but . . ." She was surprised to feel the sting of tears in her eyes. She fought them back, not wanting to put him in a bad spot with a crying woman.

"The job I have would be to round up more of the wild longhorns running in the hills around my property. It was my ma's hope, and mine, that we could build up the herd to about fifty cows. I think the grass in this canyon could support that many. And we'd have enough cattle to sell a few head every year, while letting the others grow and multiply. But those longhorns are wild as cougars and about as dangerous. It's not a job you're likely to want."

Roy was silent for a bit. Then he said, "And that's your confession? It doesn't seem like something that needs confessing."

Netty realized she was staring at her hands clamped together into one big fist in her lap. She looked up to see Roy's slight amusement.

"No, that's not it. Though I wonder if I'd been clear about the hard, dangerous job I want you to do whether you'd have agreed to sign on."

"I can round up longhorns. I'm good with a lasso, and my horse is a top cow pony. So yes, I'd have agreed to work for you."

She glanced at Jeremiah, whose full attention was on devouring his chicken.

"How about if . . . if I can't pay you?" She lifted her chin in time to see his brows arch up nearly to his hairline.

"That sounds like it'd be a pretty poor job."

She detected a note of humor in his voice. Was that because he was planning to start laughing at her . . . and then walk out?

"My thinking is that if we can round up a few extra cows you can sell them as your own."

"Aren't the cattle running wild unbranded? Couldn't I just round up a few for myself? I'm not sure how me rounding up cows for you, then cows for myself, is in anyway a payment from you. In fact—"

"I understand." Netty cut him off. "I need you, but you don't need me—not at all. Enjoy your meal. You're welcome to sleep in the small house, but I don't expect you to stay. After you saved me today . . . and saved my son . . . I repaid you with lies and . . . and—" Her voice broke.

Not with tears. Close but not quite. Shame made her words stumble to a stop.

Lifting her chin and squaring her shoulders, she met his eyes. "You've done us a fine turn, Roy. We'll remember you with respect and fondness."

Saying good-bye. Fighting down her fear of the future. But that wasn't his problem. She had to take care of herself. Surely she knew that by now. She wasn't about to crumble just because—

"I'm not going anywhere, Netty." Roy jerked her out of the encouraging talk she was giving herself, which only sent her in a downward spiral.

She sniffed. "You're not?"

He looked around the room, but she sensed he was looking through things. "This is December right?"

That got a smile out of her—well, that and him saying he wasn't going anywhere. Her spirits rose up as if they were carried on wings of eagles.

"It is tomorrow. This is the last day of November. We had a day of Thanksgiving, though not the usual feast." She smiled at her sweet son, who still ignored them while he shoveled gravy and arrowroot into his mouth. She ruffled his dark hair with one hand. "But we found much to be thankful for, didn't we, Jeremiah?"

Roy set his fork on his plate. "I counted nine head of cattle in your canyon, including the calves."

"You found time to ride out amongst them?"

"Yep, just looking around to see what chores needed doing. Nine head, though I didn't ride around every copse of trees . . . so I coulda missed a cow here and there."

"Nope, nine's right."

"A bull, five cows, and three calves that look like they were born in the spring. I noticed they were branded."

"I got those three done early last spring. The calves come early down here, mostly." She thought of that killer longhorn who'd just had her baby today, out of season. She didn't think she'd brand that one. Mama probably wouldn't stand for it. "Just finished up before Ma died. I've been mighty worried about next spring."

"And the calves look weaned and are doing well," Roy added. "You've got a lot of red in your herd, and some of them are full-bodied, fatter than your usual longhorn. I'm thinking a Hereford bull ran with some of the wild ones for a while."

"That's my guess, too, but if he's out there, I've never come across him. He might've done his years with the herd and be long gone or died of old age by now." Netty held a chicken thigh but didn't want to take a bite and be chewing when she had to answer his questions.

"So you want fifty cattle. Do you want fifty adult cattle, or can we call your calf crop among the fifty."

"I'm counting them." How could she ask him to bring in that many cows? Pa's herd had been that big, but Netty had thinned the herd many times in the years Pa and her brothers and husband had been gone. She'd done her best to round up more cattle, too, but they'd been falling behind.

"So you need forty-one more cows." Roy took a hearty bite of chicken as if that wasn't a number that scared him any. She wondered how much experience he'd had with longhorns.

"You're really going to do it? Stay until I have my herd of fifty?"

"Yep, and I'll do a gather that includes a few for myself. If I can use your canyon to hold my cows along with yours, eat at your table, and sleep in the cabin, that's worth a month's wages to me."

"Really, Roy? I know it's not fair, but I do have something of value to give, don't I? And you can stay until you get a nice bunch to sell. We'll hold them on my grass long enough to gentle 'em down if the new bunch is too wild. Most of my cows are calm, except for Cyclone, and by then those three calves will be old enough to sell. Maybe we could do a drive to the railhead and sell a few for us both. Some cash money and a trip to town would make our winter much easier."

He'd cleaned his plate so Netty was quick to scoop up some of the pear sauce in a bowl and set it in front of him.

"What's this?" he asked, sounding more like he was curious than afraid. He dipped his spoon in the still-warm bowl of fruit.

"Prickly-pear sauce."

He froze, the spoon most of the way to his mouth. His eyes met hers. "Uh, isn't, umm, that is, isn't prickly pear a cactus?"

She smiled. "I promise there are no spines in there to stab you."

He hesitated, studied the spoon carefully, then shrugged and took a bite. He sighed like a purely contented man.

"If you can cook like this, Netty, it's more than a fair deal. I'm a yondering man, for a fact. But now and then I stop and get to know a place. That's the whole point in yondering, finding out about the world, not just walking through it. I was in the mountains of Idaho last winter, and a more bitter cold part of this earth you will never see. I think spending a chunk of the cold weather months here in Texas'll be a big improvement. Besides, I'd like to stay long enough to get familiar with it."

He ate another spoonful of prickly pear sauce. "If I catch a cow a day and most with a calf at the side, I can be done by Christmas. I can hope to do better, but that'll be my goal. A few better and that'll get me my own cattle to sell by Christmas. However fast I go, I'll work until I have enough, but Christmas will be my goal."

"It's like Advent," Netty smiled.

"Advent?" His brow furrowed as if the word made no sense. And maybe it didn't to him.

"My ma always made the month of December a journey to Christmas. She talked about Mary and Joseph on their way to Bethlehem. Each day was a step along their journey, and she'd have a story or a small gift or special cookies each day as we journeyed toward the birth of our Savior."

"Advent." A kind smile bloomed on Roy's face. "I like the idea of it. Our cows can be the steps along our journey. Come Christmas Day you'll have yourself a nice herd, big enough to sustain itself and keep you and your son on your land and well fed. And it gives me pleasure to be the one who'll give you this gift."

She smiled back. It took all she had not to thank him yet again for saving her. The warmth in her heart for him went deep, and she didn't want to embarrass him with a big fuss.

But she could thank him for other things.

"Staying here, rounding up wild cattle for my herd, Roy, God bless you for it. You're the true gift. I appreciate and thank you for it."

"My pleasure, Miss Netty. Now we've had us a serious talk and neglected this fine meal." He looked at Jeremiah who was gnawing on his second chicken leg. "We'd better get our share while there's still some left."

Netty laughed and handed the bowls to him, and the man ate like she'd fed him only the finest. She had to shoo him out or he'd've helped wash the dishes.

As she swung the door shut on his retreating back, she wondered what had brought this man to her at the exact right moment.

She believed with all her heart and soul that it was a Christmas miracle.

CHAPTER SIX

For whom the Lord loveth he chastens.

As another bramble bush whipped him across the face, Roy thought he remembered more in that verse. Something about being scourged.

For the life of him he didn't know what he'd done wrong, but God appeared to be teaching him some loving lesson that included chastening.

Roy fought a hard inner battle to stay grateful as a longhorn twisted and ducked his lasso and dodged into a thicket. He roped the thick brush, but the young bull ran free. He grumbled under his breath and pushed forward carefully to avoid the scratching branches. His stallion wasn't having any fun either.

He dodged a mesquite bush. They grew everywhere, along with prickly-pear cactuses taller than he was. The biggest he'd ever seen. Running afoul of one left a man sour and cranky. He tried to imagine Netty doing this, thinking how hard it was going to be for him to keep from strangling her for tricking him into this job.

"There's a right way and a wrong way to throw a lasso in a thicket, Roy."

His control slipped a little, and he looked up from where the voice came. "I reckon I've tried a whole lotta wrong ways, Miss Netty."

Netty sat on a high rock with Jeremiah beside her. She'd saddled up with him this morning and showed him the land and where the cattle were.

Supposedly.

Then she'd left him to the most frustrating morning of his life. Maybe not counting the war.

When he reported on how things were going during the noon meal, she and Jeremiah had followed him out here.

Both of them stayed well out of danger—a lucky pair.

"I can show you the right way, if you want," she said. "It's still hard, but it can be done."

Silence stretched between them as he freed his lasso, coiled it, and rode to where she and Jeremiah perched. Roy gritted his teeth so he wouldn't say anything sarcastic.

"If it was easy, I wouldn't need help," Netty said, looking guilty, like maybe she knew same as he did that this was an impossible job.

Netty reached over and took his rope. "A big loop will never work."

"Hard to get a loop over a spread of long horns without a big loop."

She nodded silently. "Not much about this is easy."

She pulled the loop to a respectable size, and with a sudden flip of her wrist, she threw it forward, the loop more flat than round. It snaked in between a couple of mesquites and roped a prickly pear.

"You're good at that." His spirits lifted. That *would* work better. "Let me try."

"It comes quick." Netty told him a few other bits and pieces about what ranching in the Big Bend area of southwest Texas was like.

Not too much different about it. Except roping. And the longhorns seemed to have particularly bad attitudes.

"Do they all try and kill you? Because I've worked wild longhorns other places and they seemed more willing to run, and most of them let themselves be herded. Here, they just attack."

"Not all of them. Plenty run."

That was the plain truth.

"But never in the direction I'm trying to herd them." Roy sighed and tipped up his dusty cowboy hat.

"I think the heat makes them feisty. We're living in a land where everything bites or stings or stabs—and a lot of 'em throw in a little poison while they're at it. Sometimes if you're not having a good day, you'll find something that does all four."

"A longhorn with poison-tipped horns. That'll probably come next."

Netty shrugged and handed over the lasso.

He had trouble, as anyone does learning some new skill, but he finally mastered it.

"Those longhorns move as quiet as ghosts." Netty added. "Sometimes I'll be riding along looking for cattle and glance at a mesquite thicket and realize a big old bull is only a few feet away from me, staring. Makes a person nervous. Makes you wonder who's being hunted."

A little chill slithered down Roy's spine because he'd had the very same thought. "It's like they pick a spot and wait for their prey to wander by. I've never considered it before, but we're real lucky longhorns aren't meat eaters."

Netty shuddered, then grinned at him. "We'll stay up here."

She'd found a spot on top of a pile of boulders near the highest point of a draw. The bull he'd just tried to catch had gone over this slope. Roy paused a second to wonder if he was being lured into a trap. Next, those devils would learn to read and write and start campaigning for their voting rights.

"I'd really hoped I'd ride out here, find a couple of small herds, drive them in, and you'd have your fifty head of cattle by the end of the day."

She looked surprised. "You thought it'd be that easy?"

Roy shrugged. "A man's allowed his daydreams."

"I guess." She giggled and reined her horse to head back to the cabin. "Holler if the cows start winning. If they toss you in a gated canyon, Jeremiah and I'll come to your rescue. We'll try our best to get you out."

That made him chuckle, and it gave him the backbone to ride down into the shallow draw. As the sides rose around him, he noticed hoof prints on the rocky ground. Cattle definitely came this way. But now he'd stopped dreaming about being a big success on his first day.

Just one, Lord. Let me get at least one more cow in Netty's canyon today. I'll be glad to accept that as success, and keep at it every day until Christmas . . . or until I get fifty cows.

Roy hesitated on that part of his prayer and hoped he hadn't just committed himself to a life sentence.

Because right now, one day into his Advent Cow Journey, it looked to be more than he had bargained for.

Well, if Joseph could get his great-with-child wife from Nazareth to Bethlehem in twenty-five days—Roy paused to consider whether that exact number of days for the journey was in the Bible or not—but anyway, if Joseph could do it, then surely Roy could do it.

Since she seemed to annoy him, Netty had left Roy to his pursuit of unhappiness, and she and Jeremiah rode back to the house to make supper.

The meal was ready before he got back. She was glad she'd made chicken stew because it could be put on a low heat and kept warm for a long time.

Finally, he rode in with a lassoed longhorn.

"He got one, Jeremiah!" Netty turned and grinned at her son. "You stay in here. I'm going to open the gate."

Jeremiah nodded and stood at the window to watch. Netty rushed out, well ahead of Roy, to open the gate before her movements could spook the cow.

Netty stood way back, giving them space, wincing as Roy approached with the cow he was leading.

Honestly, leading was the wrong word. It was more of a battle. Or a fight. With parts that were a little bit of a dance.

Roy's horse really was a top cow pony. It kept dodging away from those slashing horns and wicked hooves. Charging and retreating. The horse kept the rope taut, not easy when the cow was charging you.

But the horse was good. Roy was his equal and stuck to his saddle like a burr. The two of them used the cow's ferocious attacks to make forward progress. Slowly but surely, they approached the canyon. With a few quick moves, Roy dragged the cow in, flipped his lasso free, and raced out before the cow could attack them. He caught the gate while still on horseback and swung it shut.

Netty had been prepared to close it for him, but it was done before she got a chance.

The cow slammed her head into the gate, but this wasn't Netty's first roundup. She'd built that gate to last—Cyclone's escape notwithstanding.

Roy turned his horse to face her. He was breathing hard. His horse was breathing harder. Cool as it was, they were both soaked in sweat and worn right down to the nub.

"You go in and wash up, Roy. Dinner's ready. I'll brush your horse down, then be in."

He rolled his eyes at her and rode his horse toward the barn. Like all western men, he tended his own mount.

The cow head butted the gate again.

Netty couldn't be gone long from Jeremiah, but she turned and waved at him, watching through the window. He smiled and waved back. He was fine.

Roy led the horse toward the barn. She caught up with him, and he stripped his horse of its leather while she pitched some hay into its stall. They worked together to give it a good brushing, then left it in the stall rather than turn it outside. The poor horse needed a long rest.

Together, they hurried to the house. When they stepped in the door, Jeremiah was already sitting at the table patiently. He'd had to grow up too fast since Ma died.

After washing up, Netty began filling plates. They all ate in silence, mealtime being serious business on a ranch.

After Roy cleaned his plate, he looked up. "You can't keep serving chicken every day. Your flock won't stand the strain."

Netty laughed. "True enough."

"I'll try to bring in some game tomorrow. I didn't think of it today, but I saw a couple of deer and plenty of birds I could've caught. I hope by noon I can have something for the pot and still get my cow for the day."

Netty's smile faded. "Sorry it's such a rugged job. I should probably just get out of here. Go to the nearest town and find work."

She looked at Jeremiah, who had laid his head down on the table fast asleep. She ruffled his hair.

He pushed at her hand and mumbled. "Stop fussin', Mama."

Her heart ached to think of what she'd do in a town. There'd be school for him, but what job could she get? Where would they live? She knew nothing of life away from this ranch, but if she had to—

"Don't give up on the land, Netty. Let me carry Jeremiah into bed, and we can talk more about what we need to do." Roy stood and gently lifted Jeremiah into his arms. "Which room?"

We? Roy had said "we" as if this was his problem as well as hers.

Netty led the way and they undressed Jeremiah down to his woolen underwear that he slept in and together Netty and Roy tucked the boy into bed. Netty said his prayers for him. He was too groggy to do more than mutter "amen."

CHAPTER SEVEN

Roy led the way to the kitchen and picked up licked-clean plates off the table.

"Let me do that. You've put in three-day's work already today."

By the time Netty quit talking, Roy had mostly cleared the table, so he said, "I'll pour some coffee then and . . . well . . . I have some questions if you're willing to answer them."

This had been eating at him all day. Should he mention the cabin he lived in and what was in there? Or should he keep his mouth shut? Maybe he should make sure it was all right to move things. Or maybe he should just leave it be. The condition of the house spoke to him of a pain she couldn't face. A pain so deep she couldn't be rational about it. Her husband, the love of her life, was dead. For Roy to speak of it—

He'd gone back and forth on the problem while he fought through brambles and mesquite thickets and dodged horns and hooves and prickly pears.

Netty poured steaming hot water into a dishpan and started washing dishes.

Now that she had her back to him, it helped him decide to ask. Or maybe he was just so tired he couldn't remember why it was a bad idea. "Netty, the cabin I'm staying in, it looks like a shrine."

He wasn't sure that was the right word.

"A shrine?" Netty whirled around so fast she sprayed water off her hands, splashing him. "What does that mean?"

Frowning, she stood silent, her hands dripping.

Her reaction shocked him, but he kept talking. "Nothing has been touched—it looks like for years. I-I don't feel quite right about moving things. I don't want to disrespect your husband, but—"

"What did you say?"

"About the house. Your cabin—the one I'm living in."

"This is my cabin. The one you're living in was my ma's. When we got the word that Pa had died, she came over here and then we just kept getting bad news. A letter about Ralph, my husband, then my two brothers, Buck and then Willie."

Her forehead furrowed as if it hurt to think. "She brought the clothes on her back, but she finally went back and got the rest of her things."

Roy hadn't seen any women's clothes. "And you never went over there?"

With an impatient shake of her head, Netty asked, "What did you find exactly?"

"There's a dinner plate that still has food on it. Everything in that house looks like it was abandoned, as if your ma ran from her home and never returned. I had the notion that you might think of it as an almost sacred place that held memories of your marriage. But if it's where your ma lived, then maybe that's how she felt."

Except Roy didn't think that quite explained it. Why hadn't Netty gone in there and gotten blankets and pots and pans? "How long ago did your menfolk die?"

Netty was silent. He could tell she was thinking back because her gaze looked through him into the past.

Roy walked toward the dishpan. His movement startled her back into the present, and she turned.

"Let me help." He picked up a dish towel. "I'll dry."

She'd already washed a few things, so he picked up a plate and dried it. That got her back to washing.

"They all ran off right away. Right after war was declared. It was the oddest thing. Pa was just plain too old. My Ralph, he had a wife and small child to think of. Willie was nineteen years old, and I suppose about right for soldiering, but Buck had just turned fifteen. He had no notion of war." Netty handed him dripping dishes as she talked.

"Ma tried to stop them. I tried to stop them. It was like the chance to go warring was more important to them than making sure Ma and I and Jeremiah could survive here on our own. All four of them just slung their rifles on their backs, got up on their horses, and rode off."

"So they left right away then? Years ago?"

"Word reached us in the middle of 1861 that Texas had seceded from the Union. Five years ago. Nearly five and a half now. It'd happened months before, but no one from our ranch had been to town so we didn't know. Los Combarse is a forty-mile ride, and the going is rough."

"I've just been on that trail and that's the absolute truth."

"Off they went." She handed him a bowl. "I went to Los Combarse far more often than usual after that—once a month at least. We sent letters, and once in a while we'd get one. It was about this time of year we received word that Pa died. He'd been gone a year and a half. Up until then, Ma and I had lived in our own homes, but, of course, we were together a lot. Me running the ranch, and Ma mostly tending Jeremiah.

"He was a year old when Ralph rode off. We had a couple of milk cows, and I'm a decent shot so we always ate. Ma could garden. I'd once in a while find a wild cow and drag her in out of the hills and into the canyon. We had this dream that if we could get enough cows to build a herd that would sustain itself, life wouldn't be so hard. I'd gentle them down, mainly just by riding amongst them and feeding them a bit of hay. They didn't really need it, but I wanted them to think kindly of me."

"Instead of being determined to kill you?" Roy asked with a smile.

She smiled back. "Yep, that gets mighty old."

"So your ma got a letter about your pa and walked over here and just never left?"

Netty handed him the last dish. "I reckon she did. It was a heartbreaking thing. Worse because we'd been so angry at them for so long. And then when Pa died, we just clung to each other. Before we'd gotten used to a life that'd never have him in it again, we got word about Buck, my little brother." She shook her head. "He should've never gone."

Roy handed her the dry dishes, and she stowed them in a cabinet fixed to the wall. It looked like a wooden box they'd gotten supplies in, but it worked well as a cupboard.

"Then Ralph. He'd been fighting over three years when he died. He had a four-year-old son he never saw walk nor talk. Willie was the last. He died just a few months before the war was over."

The dishes done and packed away, she took the towel from his hand and hung it to dry, then she poured him a cup of coffee. It'd taste good on a cool night.

She got one for herself, and they sat at the table.

"We never did go back to that house. Mine was newer and larger, but mostly it wasn't full of so much pain. So many memories of growing up. I was married to Ralph for a year and that was plenty to mourn, but nothing like losing all of them."

Roy sipped his coffee, then said cautiously, "So I can do as I wish with the things over there? Surely your ma had linens, and there's fabric in the clothes your pa wore that can be used for Jeremiah."

Nodding, Netty said, "Of course, I need to go through it. I'll do it in the morning. I'm sorry. It's got to be filthy. I never even thought—"

"Let me do it, Netty. I'll bring things over. You don't have to go into that house."

Her chin came up. He'd seen her grief, but now he remembered a woman dodging a longhorn, shouting instructions to her son stuck in a tree. She'd taught Roy how to throw a rope in a mesquite bramble for heaven's sakes. Underneath the hard blows her life had dealt, Netty was as strong as a harsh life in the Texas frontier could make a woman.

"I'll do it. You head out hunting while I go through that house."

"You don't have to."

Nodding, she said, "It's weak to avoid it, and I'm not giving into that weakness. I thank you for mentioning it so I can get to the job. I appreciate you offering to take care of things over there, but I need to. It's part of facing up to the life I've got now."

"That sounds wise to me, Netty. All right. I'll get us a deer while you roam through that house."

"Then leave the deer and go cow hunting while I butcher it and get a meal on. The noon meal if you get back fast enough."

"Sounds like we've both got a busy day laid out." Roy and Netty stood at the same moment. Suddenly, they were too close. Eye to eye. Hers so green they made him think of life and growth and the comfort of plenty. Being so close caught him somehow, and he didn't head out the door.

A tug he'd felt before, though not this strong, shocked him, and he felt himself lean forward, reach out to rest his hands on her. She didn't run like she probably ought to.

"Mama!" Jeremiah's cry jerked them both away from the edge of whatever madness had come over them.

"Cyclone! No, Mama!"

Netty whirled toward the bedroom. "It's a nightmare. He had one last night, too. I'll see you at breakfast."

Then she was gone. And she hadn't just been running to help her son; she'd been running away from him.

Very wise of her, since he was a yondering man, and she was a settled woman.

He left the house as fast as she'd left the room. He wondered why his foot wasn't as itchy to travel as usual. But it'd come. It always did.

Chapter Eight

Netty stepped into Ma and Pa's house the next afternoon, Jeremiah at her side, with Roy well down the trail after cattle.

He'd brought her a javelina, and she'd butchered it, and they'd feasted for dinner. Then she'd salted the side pork and hams. There would be roast pork for supper and sausages for breakfast if she could get to work making them, but it was when she'd finished salting down the pork and was considering how to prepare the sausage that she realized she was stalling.

Now here she was. When she entered the old homestead, pain swept over her like a Texas sandstorm. Jeremiah rushed past her and started exploring. His high spirits felt like a slash across her heart.

Her parents were fine and loving people. Pa, the old coot, should have never gone to war. He was in his fifties for heaven's sakes. He would have cherished a grandson and raised him to be tough and honorable and kind. Ma had doted on Jeremiah. In fact, in many ways, Jeremiah had held up Ma and her. His needs, simple but never ending, had forced them to live, to think, to move through their grief.

Pa was a man of strong faith, and he and Ma had raised the family up in the way of the Lord. Netty carried on their teaching, so Jeremiah would know about God. Jeremiah would remember his grandmother at least some. But he'd never know the loving hand of his grandfather or the love of a father or uncles either.

All of this hit hard as she stood just inside that door.

Jeremiah dashed into a bedroom—there were two in the back of the house—then out and into the other, so alive and happy. It was a reminder to Netty that he was growing up strong and straight. No, she didn't have help, so she would do it by herself.

After the first wash of mourning, what came to her next were happy memories. Fond memories, funny, annoying memories of her younger brothers. Loving memories of Pa and Ma. Even affectionate memories of Ralph.

She'd not thought through what abandoning this house really meant. In an effort to avoid the pain of the past, she'd denied herself the solace of her family memories. Now she was here, and the air was rich with the laughter of growing up in this home.

The lighter thoughts got her moving. She was delighted to see a good-sized stack of canned food on one shelf.

And Ma had several kitchen linens she could use. Towels, a tablecloth, dish rags. Nice, practical, well-worn things that would extend the life of the few things she had that were being used and scrubbed over and over.

She found a pair of seasoned, cast-iron skillets—one of them Ma used every morning to fry eggs. Netty remembered Ma so carefully teaching her how to use it. She clutched the handle and relived that precious relationship with her loving mother.

Netty also found a bigger coffee pot than she had and a sturdy saucepan. Besides that, Ma had far nicer plates and silverware than Netty.

And canned goods, peaches, and other preserved food that looked to have passed the years safely.

What a waste not to have used these things.

"Mama," Jeremiah yelled from her brother's bedroom, "there are clothes in here that might fit Roy, and Willie must've gotten ahead making bullets because he has some here. There's lots of other good stuff."

The more Netty dug through the house, the more she remembered. It was like her life had started on the day Ma came to the house with the letter about Pa. They'd stayed at Netty's house and given their old life no more thought. But this house was well-stocked and well-furnished. Ma had a nice kitchen table and some chairs. Three bedsteads. A bigger cast-iron stove than Netty had.

Of course, she couldn't just take everything up to her place. With Roy living here, he'd need some things. But now that she knew it was all here, she was excited and didn't feel so desperate. Not that they'd ever starve. There was abundant food here on her ranch. She could snare rabbits, and they could feast on prickly-pear cactus. The fruit was sweet, and the pads, once stripped of stickers, were tasty. Not to mention berries and nuts.

But adding these cans of food to their diet would give them some variety.

Jeremiah bolted out of her parents' room, clutching something in his hand. "Look at this toy, Mama."

Netty leaned down, loving the pleasure in her son's eyes and the smile on his face. He handed her a little figure, about two inches high, that she lifted to eye level.

Her heart clutched with poignant memories when she saw what she held.

"This isn't a toy, sweetheart. This is part of your grandma's nativity set."

She looked at the carved-wood shepherd she remembered so well. The little figure carried a lamb draped around his neck, the kind shepherd giving the wooly baby a ride on his shoulders. It was as if the warmth of a fire on a cold day burned inside her. Her heart eased away from the grief she didn't know she still felt. Her hand shook as she held the little shepherd.

"What's a nativity set, Mama?"

Jeremiah's words twisted something inside her, pushing back the warmth.

Dear God, forgive me. My son doesn't even know what a nativity set is.

Guilt warred with the pleasure of holding an old family treasure in her hand. "Where did you find this? There should be more pieces. Let's take them back to our house. I'll show you how to set them up, and while we do, I'll tell you all about a nativity set."

"I didn't see more, Mama, but I only just opened a box I found under the bed."

Back before their menfolk rode off to war, Ma had decorated the house for Christmas every year. Netty hadn't thought of those decorations for years.

She remembered how they'd put things up one by one, and Ma had told old stories. Her mother's great-grandmother had brought the nativity set here from England. It had been passed down through the generations and always set out on the first day of December. Each piece came with a story of the part that piece played in Jesus' birth. And then Ma told how the family had moved to America and spread out all over the country—even to Texas.

Those stories of family history and the faith of her ancestors had deeply blessed Netty growing up. Yet she'd failed to share them with her son. Well, not anymore.

"I'll tell you all about it, Son. Your grandma always made it so much fun when we set out the nativity set, and I remember all the stories she told me. Now I'll pass them along to you."

"What kind of stories, Mama?"

"Stories about Christmas." She smiled and rested her hand on Jeremiah's head as they walked back into Ma and Pa's bedroom together. Jeremiah dropped to his knees and pulled an old wooden box out from under the bed. It contained more treasures than just the nativity. All precious.

"There should be a baby Jesus in with the other figures." Ma had always kept the baby Jesus in a special, separate place. She always placed the Christ Child out so they could see him, but not yet in the manger. Then on Christmas Eve their Savior came. Tears burned in Netty's eyes as she thought of how she'd loved that moment when Pa read the Christmas story from the Bible, and Ma had let the children take turns placing the baby in the manger. How had she forgotten all of this?

After going through the box, she left everything else behind except Christmas decorations and a can of peaches. They'd have the peaches for supper along with salted side pork and the arrowroot. After they ate, she'd include Roy in their decorating. Maybe tomorrow while he was working his heart out, she'd go chop down a scrub pine and bring it inside to decorate. A tree to put presents under.

Of course, she'd have to scrounge around and find some presents.

Last night, Netty could tell Roy had been nervous about bringing up the subject of the old house. But she was so glad he'd done it. One more thing she needed to thank Roy for.

CHAPTER NINE

This was another day to blame on Netty.

Roy clung to the pommel of his saddle as his stallion tried to outrun Death.

Okay, outrun a cow, but it was the same thing.

He wondered what they'd name this one. Cyclone was taken, and Tornado would be too much of a copy. Grim Reaper would be his choice. If the cattle kept up being this hard to catch, he was going to see if his Bible listed names for the Four Horsemen of the Apocalypse. They could run through those names next.

This morning, Roy thought he'd come up with a great plan. He'd gotten the idea while hunting a javelina. That's what Netty called it. It looked like a wild pig to him. He'd seen a couple of young longhorn calves and wondered if they were old enough to graze. He might just catch them and give up on the half-ton killers he'd been chasing. But so far, the ones he'd come across seemed a little young to take without their mothers. So while he hunted, he stayed on the lookout for cow-calf pairs, thinking to come back to this area after he put food on the table. Seemed like a sound idea.

Then on the ride home with the javelina draped over his saddle, he wondered more about the calves. They were a lot less deadly than the mamas. And they'd grow up, right?

He didn't discuss his plan with Netty because he thought it might make him look like a coward in her eyes. He wanted to delay admitting that.

After the noon meal, Roy'd headed right back to where he'd shot the javelina that morning. He spent long hours hunting calves with the speed and agility and temperament of cougars. Finally, his chance came and he dropped a loop over a little red-and-white spotted heifer.

He'd jumped off his horse and hog-tied the calf, feeling like a genius. Then he heard the low-throated woof of a cow getting ready to charge.

Whirling around, he saw a mama coming for him, head down, horns ready. And he'd swear she might've had fire shooting out of her eyes.

He seemed to grow springs on the bottoms of his feet because he leapt on his horse, the calf still in his arms, then raced for Netty's canyon.

His cow pony had zig-zagged out of the worst of the broken hills where he had to dodge rocks and boulders. The cow had almost gotten close enough to sink one of those killer horns into his hide several times. Now on even ground, his horse ran flat out for its life, and thankfully, the cow couldn't keep up. But he gave her full credit for persistence, cuz she was still back there charging after her baby.

"Netty!" Roy screamed. Well, not *screamed* . . . that was something a girl would do. He shouted. At the top of his lungs. It might've been a little high-pitched. But it was definitely *not* a scream. He needed that gate open. She'd never hear him unless he hollered real loud. And there wasn't going to be a chance to climb off his horse and deal with it himself.

"Netty, open the gate."

Netty rushed out of her ma's house and turned to look back. He couldn't hear anything at this distance, but Jeremiah's small hand slammed the door shut. Netty seemed to judge the situation in a single glance, then sprinted for the gate.

Roy charged through the barely opened gate, the cow on his heels, then pivoted, pulled loose the pigging strings from the calf's feet, bent nearly double, and laid the calf on the ground. His stallion leapt into a gallop with a single stride. Roy escaped the enclosure before a quick glance back told him the cow had broken off her attack. She was busy nuzzling her baby.

Then Netty shut the gate and sagged back against it, her breathing hard.

He dismounted, or maybe he just plain fell . . . but not all the way to the ground, so it didn't count as collapsing. His legs felt watery. His knees quaked like an aspen tree. His hands trembled where they clung to the saddle.

Netty called, "Come on out, Jeremiah." She walked toward Roy and his trembling horse. "This critter will have nerves of iron by the time we're done with this chore."

Yep, or it'd die of fright.

Roy let Netty take the sweaty reins of his horse, and only when it moved did he realize his cow pony was holding him up. He stood on his own unsteady legs just as Jeremiah ran up and plowed into his side.

Slinging his arms around Roy's legs, the boy almost knocked Roy over, but after he survived the first impact, Jeremiah's grip actually helped him stay upright.

"I saw you bring in that cow and calf. You're really good with cattle."

"I don't know if I'll do it that way again. I was afraid that cow was gonna catch me, but my horse came through."

Roy patted the boy's shoulder as he watched Netty lead his stallion past the barn. She was going to walk it for a while, a mighty good idea, because a run like that in the cold and then just stopping could harm the horse.

"Well, you were fast as lightning. You've only been gone a couple of hours." An excited Jeremiah seemed to want a repeat of this day's madness. "And you got a mama and baby. At that rate you could bring in sixteen cows and calves working an eight-hour day."

The boy seemed so proud of him. Roy took a deep breath to calm himself and took off for the barn, walking steady. He watched Netty leading his cow pony around to cool down and wondered if a man stiffened up same as a horse. Although *Roy* hadn't been running. Still, his heart was banging against his chest, and since he was soaked with sweat, he shivered in the forty-degree weather.

"Let me stretch my legs a little and go check on how my horse is doing." And he could walk with Netty for a while.

Roy ruffled the boy's hair, and the two of them ambled toward Netty and the poor shaky dun.

When they caught up to her, Netty looked at them, her face a shade of red that near to matched her hair. Her pretty green eyes watered. Almost as if she was fighting against showing any expression . . . or trying hard not to cry.

Roy's mind rabbited around in his head. Was it the house? Had she gone in there? Well, of course, she'd gone in there. He'd seen her come out. Had that stirred up life memories of her love for her dead husband? Was that what was goading her to tears and ripping her up inside?

He never should have suggested it. Why couldn't he just keep his stupid mouth shut? Roy didn't want any woman shedding tears, not over something he'd done. He opened his mouth with no idea what to say to make it better.

Then Netty erupted with laughter.

Netty still broke into laughter every few minutes even as they finished supper.

Roy furrowed his brow. "You've been laughing at me long enough."

That set her off even more. Helplessly, she waved a hand at him. "It's not y-you. It's just the look on your f-face."

"That's me. Don't say, 'it's not you' then say it's me."

"That cow. That squirming calf. The sound of you screaming, it was just so—" She almost bent double laughing.

"I was not *screaming*. I was shouting."

She broke down again, wiping tears from her eyes, as she tried to hold back her glee.

There was a little milk left in Roy's glass. He drank it quick to keep from dashing it in her face. That might calm her down, but it wouldn't make him much of a hero.

Then Jeremiah giggled.

"You don't need to start, young man. You were in the house. You didn't see me."

"Yep, I did. I watched out the window." He giggled some more and clamped both hands over his mouth, shaking his head. Then he said,

"I'm not laughing at you, honest. Mama's just funny, so that's making me laugh."

Roy looked at Netty for a long stretch of time and then found his own lips quirking up into a smile. "You're right. She *is* funny."

In fact, he'd never seen her purely happy like this, and even if her laughter was at his expense, still, he'd given her that. The thought pleased him until he chuckled himself.

They cleaned up after the meal, all three smiling and acting silly.

And then Netty bribed Jeremiah into getting ready for bed with the promise of decorating for Christmas.

The boy raced back in minutes in his clean woolen underwear.

Roy watched while Jeremiah helped Netty arrange a nativity set. Roy heard family stories, some so old they went back to the beginning of America. Some took them across the ocean.

As she talked, she set the pieces in a strange order Roy didn't understand. There was a wooden stable with a little manger. She sat that on the mantle over the fireplace, but instead of putting the other figures beside it, she put the three wise men in the farthest corner of the kitchen. The shepherds were placed on the floor right to the side of the hearth. Netty then set Mary and Joseph against the wall that ran at a right angle to the fireplace, and the angel took up a position on the kitchen table . . . right beside the salt cellar.

He only noticed in passing where she set them because she spoke the whole time, telling old family stories.

It was the nicest evening Roy had spent since . . . he mentally shook his head . . . but there was no denying it was since before the war. Years and years it'd been since he'd had an evening with good food, a warm home, talk of Christmas, and the rich feeling of a family that had loved for generations. He'd experienced that during his childhood, but all his kin were dead and buried now.

That old life was long gone and forgotten.

Roy sank lower in a comfortable rocking chair. Netty already had one, but there'd been another in her ma's house, so she'd brought it over. Now they could both rock.

So much tension and loss and grief drained out of him it was as if the years and the horror of war melted away into his past, rather than him carrying around that crushing weight every day.

A hardness inside him that he'd paid little attention to softened as well. Since this old world was such a dangerous place, he'd always thought he needed to be hard and tough to survive. It was safe to keep moving. Safe to trust no one. Since the war, he had thought of himself as an angry man, but now he recognized that shell was made of pain and grief. He'd hardened himself to keep all the gentler feelings out—the ones he'd had for his parents and the rest of his family who'd died in that nightmarish war.

Roy closed his tired eyes, just to rest them for a moment, and listened as Jeremiah's childish voice asked questions about every word Netty said. She answered as they picked up each small figure from the Christmas story.

Her mother's love come to life in words and a tone that wrapped itself around Roy's lonely heart.

CHAPTER TEN

"Roy, Roy wake up." Netty's whispers reached inside his blissful dreams of childhood Christmases.

When he blinked open his eyes, he realized he'd been sleeping.

She smiled. Not laughing now. A smile so sweet a man might well go to great lengths to wake up to that smile for the rest of his life.

She wordlessly dipped her chin down. His eyes followed the gesture. Jeremiah had fallen asleep in her arms.

"He's so heavy," she whispered. "I can't get out of this chair without jostling him so bad I'll wake him up."

Roy was on his feet before she could finish. He slid his arms under the boy cradled in her arms. For just a second, with his arms under the boy, Roy was only inches from Netty. Their faces close, their arms touching, a child cradled between them, connecting them.

His gaze met hers, and she gave him a smile he'd never seen before, a smile just for him, just for now.

If listening to her tell stories had softened the shell he didn't know he had, then her smile slipped past it all the way to his heart.

Then she looked away. It hurt.

Until he realized she was looking at her son. The boy was far too big to be held this way. But Netty watched her child's face as Roy lifted him. Part of her probably hoping he wouldn't wake up—but Roy thought it was more than that. She'd enjoyed being close to her son for a time.

Roy doubted the little guy let her hold him and rock him much anymore. She was wise enough to cherish the moment.

With the boy in his arms, he stepped back enough to let her rise from the rocker. He wondered how long she'd sat with two of them asleep.

Now she led the way to Jeremiah's room. He was already in his night clothes so they just tucked him under the covers. He stirred a bit when Netty kissed his forehead. But his eyes stayed closed, and they slipped out of the room.

He heard the wind, not howling by any means, but it was a blustery, cold night, cloudless so the moon shone its icy white light down through the windows and lit up the room until, with the lantern light and fire blazing, it was nearly bright as day.

Everything about this night made him feel cozy, and it beckoned him to stay. Which meant it was time to go.

"It will be a chilly walk to your cabin, Roy. Would you like another cup of coffee before you go?"

"That sounds good." That was not what he planned to say. But he followed her to the stove, as if he couldn't sit in front of the fire and wait. As if he didn't want to be that far from her.

Then he noticed the angel sitting on the table. "Why did you spread out the pieces of the nativity like you did? My ma always put out a set like this at Christmas, but she grouped them all together on top of the mantle."

A smile so full of love bloomed on Netty's face, Roy had to remind himself to breathe.

"It was my pa that wanted them placed like this." She pointed to the corner of the kitchen and the wise men. "We think of them as coming to see Jesus on the night he was born, but then when Herod orders all boy children under two years of age to be killed, Pa said that might mean the wise men didn't get there all that soon. If they set out for Bethlehem following the star when it appeared over Jesus in the manger, it might've taken them two years to get there."

Netty picked up the little angel. It was only about three inches tall and a fine shade of stained oak—a perfect match for the rest of the set. "But I've always wondered if, instead, they saw the star over their own heads two years before Jesus was born. And it guided them for all that time."

Netty turned and pointed to Mary and Joseph. "They had to travel from Nazareth to Bethlehem because of the census, but why would they still be there two years later? They didn't have to stay there, did they? So that makes me think the wise men got there right away."

She looked at Roy expectantly, as if she wanted him to have the answers. He said, "I like the idea of them showing up right when Jesus is born. Especially because Jesus is only a few days old when they go to the temple, and the story seems to be told in order. Why talk about the night of his birth, then something that happens two years later, then go back to the baby just a few days old, then jump back to the story of Herod and the wise men. Of course, I think those stories are in different books of the Bible so maybe it's not in as straight of order as I remember."

Nodding, Netty said, "I like thinking of them showing up, too, but it doesn't matter when. What matters is making our peace with God and believing in Jesus. This is just the details of a beautiful story, and we like to think we know how it was, even though we don't."

"So the wise men are in that corner then, because . . ."

"They come from far away in the East. They traveled, possibly for years, to reach Bethlehem. When Ma and Pa set out the nativity, they'd move the travelers a bit each day. The wise men first because they had so far to come. The last week we move Mary and Joseph closer and closer. They reach the stable on Christmas Eve." She held up the angel. "And then the angel appears."

Netty reached into the box that had held all the figures and pulled out a manger with the baby Jesus in it. "On Christmas morning, when Jeremiah wakes up, he'll find Christ the Savior is born. Then shepherds come in from the pastures. Finally, the wise men get there with their gifts."

Netty tucked the baby in a manger back into the box and set the angel back on the table. "Every night until Christmas, I'm going to read a bit of the story of Jesus. I'll tell Jeremiah stories of our family, and I'll move the pieces closer every day to the stable. Together, we'll take the journey all these people made toward the birth of our Savior."

"That's a beautiful tradition, Netty."

Roy was so caught in her story it crept into his senses like the aroma of the crackling fire. He looked at her in a room washed in moonlight and firelight. It tugged on his lonely heart until it was all too much to resist. He caught Netty's arms gently before she could turn to get the coffee and held her so she faced him.

Her green eyes glowed like jewels in the light, and he leaned forward and rested his forehead against hers.

He said what had been awakening in him. "This has been one of the best nights of my life, Netty."

It seemed unwise to care so much for a woman when he knew he had to leave. But he did care, and it was a pure waste of time to deny it.

"I lost my family in the same war that took yours. But my family stayed home from the fight. I was the only one who went. I came home to find our home burned, my family dead. There was nothing left."

"Oh, Roy, I'm so sorry." Her arms came around his shoulders in a hug.

"It's been so long since I've touched another person, at least touched them in gentleness."

"You can add to our celebrations, Roy. You can share your own family stories."

She rested her head on his shoulder and held him, holding on tight as if she could give back to him all that he'd lost. And maybe find some of what she'd lost, too. She'd had Jeremiah to hold and, for a long time, her ma. But from her iron grip, he suspected she'd been nearly as lonely as him.

"I don't know if I can bear to talk of my family. I left everything I knew because I couldn't stay. My heart wasn't in rebuilding without my family."

"I at least had Jeremiah, and at first Ma. You had no one?"

"I had . . . there was . . . I . . ." He cleared his throat. "I was promised to a woman—Lucinda. But when I told her I had to leave, that I wanted us to start again somewhere away from the painful memories, she refused and broke off our engagement. We were both from grand homes with big, prosperous farms. We'd grown up as neighbors, and it was natural as the sunrise that we'd marry and continue in the life we'd always known. But I had to leave. I had no heart for starting over back there. She found someone who hadn't lost so much. And she found him so fast I had to wonder if she'd been planning all along to break our engagement."

His words and feelings, which had been long buried since the war years—his grief—felt as though they were wrenched from deep inside his chest. "It didn't matter. I didn't have anything left for her. My heart was dead."

Roy stopped looking into the past and pulled back a bit from Netty. He brushed one of her escaping curls off her forehead. "Until tonight when I listened to you tell stories to your son. I haven't felt such pleasure in years."

And he leaned forward to kiss her, then stopped and knew himself for a fool. He had no business kissing her when everything about her was settled and permanent, and he had no plans to stay. It would be just like what happened with Lucinda. The pain of those memories shoved a few of those shields up around his heart.

He wondered what Netty would say if he asked her to ride off with him. The three of them could wander together.

He pulled free of her hug. At first her arms had been generous and healing, but now they felt like clinging vines.

"I'd best get on to my own place, Netty." He turned and plucked his coat off the nail by her door, then slipped it on. Grabbing his hat, he turned back and saw her watching him, silent, confused.

His hands slid nervously around the broad brim of his hat, turning it in circles as he forced himself to say what had to be said.

"Your stories were wonderful, and I appreciated hearing them. But I let the warmth of your family distract me from what I know to be right. I'll be moving on after we get the job done of rounding up a herd of cattle. I should never have held you as I did, and I'm sorry. It won't happen again."

He turned and dashed out into the night, running.

Same thing he'd been doing for a long, long time.

CHAPTER ELEVEN

Netty found she could cook a man breakfast, give him jerky and hardtack to pack in his saddle, pour him three cups of coffee, and never once look him in the eye.

Part embarrassment, part fury: both turned her face blazing red. She had fair skin, and she'd always been plagued by blushes. And she had a temper to go with her red hair. It all showed on her face.

Which she did her best not to let Roy see.

A few glances told her he was doing his best to ignore her just as much as she was trying to ignore him, so they never exchanged more than a terse, unavoidable word.

"More coffee?"

"Yes, please."

"I saw a few head of cattle up in that break to the northwest of the ranch. You might check there."

"Thanks, I will."

Jeremiah was full of talk about the nativity set, so his excited chatter filled in what would've been the most awkward meal ever shared in the history of the world.

To give him his due, Roy ate fast and ran out almost as fast as he'd done last night, the low-down, stinking polecat.

Netty kept up her mad long enough to give Roy's cabin a thorough cleaning. She picked through everything and found so much that would make her life easier. Ma had fabric and thread they'd forgotten about.

They'd missed so much, but they'd been busy surviving each day and hadn't thought much beyond food and sleep and loneliness.

Now Netty saw that part of their pain had come from all they lacked. Making their lives physically better would have been a comfort to them. She needed to remember this if she ever met someone who was grieving. She could help them through the loss by helping them to be kinder to themselves.

And that's when a light went on in what she now realized was a dusty, unused part of her brain. She was thinking of someone, someday, who was grieving. But she didn't have to wait. She knew someone right now.

Roy.

As easy as that, the anger she'd been nurturing, along with her embarrassment, faded. Roy had held her last night, and she'd believed he cared for her. And then he'd told her it was a mistake and he'd run.

But why was it a mistake? Only because he was a traveling man and he didn't intend to give up his wandering ways. But he'd said himself the plans of his growin' up years had been to help run his pa's farm. He'd only changed those plans because of grief.

And here she stood, a woman who'd just had a mighty bright idea about how to help a grieving soul.

She'd make him comfortable. By gum she was gonna make him so comfortable he never wanted to leave.

And then she thought of the job he'd taken over from her, rousting those crazy, wild longhorns from the broken hills and thickets.

Not much comfortable about that.

But Netty had been good at it when she had to do it by herself. Maybe she should go back to it and let Roy stay home and care for Jeremiah.

That'd probably set wrong with him.

Men!

Nope, he'd never stand for such an idea, so what could she do instead? All she could think about was how much he'd enjoyed last night.

The quiet talk, the time together, the Christmas memories, the fire, and good food. She'd give him more of that until he'd given up on his mourning and rejoined life.

A woman who'd rounded up and hogtied stray longhorns for a living surely oughta be able to hogtie herself a man.

She'd leave using an actual rope as a last resort.

"Jeremiah, I need to get back to our cabin and start a noon meal. Roy'll be in soon." She regretted now she'd given him jerky and hardtack. She hoped he didn't take a notion to stay out all day.

Because she was a fair hand at cooking. Ma had taught her how to make some fine meals. And Netty had found a few ingredients here in Ma's house that'd make a meal mighty tasty.

Jeremiah came out of her brothers' room, carrying what was about the last of what she could use in there. But she might come and sort through things again later. No telling what she might think of in her currently creative mood. Her brothers hadn't had much for clothes, and what they did have they'd mostly worn on their backs or carried in their saddlebags. But they'd left a few things behind.

As she and her son walked to the house, Netty pondered just how she could turn a few forgotten things of her brothers into the best Christmas present a lonely man ever had.

Her first smile of the day snuck onto her face as she lengthened her stride, eager to start cooking.

"What is that smell?"

Roy sniffed and blinked his eyes as he entered the cabin.

"I made prickly-pear pie." Netty opened the baking chamber of her iron stove and pulled out a bubbling, golden-brown pie. The sweet dried fruit of the prickly pear, with honey and the last of her cinnamon, filled the house with a rich aroma.

Then she set it to cool and dished up what looked like . . . "You fried a pork chop?"

"It's javelina, but yep, I reckon it's close enough to a pork chop."

She set the arrowroot on the table followed by a bowl of gravy she'd contrived from the pork-chop drippings.

There were fresh biscuits and a pot of honey and a dish of fresh-churned butter. She hadn't bothered with churning for a long time, either, but she'd found Ma's butter churn along with everything else.

Roy might not be speaking to her, but it was hard to tell. He sat down to that table like a hungry man, and how could he be anything else?

He was so busy chewing that, except for a few compliments and many sounds of pleasure as he ate, his mouth was too busy for talking.

And that was the way it should be. He needed to fill his belly to get the energy he was gonna burn off this afternoon.

If there was any awkwardness, Netty was going to get them both through it. "You brought in another calf with the cow on your heels."

Roy looked up as if the sound of normal conversation shocked him. "Uh . . . yep, I sort of did it by accident yesterday. I had a notion I could just start catching calves and forget about those nasty adult cattle. But, of course, I grabbed the calf and here came the mama. I felt like a rat that'd stepped into a baited trap. As if the cow had set her calf out there to catch me when I stopped."

Netty laughed, delighted that Roy had the energy to tell a joke.

"But Jeremiah's the one who said it was a good idea, and I should do it all the time. I was more careful today. I scouted around and made sure to find a calf that had wandered a little ways from its mother."

"That ain't easy," Netty said. "Because even if they do wander, the minute they get spooked they run for mama."

"Yep. But I did more sneaking this morning than regular riding. I caught this calf, and I wrapped my hand around its mouth so it couldn't bawl. I got a good head start before the cow even noticed I had it."

"I've been rounding up wild longhorns for years, and I've never thought of kidnapping calves," she said.

Roy snorted, but it was close to a laugh. "You make it sound like a crime, but there ain't no law against it."

"And no sheriff even if there was a law. And I'm sure not gonna go form a posse." Netty finished the last piece of her pork chop and stood to fetch the pie.

"I'll get another pair this afternoon," Roy said, sopping up gravy with his biscuit. "At this rate it won't take me until Christmas. I'm bringing in four cows a day."

Netty set a slice of pie in front of him, thinking fast. If he brought in two at a time and maybe twice or even three times a day, for heaven's sakes, he'd be done in a week. She had to keep him here. "You don't count a cow and calf as two do you?"

Roy halted a fork of pie about halfway to his mouth. "Uh, yep, I do count them as two."

Trying to pretend in just the right way, without overdoing it, Netty gave a tiny shrug—a tiny disappointed shrug—and said, "Oh, I was thinking it was just the cow that counted, but I suppose . . ."

She let her voice fade away and concentrated on her pie.

"Netty, it doesn't matter. I'll make sure the herd is a good size. If you want mostly all cows, then that's what I'll get, but you said you had about nine head of cattle and that number includes calves."

"Counting a pair as two, I just . . . the calves won't be ready for market anytime soon. No, your way is fine."

Roy nodded absently as if he agreed with her, but she could see him thinking, changing his plans a bit, realizing it was a bigger job than he'd thought. She had to keep the man around long enough to realize he couldn't live without them. Sure she'd taken care of men all her life, her and Ma together. But she didn't know much about bringing a wild one into the herd . . . so to speak. Yes, she'd brought in Ralph, but he'd wandered onto the property and just stayed. A stray dog came to mind.

"This was a delicious meal, Netty." Roy ate the last bit of his pie. "And don't you worry. I promise here and now that I won't leave until the job is done to your satisfaction. Now I'd better get on back to the roundup."

He ran a rough yet gentle hand over Jeremiah's hair, then smiled. "Thank you for such a good idea about catching calves."

Jeremiah grinned up at Roy and shrugged one shoulder as if the compliment embarrassed him yet pleased him at the same time. "And Netty, thank you for this feast. I'll go hunting again tomorrow if you can get by until then."

"Tomorrow would be just fine, Roy." He could plan all he wanted, but Netty was the one who had his life planned for tomorrow and every day . . . for the rest of his life.

He walked out, then turned and poked his head back in. "When I come back next time, if I can get another calf, I'm going to fire my gun from a distance so you can open the gate."

"That's a perfect idea," Netty said. "We'll be ready."

He settled his hat on his head and strode to his horse.

"As soon as I'm done here," she said to her son, nodding at the soapy water for dishes, "let's go finish cleaning Roy's cabin, then get started on dinner."

"Maybe we'll find more good stuff!" Jeremiah jumped up from the table and dashed out the door.

Netty finished washing dishes, then went after her eager son. As she walked to the old cabin, new memories of her family surfaced. Ma had always stayed in the house and did all the cooking and sewing and washing and cleaning. She realized she was doing the same thing now that Roy was here. Roy was even doing the barnyard chores of gathering eggs and milking and haying the cow. Netty hadn't given Ma enough credit. It was a lot of work to keep a home running and a family fed and clothed.

As a newlywed, Netty had followed in her mother's footsteps, and then in a little while, she found out Jeremiah was on the way. But still Ralph had left with her pa and brothers, and Netty had suddenly found herself doing all the chores the men usually did while Ma worked inside. Netty had toiled alongside Pa a lot as a youngster, so she knew the way of running a ranch in wild country.

When she'd taken over Pa's side of things, it seemed to Netty like she did all the work. She hadn't respected all Ma had done, not nearly enough. She said a prayer that she would bring the same hard work and skill to this job that Ma had.

And she prayed for Roy's safety because, even though he had a good bit of humor about his calf kidnapping, the man was in danger out there. Nobody knew that better than Netty because she'd done it.

While she cleaned and sorted, enjoying revisiting good moments from her childhood and telling Jeremiah old stories of his father and grandparents and uncles, she prayed for Roy.

A thought whispered in her mind.

Roy needs to share happy memories.

When she had a thought like that in the middle of prayer, she paid close attention. God didn't always speak with a fingertip that burned words into stone.

The clearest thought she had was that Roy wasn't wandering, he was running. If he could start sorting through some of his own memories, he might be able to stop running.

Tonight, after the best meal she could make, they'd spend time again with the nativity set, moving the kings along on their journey.

She'd share her memories and coax him to share his.

CHAPTER TWELVE

Roy needed their help with the gate every day—often more than once. The days passed, Christmas drew near, the herd grew, his horse's nerves held out, and Roy wrangled with death all day every day.

Netty kept making his cabin more like a home, and her home cooking was enough to make a man long for the end of the day. Every night, she moved her nativity set figures and told family stories.

The killer longhorns helped distract him from how strongly drawn he was to Netty, so that only made him work harder.

The only sour note—not counting the razor-sharp horns slashing at him, and that was a sour note—was that Netty kept nudging him to talk about his own family.

The memories made him so sad he didn't want to turn his thoughts there. She didn't badger or nag, she just gave him a chance every night while they talked.

He always changed the subject. As long as she accepted his silence on the past, they got along fine.

He rode in on Christmas Eve, excited to tell her he'd brought in the fiftieth cow. He'd done it. There were close to fifty calves, too, and enough bulls to keep the herd growing.

Roy had found bulls would sometimes jump in to fight for a kidnapped baby, so he bagged a few of them.

Now Netty had nearly one hundred cattle in her canyon, enough to support her son and herself from now on.

But before he could say a word to her when he walked in the door, he smelled something so good he could almost feel the burn of tears. Only *almost,* cuz men don't cry.

"You made cinnamon rolls." The delicious scent washed over him. His own ma had made cinnamon rolls every year on Christmas Eve, enough for a treat by the Christmas tree, and plenty left to go with Christmas breakfast. His ma had made the best cinnamon rolls in the whole county. To Roy they had tasted like love.

It woke up a hundred happy memories from his childhood.

"My ma used to make them a lot, and we always had them for Christmas breakfast."

The flooding memories distracted him for a minute . . . but then he saw Netty and forgot all about the rolls.

She had as powerful an effect on him as the scent of cinnamon rolls.

She wore a dress. He hadn't known she even owned one.

Her hair was pulled back on her head in a way that left her bright red curls dancing down the back of her head and all the way to her shoulder blades.

She paused from turning the cinnamon rolls out on a big platter and looked over her shoulder as he walked in. She smiled, and then her smile changed and her eyes flickered to his lips.

He wasn't sure what expression he had on his face. Hungry, most likely, or she read it as such. When what he really felt was a longing so deep he wondered if men *could* cry.

Because the longing he felt was for home. And at this moment, he felt like he had walked into his home.

Jeremiah had run out and tended the gate. But he'd run back into the house and was busy setting plates on the table. When he saw Roy, a smile bloomed on that boy's face that made a man forget all his aches and pains. And settled his longhorn-shaken nerves. With a clatter of plates and silverware, Jeremiah dropped what he carried on the table, then ran to throw his arms around Roy's legs much like he'd done since the first time Roy had brought in a kidnapped calf.

The happiness shining out of the boy's brown eyes made Roy wonder what this little one might want that Roy wouldn't get for him.

Which brought to mind Christmas presents, but Roy hadn't had time to think of such things yet. He hadn't had such thoughts in years.

"You brought in six cows today, Roy." Netty's words made him feel proud and strong.

"Now, Netty, just three cows." He smiled.

She blushed slightly. "I was teasing before about pairs not counting as two." She'd said this more than a few times. "Of course, they are two. I just wanted—"

"I forget to fetch eggs!" Jeremiah whirled toward the door and raced out.

The door slammed hard, and Netty gave it an exasperated glare, then went back to tending her cinnamon rolls.

They had a minute or two alone. Now was Roy's chance to tell her he'd gotten enough cows. Except he really wanted her to finish that sentence.

"You just wanted what, Netty?" He walked toward her like she was a magnet, and he was nothing but a pile of iron filings.

Frantically, she shook her head. "Not important. I've got a roast turkey in the oven. Jeremiah and I went hunting this afternoon, and I bagged a small one. It'll feed us today and tomorrow. To roast a bigger one, I'd've needed to start it cooking earlier."

Roy didn't like changing the subject. He was very interested in what Netty wanted. But he'd push it later. Right now he had little interest in annoying a woman who'd made cinnamon rolls and roasted a turkey.

"It all smells just like Christmas, Netty. The turkey, the bread, the cinnamon . . ."

"Yes, Ma had a fair supply of food, and I thought I'd found it all. But today when we were cleaning in there, I found a small tin of cinnamon. I used the last of mine a while back, so I couldn't have made the rolls without it. And I found her big roasting pan, and that's what gave me the idea for a turkey."

She was relaxed now. He'd let her talk. He'd pick his moment to push her about that broken off sentence when she said, "I just wanted—"

He'd make sure they got a chance to talk after Jeremiah went to bed tonight.

"Can I really have a cinnamon roll? You're not going to make me wait so I don't spoil my dinner?"

That put the smile back on her face and the pink of her cheeks turned a more normal shade. "You sure enough can have one right now."

She picked up the platter, turned from the stove, and set it on the table. Then she got him a fork and a small plate and added a cup of coffee. After serving him, she got herself a cinnamon roll. It looked like she couldn't wait either.

"You haven't had these in years, have you?" Roy asked.

"Nope. And I can tell by the way you're looking at them and smelling them that you've had them before, too—but not for a long time."

"My ma's were the best." Roy took a bite of the warm, sweet bread and hummed with pleasure. "I might be wrong about that. These are the most delicious things I've ever tasted."

Netty took a bite, too, and sighed with pleasure, then she laughed. "Me, too. I think it helps that we're hungry, and it's been so many years. I haven't had time or inclination to do any fancy cooking. Until now. We're eating better because, thanks to you, I've got some energy for the kitchen. Not to mention I keep thinking of how hard you're working, and I want to make a good meal for you."

"You're doing great." As he ate through the roll, Roy said, "So any more treasures at your ma's house?"

"I think I've finally found everything, but besides the cinnamon, the best things I found today were outside. Some scrub pines and a bittersweet vine. I brought back a tree." She pointed across the room. "We'll hang the bittersweet around the house."

Roy looked over his shoulder and realized he'd been smelling pine along with all the other aromas. It had added to the feeling of home at Christmastime.

"We've got the last moves for the nativity set. Hanging the vines around the tree will make things festive for Jeremiah tonight."

"For all of us." Roy smiled.

"Yes." She returned the happy look. "All of this will help him remember how special tonight is and understand the meaning of Christmas when he wakes up to see the baby Jesus in the manger."

Roy took a long pull on his coffee. The weather had been decent today, but not so warm the coffee didn't feel almost as good as it tasted.

They'd nearly finished their rolls when Jeremiah came back, carrying a basket very gently, with four eggs in it. "I found more, Mama. They're really laying."

"I must've scared them when I fried that chicken."

Roy laughed from his belly. Netty's eyes sparked, and she joined in.

Jeremiah giggled as he gently laid each egg in the bowl Netty kept by the kitchen window, already half full of eggs.

Netty served Jeremiah a cinnamon roll and gave him a glass of milk and they talked of Christmases past. For the first time, Roy's happy memories were so strong he couldn't keep them inside, and he added his stories to hers.

Chapter Thirteen

Netty moved the three kings to the mantle, still a foot back from the manger. The shepherds were close. Joseph and Mary now stood under the shelter of the wooden manger. The angel hung from a little hook at the manger's peak.

She told Jeremiah about the wise men coming from the Far East, but she didn't really know where the Far East was except it was far.

Then she sat on the floor by the flickering fireplace and listened to the wind gust outside and spoke of how the baby would be there come morning. Jeremiah snuggled close in her lap, settled, and full of good food and happiness.

Netty listened to the blowing wind and said to Roy, "I can feel it now. How unsafe it's been here for us."

Roy's forehead crinkled. He was thinking so hard it had to show on his face. He often did that. Netty was amazed at how quickly she had come to know his expressions and what they meant.

"Unsafe? Well, it's Texas, and add to that it's the desert and you have a herd of longhorns. There ain't much safe about it."

That made her smile. "All so true. I'll tell you the last time I felt safe, Roy."

She looked at Jeremiah, nestled in her arms, his head in the nook of her arm and her chest. His eyes looked heavy. Her story needed to be told, but not in front of her son. Jeremiah's eyes slid the rest of the way shut, and he fell asleep in her arms. He was so precious. His dark hair and eyes, so much like her father's black Irish coloring. Not much of Ralph in him, thank heaven.

"The last time I felt safe was when I'd been married about three months." She couldn't bring herself to look at Roy as she talked. "That was the day I told Ralph I was sure a child was on the way."

She thought all the way back to that day. "I never dreamed he wouldn't be happy. I never dreamed he'd act like I'd done something bad." She looked up at Roy, trying to read his expression.

"Doesn't a married man expect to have children?"

Netty shrugged, glanced down at Jeremiah, and said quietly, "One with any brains does."

She went on. "That was the day I realized he'd married me because Pa had a settled ranch, and with Pa and my brothers, he expected to have things easy, all laid out for him. But he always had it on his mind to move on. I-I knew he had dreams. He talked of gold strikes and nonsense like mansions and wearing a suit every day. A cook to prepare things, carriages with hired drivers, and I'd wear silk dresses. He'd talk of it, but it sounded like a man having fun dreaming, not someone serious about wanting more than our life.

"Then I told him we had a child on the way. I was so excited. He acted like I'd wrapped a halter around his head and staked him out with a picket pin. I could see a man who wanted a way out. Nothing has ever hurt more, except for Pa dying, but this went so deep. It was as if he'd robbed me of something precious, that first moment of joy at the coming of a child. He couldn't go back and make that right."

"But he didn't leave?"

"Not right away. But I always expected him to want to go. I realized I'd been prepared for the day he'd say we were heading west, and I'd have to follow my husband wherever he went. That's in the Bible, right? But I was afraid. After I'd told him about Jeremiah and he'd acted so badly, I wasn't so sure I'd go along if he left. I wasn't even so sure I'd be invited."

"And then came the war."

"But it wasn't the war taking the men away that stole my feeling of safety. It was knowing I was married to a man who didn't love me. Who didn't love the life he had." She looked down and ran one stroking hand over Jeremiah's soft curls. "Who didn't love his son."

There was a stretch of silence before Netty said, "And then you came and pulled me out of that pit. The feeling didn't happen that first day, although it began then. But now, for the first time in seven years, I feel safe." Her green eyes came up and nearly burned into his blues. "But I know it's not forever because you're a man on the move, too, Roy. You've got big dreams. That doesn't mean I can't enjoy the feeling as long as you're here."

Then she asked the question she'd hinted at many times. This time she wasn't going to let him dodge answering. "What made a man so settled on a nice farm start to wander? Was it as simple as losing your family and having your home torn apart? I reckon that's reason enough."

"It wasn't having my family and home torn apart. I wanted to leave, start over, but I didn't want to wander. I wanted to build what my father had built, just somewhere else. What's made me wander was having my heart torn apart by the woman who'd promised to marry me."

"You told me before that you were engaged."

For the first time since it happened, Roy realized just what that meant. Promises had been exchanged. Loyalty went with that promise. No vows, but sticking together through good times and bad started with that promise, didn't it? With the right woman it did.

Until now he couldn't think of Lucinda without pain and anger. He'd told himself it was the war and death and grief. But it was Lucinda's betrayal that'd changed him. He'd always blamed himself instead of her. Until now. Until he met Netty, who knew what it meant to have a man who couldn't stick to anything.

"Yep, to a woman named Lucinda."

Roy was sitting in a rocking chair in front of the fire while Netty cradled Jeremiah on the floor. He rose and said, "Let's get him to bed. He can dream of Christmas morning."

Netty let him take her son, then she stood and followed him.

They laid him down, and Netty tucked in his blankets, then they stood side-by-side in the doorway and looked at him.

"Let's go." Roy rested his hand on her shoulder. "I'll tell you why a faithless woman made me into a wanderer."

Netty nodded, then he slid his arm around her shoulder as she turned, and they walked together back to the fire. This time Netty headed for the other rocking chair rather than sitting on the floor, but Roy stopped her and turned her to face him.

He almost pulled her close. Kissing her was long overdue, but before he could, he had something to say.

Something a lot more important than what happened with Lucinda, but he had to start there.

"When I came home from the war, like I told you, everything was gone."

Nodding, Netty said, "Your family dead, your home burned, your land lost to you."

"I still wanted home, but not that home. I wanted to get away from all the old tensions left from the war. The West drew me. Many families were heading west. There were homesteads to be had, and I saw myself settled in a new land—with Lucinda and a new family. I was heartbroken over all I'd lost, but I still cherished the life I'd been raised in, and I wanted it for myself and my wife and children, just not there where the grief was so alive and painful."

Netty gripped his hands as if she'd never let go. She was exactly what Lucinda was not. He continued, "But Lucinda didn't want that. She didn't see a life in the wilderness as anything but back-breaking work."

Arching a brow, Netty added, "She had that right."

Roy laughed. "Yep, I reckon she did. But I didn't see it quite clearly then. I told you we were prosperous, but I see now that Lucinda's family was a bit more than prosperous. They lost everything in the war, too, but unlike my family, who'd all worked hard to prosper, Lucinda had been raised with servants, a housekeeper, and a cook. I hadn't realized just how cosseted she'd been. She had no interest in hard work to build a new life. She just wanted someone to hand it to her. And I had a neighbor who hadn't been wiped out who was able to do just that.

"Lucinda chose an easy life over me. I've never blamed her for that, but it's only since I've been here that I've realized she *is* to blame. She chose comfort over love, and I reckon that means she didn't really love me at all. She was a shallow woman who didn't stick through bad times, and I'm lucky she betrayed me before the wedding because she'd've likely done it after if things got hard for her. That woulda been a sight worse."

"So you're angry with her now? That still seems like she'd got a lot of a hold over you, Roy."

Shaking his head, Roy said, "I was angry, but only for a while. It was like the blame I felt myself and the grief of losing everything I loved were all twisted up in a knot inside. And once I got that knot untied, the anger rushed through me but is gone. And with that out of my thoughts, I've been able to think back, past all that hardship, to the joy of my childhood Christmases and the love of my parents."

Now Roy rested one open hand on her cheek. "And that's because of you, Netty."

"Me?"

"Yes, you. With your stories of the Christ Child and the journey to Bethlehem from all directions, and the memories of your family, and even the cinnamon rolls, I found that the knot of grief and blame was strangling all my love for you."

Netty gasped. Her eyes lit up fresh and evergreen like the tree behind them. Her pretty lips opened in surprise. "You love me?"

A smile bloomed on Roy's face as bright as the sunrise on that first Christmas morning. "Yes, I love you. You've helped me realize that I haven't been wandering, I've been searching. Searching for love. Searching for family. Searching for home. And I've found it all here with you."

"Oh, Roy, I love you, too." She flung her arms around his neck.

"You'll marry me, won't you, Netty? Just as soon as we can get to town to see a parson?"

She straightened away from him, nodding. "There's one in Los Combarse. We can ride in tomorrow. We'll have to push mighty hard, but I always made it to town and back in a day."

"Then we'll push hard and do it because I want our life together to start as soon as we can say our vows." Roy pulled her close and just held her. Held his future and his hopes and his home right here in his arms.

Netty held him tight. And he knew she always would.

"For better or worse, Netty, I promise to stick through it all. I haven't even told you I've got enough cattle. Your herd now has fifty cows. It's your Christmas present."

"Thank you, Roy. I wanted that herd so badly, but now it doesn't hold a candle to the gift of being in your arms."

Roy settled in beside her in their rockers. He planned to do some talking and tell her all about his family. He was suddenly bursting with memories he wanted to share with someone.

"Instead of longhorns for Christmas," he said, "I'm thrilled and honored to offer you my heart."

"And I give you mine right back."

Roy reached across from his rocker, and she gave him her hand. They sat together before the fire. He turned to look at the little group of figures in the nativity, together after their long journey, finally together, finally all in place as God declared it in the fullness of time.

Roy felt as if he'd taken that journey with them and reached a destination blessed by God. He'd found home and love—the best Christmas present a man could ever have.

Connie's Christmas Prayer

ANNA SCHMIDT

The sparrow hath found an house, and the swallow a nest for herself, where she may lay her young.

    —*Psalm 84:3*

CHAPTER ONE

Arizona Territory
December 1868

Constance Lancaster wondered if she might have to spend the rest of her life serving rough-looking cowhands and prospectors in the small café her mother owned. But Constance—known to her friends as Connie—longed for the life she had left behind in St. Louis—the good times the family had shared, her schoolmates with whom she had confided her hopes and dreams, and the hustle and bustle of life there.

Compared to St. Louis, Whitman Falls in the Arizona Territory was positively primitive. She missed the house they had lived in—an impressive three-story dwelling that had been the envy of all her friends. She missed the lavish parties her parents had given several times a year—especially the Christmas ball.

That life had come to an end when her father died suddenly, and a parade of angry men knocked at the door of the large house, demanding to be repaid for loans they had made to him to keep his business afloat. Distraught and humiliated, her mother had sold everything to pay off the debts. But her breaking point came when friends and neighbors turned away. Some even crossed the street to avoid contact.

After that Connie and her mother had joined a wagon train headed west to California. Lettie Lancaster had promised her daughter a new and better life, but when they reached Arizona, Lettie admitted she could go no farther. The wagon and supplies had used up the last of their money, and she and Connie were running out of food.

The other travelers on the wagon train had stayed a few days at Fort Lowell while the wagons were repaired and the livestock rested. The wife of the fort's commander had been the one to suggest that Lettie would be the perfect candidate to take over a small café in the growing cow town of Whitman Falls. The owners had recently packed up and headed back east and abandoned the place.

"I can cook," her mother had muttered, and that seemed to have settled the matter. Now with Christmas only a few weeks away and the start of a new year a week after that, Connie could see nothing but more work and boredom in her future. She had to find a way out of this town. Perhaps if her mother remarried, then there would be nothing to stop Connie from returning to St. Louis. Her friends had written her—at least one had—and she was fairly certain she would find a welcome there.

With a sigh, she turned her attention back to clearing the counter where three cowhands had just finished their supper. Another customer sat alone at the table in the back corner, his black Stetson set low over his forehead, shading his eyes. That was another problem with life on the frontier—not a decent-looking man to be found. And certainly not one that ever seemed to have so much as cracked the spine of a book. Her mother, an educated woman who loved poetry and art, had passed on her passion for reading to Connie.

The men at the counter spoke in low voices, eyeing her from time to time, but limiting any actual communication to raising their coffee mugs to request a refill. They all appeared to be the right age for her mother, but out here life took a toll on people—these men might be too young. And not one of them looked like someone who might read a poem or admire a painting.

Still lost in her revelry, she picked up the coffeepot, and as she turned to pour, her apron pocket caught on a nail. The coffee sloshed onto her hand, and she cried out in pain.

The three men at the counter stared but did not move. Only the cowboy who'd been sitting alone came to her aid.

"Let's get something to cover that," he said, and in a matter of seconds he relieved her of the coffeepot, took a gentle hold on her injured hand, and reached for the pan of congealed bacon drippings her mother kept next to the stove. With slender, surprisingly clean fingers, he spread the grease over the burn.

"Want me to go for the doc?" one of the men at the counter asked.

"Of course not," Connie replied, snatching her hand away and smoothing out the glob of grease. "Here." She tossed the cowboy a flour sack towel to wipe his hands on. "Thank you," she added.

To her surprise, the man began tearing the sack into strips. "Best wrap that," he said, and before she could react, he had once again taken hold of her wrist and wound the soft cotton fabric around the wound. In the dimly lit interior of the cafe, she continued to focus on his hands— tanned to a deep golden brown that reminded her of caramels. At the same time, she realized that unlike most of the men who frequented her mother's establishment, this man smelled nice—a mix of soap and the lime aftershave the barber down the street slapped onto his customers' cheeks.

"I haven't seen you in here before," she said, knowing full well that her mother would be horrified that she would engage a total stranger in conversation. Judging by the smoothness of his clean-shaven jaw, he appeared to be too young for her mother, but perhaps he had a friend— or a father.

She saw the corner of his mouth quirk into a semblance of a smile, but she still could not fully see his face because of the hat—a hat she saw now was made of a soft felt with a thin braided leather band around the crown and accented with a small, bright red feather. He wore a blue homespun shirt with no collar and black wool trousers. He'd left his outer coat—a heavy, tanned, sheepskin jacket—on the chair. "Are you passing through or . . ."

The other three men leaned closer, their curiosity matching hers.

"No, ma'am." He tied off the ends of the fabric and released her. At the same time, he tipped back his hat and looked directly at her for the first time. "I plan to settle here—if that suits you." The light from the lantern hung over the counter showed that his eyes were a startling shade of blue-green, deep-set beneath the ridge of his forehead, and eyebrows that arched with his last comment.

Connie felt her cheeks grow hot, and she saw the three customers exchange grins and nudge each other with their elbows. "Go or stay," she said with all the nonchalance she could muster. "I can't think why my opinion would matter." She retrieved the coffeepot and refilled the mugs.

"Oh, it matters," she heard him murmur as he returned to his place in the corner.

He put his coat on and gathered his dishes—the ones Connie's mother had served his supper on when Connie had been late coming from her lessons with Reverend Cantor. He carried the dishes to the counter and set them down, along with a single gold coin. Connie and the three men stared at the coin while he tipped his hat and headed for the door.

"Wait! Sir, this is too much, and I haven't change for . . ."

He paused, his hand on the doorknob. "Well, I wasn't expecting change," he said, "but not wanting to offend you, how about I come back tomorrow for supper and then we can call it even?"

Connie was pretty sure the coin would pay for a week's worth of suppers. "Tomorrow and three days more," she bargained.

She saw the full flower of his smile. "Won't say no to four well-cooked meals, Miss. See you tomorrow." He paused and looked back at the men at the counter. "If any of you are looking for work, I'll be needing some help out on my ranch."

The three cowhands glanced at each other, slapped down some coins—not gold—as they gulped down the last of their coffee and followed him outside.

It had started to snow, and as he and the others passed by the window, Connie saw him turn up the collar of his coat against the cold north wind. As she cradled her injured hand, she realized she didn't know his name.

Isaac Porterfield had learned to make decisions based on the feeling he got for a particular situation. That's how he had decided to volunteer for the Union Army and, once the War Between the States finally ended, it was how he had decided to head West and work as a scout, leading wagon trains of settlers across the Plains. On one of those trips, he'd ended up in Colorado helping a friend mine for silver. The two of them had made a good deal of profit. His friend had married and now owned most of the real estate in the town of Roaring Gulch. He'd wanted Isaac to partner with him, but sitting inside an office juggling bank accounts and such was not Isaac's idea of the life he wanted.

So Isaac had taken his cut of the profits, converted it to gold, and headed south into Arizona Territory where he had been immediately captured by the unexpected beauty of the region's grasslands and open range—a surprise because he had been told this was barren desert country. Even with everything covered in an early snow that had struck this high country in October, he could see the splendor of the land, could imagine building a home there, starting a ranch, raising a family.

And so he had taken ownership of several hundred acres of prime land that included a barn, a one-room cottage, and other outbuildings outside of Whitman Falls near Fort Lowell—the military base for a regimen of soldiers charged with keeping the peace between the landowners and what was left of the native population. As a former soldier, he was welcomed at the fort and had spent most of his time there since coming to the area—until today.

Building a life went beyond hiring dependable help, putting up a house, and becoming part of the community. It meant finding the right woman to share his life and a future with. His first idea had been to attend church services on Sunday in the hopes of meeting people and starting his search for that woman, but he was not a patient man, and Sunday was still four days away. Surely, there was no harm in spending some time in town, getting to know the locals. For one thing, having managed the large ranch on his own for weeks now, he needed to find some cowboys willing to work for him.

But when he rode into town, the weather had been against him. A cold north wind and the threat of more snow had left the streets deserted. The mercantile had been empty of customers other than a couple of old coots warming themselves by the potbelly stove. Neither the hotel nor the local saloon seemed to hold any promise. Earl Gladstone, the banker, had mentioned the café, and so, hungry and discouraged, he had decided to get a solid meal before riding back to the fort.

The woman who served him a plate of beef stew with a side of cornbread and a mug of black coffee was old enough to be his mother, or at least his elder sister. She was friendly, but distracted and clearly overworked. She kept glancing toward the door, and when he had asked if she was expecting someone, she huffed and replied, "My daughter, Constance. I was expecting her an hour ago, but she's probably got her nose buried in some book and forgotten the time. I want her to finish her schooling. I made arrangements for her to sit for lessons with Reverend Cantor between doing her chores and working here. But she's a dreamer, that one—not like my others. 'Course she's the only one I've got with me now. The others are all out on their own. You got any children, Mister?"

"Not yet."

"My advice? Pray for boys. A girl will drive you to an early grave." And with that, she had turned back to greet three cowhands entering the café and bringing with them the cold air and a flurry of snow.

A few minutes later when he heard the door open a second time, followed by a flood of apologies from the young woman who entered, he knew this must be the daughter. He knew something else as well. He knew that seeing her with her windswept hair the color of an Arizona sunset, he was struck just as he had been by the land and the dream of a ranch and a family of his own. Seeing her, he felt like he'd found the right woman to make that dream a reality. Of course, he could buy the land—already had. And he could buy enough stock to get started on a herd. He could buy what he needed to make do with the small cottage already on the land while he built a proper home.

But he couldn't buy her.

And so he had sat in the corner, finishing his meal and thinking how best to approach her without scaring her off. He had watched her go about her work, trying without much success to make amends for her tardiness. After a while, the mother had untied her apron, put on her coat and hat, and announced she was going home.

"You close up at seven, Connie—and not a minute earlier, do you understand? Folks have got to know we're open the hours we say we are." The older woman had tapped on the painted notations on the glass door—OPEN 7 A.M. —7 P.M. MONDAY—SATURDAY.

The girl rolled her eyes as she closed the door behind her mother. After checking to be sure the men at the counter had no requests, she lifted the coffeepot in Isaac's direction to see if he wanted a refill—an offer he waved off. She immediately pulled out a book that she'd apparently hidden in her cloak and took a position on a high stool near the lantern. She opened the volume to a page she'd marked with a piece of ribbon.

He watched her as he continued to enjoy his supper. The portions were generous and the food tasty. It was the kind of Midwestern fare he'd grown up eating, and although he was fond of the Mexican influence on much of the food served throughout the Southwest, now and again there was something to be said for a bowl of beef stew—the meat tender from slow cooking and the potatoes and carrots plentiful.

Her mother had called her "Constance"—*constant and true*. Isaac smiled at the irony that she had arrived late to relieve her mother, so not exactly constant. Maybe more true to those dreams her mother had mentioned. He wondered what it was she wanted—what she longed for.

Once she had removed her coat, tied on her apron, and twisted her hair into a no-nonsense bun at the nape of her neck, he realized that she was older than he'd first thought—eighteen or nineteen, if he was any judge. Most females on reaching that age had marriage and family in mind. He wondered if Constance would fit that mold. Her mama had called her a dreamer, and the way she was engrossed in whatever she was reading, Isaac felt inclined to agree.

He'd turned his attention to the increasing snowfall outside the window when he heard her cry out. He saw the coffeepot she held teetering as she stared at her hand and bit her lip.

"My fault," she managed when the cowhand apologized.

Isaac stepped behind the counter and relieved her of the pot while taking hold of her wrist and finding the bacon fat. Her skin had already turned red in spots where the coffee had splattered. He'd barely had time to notice that her skin was soft as a well-tanned piece of leather when she snatched it free of his hold and tossed him a flour sack. Instead of wiping the grease from his fingers, he tore the sack into strips and once again took hold of her hand, wrapping the soft cloth around it. He'd liked the way her hand fit in his. He also liked the way her hair smelled of lavender and shone in the lamplight.

But choosing a wife wasn't something a man did based on a feeling. It wasn't the same as choosing a place to settle because in choosing a location, one could always move on. Marriage was a commitment for life. He'd searched for flaws. But when she spoke, her voice came deep—husky. She seemed interested in him—asking his plans for passing through or staying on. Surely that was a good omen.

When Isaac tried to flirt with her a bit, she turned away with a shrug. "Go or stay," she'd said as if she could not be less interested. On the other hand, when he put the dishes on the counter along with that gold coin—that got her attention—not to mention the attention of the other three customers.

Isaac knew instantly that he'd made a mistake. He'd been showing off—wanting to impress on her the fact that he was a man of means. But in a place like Whitman Falls, the law was a sometimes thing. If those three cowboys decided to ambush him, there wouldn't be much he could do about it. He'd kept an eye on them even as he made the bargain with Constance to return for the next four evenings. Once again, he made a decision based on nothing more than a gut feeling. He took a chance and offered the three cowboys work on his ranch if they were interested—and they were.

Outside, the snow started to accumulate in windblown piles around the rough, wooden boardwalk that ran the length of the town from the saloon at one end to the café at the other. He made arrangements for the three cowhands to come to the ranch the following day, then unhitched his horse—a black stallion he'd bought shortly after coming to Arizona—brushed snow from the saddle, and rode slowly out of town. He used the time it took to get from town to the fort—over an hour—to further indulge his dreams of a large working cattle ranch, a rambling adobe house, his children playing in the courtyard, and his beautiful wife running to welcome him home. A man could be content with such a life.

CHAPTER TWO

The stranger was already seated at the table in the back of the café when Connie arrived the following afternoon. Once again, Reverend Cantor had kept her late for her lessons, chastising her for her inattentiveness.

"Sorry, Pastor. Mama's gonna worry if I don't get there soon," she called as she rushed out the door, cradling her books against her chest. Her heavy silk scarf—a treasure from her days in St. Louis—and open coat billowed behind her as she ran down the town's main street.

She arrived at the café red-cheeked and out of breath. "Sorry, Mama," she managed even as she glanced toward the table in back.

"Look at you," her mother said in a hushed but no less exasperated tone. "Go in back and fix your hair, then see if Mr. Porterfield requires any more cornbread or coffee."

Mr. Porterfield. Since he was the only customer in the place, there was little question who her mother meant. In the cramped area that served as the kitchen, Connie stood on tiptoe to get a view of her face in the piece of broken mirror they had hung above the shelves holding the crockery. Hairpins stuck out like the quills of a porcupine. Quickly, she collected them and stuck them between her lips as she gathered her long thick mass of hair—red and unruly—and twisted it firmly into a rope that she wound around her hand and then stabbed with the pins to hold it secure. She pulled a bibbed apron made from flour sacks over her head and tied the sash in back before returning to the counter to pick up the coffeepot, using her other hand.

"More coffee, Mr. Porterfield?"

He looked up from a book he'd been reading, and she saw he wore a pair of wire-rimmed eyeglasses. For some reason, that made her smile. And when he smiled in return, she felt the coffeepot wobble dangerously.

"Careful there," he said as he reached up and steadied her by taking a grip on her forearm. "Can't have you risking a burn on your one good hand, can we now?" He held up his mug. "Just half."

Speak, she ordered herself as she poured the coffee. "What are you reading?"

He glanced at the book as if seeing it for the first time. "This? It's a book about cattle ranching." He pushed the glasses back onto the bridge of his nose. "Probably not as interesting as the book you were so engrossed in yesterday."

She shrugged and then, aware that her mother watched from the counter, she glanced at his plate—wiped clean of any trace of his supper. "There's pie," she said and once again was rewarded by his smile.

"Well now, that's an offer that would be hard to refuse, Miss Lancaster."

"It's Constance—Connie," she said softly, embarrassed by his formality and, at the same time, wondering if he was teasing her.

He stuck out his hand the way men did when introduced to someone. "Pleased to make your acquaintance, Constance. I am Isaac Porterfield, and I hope you don't mind if I call you by your given name? Connie is a name for a girl, not a grown woman."

Outside, the snow had started to fall again. Her mother edged closer on the pretense of wiping the window ledge where the cold met the heat of the café, leaving rivulets of water on the window and its frame. But Connie knew that her real purpose was to better hear their conversation. "Constance, there are dishes to be dried and put away. Mr. Porterfield, will you have more cornbread?"

"I'd like that, ma'am, but your daughter mentioned pie. Given the choice . . ." He grinned up at Mrs. Lancaster who ducked her head in a girlish way and smiled back at him.

"Pie it is then." She turned to go and fill the order but stopped when her daughter lingered. "Constance, chores," she said and waited until Constance preceded her to the kitchen before picking up Isaac's dishes and following her.

Isaac—a good biblical name, Connie thought. Surely that boded well for the man. And so what if he was younger than her mother? "Mr. Porterfield seems to like your cookin', Mama," she ventured.

"Don't pretend you don't know that it's you these cowboys come in to see, Missy. Although I will admit that Mr. Porterfield is the first I've seen that I would give one minute's second look to." She cut the pie into eight even slices and scooped one onto a saucer. "I will also own to bein' relieved. From what I've been able to gather from Mr. Gladstone over at the bank and Mr. McNew at the mercantile, he's come to stay. Not like the others who are here for a season and then move on. He's bought a large parcel of land and aims to settle there. You could do worse."

"So could you," Connie said before she could censor herself.

Her mother laughed as she dropped the pie knife into the soapy dishwater filling the pan in the sink. "Me? Don't talk foolishness. That man is young enough to be my . . . little brother."

"And he's old enough . . ." Connie started to reply, but both she and her mother froze when Isaac stepped around the doorway, holding the coffeepot in one hand and two mugs in the other.

"Didn't mean to eavesdrop, ladies," he said. "I was just thinking with the weather and all that it's unlikely you'll have more customers this evening, and maybe we could enjoy a slice of that pie and some coffee together. Today's my birthday. I just turned twenty-five." He headed back to his table, the heels of his leather boots clicking on the bare wooden floor.

Over warm apple-cinnamon pie and coffee, Connie's mother questioned Isaac relentlessly. Where was he from? *Originally, the western hills of Pennsylvania.* Were his folks still back there? *Yes, along with his two brothers and three sisters.* How did he end up in Whitman Falls? *Long story, ma'am.* And the most mortifying question of all to Connie, *Why hadn't he married?*

He answered every question directly, even giving them what he called the short version of how he had come to settle in Arizona, with no sign of annoyance at Lettie's prying right up to that last question.

"Why haven't I married?" Isaac repeated as if needing to be sure he understood. He leaned back in his chair, his mug of coffee in hand. He took a swallow and looked first at Connie's mother and then allowed his gaze to shift to Connie. "I guess the short answer is that until now I haven't found the right woman."

There it was again—the reference to her as an adult—a woman, not a girl.

"And now?" Lettie Lancaster pressed.

"Well now, ma'am, the thing is that marriage takes two, and just because I'm of a mind to move in that direction doesn't mean the lady in question is." He looked over at Connie and smiled. She felt heat rush to her face.

"Or her mother, young man." Both Connie and Isaac shifted their focus to Mrs. Lancaster. "If you wish to court my daughter, Mr. Porterfield, then in the absence of her father, I expect to have my say in the matter."

"Mama, please," Connie whispered, unsure if she was pleading with her mother to stop embarrassing her or to agree to this ridiculous idea. But it really didn't matter because her mother and Isaac Porterfield continued to talk as if she were not there.

"That goes without saying, Mrs. Lancaster. Let me make my intentions clear." He proceeded to present his case, pointing out that the land he had purchased already had a small house that would do until he could build something more substantial. Her mother nodded approvingly.

Connie seethed.

He spoke of the importance of family—stating that, should they marry, Constance's mother would always have a place in the home as well. Her mother smiled.

Connie stood.

They looked up at her.

"Mother, if I could please speak to you in the kitchen?" She did not wait to see if her mother followed, but gathered the pie saucers and forks and walked away.

"That was rude," her mother whispered when they were alone.

"The days of arranged marriages are in the past, Mama, and yet the two of you were planning my life without allowing me any say," Connie countered. "How is *that* not rude?"

"I thought you were drawn to the man. You certainly went on enough about him last night when you were explaining how you burned your hand. I was just making sure that—"

"He is a nice man, but Mama, he is planning a life *here*. What about what I want? What about St. Louis and my friends?"

"Your friends? You mean all those who have written to you since we left? I must have missed seeing so many letters going back and forth."

"Daphne wrote . . . twice." *And then not again in spite of two more letters I sent her.* Connie saw the folly of that argument. "The fact is that I am nearly nineteen, Mama, and surely have the right—"

Her mother's laughter interrupted, laced with bitterness rather than humor. "You wish to discuss rights? Very well. Perhaps you might explain what gave your father the right to take everything we had and fritter it away? What gave those businessmen he owed money to the right to put us out of house and home without compassion? And where do you get the *right* to question me when all I have done for the last year is try and make a decent life for you?" Her lower lip quivered with emotion even as her weary eyes filled with tears she was too proud to let fall.

Humbled by her mother's distress, Connie hugged her and felt the tears release and dampen the shoulder of her dress. Outside the doorway, Isaac cleared his throat. When Connie looked at him, he frowned.

"I didn't mean . . . that is, if you would agree to let me—"

"You should go, Mr. Porterfield," Connie interrupted. To her relief, he nodded, collected his hat and coat from the hook by the door, and left.

CHAPTER THREE

Isaac avoided the café for the next two evenings. It irked Connie that she kept watch for him, and there was no denying the way her heart raced when she saw him exit the bank across the street late Friday afternoon.

Then she found a spot near the window where he wouldn't see her and watched as he entered the mercantile. He left there fifteen minutes later with two small packages wrapped in brown paper and tied with string. He placed them in one of the saddlebags that straddled his horse's hindquarters and glanced once at the café, stared for a long moment, and then mounted his horse and rode out of town.

On Sundays, the café was closed, and Connie attended church with her mother. They sat in the next to last row, mostly because Lettie was intimidated by other women who arrived with their husbands and families and chattered on about the latest meeting of the ladies' auxiliary—an organization they had invited Connie and her to join. But because of the need to keep the café open until seven to serve customers working late in their shops or cowhands passing through town on their way to the next job, her mother had politely declined.

Still, Connie could see how her mother longed for the companionship of the other women. Back in St. Louis, Lettie had been involved in many church and community activities and had been held in high esteem by her friends and neighbors. Here, she was just the woman from the wagon train who had stayed on to take over the café.

"Mama, why don't you plan to attend the meeting this coming week?" Connie whispered as they waited for everyone to settle in and the service to begin. "I can manage for one evening on my own. They'll be planning the Christmas Eve reception, and you were always so good at things like that back in St. Louis."

Connie saw that her suggestion had surprised—and pleased—her mother. She felt as if she had given her a gift. A Scripture flashed through her mind: *'tis better to give than receive.* "I mean it, Mama. You've been so busy trying to make sure I was all right that you've not even thought of what you might want. It's time you did something you enjoy."

Before her mother could protest, Connie leaned forward and tapped Mrs. Gladstone—the banker's wife and president of the auxiliary—on the shoulder. "Forgive me, Mrs. Gladstone," she said, "but I overheard you and the other ladies speaking of the need for help with the Christmas Eve reception."

"Oh, Connie dear, that would indeed be a godsend. We are so very short-handed this year."

"Mama was quite involved in planning such events when we lived in St. Louis."

Mrs. Gladstone turned so that she could see Lettie, who sat with her hands folded in her lap and her face flaming red with embarrassment. "If you could find some time, Mrs. Lancaster," the banker's wife whispered. "Let's talk more after the service."

Hattie Olinger had just pumped the organ to life and played the prelude that indicated the beginning of the service. Reverend Cantor took his place behind the pulpit and waited for all to stand and join in the opening hymn. A couple of latecomers hurried to take their seats, and instinctively, Connie moved closer to her mother as someone stepped into their row. She couldn't have been more surprised when she glanced up with a welcoming smile and the offer to share her hymnal and saw Isaac Porterfield grinning down at her.

———

Isaac had never been much of a churchgoing man. For the last several years, his lifestyle hadn't put him in the vicinity of too many churches, and he tended to do his praying under the stars or during the battles he'd fought during the war. Still, he considered himself a deeply religious man. Now that he was settling down—building a ranch, looking to marry and start a family—it seemed that regular churchgoing was important for a life like that. Of course, the fact that he was pretty sure Constance Lancaster would be there with her mother made getting up before dawn to tend the stock and make the ride into town a lot more palatable.

Now, as he slid into the pew next to Connie and took hold of the hymnal she offered before she had a chance to change her mind, he wondered if it was Divine Providence that had led him to this woman. He knew next to nothing about her, but the way she had stood up for herself that night in the café told him a great deal. This was a woman who knew what she wanted and wasn't afraid to say so. Of course, at the moment what she wanted was to head back to St. Louis, but with time he felt pretty sure he could persuade her otherwise. She was smart and willful, and those were qualities that would serve her well on the frontier.

She also had a fine singing voice, he realized, and that made him smile.

"Stop that," she muttered as the music ended, and he put the hymnal in the rack of the pew in front of them and sat.

"Stop what?" he whispered as the congregation settled in for the Scripture reading.

"Smiling like that. People will talk."

As far as he could see, not another soul glanced their way, and since they were seated near the back of the church, most folks had their backs to them. "Sorry," he whispered. "Just can't seem to help it when you're around."

Reverend Cantor cleared his throat and began to read the story of Mary and Joseph going to Bethlehem. He stopped the reading short of the actual birth of Jesus, but took it to the point of kings being told of the impending arrival. Constance seemed totally engaged in the story, as if she were hearing it for the first time. Watching her features come alive with the telling of it, Isaac had to admit that he'd seldom really listened to the timeless words. They had become rote to him as they had for so many others who'd heard the same passage year after year since childhood, but Constance truly heard the words and appeared to understand the miracle they foretold.

And in that moment, he clearly saw a future with her—one filled with laughter and love and adventure. There was something in her face, in the way she leaned forward as if to come closer to the words and story, that told him this was a woman drawn to adventure.

As the organist pounded out the postlude, Isaac stepped into the aisle and allowed Constance and her mother to precede him from the church. Outside, Mrs. Lancaster waited for him to shake hands with the preacher and then motioned him forward. Her daughter was engaged in conversation with a trio of young women who seemed quite excited about something.

"Good day to you, Mrs. Lancaster," Isaac said by way of greeting.

"How interested are you in getting better acquainted with my daughter, Mr. Porterfield?"

Isaac smiled. He liked this woman. When she had something on her mind, she had no patience with small talk. "Quite interested," he replied. "Is that agreeable with you?"

She waved a dismissive hand as if his question needed no response. "Then may I suggest that you make sure you attend tonight's sleigh ride and caroling party? The young women talking to Constance are the organizers, and I am quite sure there will be at least three cowhands along as well."

"Perhaps one of those cowhands has his eye on your daughter," Isaac suggested.

"She won't pay them any mind."

"But you think if I were there—"

"Stop fishing for compliments, young man. My daughter is miserable. She sees no future for herself here and believes she would be happier if she could return to St. Louis. The truth is that—like me—she has been abandoned by every friend she ever had there. She needs to find her happiness here."

"I'll do my best," he replied, fighting a losing battle with a smile. He saw Constance glance their way and frown. He nodded to Mrs. Lancaster and moved away. Mrs. Lancaster pursed her lips and cocked her head in her daughter's direction, sending the clear message that there was no time like the present for him to take action. But Isaac would handle things his way.

Connie was reluctant to go on the sleigh ride, but Eliza McNew, whose parents ran the dry goods store across from the café, had finally persuaded her. "Come on, Connie, it will be such fun. And what else have you got to do tonight?"

Eliza had a point. She could spend another long evening sitting across from her mother in the small parlor of the house they occupied behind the café, or she could spend time with people her own age, talking and laughing and momentarily forgetting how much she missed the Christmases she had known back in St. Louis.

"All right, I'll go." She sighed.

Eliza laughed. "Oh, Connie, if you could see your face. You look as if I'm dragging you off to the gallows rather than inviting you to an evening of fun—and, who knows? —perhaps romance? See those cowboys over there? Every one of them has agreed to come tonight."

Connie blushed as she glanced toward a group of young men. Her gaze settled on Isaac Porterfield, who happened to be walking past them. She so wanted to ask Eliza if Isaac would be among that group, but she refused to let anyone see that the tall, broad-shouldered, best-looking man she'd ever seen had caught her eye.

"I have to go," she said. "Mama's waiting."

"Dress warm," Eliza called as she hurried away.

Because she had lost track of time helping her mother cut the dried fruit for the fruitcake they were preparing for the church's Christmas Eve reception, Connie arrived as Eliza and the others were already crowded together on the sleigh's wooden benches. The driver had the reins in hand.

"Wait. I'm coming," she shouted as she ran toward the church, her scarf trailing behind her in a streak of scarlet against the white of the snow. As she got closer, she saw that several others had apparently decided the sleigh ride and caroling were a good idea. The sleigh was jammed with people.

"Sit up front," Eliza said. "There's room by the driver, and we still have to stop for Lucille."

With no other choice, Connie hurried forward and looked up straight into the eyes of Isaac Porterfield. "Welcome aboard, Miss Lancaster. Or would it be all right to call you Constance?" He offered her his hand.

Connie glanced back at Eliza who grinned and shrugged before settling back into her seat between two of the cowboys Connie had seen in the churchyard. "It's my name," she grumbled, "so I suppose so."

"Give me your hand, Constance," Isaac said softly.

And because it sounded like there just might be a double meaning to those words, Connie ignored him and pulled herself up and onto the seat, settling as far as possible from him. The sleigh was really a buckboard on runners, the team of horses clearly anxious to be on their way. They snorted and pawed the ground and tossed their massive heads, setting off the jingle of the bells that decorated their harnesses.

"Everybody back there ready to go?" Isaac shouted and was answered with a chorus of agreement. "Not exactly a one-horse, open sleigh, but let's make do, shall we?"

The others all laughed, and someone started singing the tune made popular years earlier as a song to celebrate Thanksgiving.

Dashing through the snow . . .

As they belted out the chorus and moved away from the cluster of buildings in town to the countryside, their voices rang out on the cold, snowy night air. Connie noticed that no one sang with more gusto than Isaac. To her consternation, his enthusiastic—if slightly off-key—rendition warmed her heart.

To her surprise, caroling in Arizona was nothing like caroling back in St. Louis. There, they went house to house and often enjoyed a treat of hot chocolate or cider with the family before moving on to the next. Here, things were different.

Just outside of town, Isaac pulled the sleigh to a stop at the home of the Baxter family, owners of the livery stable. Their daughter, Lucille, was younger than the other girls Connie had gotten to know. She was also heavier and stronger.

"Scoot over." She scrambled aboard the sleigh. The sheer force of her bulk forced Connie to move close enough to Isaac that their shoulders touched. "I heard you all comin'," she said, including the others as she settled herself onto a good half of the seat.

Isaac snapped the reins and the team picked their way through the snow.

"How about "Silent Night"? Lucille might be younger, but she had no problem taking charge.

"Seems appropriate," Eliza agreed. "Connie, you start us off. You have the best voice of the bunch of us."

Connie was pleased by the compliment—and doubly so when she heard Isaac murmur, "I agree."

"Maybe we should save our voices until we reach the first house . . . or ranch," she suggested. The night air was raw and moist and ripe for causing throats to close and voices raised in song to falter.

"Oh, we don't go house to house," Lucille replied. "I reckon that would take us all night, the ranches being so far apart and all. We just ride and sing."

"But the point is—" Connie started to protest.

"The point—as I understand it—is that whoever is in range hears us," Isaac explained. "More often than not, it's a bunch of lonesome cowboys watching the herd or soldiers on patrol trying to stay warm and awake through their shift."

Behind them, the others talked and laughed. Next to her, Lucille let out a heavy sigh as she cast longing looks toward the back. On her left, Isaac started to hum the opening notes.

" . . . holy night," Connie sang softly and then, turning to look at the others, raised her voice. "All is calm . . ."

Conversation ceased as everyone joined in. " . . . all is bright."

And it was—so very bright. She could not recall a night that had been more perfect or a sky so filled with stars. Continuing to sing, she tipped her head back, raising her face to the heavens and savoring the sheer magnitude of her surroundings. And for an instant, she felt something she had not felt since leaving St. Louis—she felt, if not happy, at least content.

They sang all the verses to the beloved carol and then launched immediately into "The First Noel," followed by "O Come All Ye Faithful." The sound ricocheted around the open land, bouncing off buttes and mesas as they glided along. After a while, Connie noticed one or two singers had dropped out. When she glanced back, she saw one couple close together, the girl's head resting on the boy's shoulder. Her eyes widened in surprise when she realized the girl was Eliza.

Feeling as if she had intruded on some very private moment, Connie faced front and sat up straight, more aware than ever of the way her shoulder rubbed against Isaac's in rhythm with the horses' movement.

"Getting late, folks. Guess it's time we head back," he said to no one in particular. A chorus of groans followed but no objection.

Just when Connie thought she might not be able to stand the silence or the closeness to Isaac one minute longer, Lucille began to sing "O Holy Night." The sweetness and innocence of her voice brought tears to Connie's eyes. Tears that she allowed to fall without trying to stop them. The melody brought back memories of Christmases past—Christmases when her family had been all together and happy—Christmases that would never come again. Everything was different now, and she understood that nothing she could do—not even going back to St. Louis—would change that.

As Lucille's vibrant voice reached the final notes of the carol, Connie once again looked up at the stars. She thought of all her mother had had to overcome—her losses so much greater than Connie's. After all, Connie had already found new friends, even if she did keep them at arm's length with the idea that their friendship was temporary until she could return to St. Louis. Her mother had lost everything—her friends, her home, and most bitterly of all, the love she had cherished. In a moment of unexpected clarity, Connie suddenly felt the twist of her strengthening resolve to find contentment in the life she faced here and now.

"Are you all right?" Isaac asked softly.

"Yes," she replied. "I will be."

He grasped the reins in one hand and with the other he pulled a kerchief from the pocket of his sheepskin coat and pressed it into her hands. She looked directly at him for the first time since boarding the wagon.

"Thank you, Isaac," she whispered as she dabbed the soft, warm, fresh-smelling cotton to her face.

"My pleasure, Constance."

Not long after the last notes of Lucille's solo faded, they reached the Baxter house. Nimbly, Lucille jumped down from the high seat, grinned, and waved as she started for the front door where her father waited.

"Wake up, sleepyheads," she shouted. In the back of the wagon, straw and fabric rustled as the others realized they were almost home. Lucille laughed as she and her father went inside and shut the door.

"How about one more round of the jingle bell song?" one of the cowboys suggested.

"It's late. Something softer," Eliza replied. "Connie, what was your favorite back in St. Louis?"

"Well, it's not exactly soft, but "Joy to the World" was always how we ended our caroling."

"'Joy to the World', it is," Isaac said, and he launched into the chorus.

It seemed only natural to link her arm with Isaac's as she joined in the singing along with the others. Their voices were loud and boisterous as they approached the church where parents waited for their daughters and cowboys would mount their horses for the ride back to the bunkhouse. When they reached the third repetition of "let heaven and nature sing," Isaac entwined his fingers with hers—and Connie did not pull away.

CHAPTER FOUR

Isaac hadn't missed an evening of supper at the café since the night they went caroling. He always arrived around six-thirty, and Mrs. Lancaster always kept a plate of food and a piece of pie waiting for him. He sat at the counter with other customers, often calling them by name, discussing something in the news and seeking their thoughts on ranching. It was clear that he was well-liked and respected by the cowhands who were regulars.

One by one, the others paid their bills and left, but Isaac always lingered, carrying his dishes to the kitchen and pouring himself a second cup of coffee.

After a week of the three of them working together and talking about everything from politics to poetry, he was still there when Mrs. Lancaster locked the front door and pulled the shade to indicate the café had closed. Constance—for that was how she had begun to think of herself—washed the dishes while Isaac dried, and her mother kneaded the dough for making biscuits the following morning.

"Constance, finish readying the dough for me, if you don't mind," Lettie Lancaster said. "I promised Mrs. Gladstone I would meet her and the other ladies at the church to finalize plans for the Christmas Eve reception."

Connie saw right through her mother's ploy—and from the twitch of his lips as he fought a smile, she suspected Isaac might be in on this little scheme to leave them alone together. "But it's so late. Isaac, perhaps you would be so kind as to walk my mother to the church—just to make sure she gets there without incident?" She had to bite her lip to keep from laughing when she saw Isaac glance at her mother—the two of them sending silent messages with a look.

"Don't be ridiculous, child. I'll be perfectly fine." Lettie removed her apron and hung it on the hook by the stove before putting on the coat that Isaac gallantly held for her and wrapping her wool shawl around her head and shoulders. "I'll see you at home," she said as she hurried out the door.

Constance dried her hands and finished kneading the dough, plopping it into a large bowl and covering it with a towel so it could rise. "You should go," she said as she busied herself with wiping the excess flour from the wooden table. The kitchen quarters were so tight that she could hardly avoid bumping him with her elbow or feeling him so near that she could hear him breathing.

"And if I stay?"

"People will talk. People are already talking." She scrubbed the table as if it had been stained by a disastrous spill.

"And it bothers you to think you—we—might be the objects of gossip." He let out a breath, folded the towel, and hung it over the edge of the counter. Then he leaned against the sink, one booted foot crossed over the other, his arms folded over his chest. "Why do you care?"

She stopped wiping the table and turned to face him. "I . . . we . . ."

He shrugged. "I mean, isn't it true that your plan is to return to St. Louis at the first opportunity?"

"I . . ." she began and then she looked at him, seeing him clearly for perhaps the first time, in spite of the dim light from the lantern that cast shadows over his features. "St. Louis is my home," she said defensively.

"Not really. From what your mother has told me, there is no longer a home for you there." His voice was soft and gentle, but the words were a harsh truth she did not wish to hear.

"Well, it's the only home I've ever known." She spoke through gritted teeth and over the lump of despair that rose in her throat. "I'm not stupid, Isaac. I am well aware that St. Louis is in the past. But this isn't exactly home either. I just wish I could figure out what the future might be."

Unaware that she'd begun to cry until he held out his arms to her, it seemed the most natural thing in the world for her to take the single step that allowed him to wrap her in his embrace. "I'm sorry, Constance.

The last thing I want to do is upset you. I wish there were some way I could make you see the beauty of this place. It's not St. Louis, but it has a splendor that is unmatched by any other part of this big country of ours. I know because I've seen a lot of places."

She felt the thumping of his heart beneath her cheek, but she didn't move. "Men are more fortunate than women," she said. "You can go anywhere and no one thinks anything of it."

"I guess that's right, but out here, Constance, a woman can make her mark. Out here, there are not so many rules, and a woman can do things she would never think of doing back there." He rested his chin on the top of her head. "And together we could—"

She pushed away from him, but while he loosened his hold on her, he did not let her go. "Why me? Why not Eliza McNew or one of the others? You set your mind to court me, and I want to know why."

"Fair question," he said. "If you've finished in here, how about taking a ride with me?"

She hesitated. "It's awfully late—nearly eight o'clock already."

"We could stop by the church and let your mother know you're with me," he suggested as if the fact that she would be out alone with a man were perfectly normal. "You want answers and that means showing you something."

She felt the thrill of adventure race through her veins. She thought of all the things her mother had done since her husband and Connie's father died that went against everything she'd been raised to believe was proper. Riding off in the night with Isaac would test her mother's determination to have her daughter settle into a life in Arizona. Her mother would be horrified at the very idea. She would forbid it and maybe then she would listen to reason when Constance made her case for starting over somewhere else.

Constance smiled. "All right. But don't get your hopes up."

Not only did her mother give her permission for the venture, she placed her hand on Isaac's arm and said quietly, "I expect you to make certain that her reputation is in no way compromised, Mr. Porterfield. That includes making sure she arrives home unseen by others, no matter what the hour."

"Yes, ma'am. You have my word."

Once again the two of them seemed to be in cahoots, with Constance having no say at all. "But, Mama," she whispered, keeping her voice low as Mrs. Gladstone and another lady glanced their way.

"I know you question my motives in this, Constance, but please trust me to know what is best for you. Opening your mind—and heart—to new possibilities is something you need to consider." She kissed her daughter's cheek and hurried back to the meeting.

Constance heard her telling the other women that Isaac Porterfield was a true gentleman, having just stopped by to seek her permission to see her daughter home. It wasn't a total lie, but neither was it the entire truth.

She waited inside the stables while Isaac hitched his horse to a sleigh outside. "We'll take the regular roads and trails," he said as he worked. "No reason to go cross country." He covered the seat with a buffalo robe and held out his hand to her. "Milady."

She settled herself in the warmth of the bison fur, and Isaac handed her a woolen blanket to cover her legs. He climbed in next to her and took the reins, clicking his tongue to set the horse in motion. He did not speak again until they were well away from town, nor did he look at her. Instead, he kept his focus on the road ahead, his shoulders tense as if he had forgotten she was there next to him.

"Where are we going?" she asked.

He ignored the question. "Back there, you asked me why I have chosen you. The simple answer is I don't know why, but there was something about you the first time I saw you that was so like the feeling I had when I first saw the land here."

She couldn't decide whether to be miffed or flattered, so she said nothing.

"That first Sunday in church—the way you listened to the sermon . . . And the other night when we all went caroling, I saw the way you looked at the sky and the stars. It seemed to me that maybe in that moment you were seeing what I saw when I first came out here. The majesty of it all. When I see the land and the sky unsullied by man, I know God is there. What I want more than anything is to take the land

I bought and build something . . . I don't know . . . something that honors him."

He stopped talking and once again focused on the road. After what seemed like a long time, he muttered, "Not good at putting it into words, Constance."

"Your words are beautiful, Isaac. I just don't understand what all of that has to do with me."

He looked over at her. "I can't do it alone. Oh, I can work the land and hire the help I need, but to make it last—to make sure that years from now the land will still be here—open and free—and that the love and appreciation for this gift God has given us will be carried on long after I'm dead and buried . . . I can't do that alone."

"You need a wife," she said. "Someone to bear your children." She placed her gloved hand on his arm. "That doesn't answer the question of why me, Isaac."

"No. It's more—so much more than that, Constance." His voice had taken on a passion that she found exciting. "I want someone I can *share* my life with, someone I can talk to, someone I can laugh with, argue with—and make hard decisions with. I want someone who will not be afraid to ask questions and stand her ground. And I think that woman may be you, Constance Lancaster. Truth is, every moment I spend with you only makes me more certain."

"You hardly know me," she protested.

"And you hardly know me, but what if we could make it all work? The only good thing I took away from the war was that time moves on, and we either live our lives to the fullest or face the regrets of not doing so." He urged the horse up a steep trail. When they came to a stop at the top, he jumped down and tied the reins to a juniper bush, then held out his hands to her. "Come on."

She hesitated before letting him help her from the sleigh. He was still holding tight to her hand, as he broke a path for her through the deep snow to a cluster of trees. "Look," he said and pointed through the trees to an opening where ice hung from rocks and cliffs and she could hear the merest trickle of water.

"It's like something out of a fairy tale," she whispered, instinctively lowering her voice as if she were in church. She edged closer for a better view. "Is this part of your land?"

"No, but it's the water from this falls that forms the creek that runs through my ranch."

Connie had always thought of Arizona as barren and dry. When she and her mother had first arrived in August, it had been so terribly hot that she felt as if her skin was on fire. But now, she stood in a powdery snow on the edge of a high cliff where water had frozen around the rocks and boulders to form a kind of ice palace. The full moon and starlit sky, reflecting off the ice, made it even more beautiful.

"If you lean out a bit, you can see the ranch down there." He pointed and then wrapped his arms around her waist to keep her from falling as she strained to see.

"Oh, I see a little house."

"It'll do for now, but I want to build a bigger place—one that will be right for a family. And the place needs a bunkhouse in addition to the barn there."

"I want to see it up close," she said excitedly.

He pulled her back from the precipice. "Another time—in the daylight," he promised. "For now, you're shivering, and I need to get you home."

As she followed Isaac's footsteps in the snow back to the sleigh, she was shivering all right, but not from the cold. From excitement. Isaac was building his future here, and others would as well. Perhaps in time she would find her happiness here after all, for even if she returned to St. Louis, she'd still have to start over as her mother had.

On the other hand, building a new life was one thing—building that life with Isaac Porterfield was something quite different.

He'd made a mess of things. Isaac knew it the minute they started back. Instead of talking about the life they might have together or even the beauty of the land, she said nothing, just rode along next to him as if lost in thoughts of her own. When he couldn't stand the silence any longer, he drew in a deep breath and watched it cloud as he let it out. "Look, I know you have fond memories of your life back in St. Louis, but—"

"Not all of them were good memories," she admitted. "After my father died, it was as if everyone we'd ever known or trusted abandoned us. I thought that what he did had not touched my life—*should* not touch my life. I had done nothing wrong, so why should I have to pay for his mistakes?"

Isaac was surprised at the anger in her tone. "I'm sure your father—"

"I'm not blaming him. He did everything he could to give us a wonderful life, but . . ." She turned to him. "Isaac, I've been praying for all the wrong things. I'm selfish and so full of wanting what I want without considering Mama or anyone else. Our life is here now—hers and mine—and I need to accept that and listen for what God's plan for me will be."

Isaac hoped with all his heart that somewhere in God's plan was a place for him as part of her life, but he would not push her. "It seems as if we're both kind of fumbling around trying to find our way."

And then she said the one thing he had not expected.

"What if God sent you to me, Isaac? After all, you came into my life just when I was at my lowest point, feeling sorry for myself, feeling lost. What if we're supposed to figure this all out together?"

They had reached the stable, and Isaac's intent was to tie the horse to a hitching post, walk her home, and then return to curry the horse and put the sleigh away.

"Sleep on it," he suggested, even though his heart raced with hope. "Tomorrow, we can talk more."

He climbed down and turned back to help her. "That sounds like the wisest plan," she agreed, and to his surprise, she stuck out her hand to shake his as if the two of them had just struck a business deal. Whether it was because he'd had such high hopes for the evening and been disappointed or he was just tired of doing the proper thing, he ignored her hand, lifted her from the sleigh and did not let go.

"One more thing for you to think on while you sleep," he murmured as he held her close and kissed her forehead.

The embrace was unexpected, and yet Constance had to admit that she had thought about what being in Isaac's arms might be like. So many men—especially those on the frontier—had heavy beards or at least a moustache, but Isaac remained clean-shaven, his mouth and jaw fully revealed. Of course at this hour, after a long day, his cheek was covered in stubble that on him somehow appeared attractive.

His arms held her close, but she remained aware that she could step away any time she chose. He was the one to pull away first, and the air between them fogged by their combined warmth hitting the chill of the night. It was not her first romantic embrace. She had shared that with Billy Goodman back in St. Louis. But Billy was a boy, while Isaac was a man, and it occurred to her that in a situation like theirs such details could make all the difference. What she knew for certain was that she wanted to embrace him again—and again.

"Let's get you home before the rooster crows," he suggested.

"It's not *that* late," she teased.

"I'd like to see you during Christmas," he said.

"Are you coming to services on Christmas Eve?"

"Sure, but from what I've been hearing your mother saying, you're going to be pretty busy helping out with the reception."

"Well, there's always Christmas Day," she suggested. "Maybe we could ride out to your ranch and you could show me around?"

"I'd like that—a lot." He wrapped his arm around her shoulders and pulled her close as they began the short walk from the stable to her house. "I like the way we fit together," he said as they walked. "Like two pieces of a puzzle."

She liked the way they fit as well. In fact, there was a lot about Isaac Porterfield that she liked.

But in the bright light of day, she began to have second thoughts. And when after two days Isaac Porterfield had not come to town or sent word, she wasn't sure whether to be irritated—or worried.

Something wasn't right.

Isaac rode slowly over his land checking the herd. Across the way, the three cowhands he'd hired spread out to do the same. Bunker—one of the men he'd hired—galloped toward him.

"Looks like the count's off, boss," Bunker said. He took a small notebook from his coat pocket and chewed on the stub of a pencil as he turned the pages. "I figure there's two steers and a calf gone missing."

"I saw George Johnson the other day," Isaac remarked, "and he said he's come up short as well. You think they got separated from the rest of the herd?"

Bunker snorted. "I think they got *in-ten-tion-al-ly* separated by somebody looking to bolster their own stock." He followed his words by spitting a stream of tobacco juice at a cactus.

Isaac knew the man was probably right. He had just started to build his herd and hadn't yet branded his livestock. He had only three hired hands and himself to keep watch. Truth was, stealing from him would be easy.

"Let's move the herd in closer to the ranch," he said.

"Sounds like a good idea, boss. You know with Christmas and folks tending to go into town pretty much every evening, that leaves the door wide open for whoever's behind this."

Isaac didn't miss the veiled reference to the fact that he was the one going to town every night and leaving the trio of cowboys in charge. "I'll be right here," he said. "Tell the others we'll work in shifts—two on and two off. We'll keep the stock bunched in a smaller area so they're easier to watch."

Bunker nodded. "Maybe I can round up one or two other men."

"Do that." He shook hands with Bunker. "I have to go into town one more time, but I'll be back before sundown."

Bunker grinned. "You oughta marry that gal and move her in out here so you don't have to keep going back and forth." He slapped his horse's haunches with his hat and rode away.

"I plan on doing that very thing—if she'll have me," Isaac muttered as he watched the man ride off to tell the others the plan.

Chapter Five

Constance could not have been more surprised when she saw Isaac ride into town. Christmas Eve was yet a day away. After not seeing him since that night he'd shown her the frozen falls above his ranch, seeing him that morning made her heart race with relief—and delight. He cut a fine picture sitting tall in the saddle of that black stallion. She stood outside the café, leaning on the broom she'd been using to sweep away the coating of dry snow that had fallen during the night, and watched him.

He saw her at about the same time, and although he acknowledged the greetings of other shopkeepers and riders he passed, he came straight to the café.

"Good morning," he said as he dismounted and wrapped the reins around the rough hitching rail. He focused all his attention on her and strode toward her with purpose; Constance kept the broom between them as a barrier.

Isaac stopped just short of being toe to toe with her, removed his hat, and twisted it nervously in his hands. "Constance, I can't be at the service and reception tomorrow."

He looked so serious. She inhaled sharply, knowing her face reflected her worry. "Has something happened?"

"There's been some trouble at the ranch."

"How can I help?"

He smiled and ducked his head. "Not really anything you can do. I just wanted to let you know I wouldn't be here tomorrow. I didn't want you to think I'd just abandoned you."

"I wouldn't think that," she protested, but she had. All throughout the day before, she had convinced herself that the closeness they had shared meant nothing to him and that he had decided he made a mistake in courting her.

"So I wanted to give you your Christmas gift now," Isaac said.

Connie propped the broom against the café wall as he walked back to his horse, unbuckled the saddlebag, and retrieved two small packages. "This is for your Ma," he told her, handing her the larger of the two. "And this one is for you. I thought you could put them under your tree and open them on Christmas Day."

She thought about the bolo tie she'd bought him on their account at McNew's General Store. Eliza's father had agreed to allow her to pay it off at ten cents a week.

"This is no way to exchange gifts," she said, pressing them back into his hands. "What if Mama and I ride out to your ranch on Christmas Day? We'll bring food for you and your hired hands, and we can open our presents then."

"I don't know, Constance. I don't like the idea of you and your mother being out alone—even in the daytime." He sounded worried.

She put her hand on his sleeve. "What's going on, Isaac?"

He sighed deeply and told her about the cattle rustling they'd discovered. "It's not just my herd. George Johnson and others have also lost stock. And until we know who we're after—and how many of them there are—it's just not safe. I would love to have you see the ranch—and your ma as well—but I can't come get you. We're shorthanded, and I won't ask my men to do anything I'm not there to do with them."

"But—"

"This is dangerous, Constance. Whoever is rustling our cattle is desperate, and if challenged they are likely to start shooting. I don't want you in the middle of anything like that."

She placed her hands on her hips and looked up at him. "Now you listen to me, Isaac Porterfield. My mother and I are not some wilting roses in need of your protection. I would remind you that we took a wagon halfway across the frontier without help. Well, there were other wagons, of course, but—"

He placed a finger on her lips. "Stop talking and listen. It's too dangerous. I won't allow it."

What did he just say? She moved a step closer to him. "I don't know what you think gives you the right to make decisions for me."

"I didn't."

She jabbed her finger into his rock-hard chest. "*You* stop talking and listen," she demanded, mocking his words to her. "I will do what I please. But if you don't want me at the ranch, just say so."

He took hold of her shoulders. "Constance! I want you with me for the rest of my life, all right? But when there are dangerous men out there, I do not want you taking unnecessary risks."

All she really heard was "the rest of my life," and that stopped her. Things were moving so fast. Was she ready to make a "rest of my life" decision? Was she ready to pledge her love to this man—this veritable stranger?

Apparently, he saw her confusion—although he may have misread it—and he gentled his tone and stance. "Constance, if you want to come out to the ranch, let me see what I can do to make the arrangements. The rustlers have struck at night, so perhaps we can enjoy the day. The men will be missing their Christmas dinner—that's certain. Some of your ma's home cooking would be the perfect gift."

Isaac placed the gifts back in his saddlebag. "I'll speak with Elliot Baxter over at the livery, and you talk to your mother. Tell her to buy whatever supplies she might need and charge them to my account over at the mercantile. How about I have a driver call for the two of you first thing Christmas morning?"

His charm and enthusiasm were hard to resist, but Constance was determined to have her say in the matter. "It seems to me that now you have turned this whole business into *your* idea, everything is possible."

"You wanted to come on your own."

"You won't *allow* that. Isn't that the word you used?"

He shifted uncomfortably from one foot to the other and pushed his hat back like he needed to see her better. "You're twisting my words."

"And you are treating me like somebody who hasn't the sense God gave her. You said yourself the rustlers work at night. My mother and

I will come—and go—in broad daylight." She grabbed the broom and turned to the door, but looked over her shoulder before entering the cafe. "You keep any chickens on that land of yours?"

"Yeah. Why?"

"Laying or eating?"

"Both. Why?"

"Best have your men round up two or three and clean them if you want meat with that Christmas dinner."

It snowed through the night, and the heavy gray clouds that blocked the sun on Christmas Eve morning foretold more snow to come. The wind picked up, and given the weather, Isaac hoped Constance and her mother would stay in town if the weather was bad. On the other hand, perhaps by tomorrow the storm would have passed.

Clearly, he had underestimated Constance's determination to make sure that he and his men had a proper Christmas meal. Around nine that morning, as the wind made it hard to tell if it was just stirring up snow already on the ground or if fresh snow was falling, he heard the jingle of harness and the snort of horses. Moments later, he heard voices raised in song. His three hired hands had been gathered around a campfire near the corral trying to stay warm, but when they heard the singing they moved closer.

"What's up, boss?" Bunker asked.

"Beats me." But as he and his men watched as a buckboard filled with people—and accompanied by at least half a dozen men on horseback—came closer, Isaac felt willing to bet that Constance had something to do with it. Sure enough, he saw her seated next to her mother and Reverend Cantor, who drove the wagon.

"Merry Christmas," she called out as the horses came to a stop and people began climbing down and stretching their arms before turning back to help the children. The women carried covered dishes and baskets laden with food. The men set to work unhitching the wagon and leading the horses to the corral. Isaac went immediately to Constance who had climbed down and was now helping her mother.

"What's going on?" He directed his question to Constance, but it was the minister who offered an explanation.

"Constance told us about the trouble you and the other ranchers are having, so we decided to divide up into groups and come see what help we could offer. Another group of folks are on their way to the Johnson place and a third to Arnold Keller's."

Earl Gladstone stepped forward. "One would hope that even thieves would respect the holiness of the season, but one can never be too sure or too careful. The ladies have brought food, Mr. Porterfield, and the men have brought their horses—and their weapons—to join you and your men in keeping watch."

Isaac turned to Constance who stared at the small cottage, frowning. Then she spotted the campfire and sighed with something akin to relief. "Mama, we'll have to call upon our experience with the wagon train and cook the chickens over an open fire."

"There's a fireplace and cook stove in the house," Isaac said, somewhat offended that she thought his accommodations were so primitive.

"Excellent," Mrs. Gladstone said. "Follow me, ladies."

And they did, baskets and covered dishes in hand, their boots breaking a trail through the snow, their voices raised in excited chatter. When Constance prepared to follow them, Isaac blocked her path and relieved her of one of two baskets she carried.

"Allow me." He smiled and fell into step beside her, but she didn't say a word to him. He saw Eliza McNew glance back at them, but Constance kept her focus on following the trail the women broke. "Still mad at me, I see."

"If I were mad at you, I wouldn't have come," she replied.

"I suppose you are right. And you thought coming a day earlier and bringing half the town with you would make a point?"

"It's more like a third of the town. As Mr. Gladstone explained, we had to spread out a bit. And what point would I be making?"

"That you are perfectly capable of managing your life without my help."

"There's that. Or you might look at it another way and see that I was concerned about you—and your men."

"I admit to liking that reasoning a good deal more."

They reached the house, and the other women inside all talked at once as they decided where to set up the food. Isaac was glad he had at least made an attempt to tidy the place up in the hope that Constance might come, although he had intended to do a better job of it later today. It was important that she see the possibilities in the house—that she imagined herself there. But with the small cottage bursting at the seams with women and children, he doubted it held much appeal for Constance.

The night he had taken her to the falls, she had talked a little about the house in St. Louis where she grew up. He, too, had spent his childhood in a large house like that, and he could imagine the kind of memories she had of Christmases there. *Well, maybe the time has come for making new memories.* He stood in the doorway and watched Constance join her mother and the other women.

"Isaac, we're going to need a place to serve and sit," Mrs. Gladstone said. "Perhaps the barn would do. Oh, and I think Reverend Cantor is planning to offer a service before we have our meal. Hopefully, he'll be brief."

All of the women turned to look at him, waiting expectantly for him to do their bidding. He pushed himself away from the doorjamb. "I'll get some of the men to help set up the barn. Constance, maybe you could come and show me what's needed?"

"Excellent idea," Mrs. Gladstone said as she relieved Constance of the knife and bowl of potatoes she had started to peel, passing them to Eliza. "Shoo," she added when Constance seemed reluctant to leave with Isaac.

They walked out to the barn, passing the corral now crowded with horses as they went. Isaac saw Bunker talking to the men who had come from town. The way the men listened, nodding and stroking their beards, their faces lined with concern, told Isaac that they were getting the details of the recent cattle thefts. Bunker seemed like a good man, and Isaac was glad he'd hired him. He could trust the cowboy to organize the others.

"We'll need something for at least the older folks to sit on during the service and after as they eat their meal," Constance said.

She ticked off a list on her fingers. She wore a pair of thick, woolen gloves and had wrapped her shawl around her shoulders and head against the biting wind. At her throat, he caught a glimpse of that red silk scarf she often wore.

"There are some hay bales," Isaac suggested. "Maybe the younger ones can roost on top of the side walls of the stalls or sit up in the hayloft."

"That wind is fierce," Constance said as she pulled her shawl closer and shivered.

Isaac closed the oversized double doors at one end of the barn. "Better?" He saw that she had pulled off her gloves and rubbed her hands together as if to restore circulation.

"It helps," she admitted.

He walked over to her and took her hands between his. She did not pull away, but rather stared at his larger hands covering hers. "I'm glad you came today, Constance. Of course, I'm not sure how I feel about you bringing so many others along."

She fought a smile. "I thought you were worried about Mama and me traveling alone."

He laughed. "You've got me there."

The barn door creaked open behind them. "Need any help in here, boss?" Bunker asked.

Constance pulled her hands free of his and busied herself with brushing loose hay off a worn, warped split-log table.

"We're going to need somewhere to put the food," she said as she tried to drag the heavy table from its place near the wall.

"Let me help you with that, miss," Bunker said, rushing to her aid. "Mighty nice what you and the other ladies are doing. Didn't look like it was gonna be much of a Christmas 'til you all showed up."

"Oh, Mr. Bunker, it's going to be a wonderful Christmas," she said, and when Isaac realized she looked at him and not Bunker as she made this declaration, he felt a warmth rush through his body that belied the cold blustery day.

They had endured Reverend Cantor's rambling sermon and everyone had gathered in the barn, lined up to fill their plates with the bounty of food when Bunker motioned for Isaac to join him outside.

"Got some bad news, boss," he said. "Looks like them rustlers decided to take their chances in broad daylight."

"How many did they get this time?"

"Three, near as we can tell. The good news is that with the fresh snow overnight they left a trail. Me and the boys thought we'd follow it, but that leaves the herd unprotected, and maybe the rustlers made those tracks to throw us off."

Isaac glanced up at the sky. "Weather's getting worse. If we don't go now, any tracks will be covered over by this wind and more snow." He stepped back inside the barn and, explained the situation to Reverend Cantor, who took charge, clapping his hands and calling for everyone to gather round. The Reverend explained what was happening and then asked everyone to join him in prayer. The men removed their hats as the women shushed the children, and the minister raised his eyes to the rafters of the barn and prayed for the men that they might recover Isaac's property, apprehend the culprits responsible, and make a safe return to their families and loved ones.

"Amen," the group murmured in unison, and the barn that had been so silent and still, became a beehive of activity. A trio of men set out to alert the soldiers at the fort of the theft, while the others prepared to follow Bunker back out to the range. All around him, Isaac saw women wrapping wool scarves around their husband's necks and standing on tiptoe to kiss them good-bye.

"Let's get started," he called out and headed for the corral.

Isaac was checking the cinch on his saddle when he felt someone touch his shoulder. He looked around to find Constance next to him, her hair coming loose and blowing in the strong wind. "Take this," she said as she pressed the familiar red scarf into his hands. "You can use it to cover your face against the cold."

He tied the scarf around his neck, relishing the warmth of it and the lingering scent of her. "Sooner or later, Constance, we will have that Christmas I promised you."

She touched his cheek, her hand smooth and gentle. "Hurry back, Isaac. We have a great deal to talk about." She pressed her fingers to her lips and then to his, surprising him so much that he felt incapable of a response. And then she was gone—stepping back into the gathering of women and children waving as the men rode away.

Chapter Six

"Isaac Porterfield could not take his eyes off you, Connie," Eliza whispered as they helped pack up the food and other trappings of the meal in preparation for the return to town. "People are already buzzing about the way you two look at each other. Has he asked you to marry him yet?"

"Don't be silly. We haven't known each other long enough." Connie avoided looking at her friend.

"Out here, things tend to happen different than they might back where you come from. Faster. It's kind of a situation where folks think life's too short to dillydally. Sure seems to me the way he came in here and bought all this land and a good start on a herd and hired those cowboys and all, Isaac Porterfield is a man who doesn't dillydally."

"What are you girls whispering about?" Neither of them had seen Mrs. Gladstone edging their way.

"Nothin'," they murmured in unison.

"Well, we're almost ready to go, and the sooner the better given the way that wind is blowing. Now hurry up and finish putting away those leftovers. Mr. Porterfield and his men will appreciate them once they return."

"Yes, ma'am."

It had been decided that, with the weather deteriorating and the fact that darkness would come sooner because of it, the women and children should return to town. The buckboard on runners had just pulled up outside the cabin, and the women loaded them with the baskets and supplies they had brought for the meal. One by one, they climbed aboard.

Just before it was her turn to step up, Constance remembered she'd brought the Christmas present intended for Isaac with her. She'd left it behind with a tin of tea on a shelf in Isaac's kitchen for safekeeping. She still wanted them to open their gifts together, so while the others loaded the wagons and settled themselves and the children for the ride back to town, she ran back into the cabin.

The package wasn't where she'd left it. She hurriedly searched the other shelves and only realized the others had left when she heard the distant sound of voices raised in song. She ran into the yard waving her arms to call them back, but they'd moved too far away and the wind was too strong for them to hear her calls.

Surely, someone would realize she was not with them—her mother or Eliza—and they would come back for her. She hurried back to the cabin to wait.

Once inside, she closed the heavy wooden door and latched it. With the shutters also fastened tight, the only light came from the embers of the fire they had left banked in the hope that Isaac and the others would return soon. She pulled off her gloves and warmed her hands, then added two split logs to the fire, enjoying the way they caught and flared to brighten her surroundings. Outside, the wind moaned as it caught in the cracks between the stone exterior or found its way between the wide boards of the shutters. But inside, she felt warm and safe.

She looked around, seeing the one-room cabin as it must appear to Isaac when he came home at the end of a long day on the range. It had a certain charm, but he was a terrible housekeeper. The rumpled bed had been hastily made, dried leaves clung to the corners, and dust settled on the window ledges and shelves. She spotted the missing package where it had gotten pushed behind a canister of sugar. She put the gift in the pocket of her skirt for safekeeping.

She opened the door twice to see if she could hear the others returning for her, but all was silent except for the wind. With nothing to do but wait, Constance set to cleaning. She filled a tin dishpan with snow from outside the door and set it near the fire to melt. In the meantime, she found a broom and swept the stone floor. She wiped down the few pieces of furniture—a rocking chair with a cane seat, a high-backed straight chair positioned near the table in front of the fireplace, and a small bookcase stuffed to overflowing with books—a collection that surprisingly included poetry and the works of Shakespeare in addition to several volumes on ranching and world history. There was also a Bible—its leather cover cracked and the thin pages dog-eared from use.

The largest piece of furniture in the room—aside from the bed—was an ornate rolltop desk. She carefully opened the top, half expecting papers and other items to tumble out, and was astonished to see everything in pristine order. A thick, black ledger lay open to a page of figures and inventory listings. Next to that, a brass inkwell, two pens, and a nib brush for cleaning the residue of ink from the points of the pens. The built-in slots were filled and labeled—*bills owed, bills paid, receipts,* and so on.

She sat in the wooden, straight-backed chair next to the desk and studied a small framed photograph that showed a man and woman surrounded by several small children—a girl and two boys. She guessed the faded image must be Isaac's parents and siblings. She set the photograph back on the desk and closed the rolltop. She tested the snow she'd melted and found it warmed by the fire. Carrying it to the dry sink, she washed the few pieces of crockery she found on an open shelf next to the window.

Finally, Constance pulled back the covers on the bed and remade it, fluffing the straw in the mattress and folding an extra quilt into quarters before laying it across the foot of the bed. She smoothed the layers of linens and blankets, noticing a small rip in one. The next time she came, she resolved to bring needle and thread to repair it. She climbed the ladder to a small loft where she found more books, still in boxes, and decided to leave the job of dusting them for another day. All the while, she found herself imagining living in this space with Isaac.

After checking again for any sign of someone coming for her and noticing dusk setting in, she sat in the rocking chair next to the fire and picked up the worn Bible. As was her habit, especially when restless with her thoughts unsettled, she allowed the good book to fall open, ran her finger down the page without looking, and then read the passage. Invariably, the words always seemed exactly what she needed to put things in the proper perspective.

Today was no exception.

She held the Bible closer to the light spilling from the fireplace and read aloud. "Isaiah, chapter 43, verse 18: Remember ye not the former things, neither consider the things of old."

Well, that certainly seemed to fit her situation. She had been dwelling on the past for months now, wishing for things that were behind her. She had clung to a vision of a life that used to be, but now she admitted those things would not come again. She read the next verse.

"Behold, I will do a new thing; now it shall spring forth; shall ye not know it? I will even make a way in the wilderness."

"I will do a new thing," she repeated softly as she marked the passage with her finger and looked around the cabin. "God will make a new life—not for Mama, but for me."

But would that life be in this wild country? And was it possible that God had sent Isaac Porterfield to show her the way?

Isaac and the other men pushed their horses across the open range, riding straight into the wind and blinding snow. Rusty, the cowboy who had discovered the theft, led the way. Because Isaac had brought the herd closer to the ranch, it was not long before they reached the spot where the tracks had been. Only now, as Isaac had feared, they were mostly covered over. He reined his horse to a stop, slid from the saddle, and knelt to examine the ground.

"They lead that way—toward that canyon," Isaac shouted above the howl of the wind. He pointed to a narrow opening between two rock formations in the distance.

Bunker knelt next to him and nodded. "Makes sense. They leave the stock there while they go steal more and then move them all out together—most likely after nightfall. What do you want to do, boss?"

The scarf Constance had tied around his neck caressed his chin, reminding him of her fingers touching his lips. "Let's go get our property," he replied through gritted teeth.

Isaac and Bunker mounted up, and he signaled the others to spread out and keep watch while they rode toward the canyon.

"They'll have left a man to keep watch," Isaac said as they rode side by side. "Best not raise his suspicions."

"What do you suggest?" Bunker asked.

"I'll act like I'm just circling the herd with the others. You create a diversion so I can slip down that trail yonder and go into the canyon from the rear."

Bunker spit out a stream of chewing tobacco, leaving an ugly brown stain on the snow. "What if there's more than one man?"

"I thought of that. It's more than likely that the others are off stealing from the Johnson or Keller herds. But just in case, how about you get two of the men and follow me into the back of the canyon? If there's more than the lone lookout, I'll bide my time 'til you get there."

They exchanged nods, and Isaac rode slowly around the herd, picking his moment to peel off toward the narrow trail. It occurred to him just then that trust was a big part of life out on the frontier. Trust in others and trust in his gut to make the right decisions. He certainly had come to trust Bunker, and it felt good to know he had a man like that in his corner.

He urged his horse up a narrow trail to the top of a rock formation that gave him a view of the canyon below. As they'd guessed, there was a lookout—a lone figure crouched on the edge of a cliff across from him, but no sign of anyone else. Half a dozen steers milled around below. He slowly worked his way down the path that led into the canyon from the rear, keeping his eyes on the lookout as he approached the stolen livestock.

Behind him, Isaac heard the soft plod of Bunker's horse. He held up his hand, warning the cowboy to hold up. He checked once again for signs of other rustlers. Seeing none, he dropped his hand and kicked his horse to a full gallop as he raced forward into the canyon, yelling and startling the steers so that they headed for the opening. From above, gunshots rang out, and he realized the lookout was firing at them. All he could do was pray that neither he nor any of the others would be hit.

In less than a minute, they had driven the stock through the narrow opening of the canyon and back out to where the rest of the herd and cowhands waited, but a group of riders—the other rustlers—rode full out across the range, firing their guns. To Isaac's relief, his men were ready. Some of them returned fire as the rest steered the stolen cattle back into the herd. At Isaac's signal, they moved the herd toward the ranch, putting distance between them and the rustlers.

"They won't come after us," Bunker assured him, coming alongside once they'd moved far enough away that the shots had no effect.

Isaac felt a searing pain in his left thigh, knowing he'd taken a bullet, but trying to keep his voice steady. "You think they're done for tonight?"

"I'd say so."

"Then tell those men who came from town to head on home. At least they'll be home with their families for Christmas. You and the others keep watch tonight, and tomorrow I'll hire more help to relieve you."

Bunker nodded. "You been hit," he said, pointing to the splotch spreading on Isaac's trouser leg—a stain large enough to be noticeable even in the gathering darkness.

"It's not bad. I'll head on to the cabin. I'll treat it there. Then I'll come on back to help you and the others." He didn't want to admit that he felt dizzy and sick from the pain. He'd been wounded in battle during the war, as well as in his role as scout, and this felt like something he could take care of on his own. "I'll be back by first light," he promised as he turned his horse and galloped off.

Not wanting to concede that he might be more seriously wounded than he first thought, Isaac rode some distance before he stopped his horse and dismounted. He took out his knife and cut the fabric of his pant-leg, now soaked with blood. Immediately, he realized that the wound went deeper than he'd thought. He grew weaker by the minute, in real danger of passing out, and knew he needed a tourniquet to stem the bleeding.

Think.

Too faint to reach his horse and the rope looped round the horn of the saddle, Isaac realized the only possibility was the scarf Constance had given him. He hated to ruin it, but it was either that or black out and die from bleeding out or freezing. She would understand. He wrapped the smooth fabric around his leg above the wound and pulled it tight, knotting it around a stick to hold the tension. He used snow to wash away the blood so he could better examine the wound as his vision blurred.

He grasped a stirrup and tried to get to his feet. "Steady, boy," he instructed when the horse snorted and, took a step forward. Managing to stand after several attempts, he put his good foot into the stirrup and cried out in pain as he pulled himself up and into the saddle. A wave of sickness and dizziness threatened to overwhelm him as he clicked his tongue and sent the horse walking into the black of the night.

Constance woke with a start, struggling to get her bearings. The light of predawn filtered in through the small cabin windows. It was coming on morning, and no one had come back for her. She stood and stretched to ease the stiffness made worse by the realization that she was cold. The fire had gone out.

She wrapped herself in the quilt she'd so carefully folded when she made up Isaac's bed. It smelled of pine soap and something more uniquely him. She pulled the quilt closer and knelt to rebuild the fire. For kindling, she used the dried leaves she had swept up earlier. When it finally caught, she added a log and entertained an image of cooking supper while Isaac was outside splitting more wood for the fire. When she realized she was once again thinking of what it might be like to live here—with Isaac—she frowned. When had such thoughts replaced her dismay over the realization that dreams of returning to St. Louis and building a new life there were just that—dreams?

Her stomach growled and she felt thankful for the food the others had left behind for Isaac and his men. There was more than enough for her to have a little something. After that, she needed to consider how she might get back to town. It was Christmas morning, after all, and her mother must be frantic with worry. She scooped a helping of dried fruit compote into the one bowl she found on the shelf, picked up a spoon, and walked to the window as she ate.

That was when she realized both windows were blocked with snow. She set down the bowl and opened the door. It blew in, nearly knocking her off her feet, and banged against the wall. Drifted snow blocked the front stoop, and all she saw in any direction was more snow and a sky that with the rising sun promised to be clear and blue. The path leading from the cabin to the trail the others had taken back to town had disappeared. The rust-colored barn was the only mark of color in the entire landscape.

The barn, she thought. Isaac kept one milk cow, and there were chickens. She glanced to the right of the barn where the chicken coop sat—or rather, the little she could see of it. It dawned on her that neither Isaac nor one of his hired hands had returned to care for the livestock. She'd never milked a cow in her life, but she'd watched it done. How hard could it be?

Constance put on her coat and gloves, wrapped her shawl around her head and shoulders, and the quilt over that. She spotted an old pair of boots near the door and pulled them on. They were so big they fit over her shoes. Outside, she stepped off the stoop and sank into soft snow up to her knees. Fortunately, it was dry snow, so with some effort she could push her way forward. Progress was slow, but the exertion kept her warm so that by the time she reached the barn, she no longer needed the extra warmth provided by the quilt.

As she had suspected, the dairy cow's udder looked full to bursting. She found a three-legged stool and pulled it close to the animal. "That's a good girl," she crooned when the cow flinched and moved away. "Come on now, we need to work together if we're going to do this." She placed a tin pail underneath the animal and leaned in to assess the situation. The udder was so full that she could see droplets of milk leaking from the teats.

She took gentle hold of one and squeezed. A thin squirt of milk hit the pail. Working with both hands, her cheek leaning against the warm side of the cow, she continued the rhythm. When the cow grew restless, she switched to the other two teats and began to hum a Christmas carol, hoping to keep the animal calm. It seemed to work, and by the time she felt the udder sag and go flat, she had three-quarters of the pail filled with milk.

"Oh, how lovely," she murmured, her mouth watering at the thought of fresh milk. She got to her feet and put the stool away. What she failed to do was secure the pail, and to her frustration, the cow kicked it over, spilling the precious contents onto the dirt floor of the stall.

"No," Constance shouted as she rescued what was left of the milk and stepped quickly out of the way. "Next time, I'll be quicker."

Then she headed outside to the chicken coop. Once she had pushed her way through the snow and into the coop, she collected six eggs and wrapped them carefully in her shawl. She found a burlap sack filled with feed and scattered some for the chickens before wrapping herself once again in the quilt, collecting her shawl with the eggs and the bucket of at least some milk and starting back to the cabin.

The sun had fully risen, and the day promised to be clear and calm. *Christmas Day*. She paused to scan her surroundings but saw no sign of anyone.

She had reached the cabin and set the milk and eggs inside with the intent of gathering more firewood when she saw something moving in the distance. She shielded her eyes from the bright sunlight and recognized Isaac's black stallion picking his way through the snow toward the house.

His horse . . . but no Isaac. Constance's heart seemed to skip several beats.

The horse came from the direction of the creek formed by the falls Isaac had shown her. Perhaps he had fallen or been taken ill. He'd been out in this bitter cold through the night. Connie tried to run toward the stallion, but between her already sodden skirts and the snow, she could only manage to stumble along, praying the horse would lead her to Isaac.

She saw the red of the scarf first—the ends fluttering in the wind. "Isaac," she shouted, her heart racing where her feet refused to go.

"Constance?" His voice was weak and filled with disbelief.

"I'm coming. Don't move." She grabbed the horse's reins and pulled herself up and onto the saddle. "Let's go." The horse didn't move. "Come on."

Nothing.

A clicking sound came from Isaac's direction, and the horse walked straight to him. "Good boy," she whispered.

Isaac sat in a pile of snow, his back against a fallen tree. He was pale and coughing, but when he saw her he managed a grin. "Fancy meeting you here, Miss Lancaster."

"What happened?" She was all business as she slid from the horse and hurried to his side, bringing the quilt with her.

He told her the brief details while she wrapped the quilt around him and knelt to examine his leg. "There's a hole," she said.

"Yeah. It's just a flesh wound, but it would be best if we could get the bullet out."

In spite of the cold, sweat beaded his forehead. His hat sat next to him on the ground. She brushed his hair from his brow. "Do you think . . . can you stand?"

"Get the rope," he said, ignoring her question.

She did as he asked. "Now what?"

"Tie it under my arms and across my chest, then tie it to the stirrups—one end to a stirrup. Make the knots tight as you can."

"Isaac, I am not going to allow this animal to drag you through the snow."

"Then come up with another idea."

His head fell forward. At first, she thought he'd died, and she screamed as she knelt next to him and cradled him against her body.

"No, please," she prayed. "Give us a chance, please." In that moment, Constance realized how much she had come to care for Isaac. Tears rolled down her cheeks as she rocked him back and forth. "Please," she begged.

When she felt his hand tighten on her arm and realized he was not dead after all, she raised her eyes to the brilliant blue sky and whispered, "Thank you."

Then she set to work. She managed to secure the rope as he had suggested. She even thought to tie it around the quilt to form at least that much of a buffer between his body and the snow. Then she took hold of the reins and walked slowly toward the cabin, following the trail she and the horse had made coming to Isaac's rescue. A thin stream of smoke rose from the chimney, and she felt immediately grateful for the blessing of the warmth of a fire that would be there when they finally arrived.

But reaching the cabin and getting Isaac inside were two different matters altogether. She unfastened the rope from the stirrups, led the horse to the corral, and then pulled Isaac's unconscious body inside, inch by inch. She pulled him as close as possible to the hearth, then stood, hands on hips, to catch her breath. Her mind skittered from one thought to the next as she tried to think what to do.

Isaac moaned, and his eyes fluttered open.

"Tell me what to do," she said.

"Whiskey," he managed and pointed in the general direction of a cupboard next to the dry sink.

"Isaac Porterfield, this is hardly the time for spirits."

"Clean the wound," he rasped.

"Oh." She hurried to the cupboard and pulled everything from it until she found a dust-covered brown bottle in the back.

When she returned to his side, he had pushed himself to a half-sitting position and held a knife in one hand. "Give it to me."

She did and was horrified when he raised the bottle to his lips and took a long swallow. He shuddered and handed her the bottle. "Now pour what's left on the wound," he said. He growled when she hesitated. "Do it."

She did as he asked, trying without success to ignore the way his body stiffened and his lips went white with the effort not to cry out.

He handed her the knife. "Use your finger to probe, and when you feel the bullet, dig it out."

Again she hesitated, her hands shaking.

"You can do this, Constance."

The light from the fire coupled with the sunlight pouring in through the open cabin door gave her a clear view of the gaping wound. The bleeding had stopped, thanks to the tourniquet. The whiskey had cleaned the area, and she realized she could actually see a glint of metal near the surface of the wound. "I can see it."

"Slow and steady," he said, but his voice sounded far away, drowned out by her words; she was praying as she had never prayed before that God would give her the skill and the courage to do what was clearly necessary to save Isaac.

CHAPTER SEVEN

Isaac fought to stay conscious, but once the bullet was out and Constance had started ripping something she had found into strips to bandage the wound, he lost that battle. The next thing he knew, he awoke in his own bed to the sound of "O Come All Ye Faithful"—sung with gusto by Constance.

So he wasn't dead . . . and the fever had broken. He threw back the blanket she'd covered him with, straightened his leg, and groaned. It was stiff and sore and a stain of blood colored the fabric she'd used for bandages. On closer examination, he saw that what she had ripped into strips was his one good shirt.

"Constance!" What he intended as a shout came out as a raspy croak, but she apparently heard him. She rushed in, dropping the bundle of fresh evergreens she carried, and hurried to his side.

"Merry Christmas, Isaac," she said as she felt his forehead for fever. Apparently satisfied that he was improving, she got to her feet and bustled around the small space, setting the greens in a bucket filled with snow. Then she set two places and pushed the table closer so he could sit on the side of the bed to eat. "You must be famished. Fortunately, when the others left yesterday, they left a good deal of the food for you and your men."

"Where are my men?" He pushed himself upright and watched her work.

"Mr. Bunker came by and looked in on you. He was worried after you rode off—such a sweet man. He helped get you into bed and assured me I had done everything just right. Then he checked on the livestock and cleared a path to the coop so I could get to the chickens more easily."

"And where is he now?"

"Oh, he went back to watch over the herd. He told me to say you are not to worry because the militia from the fort caught up with the rustlers and have them in custody. Oh, and some of the men from town refused to leave, so Mr. Bunker says they can manage for a day or two while you rest. I made him promise to send someone back for food."

He watched as she filled a plate and set it on the table, then filled the tin cup with steaming coffee that smelled better than any coffee he'd ever drunk. Finally, she set a small wrapped box next to his plate. "Can you make it to the table if I help you?"

He wrapped his arm around her shoulders—aware once again of the way the two of them seemed perfectly fitted to each other. She helped him to his feet, and he hobbled to the chair she'd pulled closer to the bed. As soon as he settled into it, she pushed the table closer, got food for herself, and sat down.

He was about to attack the food when she bowed her head and folded her hands. "Heavenly Father, we are so grateful for the many blessings you have given us on this holy day. Thank you for bringing Isaac safely home, and thank you for this food, and most of all thank you for the miracle of this day and the promise it holds for us in all the days to come. Amen."

"Amen," Isaac murmured, moved more than he cared to admit by her words.

"Aren't you going to open your present?" she asked, and he realized she seemed nervous.

"How about we wait until we eat and then you can get your gift from my saddlebag and we can open them together?" He focused on his food, fighting a grin. If there was one thing he'd be willing to bet it was that Constance Lancaster loved presents and had no patience for waiting to open one.

"Well—"

"I'm teasing you, Constance. Go get your gift and let's open them together."

She smiled sheepishly. "I was hoping you might say that, so when Mr. Bunker helped me put your horse away, I took the liberty of bringing my gift—and Mama's—inside." She reached into the pocket of her skirt and produced the small flat box. "You first," she insisted.

It had been some time since he'd received a gift, and he was surprised to realize that he felt both excited and anxious at the prospect. He fumbled with the knotted string until finally an exasperated Constance pulled the string free of a corner and the paper fell open. He lifted the box lid. Inside was a braided leather bolo, its ends anchored by beautiful turquoise stones.

"Do you like it?" she asked shyly.

He put it round his neck. "I've never had anything so fine," he said. "Thank you." He grasped her hand and squeezed it. "Your turn."

It took only seconds for her to rip away string and paper and open the box. He waited while she slowly lifted the locket on its long gold chain from the wrappings. He realized he actually held his breath. "It was my grandmother's," he explained. "She gave it to me when I left home and said that one day there would be this woman and I would know right away that she was meant to wear it."

To his delight, Constance clutched the necklace to her heart and grinned at him. "A wise woman, your grandmother," she said. She turned her back to him and put the chain around her throat. "Help me fasten it."

His fingers shook slightly as he lifted her hair and locked the small clasp. "Do you think then that one day we might—"

She turned to him and placed her hands on his cheeks. "Yes, Isaac Porterfield, I am more certain of that than I've ever been about anything else."

"Even St. Louis?"

"St. Louis was the only place I had ever been happy—or thought I had. But now I see that happiness isn't a place—it's being with people you can count on and share your joys and sorrows with. It's finding someone who, when he looks at you and you see yourself reflected in his eyes, you feel loved—cherished and safe."

Suddenly, Isaac felt the need to temper her passion. "We'll have our hard times, Constance. Life out here is not easy, and it can get pretty lonely."

She placed a finger on his lips. "Shush," she said softly. "We'll have more good than bad, and as long as we have each other, we will never be lonely." She fingered the locket. "I will wear this until the day I give it to our oldest son with the same message your grandmother gave you."

Her face went white, and he thought she might be ill.

"Unless," she murmured and started to pull away.

He covered her hands with his. "Marry me, Constance Lancaster. Tomorrow, next week, next year—just say you will."

Once again she shushed him, only this time she did it by resting her forehead against his chest.

Feeling Isaac's heartbeat beneath her cheek felt like the best gift of all. So special, in fact, that she thought she heard bells. How appropriate to hear bells of joy on Christmas Day!

"We've got company," Isaac said, his husky voice telling Constance that he was as reluctant as she was to end the moment.

"Constance!" Her mother's voice cried out, followed by Eliza's. "Connie?"

"Best let them know you're all right," Isaac said, releasing her.

She crossed the cabin, stabbing errant pins into her hair as she went, flung open the door, and called out, "Merry Christmas!"

"Praise God," her mother said as she climbed down from the wagon driven by Reverend Cantor and hurried to embrace her daughter. "You gave us such a fright, and then with the storm and all, everyone assured me you had food and fuel here in the cabin. I knew that you've always been resourceful, so I wasn't worried on that count and . . . What's that around your neck?"

"It's a gift from Isaac."

"A Christmas gift?"

"On the one hand." Isaac had managed to hobble to the door. "And if you approve, it is also a pledge of love and marriage."

Eliza squealed with delight and climbed down to hug Constance while Lettie Lancaster frowned at Isaac. "You and my daughter were here through the night?"

"No, ma'am. She found me this morning half out of my head with pain and fever."

"Mama, we're to be married."

"And if I object?"

Constance took a stance next to Isaac. "It won't matter. I'm a grown woman."

Her mother's smile was like the sun coming out from behind a storm cloud. "Just had to be sure this is what you want." She turned to Isaac. "One thing you'll learn sooner than later about this daughter of mine . . . tell her she can't do something and she's gonna be bound and determined to prove you wrong."

"Good advice," Isaac replied.

Reverend Cantor cleared his throat to gain their attention. "Perhaps we should bow our heads in silent thanks for the many miracles of this day. Finding Constance safe and well, the proposed joining of these two young people, and always the miracle of the holy birth."

Constance felt Isaac's arm circle her waist as her mother reached for her hand. Eliza stood next to the minister and grinned and winked at Constance before bowing her head. And as she half heard the words Reverend Cantor intoned, she mentally said a little prayer of her own.

So this is what true joy feels like. So this is why I was brought to this place that seemed so desolate and foreboding and now feels like home. Thank you, dear heavenly Father, for the gifts you have bestowed on us all this happy Christmas Day.

"Amen," Isaac murmured as he tightened his hold on her. It was as if he had heard her prayer, or perhaps his thoughts only mirrored her own. Either way, they were of one mind. When she looked up at him, she saw love—pure and sweet—reflected in his eyes.

"Merry Christmas, Constance," he said softly. "And welcome home."

Meet the authors online!

Mary Connealy

Website: maryconnealy.com

Facebook: facebook.com/maryconnealyfanpage/

Twitter: twitter.com/maryconnealy

Pinterest: pinterest.com/maryconnealy

Blogs: Seekerville.blogspot.com

Petticoatsandpistols.com

Ruth Logan Herne

Website: ruthloganherne.com/index.html

Facebook: facebook.com/RuthLoganHerne

Twitter: twitter.com/RuthLoganHerne

Pinterest: pinterest.com/RuthLoganHerne

Blogs: Seekerville.blogspot.com

yankeebellecafe.blogspot.com

Julie Lessman

Website: julielessman.com

Facebook: facebook.com/JulieLessmanAuthor

Twitter: twitter.com/julielessman

Pinterest: pinterest.com/julielessman

Blogs: Seekerville.blogspot.com

Anna Schmidt

Website: booksbyanna.com

Facebook: facebook.com/writerannaschmidt

Twitter: twitter.com/13AnnaSchmidt

Pinterest: pinterest.com/an13na003

FOUR CONTEMPORARY
ROMANCE NOVELLAS

Sleigh Bells Ring

Sandra D. Bricker, Barbara J. Scott,
Lynette Sowell, Lenora Worth

Never mind a pony. The Tucker sisters have inherited their
father's horse farm for Christmas. Make that . . . a run-down
horse farm. It needs some serious time, love, and care in
order to make it ready to sell. Emphasis on love.

**To curl up with your own copy,
order from fine retailers today.**